# REFUGE

A thrilling murder mystery with a big twist

NICOLA CLIFFORD

THE BOOK FOLKS

Published by The Book Folks

London, 2021





ISBN 978-1-913516-41-3

www.thebookfolks.com

To Cliff Henneveld 1934-2020
A very responsible man

# Prologue

The Mid Wales Times – 18th April
LOCAL MAN FOUND DEAD by Stacey Logan

The body of Daniel Evans was discovered on a footpath running through Long Field – popular with dog walkers – two miles from the village of Llanagethin close to the military firing ranges on the Epynt Mountain. Alongside him lay Mollie, his two-year-old black Labrador, also dead. It is believed they both suffered gunshot wounds and died at the scene sometime during Monday evening. The bodies were found by another local dog walker, Suzie Thomas, in the early morning of Tuesday. Local police have cordoned off the area and are appealing for anyone who may have information to contact them.
Daniel Evans, 35, was born in Llandovery and was well known and respected by the community. He worked as a teacher at the local comprehensive school for ten years and was married with two young children. His wife, Joanne, is staying with relatives and receiving treatment for shock.

Local shopkeeper, Hugh Davies, said, "I've known Danny all my life, a lovely lad who grew into a really great bloke. I can't believe someone killed him, why would they? Danny was special and everyone liked him."

Ms Thomas, who found the bodies, said that she was "devastated" by her discovery. "My dog Charlie found them, he was running way ahead and not coming back. I couldn't believe it when I saw Danny and Mollie. I'll never get over finding them like that."

Police are appealing for anyone with information to contact the Incident Unit on 0845 4267391 or the local Llandovery Police Station.

## Chapter one

'Got any leads then?' Stacey peered over the top of the newspaper and smiled across the table at her partner, Ben, who was busy chewing on a slice of toast.

'You asking as you, or as your alter-ego?'

'Bit of both really.'

'You know I can't discuss this, especially if you're going to write it up for that rag of yours.'

'OK then, I'm asking as me. Got any leads?'

'No, but it's early days. The lads are still searching the area, but so far we've found nothing.'

'Maybe your boys in blue aren't looking hard enough. There *must* be something.'

'All we know so far is that they were shot with a rifle. We found a bullet in Danny but not in the dog, seems as though it passed right through Mollie.'

'So, what's your next step?'

'Interviews today, the finder of the body, the wife…'

'Don't they say that the finder is often the killer?'

He chuckled. 'I think you watch too many whodunnits on telly!'

'But they do say that, don't they?'

'Are you really suggesting that Suzie Thomas was the shooter? *Little* Suzie Thomas? You're having a laugh, aren't you?'

'Stranger things have happened.'

'Yeah, but not that. She doesn't own a gun that we know of and even if she did, I doubt she'd be able to lift it. Honestly, Stacey, I worry about you sometimes. What are you planning for today?'

'Oh, not much. Back to the ordinary and mundane. *The Mid Wales Times* doesn't get too many murders to cover, so I'm working on the flower festival at the church, then thought I'd call in at the school where Danny worked, get some comments on his death from his colleagues.'

'The flower festival I'm fine with, but the school? Do you think that will help? Stirring things up and digging around?'

'I'm not stirring things up!' Stacey was indignant. 'How could it be more stirred than Danny getting killed? I thought I could get a few quotes and maybe a follow-up story; after all, this is the biggest thing to hit the area for years. A murder in Mid Wales? I've only covered one other.'

Ben sighed and ran his fingers through his short brown hair. 'I guess there's no stopping you, is there?'

'You do your job, honey, and I'll do mine. Speaking of which, I'd better get on, I'm meeting the vicar at the church in an hour and I'm still not dressed yet!'

'What's different there? You're always chasing your tail.' He laughed as she threw the paper at him and made for the stairs.

'Have a good day, copper. Go and catch crims. You around for supper tonight?'

'No idea how the day'll pan out, but I'll let you know – if you remember to switch your phone on.'

'May see you later then, Sherlock.'

She disappeared upstairs and as Ben left the house, he heard the shower running and his partner warbling along to the radio.

* * *

Ten minutes later, Stacey was back downstairs towelling her long curly hair. Another quick cup of coffee and she was out the door, heading for St David's church at the bottom of the village, a fifteen-minute walk from her cottage.

It was a beautiful spring morning. Late daffodils swayed in the breeze and covered the verges of the little hamlet, air full of birdsong. High up, riding the thermals, two red kites circled in the mild air calling to each other, sounding like airborne cats mewing and squealing, and a large flock of jackdaws zipped around the houses chattering, as they laid claim to chimney pots ready for nesting. They were so plentiful that the flock cast a moving shadow on the grass as they whirled around.

As she neared the church, Stacey spotted the Reverend Andrew Johnson waiting for her in the porch. She waved and he raised his hand in acknowledgement.

'Hi there, vicar,' she called.

'Stacey, lovely to see you. I wondered whether you'd bother with us, what with all the other news around at the moment.'

'Life goes on and so does your flower festival. It'll be nice to have something good to write about instead of the usual rape and pillage.'

Andrew frowned at her.

'Sorry, trying to lighten the mood.'

'Poor Danny,' Andrew said. 'I've been talking with his wife and she's in a pretty bad way; in England at the moment with her parents, taken the children with her. Such an awful thing to have happened. They were a lovely couple, childhood sweethearts. I married them here at St David's.'

'You've spoken to Joanne then?'

'Only briefly. She rang to ask if I'd keep an eye on her place, doesn't know when she'll be back. She can't even plan a funeral until the authorities release his body, and who knows when that will be?'

'Shitty thing to have happened. Oh, sorry, vicar.'

'Well, yes.' He cleared his throat. 'Come on then, let's get to it. I have a busy day today. Local folk are extremely upset by this and my pastoral care is in demand. I also need to visit the school later to speak to the staff and children.'

Stacey followed him into the cool darkness of the church. The sun shone through stained-glass windows and filled the space with rainbows, adding to the splendour of the flowers that crowded every alcove and windowsill. The altar was almost buried under towering displays of blooms, their delicate perfume mingling with the mustiness of ancient hymn books and candle wax. In the nave, close to the vestry door, a small woman fussed with a large display of lilies. Her grey, unruly hair stuck up in all directions and combined with the thick, black framed glasses, made her look a little like Wellington from *The Wombles*.

She glanced up. 'Hello, vicar, Stacey. How are you? I haven't seen you in ages. How is Ben doing?'

'He's fine thanks, Suzie, busy. How about you after your awful shock?'

Suzie's face instantly lost its smile. 'I'm all right, I guess.'

'You sure? You sound very unhappy.'

'No, I'm fine, really. It was just so terrible, finding Danny and his beautiful Mollie like that on such a gorgeous morning. Charlie was full of it, chasing squirrels, rabbits, his tail – anything that moved, really – and we were having such a lovely walk listening to all the spring birds, seeing which new flowers were out. Then…'

Suzie ran out of words and seemed to crumple against the choir stalls. Sitting down heavily on the polished black oak, she began to sob quietly.

'I don't seem to be able to banish that image from my mind. Every time I close my eyes I see them, lying together at the edge of the field, and the blood… it was so, so horrid. Who on earth would want to kill Danny, such a kind man, and what sort of person shoots a dog?'

Stacey sat by her side, pulled the small woman towards her and hugged her tightly.

'It's OK, sweetheart. Much better to cry than keeping it all bottled up.'

'That's all I've been doing since I found them. Every evening Charlie and I cuddle up on the sofa to watch telly, but I can't concentrate on anything and end up in floods of tears. Poor old dog doesn't know what to make of it all. I'm usually a happy person, but this has knocked me for six, really it has.' She sobbed harder while Stacey held on and gently rubbed her heaving back.

'Have you been to the doctor?'

'Yes, he gave me sleeping pills. I mean, what else can he do?'

'How about going for some counselling?'

'The doctor offered me an appointment, but that's not for me. I've plenty of friends I can talk to.'

Gradually the crisis passed and Suzie pulled away, scrubbing at her face with a crumpled tissue.

'I'm OK. Truly, I am. I used to walk that way every morning with Charlie, but we haven't been back since. The police are all over the place anyway and I'm sure it will never be the same. I shall always be thinking of… Enough!' She stood up and moved back to the stand of flowers. 'I must get on. The police are coming to see me at eleven, still haven't given a proper statement, guess they've been busy, and I haven't finished here yet.'

'Come on now, my dear,' Andrew said. 'I think you've done quite enough. You've been here since eight this morning and you look worn out. Why not call in on Emily for a cup of tea before you go? She's over in the vicarage and would be very pleased to see you. Some others are coming in later and they'll finish off. There isn't that much more to do now. It all looks quite magnificent.'

Suzie smiled, nodded slightly and, after collecting her cardigan from a nearby pew, made her way out of the church, pulling the heavy oak door shut behind her.

The vicar turned to Stacey. 'Poor woman, having to go through all that and her living alone as well, it must be dreadful.'

'Good job she has Charlie.'

'You're right. Dogs can be such good company, honest creatures. I wouldn't be without my daft Sami spaniel. Now, do you want to take your pictures and do you actually need me to be here? As I said, I have a very busy day and must get on.'

'That's fine, Andrew, I'm incredibly self-sufficient when I have to be. Should I lock up or anything?'

'No, leave the door open. Volunteers will be coming and going all day to make sure everything is ready for tomorrow. Thank you for taking an interest in our festival. Any publicity is useful and anything to help the community move on from this point will be welcome. Focus people's minds on other things.'

'My pleasure. I won't be too long and have your leaflet I can refer to when I write the article. I must say, the place does look marvellous, everyone's worked very hard. Is Suzie a regular, or is she just involved with the festival?'

'No, she's a regular, comes to most services and is on the church flower rota. Such a pleasant soul, I do hope that she can recover from this.'

'I'm sure she will. You of all people must know that everyone has hidden depths.'

'That's very true,' Andrew said, then made his way down the aisle and out into the churchyard, closing the door softly behind him.

Stacey opened her camera kitbag, dragged out her favourite Nikon and went to work. She clicked away, delighting in the colours reflected from the windows onto the delicate petals of the flowers. She tried to concentrate, but her mind wandered back to the murder. Who on earth *would* want to kill Danny? The question rolled around inside her brain. How could such a dreadful thing happen here? This small, isolated Welsh village had never seen anything like it; to her knowledge there hadn't been so much as a burglary here, so what on *earth* had the area done to deserve a murder?

* * *

Half an hour later she finished at the church, strolled back to her cottage, climbed in her car, drove out of Llanagethin and parked in a narrow lay-by on the lane running close to Long Field. She clambered out, leant against the five-bar gate and gazed across the acres of scrubby mountain grass, edged by a small, deciduous patch of woodland.

A few hundred metres away, she could make out a white tent erected over the spot where Danny and Mollie had been found, and watched as a line of uniformed police officers moved slowly over the surrounding area, searching the ground. Every now and again, they paused and a senior officer approached to inspect possible finds, before the line started its snail-crawl again. Stacey could hear a rumble of voices and the odd crackle of a police radio, but mostly the search was conducted in silence. She watched for a while then grabbed her kitbag from the back of the car, climbed over the gate and wandered along the path.

She didn't get too far before she encountered a fluttering ribbon of blue and white tape. Camera in her hand, she snatched a couple of shots of the searchers, the tent and the vehicles parked on the grass.

'Stacey!'

She jumped and whirled round to see Mark Jefferies – a constable who worked with Ben at the local station – heading her way.

'Hey, Mark! How you doing?'

'Never mind how I'm doing. What are *you* doing here?'

'Oh, you know, being a meddlesome, interfering reporter.'

'Well, there isn't anything to see – or photograph,' he grumbled, spotting the camera in her hand. 'I can't let you in, we haven't finished the search yet. How did you get this close anyway? The rest of the hacks are on the other side of the field where we can keep an eye on them.'

'You know me, Mark, where there's a will there's a way. Anyway, being local I know the shortcuts. Found anything?'

'Like I could tell you if we had, but no, we haven't and we're nearly done. Last day today and then we're back in the office with the paperwork. Ben with you?'

'No. Like you he's working, said he was interviewing today and I don't know whether we'll get together later or not. We haven't seen you at the cottage for a while, fancy a meal at the weekend – if you're not too busy with this obviously?'

'I'll let you know. Better get back, I'm needed. Now, no sneaking round the tape, you. I'd hate to have to nick you.' His eyes twinkled, as he wagged a finger at her, before striding back to the rest of the group.

Stacey took a few more photos, including one of Mark's retreating back, then returned to the car and headed for home.

* * *

Ben strolled up the narrow path to a lime-washed cottage and knocked loudly on the front door. He gazed at the overflowing garden crammed with flowers of every colour, shape and size. Bees buzzed between the blooms as they jockeyed for position with hoverflies and the odd early butterfly. A slight breeze stirred the stems and they rustled gently against each other. He knocked again and this time heard a sharp bark from behind the house. He wandered round to the back garden and there he found Suzie, kneeling on the ground, head and shoulders buried in the undergrowth. She backed out as he approached.

'Hello, Ben. Sorry, didn't hear you knock, I'm struggling to remove the last of the weeds from this patch before the festival tomorrow. There's always so much to do in a garden.'

He chuckled.

'It all looks great to me, but then I'm not much of a gardener and wouldn't know a weed if it bit me.'

'No such thing as weeds really,' she said, 'only plants in the wrong places. I always feel bad digging them out – some are really pretty – but I'm anxious not to let the side down this year. Can I make you a cup of tea or coffee?'

'Coffee would be nice, if it's no trouble.'

'Not at all. Come into the kitchen and I'll put the kettle on.'

Followed by a panting Charlie, they went into the narrow kitchen and while Ben sat at the table ruffling the dog's ears, Suzie busied herself with the kettle.

'How you doing, Suzie?' he asked.

'Oh, you know. Trying to forget about it to be honest, although with you here there's not much chance of that, is there?' She smiled weakly.

'I'm sorry, but there are questions I need to ask.'

'Of course there are. Would you like a piece of cake, baked yesterday? We could take it out to the garden. I hate being indoors when the sun is shining, don't you?'

Suzie loaded a tray with mugs, plates, a full coffee pot and a couple of slices of buttered bara brith – a home-made fruit loaf. Not waiting for an answer, she headed back to the garden, put the tray on an old wooden table and dragged over a couple of folding chairs.

'Please, sit down. Milk and sugar?'

'Black, one sugar, please.'

Ben watched as Suzie fussed with the drinks before sitting opposite him.

'Well then,' she said. 'What can I tell you that I haven't already?'

He took a sip of the scalding coffee. 'That's good and strong!'

Suzie smiled. 'No point in having it if you can't taste it, is there?'

'This shouldn't take long, I just need to take your official statement. All you need to do is tell me again what happened on Tuesday and I'll scribble it down as we go. Sorry – but I need your date of birth.'

Suzie reached for her mug, hand trembling slightly. '26th August 1962.'

'You OK?' Ben asked. 'I'm sorry I have to do this, but I'll try to make it as easy as possible. Just talk to me – talking's good, you know.'

'Yes, OK. I'm all right really, just can't get the memory of the blood out of my head. That poor man, and poor Mollie.' She sipped her coffee and sniffed. 'It was like I told you. Charlie and I were out for our usual early morning wander and we found them lying by the side of the path.' She shivered.

'What time did you leave home? Tell me everything about your morning from when you got up, to when you found Danny.'

Suzie sniffed again, hunting in her pocket for a tissue. Dabbing her eyes, she took a deep breath and began again.

'We were up at six, like always. I made coffee, gave Charlie his breakfast and let him out into the garden for a wee while I got dressed. We left home at about a quarter to seven, strolled along the back lane and climbed over the stile at the village end of Long Field. It was a beautiful morning, same as this. A touch of mist around, but the birds were up and all singing their heads off. Charlie was being a nutter – as usual – running about chasing rabbits, normal doggy stuff. Then all of a sudden he dashed off and wouldn't come when I called him, and that's unusual. He's such a good boy.'

Suzie reached down and touched the top of her lurcher's head, stroking his silky ears. He looked up at her adoringly and leant his body on her legs, enjoying the attention.

'Where was he?' Ben prompted.

'Right at the opposite end of the field, away from the houses where the grazing begins. I could see him and called again, but he would not come back. He was standing by something, nosing at it, didn't even look at me when I shouted. I walked faster in case he'd found something nasty to roll in, sheep poo or worse, and when I got closer I realised what I was seeing…' She seemed to drift away and gazed up at the sky, tears in her eyes.

'I know this is difficult, Suzie, but what *exactly* did you see?'

'Danny and Mollie, of course. Dead. Both of them. And blood, lots of it. Danny's hands were covered in it and his shirt was soaked.' She swallowed hard. 'I knelt by his side and saw a gaping wound in his chest, there were flies everywhere and an awful smell. It was obvious he was dead. Molly was close by, her beautiful fur stained red. Oh God, I *still* can't believe it.'

Suzie began to cry, tears streaming down her face, shoulders heaving. Charlie nuzzled his mistress and she put her arms around the dog, burying her face in his grey, bristly fur. He licked her ear and she smiled briefly.

'I'm so sorry. What must you think of me, such a bloody wimp.'

'Don't worry, Suzie. A dead body is an appalling thing to find and much more shocking if you know the victim.' Ben paused. 'Was there anyone else around?'

'Not at that time of the morning. The other dog walkers don't go out as early as I do. I like the start of the day when it's just me and Charlie and the wildlife, well, what he doesn't scare off, that is. But no – no one around.'

'What did you do next?'

'Called you. I always take my mobile with me, even though the signal is so bad, in case I fall or anything. You can nearly always make emergency calls.'

'Did you ring the station or 999?'

'999. They told me to stay where I was and someone would come. They were pretty quick, I only had to wait about ten minutes before the police arrived, but didn't want to be there. Couldn't drag my eyes away. Then an ambulance came – even though it was too late for that – and before long there were people everywhere.'

'Yes, that's what happens – a circus. I was there, too.' Ben wrote for a moment. 'Is there anything else you can tell me, anything at all? You said the body was by the path in full view, did it look as though it had been moved?'

'Don't think so, there was a pool of blood on the grass where Danny lay. As I said, I found the bodies, rang for help and waited until I was told I could go home. I wanted to get away from it all as soon as possible, but they made me hang around for ages. Eventually, Charlie and I got a lift home and a female officer stayed with me for a while. She called the doctor so he could check me over, and when he arrived, she left.'

'And you're sure you didn't see anyone else in the field?'

'No, just me and Charlie and I didn't pass anyone in the lane.'

Ben scribbled some more before putting the statement on the table in front of her.

'I think I've got it all. Read this through carefully and if you agree with what I've written, sign and date the bottom. We can change anything that isn't right.'

Suzie read slowly, struggling with his handwriting.

'Yes, that's right,' she said. 'Do I sign here?'

He nodded. 'Right beneath what I've written, so nothing can be added.'

He passed her the pen and she scrawled her name.

'Would you like some more coffee?' she asked.

'No thanks, I'm a bit coffeed out now, that last one was good but very strong. I'll never get to sleep tonight if I have any more. So, Suzie, how are you *really* doing? Can I do anything for you? We have support officers who could come round to talk with you, if you like.'

'Don't worry, Ben. It'll be better for me if I can recover on my own. I have Charlie so I'm not completely alone, and guess if I can get some time between me and *it*, I'll cope better. But thanks for asking.'

'No problem. Give me a call if you need me, or if you think of anything else. Take care of yourself, Suzie, won't you?'

'I'll be fine, I'm sure. I may go away for a while to visit Mam and Da, as soon as the flower festival is over.'

'That's on for a few of days, isn't it?'

She nodded. 'Finishes after the evening service on Sunday. Saturday is the main day though. Before that people come to look at the gardens – and the church of course – but on Saturday we'll have a fair in the field at the back of the village hall with stalls, you know the sort of thing, usually a well-attended event. I said I'd help Emily run the white elephant stall.'

'I may see you there,' Ben said. 'Stacey is covering the festival for *The Mid Wales Times*, so if I'm not working I shall probably get dragged along.'

'I bumped into her this morning. I was at the church arranging the displays when she came in with Andrew to take some photos. The place does look very pretty, I think we may have outdone ourselves this year.' She picked up the tray and moved towards the back door. 'Can you see yourself out? I really must finish the flower bed. I'd hate to be known as the woman with the weedy garden. You know what they're like round here.'

'Yep, only too well!' Ben chuckled. 'Try and enjoy the rest of your day and thanks for your help. Sorry I had to bother you with it again.'

'No problem, Ben, you're one of the good guys. Stacey is lucky to have you.'

Ben sat in his car outside the cottage, wrote up his notes, then tucked the completed statement away in his briefcase. He picked up his mobile phone and dialled Stacey's number, not at all surprised when the connection went straight to voicemail.

'Hey, Pumpkin! I *knew* you wouldn't have your phone on, you are losing the element of surprise. This could turn into a stale and boring relationship if you go on like this. Not sure about tonight yet, but I'd like to see you. If I can get there, I'll bring food, so don't bother to get anything in. I can pick up a takeaway and use the blue light to Llanagethin so it doesn't get cold. I'll text you if I can't make it. Love you.'

He returned the phone to his pocket, started the car and headed towards the motorway and the Severn Bridge that would take him to England and the newly widowed Mrs Evans.

## Chapter two

Stacey pulled up on the gravel drive of her home and gazed lovingly at the cottage. It was called Noddfa, meaning refuge, and had been left to her by her favourite auntie several years ago. Built in the eighteenth century, a short distance away from the more recently built houses that made up Llanagethin, the cottage had a large garden and stunning views over wild land which made up the military firing ranges.

She had always adored the squat, traditional Welsh building and had spent many happy summer holidays here when she was a child. Her mother would see her safely onto the train in Bristol and after two changes, and an hour or so riding the single-track, Heart of Wales Line, she'd step off in Llandrindod Wells. Auntie Alice was always waiting for her on the short platform, usually with some chocolate or other goodies tucked away in her coat pockets. They'd wander through the Victorian town from the station to the car park, where Alice's battered Land Rover waited for them. Stacey loved the rattly old vehicle, the muddy floor and debris-strewn dashboard, and was exhilarated by the ride home through the mountains.

The roads were more or less deserted and they met more sheep than other traffic. The closer they got to Llanagethin, the narrower the lane became until the undergrowth on each side brushed against the ancient paintwork. If the weather was fine, she'd open the window, dangle a hand out to feel tall grasses and cow parsley slide over her skin. The truck didn't have a radio in the cab so she listened as Auntie told her what had been going on in the village since her last visit, who had left, details of any newcomers and what the local gossip was. It took nearly an hour to arrive at Noddfa and as soon as Alice pulled up outside the cottage, Stacey escaped the vehicle's confines and ran about in the garden, like a horse put out to pasture. Then inside for a proper Welsh tea with bara brith, strong Welsh tea, and cawl, a watery lamb soup with chunks of meat and vegetables floating in the broth.

Every time Stacey pulled up in the drive and gazed at the roses growing over the porch and the riotous tangle of plants surrounding her home, the memories came flooding back and she felt as though she was a child again.

Making her way round to the back, she unlocked the door and walked into the kitchen, a large room with a low ceiling and not a straight wall in sight. Dumping her bag on the table, she filled the kettle and put it on the Aga to boil. Kicking off her shoes, she sat in a worn, wooden chair and rested her feet on the table. Auntie would have a fit, she thought with a fond smile.

The answering machine blinked and she discovered two messages, one from Ben and the other from Sam Jenkins, her editor. She listened to both while the kettle boiled, then made tea and carried it through to her cluttered office, overlooking the jungly side-garden.

She dialled Sam's number using the landline.

'Stacey! How's tricks? Anything for me?'

'Pictures for the flower festival article and I've put a couple of hundred words together on it. I'll send you the lot via email. Not quite as exciting as a murder but we can't have one of those every day.'

'Not funny, Stace.' He paused. 'Anything new on that?'

'No, not much. I met Suzie Thomas at the church this morning, she was putting finishing touches to the displays there. She's very distressed about it all, especially the dead dog; she's such an animal lover. I think that might have upset her more than poor Danny getting shot. I swung by Long Field on the way back. Couldn't see much though, we're all being kept well away by the local plod. I went in the back way, so didn't see any other journos, but ran into DC Mark Jefferies. He couldn't tell me anything – wouldn't, more like – but I get the feeling there isn't much to tell. The lads were carrying out a fingertip search, but Mark said they'd more or less finished. I took a few photos and I'll send them over with the others.'

'Couldn't get to the actual site of the shooting then?'

'Not a chance today, boss. Maybe tomorrow. For now, though, I'll take a drive over to the school and round up a few interviews from folk Danny worked with, collect some background stuff. Sounds like he was a good guy though, everyone I've spoken to seems shocked he's been killed. They nearly all gave me the usual "didn't have an enemy in the world", but he obviously had at least one.'

'Unless it was a stranger killing. Or maybe something to do with the army ranges, lots of guns up there,' Sam said.

'Why on earth would a stranger come to this part of the world to kill another stranger? And an army recruit going mental? I can't see that happening. Apart from anything else, you can wander around for days out here and not bump into another living soul. You know how isolated it is – the Welsh Wild West. I wouldn't even have internet services if I didn't pay a *very* expensive monthly tariff and rent a bloody satellite dish.'

'No, Stacey, the paper is *not* going to pay for it. How many times? After all, you choose to live where you do.'

'OK, Sam, keep your hair on. Can't blame a girl for trying.' She grinned into the receiver as she pictured her short, tubby boss slumped behind his desk, like a sack of potatoes – a lumpy, *bald* sack of potatoes.

'Very funny! Ha ha. I'm cracking up here. If you pick up anything worth having, give me a shout and I'll ensure it makes the deadline for tomorrow's edition. Now get on with it and stop winding me up.'

He huffed and disconnected the call but Stacey was certain she could hear a smile on his face.

She dialled Ben's number and he answered after a couple of rings.

'Hi, you. Switched your phone on at last, then?' he said.

'Yeah, yeah, I know, just don't like being disturbed when I'm working, destroys my train of thought.'

'Good job us men can multi-task.'

She ignored his comment. 'So, where are you?'

'On the M4, about to pull into sunny Bristol to see Mrs Evans. I guess I'll be here a couple of hours or so, then I'll be on my way back. What about you?'

'Off to the local comprehensive. I went out to Long Field earlier on the way back from the church and bumped into Mark, the boys were doing the fingertip stuff, but I don't think they found anything.'

'He told you that, did he?' He sounded huffy.

'No, of course not, but apart from the line of coppers, the line of journos on the other side of the tape, a big white tent and a few cop cars, there really wasn't much to see, so I guessed that they hadn't found much. By the way, I asked him round at the weekend for dinner.'

'Oh you did, did you? Do I have to worry about anything, Pumpkin?'

'Don't be daft, not my type. I've never been into blondes. I prefer dark-haired, clever men. Are you still planning to come over for supper?'

He sighed. 'I'll try to get there, probably around eight and – as I said – I'll pick up a takeaway in town and drive fast. Indian OK?'

'Anything. It will be lovely not to have to cook tonight.'

'What, not lovely to see *me*, but lovely not to have to *cook*?'

'Oh, get on with you! I'll see you later. Love you.'

She collected her camera from the kitchen, switched on the computer and waited while the dreadfully slow connection sorted itself out, before uploading her morning's work and sending the whole lot through to the Brecon office. That done, she finished her tea, poured another cup, carried it out to the car together with her kitbag and drove slowly towards Llwyncelyn School, on the edge of Llandovery, ten miles away.

* * *

Stacey arrived at break-time and the schoolyard was full of running, yelling children. Parking in the staff car park, she headed to the main entrance and made for reception. She tapped lightly on the door before swinging it open and almost bumped into Andrew Johnson.

'Oh sorry, vicar, didn't see you there. Twice in one day, that must be some sort of a record.'

'Well, I did say I was coming. Why are you here?' he asked.

'Follow-up stuff for the paper.'

The receptionist looked up from her screen. 'Can I help you?'

'Yes please. Stacey Logan, *Mid Wales Times*. I wondered if I could have a word with the headmaster about Daniel Evans?'

'Have you got an appointment?'

'No, passing by and thought I'd drop in.' Stacey smiled her most winning smile.

'We're all very busy with this terrible business. We were extremely fond of Daniel and this has been a dreadful shock. Some of the children are utterly distraught.'

'I'm sure it's difficult for you. I'd only take a couple of minutes of his time though. It would be good to have some background from someone who knew Danny really well, for an article in *The Times*.'

'Well, I'll ask.' She huffed and picked up the phone.

Stacey sat and glanced at Andrew. 'How have you got on this morning?'

'It has been tiring. The children loved Daniel, he was very popular, but then, don't all children love their art teachers?'

'I didn't know he taught art.'

'Art *and* English. Exceptionally good at both, or so I'm led to believe.' He nodded at the receptionist who was talking on the phone. 'I'm about done for today though, so I'll say cheerio. Are you planning on coming to the festival over the weekend?'

'Wouldn't miss it for the world. Let's hope the sun stays shining. Maybe you could have a word with Him upstairs?'

Andrew raised an eyebrow and Stacey felt herself reddening. She never stopped trying to make people laugh and – often – they didn't.

'Maybe I'll see you on Saturday – if it's not raining.' He chuckled softly as he left the office.

'Ms Logan? Mr Jones *will* see you. He'll be along shortly.' The receptionist hung up the phone and resumed bashing the keys of her computer.

Stacey stood, walked over to the window and looked out, watching the mass of children in the yard. A few were running around after a football, but there were several sad little huddles – mainly girls – hanging around the edges of the netball court. Some looked as though they might be crying and others were hugging each other.

The office door opened and the headmaster strode into the room, his hand outstretched towards her.

'Ms Logan. Glad to meet you.'

She took his offered hand and shook it firmly. 'Mr Jones. Thank you so much for seeing me – especially without an appointment.' Stacey glanced at the receptionist who continued to type busily.

'Let's grab a cuppa in my office and see if there's anything I can do to help you. Thank you, Janice.'

Janice humphed but didn't look up.

They walked along the corridor, Mr Jones leading the way to his small, cluttered office. Once inside, he cleared a chair by moving a pile of papers to another one, already burdened under a tilting pile of even more paper. The whole lot wobbled for a second or two before splatting to the floor in an untidy jumble.

'Blast! That's always happening. I keep telling the powers that be I need a bigger office, or at the very least more filing cabinets. Now, coffee?'

'Yes, please, black, no sugar.'

He poured a couple of mugs from a jug on a hotplate in the corner of the room.

'I can always find room for this little wonder,' he said, patting the coffee maker. 'Couldn't get through the day without regular fixes of caffeine.' He handed her a mug and settled in his chair behind the desk. 'So, Ms Logan, what can I do for you?'

'I'm looking for some background information for a follow-up piece in tomorrow's paper. Usual sort of stuff, how long Danny worked here, what he was like at his job and as a person; a bit like a school report.'

The headmaster grinned. 'I'm good at those. Damn well should be after nearly forty years. What can I say? Danny was a bloody good teacher and there are far too few of those around these days. I'm devastated to lose him, especially under these appalling circumstances. I always thought he'd go on to bigger and better things, maybe move to a private school – they like to poach good staff – but never that he'd leave like this.'

'You've known him a while then?' Stacey asked.

'I gave him the post ten years ago, his first position. He was such a great guy and his family are lovely too. I don't know how Joanne will cope with this, never mind poor Daisy and Oscar. To lose your dad at such a young age is just awful.'

'How old are they?'

'Daisy's eight and little Oscar turned six last month. My wife and I saw them often and occasionally they came round for dinner, all of them. We'd eat early so that the children could come as well. I'm obviously not child-phobic like so many adults are.'

'So he was a good teacher and a great bloke? I'm hearing that everywhere I go.'

'Because it's true, he was one of the best. Why on earth someone would do this I can't imagine. All the students adored him and he obtained excellent results both in Art and English. He was a talented artist – some of his work is hanging in the school corridors – and his English lessons were lively and interesting. The kids looked forward to his classes. We'll all miss him.'

* * *

Half an hour later, the interview completed, Stacey mooched around the school corridors looking at paintings. There were dozens and dozens, mostly by the students, but every now and again one of Daniel's hung amongst them.

The pictures were striking. Views of the local countryside, Brecon Cathedral in watercolours, the swooping bridge over the River Irfon at Builth Wells, the metal sculpture of a dragon in the lake at Llandrindod Wells and – by the main door – a portrait of the headmaster. Stacey paused to study the realistic colours and great attention to detail. It was almost as good as a photograph.

On the opposite wall hung a portrait of a girl about eighteen or so. Tall and thin, with long black hair plaited into a thick rope draped over her left shoulder, the suggestion of a smile on her face. She perched on a desk edge, hands folded in her lap, not unlike a modern Mona Lisa. Stacey peered at the label, 'Samantha Phillips, Head Girl'. Snatching a look over her shoulder and seeing the corridor was empty, she took a couple of quick shots of both portraits to look at later, then signed out at reception, climbed into her car and headed for home through the narrow lanes.

* * *

Later that day, Stacey was soaking in a deep scented bath when she heard a car pull up outside her cottage. Hauling herself out of the hot water, she peered through the tiny window and spotted Ben struggling out of the front seat, hands full of carrier bags.

'Hey, Sherlock!'

He looked round.

'Up here! Some bloody detective you are.'

He raised his head and spotted her. 'Now there's a sight for sore eyes. Never heard of frosted glass? Good job I'm off duty or I would have to arrest you for indecent exposure.'

'You could try, copper, but I won't be taken without a struggle. Let yourself in, key's under the pot. There's some wine in the storeroom and I'll be down by the time you've got the cork out.'

She sank back beneath the bubbles and listened as Ben unlocked the back door and began rummaging about in the larder. Before she could climb out of the bath, he was at the door, two glasses and a bottle in his hands, a dandelion clamped between his teeth.

'Oh! What's with the weed?' She giggled.

'There are no such things as weeds, only plants in the wrong places. That's what Suzie Thomas reckons and I couldn't find an early rose you wouldn't miss.' He winked and dropped the flower into the steaming water. Placing the glasses on top of the cistern, he uncorked the bottle, poured two large measures and passed a condensation-covered glass to Stacey. He lowered the lid on the toilet and sat.

'Cheers!' He drank deeply, gazing at her, swishing the covering of bubbles about with his empty hand.

'Got an audience now, have I?' she asked.

Ben chuckled. 'Nothing worth watching on the box. You hungry? I picked up a selection from the Indian in Llandovery, wasn't sure what you wanted. It's in the oven keeping warm while you finish.'

'Scrub my back for me, then I'll be out quicker.'

* * *

After supper they sprawled on the overstuffed sofa, tangled together like puppies. Ben stroked her damp hair while she ran her fingers up and down his thick forearm.

'How did it go in Bristol?' she asked.

'Much as you'd expect. Joanne is in a dreadful state and the children don't really know what's going on, other than they won't see their dad or pet dog again. She's staying with her parents. They're nice people and her mother seems very capable, so I'm sure she's in the best place. Joanne confirmed pretty much what everyone else has been telling us. Danny was a wonderful father and husband, not a bad bone in his body, didn't have any enemies, no recent set-tos with anyone, no debts and she's no idea at all why this might have happened.'

'No new clues?'

'*New clues*? I'd be grateful for an old one. As things stand at the moment, we have one bullet, a body, the body of a dog and that's it. Nothing else.'

'I didn't discover much either. Went to the school and chatted to the headmaster. Did you know Danny was a talented artist?'

'What did he paint?' Ben asked.

'Landscapes, bridges, cathedrals and excellent portraits. There are a couple inside the main entrance, one of the head and one of a head girl. Here, have a look.' She uncurled her long legs, padded over to her jacket draped over the back of a chair and dug the little camera out of the pocket. Carrying it back to the sofa, she switched it on and after sorting through the images, passed it over.

'You're right, he was good,' Ben said, peering at the screen. 'Who's the girl again?'

'Samantha Phillips, head girl.'

'What a looker. I feel as though I've seen this before, but haven't been to the school since I left and that was a while ago now.'

'Yeah, I thought I recognised it too. I reckon it's styled on the Mona Lisa, see the hands and that half smile? Very accomplished.' She yawned. 'Come on, Sherlock, early night for us I think, you look done in and I need to sleep off that huge meal.'

'Early night cos you're tired? Isn't that a bit boring? I can remember when we had an early night because we *weren't* tired.'

'Let's go up anyway, who knows – I may wake up a bit by the time we get upstairs.'

* * *

A ringing phone jerked Stacey awake. Squinting at the clock by the bed she discovered it was half past two. Who the hell? She fumbled for the receiver and held it to her ear, only to hear the dialling tone and realised it was Ben's mobile that was ringing.

She nudged him awake. 'Hey, you. Phone.'

He grumbled, ferreted about by his side of the bed and found the offending article.

'Hello? What's up, Mark? It's early.'

Stacey wriggled closer to Ben's warm body and tucked the duvet around her shoulders.

'What? This is a joke, right? Well, it's not very bloody funny, I'm– OK, OK. Where's here?'

Ben listened, then said, 'I'm on my way.' He struggled to sit up. Stacey wrapped herself round his waist.

'Come back to bed, Sherlock,' she mumbled.

'I can't, sweetheart, I'm needed at work.'

'It's two thirty in the morning, whatever do they need you for?'

'Another body.'

Stacey hauled herself into a sitting position, suddenly awake. 'You've *got* to be kidding! Two in a week? No way, not round here. What is it? Surely not another shooting, that would be crazy.'

'No idea yet, but I've got to go.'

'Go where?'

'Llandovery Road, picnic area. That was Mark on the phone.' He dressed quickly while Stacey watched him from the bed.

'Can I come?' she asked.

'Not a chance, go back to sleep and I'll ring you as soon as I can.' He ran down the narrow stairs, grabbed his jacket from the banister and banged the front door on his way out.

Stacey rolled over to snuggle in the warm patch Ben had left behind, but sleep evaded her. Her brain was too busy. How was it possible there was another body? Maybe it was a walker, or a suicide, some sort of nasty accident, just an awful coincidence. After an hour, she gave up, pulled on her fluffy dressing gown and went down to the kitchen to make coffee, sitting at the table to drink. It was now four o'clock. Wide awake and wired, she went back upstairs and dressed, pulled on wellies then wandered into the darkness of the garden with a second cup of coffee, mind working overtime. What if it *was* another shooting? How could that be, here, in the middle of nowhere? What on earth was going on? It was no good, she couldn't calm her thoughts, so grabbed her kitbag, pulled on a dark green, hooded sweatshirt and went out to the car.

## Chapter three

Stacey pulled into a wide gateway half a mile away from the large, forestry picnic site, hefted the bag on her shoulder and began to walk along the lane. She was still someway off when she spotted the mass of blue flashing lights reflected on the branches of the thick conifer woodland, like a music-less, outdoor rave. It was still dark, but the moon was up and clear skies made for fairly good visibility. It didn't take her long to reach the entrance of the parking area.

She lingered for a while and watched people moving about beneath the strong lighting that had been erected at the edge of the clearing. Generators clattered loudly in the stillness of the early morning and voices echoed under the trees. No police tape blocked her way and she didn't see anyone standing guard, so she wandered slowly towards the group of vehicles. Standing in the shadow of an ambulance, she watched, trying to make sense of what she was seeing.

'Stacey! What the *hell* are you doing here?'

She whirled round to discover she was toe-to-toe with Ben and he didn't look at all pleased to see her.

'I left you in bed with instructions to stay there! Why are you here? You can see we've got our hands full.'

'Couldn't sleep. What's going on?'

'I can't tell you – you *know* that.'

'But there *is* a body, isn't there? Shot like Danny? Or is it something else? Come on, give me a clue.'

'Well, you'll find out soon enough.' He looked exasperated and scrubbed his face with his hands. 'Yes, it's another shooting, but I *really* can't tell you any more. Even if you weren't press, I couldn't. Now please, go back home and as soon as I can, I'll call you. Go on – scoot. You'll get me in bother if the boss sees you.'

Stacey gave him a brief peck on the cheek, then jogged away.

She didn't return to her car, but turned off the lane to hike up the rutted, old Roman road that wound up the side of a steep ridge. It was hard going and she was puffing by the time she reached the top. Pausing to catch her breath, she gazed out at the view in front of her as the sun began to creep into the sky above the mountains, illuminating the forests and fields. Dragging her Nikon from the bag, she pointed it in the direction of the blue lights and, using the zoom facility, was able to get a decent view of the activity below her.

A mass of vehicles had congregated in the picnic area, there were police cars in abundance, the ambulance she had leaned against, and lots of dark shadows fluttering about. She thought she spotted Ben standing in the middle of a group and hoped no one else had seen her; she didn't want to cause trouble for her partner. Ben seemed to be directing operations and another ominous-looking white tent had sprouted on the rough ground. Perching on a mound of earth between bilberry bushes, she wished she'd brought something to drink, the early morning coffee long forgotten. The sun crested the hills and spread yellow, early morning light, dissolving away the night and bringing colour to the landscape. Far beneath her a search line had been organised and for the second time in as many days, she watched as it crawled slowly forward.

Another car arrived – a dark Volvo. Stacey was sure she recognised it and searched her internal filing cabinet – of course – it was the vet's car. Why was the vet here? Maybe another dog had been shot as well? That was surely impossible. If there was a second body with another dead dog, what did that mean? Was it a stranger killing? Someone who'd come from the city with a gun and a need to kill things, like people and dogs? Had there *ever* been a serial killer in Wales? Was that what this was? Why kill the dogs?

She snapped away with her camera on full zoom, changed to a larger lens and, as the morning sky grew lighter still, she could see in greater detail. Yes, that *was* Ben organising things and she hoped he wouldn't stay angry with her. He looked stressed and again she regretted crashing in on his scene. Not the way a responsible adult would behave, more like a pushy reporter – but then, wasn't that who she was? She was paid on results, had to write stories good enough to impress her editor, so needed to be pushy.

Time passed. Eventually, a wheeled stretcher was rolled out from the confines of the tent and loaded in the back of the ambulance. A smaller bundle was carried to the vet's car and placed in the boot, then both vehicles started up, pulled onto the narrow lane and headed down the steep hill towards the main road. It was no good. She *needed* to know what was going on and knew Ben couldn't tell her. Pulling out her mobile, she was surprised to see that, on the top of the hill, she had a strong signal. She checked her watch, saw it was five past nine and rang the vets.

'Hawthorne House, how can I help you?'

'Hi, Ali. Stacey here. How's it going?'

'Hi, Stace. Bit busy at the moment to be honest, can't really chat.'

'Busy because of the shot dog?' Stacey fished.

'How can you *possibly* know anything about that? No one else does and the dog hasn't even been brought in yet,' Ali snapped.

'I know. I just watched your boss load it into his boot, guess it'll be there soon. What's going on?'

'I obviously don't know as much as you do. Where *are* you?'

'Halfway up the old Roman road, watching the police. What have they told you?'

'Not much. Look, Stace, this isn't on – really it isn't. You can't pump me for information like you do everyone else. I'm your friend.'

'I know you are. I'll come to town later and take you out for lunch to apologise for trying. See you at one.' Stacey disconnected the call before Ali could protest.

* * *

Three hours later, after she had been home for a wash and brush up, Stacey was sitting in the vet's waiting room. A mother and her two children sat opposite, the little ones cradling a newborn lamb in their arms. They stroked the soft woolly coat and laughed as the tiny animal tried to suck on their fingers. Customers came and went – mainly farmers picking up drenches and antibiotics for stock at home, and vets and animal nurses bustled in and out of doors off the waiting area. Ali was behind the counter talking on the phone when Stacey arrived. She nodded and held up her hand to indicate five more minutes. Stacey waited.

Ali ended the call. 'I'll get my coat, won't be a mo.' She disappeared into a room at the back of the building. Stacey stood and made her way over to the surgery door. It was standing ajar, so she took a breath then cracked it open and peered inside.

She was surprised to see how many staff were crammed in the small room, and lying on a table was a large, white dog. It looked like a German shepherd and she craned her neck to see more. Ali caught Stacey nosing, grabbed her friend by the arm and pulled her roughly away.

'Bloody hell, you wind me up sometimes!' she said. 'I thought you wanted to take me out to say sorry for taking the piss and now I discover you're only here to see if you can find anything out. It's a good job I know you have a better side than the hack one.'

'I was looking for you,' Stacey protested.

'Yeah, of course you were. Come on, I'll make you pay for that. You'll have to buy me a Welsh Black steak at the King's Head – *and* afters.'

As the women left the waiting room, Stacey rubbed the lamb on the top of its soft, woolly head.

'Why is it that newborn lambs are so incredibly cute?' she asked. 'Yet fully grown sheep have to be one of the ugliest animals around?'

'Don't change the subject,' Ali grumbled.

They wandered down Stone Street and into the pub, choosing a window seat at the front so they could watch the locals go about their business. Within minutes they had placed their orders, steak for Ali and a lighter fish dish for Stacey. Sipping their drinks, they chatted about their partners, their gardens and the workload due to lambing. Anything but the obvious.

Stacey couldn't stand it any longer. 'Look, Ali. I don't mean to piss you off again, but you *have* to tell me what's going on.'

'Why do I?'

'Because you're my friend, you like to help me and want me to be happy. Telling me would help me with my career and you can unburden yourself. It's always better if you tell a friend about something that's bothering you.'

'I wouldn't say it was bothering me.'

'Of course it is. I can see you're dying to tell me.'

Ali said nothing and stared out of the window, swirling ice cubes in her glass.

Stacey tried again. 'Look. I'll tell you mine if you tell me yours. How about that?'

'You'll get me the sack,' Ali grumbled. 'I'm not allowed to tell you anything, patient confidentiality and all that.'

'Does that include dogs? Do *dead* dogs get data protection rights these days?'

'You know what I mean, don't wind me up.'

'OK, OK. I *promise* not to drop you in it with your boss. I'll tell you what I *think* is going on and then all you have to do is nod or shake your head. How about that?'

Ali said nothing, gazing out the window at the few shoppers passing by.

Stacey leaned across the table and lowered her voice and recounted the early morning events. 'Ali, I saw the dog on the table, that great white thing. It's dead, isn't it? Been shot?'

Ali looked up with tears in her eyes. 'Yes, he's dead. Poor old Sabre. He was such a lovely dog, huge, but a real gentle giant and yes, it did look like he'd been shot.'

Stacey's mind shifted up a gear as she again rummaged in her memory banks. She knew that name, knew the dog, who…?

'Oh shit!' she said. 'That's Mrs Read's dog, isn't it? The woman who's doing up the old school on the edge of Llanagethin. Lots of dogs and grown-up kids, caravans and junk cars everywhere – that's right, isn't it?'

Ali just nodded and looked as though she was going to cry. Stacey reached out and covered her hand with her own.

'It's OK, love, you don't have to say anything and really, I won't get you into trouble. I won't ask anything else, let's just have a nice lunch. Look, here comes our food.'

'I don't think I'm very hungry anymore,' Ali sniffed.

'You are *not* going to waste all this good food, especially as I'm paying for it. Come on, get it down you, you'll feel better, and if you eat it all you won't have to cook tonight and that's a bonus, surely?'

* * *

After lunch, Stacey walked Ali back to the surgery then retrieved her car from the Castle car park. She drove home the long way round, past the Llandovery Road turnoff and carried on the mountain road, to enter the village from the other side. After half an hour or so she passed the Reads' place and, unsurprisingly, saw a pair of police cars parked on the verge outside. She slowed down but couldn't see anyone about – even the dogs were inside – so drove on home.

She made coffee, carried it through to the office and rang her boss.

'Hey, Sam.'

'Stacey! Ta for the flower stuff, safely received and came out well in print. *Nice* photos. What did you think?'

'Sorry, boss, haven't had time to look at it yet.'

'What do you mean, you haven't looked at it? Unlike you not to pore over every word of every article you write and then ring me up to bitch about the editing. You mean that's *not* why you're ringing? What's the matter, you ill?'

'Oh shut up, Sam. I'm not as bad as that. Breaking news – there's been another one.'

'Another what? Flower show or festival, whatever it's called? Llanwrtyd holding one on the same day to steal St David's thunder?'

'No, you prat, another murder!'

'You're having a laugh, aren't you? Another murder, yeah right. Obviously wind-up-an-editor day today,' Sam said.

'No, I'm deadly serious. Ben was called out early this morning. I followed on behind and watched the crew set up off the Llandovery Road. Then I went to town to see my friend and spotted the body of a dog in the vets.'

'A dog? That's not a murder.'

'Get with it, Sam, how many shot dogs do we get round here?'

'Quite a few actually in the lambing season. You know how trigger happy the hill farmers are when they've got young stock. Any suggestion a dog is worrying sheep and out come the shotguns – bang, bang!'

'This is different. Hill farmers don't tend to shoot the owners as well, even if they'd like to. I know whose dog it is – was – but haven't got all the details yet. I'm busy filling in the gaps, but I'll have a piece ready soon and I'll send you the pics I've already got.'

'Bloody hell, Stace, this is for real, isn't it?'

'Yes. It is. I'll be in touch.' She hung up, finished her coffee and laced up her hiking boots. Packing her favourite leather duffel bag with essentials, including a drink, she left the house locking the door behind her. Climbing over the back fence of her garden, she set out over the Epynt Mountain, heading towards the picnic area across country.

An hour later, she was trekking through thick pine forest, moving as silently as possible on the needle-covered floor. The closer she got to the picnic area, the slower she walked and before too long she could see the white police cars, a sharp contrast to the green and brown of the forest. Finding a fallen tree trunk she knelt behind it, scanning the area trying to work out what was going on. She peered through a pair of binoculars to get a closer look and was disappointed to see a small group of reporters behind a ribbon of tape on the far side of the clearing, watched over by a local uniformed officer. The cat was out of the bag then. There was no sign at all of Ben or Mark and it looked as though the search had finished. Every now and again a figure emerged from the tent and then went back inside, but nothing was really going on; it was as exciting as watching a poor game of cricket. Stacey took a few photographs, then retraced her steps and hiked back across the fields towards Llanagethin.

She found a spot overlooking the village and pulled out the binoculars again, focusing them on the Old School House – home of the Reads. A single police car was parked outside, but everything seemed quiet. With nothing further to see and nothing worth photographing, she went home.

Once she was sitting comfortably in the kitchen, she tried calling Ben's mobile and was surprised when he answered.

'Hi, Stace. Not sure I'm talking to you after that stunt you pulled this morning,' he grouched.

'Sorry, Sherlock, I couldn't sleep and I'm curious. Guess I was a cat in a previous life. I like to *know*.'

'You may have been a cat before, but that doesn't mean you've got nine lives. You'll get me in serious shit, you know, if you carry on like that. The brass'll think I'm tipping you off.'

'No they won't, they know what I'm like and I'll swear on a stack of bibles that you're being very unhelpful and won't tell me anything.'

'What do you want, Pumpkin? I *am* busy.'

'It's another of the same, isn't it? Dog and walker both shot. Mrs Read and Sabre. Tell me I'm right?'

Ben sighed heavily on the other end of the line. 'How did you reach that conclusion?'

'Went snooping at the vet's in town. It's OK, you don't need to say anything, I just needed confirmation before I filed the story. You around tonight?'

'God, you're a handful. No. Sorry, can't make tonight. Things are so chaotic here I doubt I'll get away. Might have time for a chat once I'm home, but it'll be late. I'll call you.'

'You're not angry with me, are you? I'm only doing my job and can't help it if your *Sherlockness* has rubbed off on me, can I? Just call me Watson.'

'No, it's OK. It would have come out anyway and I'm happy for you to get the scoop, as long as no one thinks I gave it to you.'

'They won't, I promise. Maybe we'll chat later then. I've got a front page to fill.'

> The Mid Wales Times – 20th April
> SECOND BODY FOUND ON THE EPYNT by Stacey Logan
>
> Another body has been discovered on the Epynt Mountain Ranges. Mrs Read, 48, of the Old School House, Llanagethin, was found in the early hours of Thursday morning, in the main picnic area just off the Llandovery road.
> Police were called out in the early hours and her body was recovered together with that of her dog, a white German shepherd, called Sabre. It is believed that both had been shot in an apparent repeat of the killings on Monday. Police have refused to confirm or deny this information, but the body of a dog was taken to Hawthorne House Veterinary surgery in Llandovery with a gunshot wound.
> The picnic area has been cordoned off and is being searched by a team of officers. No one

was made available for comment, but a press conference is being arranged and full details will be supplied then.
Police have asked dog walkers and other users of the forests and footpaths not to approach any strangers and to report any unusual vehicles they may have seen in the area. They are urging anyone with information to contact the incident room. Any information provided will be treated in strict confidence. Tel: 0845 4267391.

## Chapter four

Stacey woke early and stretched. Bright sunshine streamed through the mullion windows of her bedroom and a blackbird sang to the new day from the top of a sycamore tree just outside. She hadn't heard from Ben and didn't want to call him, still feeling sorry she'd crashed in on his scene.

Climbing out of bed, she padded to the bathroom for a shower to wake herself up, then down for coffee, sitting on the bench in the back garden to drink. She wondered what she could do with the day. The press conference called by the police wasn't until the afternoon, so she had the morning to fill. There didn't seem much point in going back to the picnic area – it was bound to still be cordoned off – but maybe Long Field would be more accessible. With a plan in mind, she poured another coffee, collected her duffel bag and stuffed a few nibbles in the front pocket, together with a bottle of water.

It didn't take long to drive to the narrow parking place on the lane and, gazing out over the field, she saw it was deserted. Tattered strands of blue and white tape fluttered in the breeze, but there was no one in sight. Locking the car, she climbed over the gate and wandered slowly along the path.

The tips of the grass were still covered with diamonds of dew and somewhere, high up, a skylark twittered. In the neighbouring field a flock of sheep munched contentedly on fresh spring grass and new lambs galloped about in small gangs. Primroses shone beneath the trees at the edge of the wood, pale yellow against the emerald green of the new leaves and moss, and here and there, an early brimstone butterfly floated on the breeze. It was hard to believe this lovely place had been the site of murder.

The further she walked, the more trampled the undergrowth and scrubby grass became, squashed by many feet. By the time she reached the actual site where the body was found, the ground was hard and flat. Bending down to inspect the spot closely, she was sure she could see some dried blood on the soil. She shuddered, took a few photographs then scanned the whole area. On her left was the open field and she caught a glimpse of a lapwing swooping up and down, trying to impress his mate. On her right was the small patch of open woodland and beneath the trees a few bluebells were beginning to open, a low, purple-blue mist floating a few inches above the ground.

Standing, she noticed a narrow track in the long grass and that some of the flowers were crushed flat. Hefting her kitbag on her shoulder, she began to follow the indistinct path. The surrounding undergrowth was also trampled in places, but this narrow track looked as though it was used regularly. She squatted down for a closer look, no hoof marks, so definitely not a sheep track. It didn't reach very far into the wood and led to the base of an old, gnarly oak tree. Walking around the trunk she peered at the ground and couldn't find any sign of a track on the far side. Returning to her starting point, she leant against the rough trunk, and stared across Long Field. With a shock, she realised she was looking directly at the spot where Danny and Mollie had been found. If she had been here when they had been shot, she would have had a perfect view. She tried to estimate how far away the blood patch was, maybe a hundred metres? More? She wasn't brilliant at guessing distances. Was it possible the killer had shot his victims from here?

Dropping to her knees, she ran her fingers through fallen leaves and dog mercury plants, but found nothing. She peered up into the branches. There appeared to be a lighter patch of wood about five feet up and when she stood to examine it, realised what she was looking at. A small piece of bark was missing. It had been ripped away and the lighter patch was the fresh wood underneath. Pulling binoculars from her bag, she scrutinised the trunk more closely, working her way up slowly to the larger branches, and discovered a clump of mud. How could mud get this far up? The answer was obvious, someone had climbed this tree recently. Maybe this *was* where the killer had concealed himself to take his shot. She snapped the bare patch and the mud before searching for a way to climb higher.

Not far up grew a jutting spur, left from a long fallen branch and using her six-foot frame she managed to grab it, braced her boots on the knobbly base of the tree and was able to haul her body into the canopy. Carefully, she studied each branch, every square inch of bark and found another missing patch. Scrambling four feet higher, she discovered a wide cleft and with little effort was able to sit in it, legs dangling each side of a thick branch. Looking back at Long Field, she saw she was looking *directly* at the kill site, thick boughs of the oak framing the view perfectly. This must have been where the sniper positioned himself and from here killed Danny and Mollie.

Stacey took shot after shot of the field, the tree, the missing bark and yes, there – another blob of mud.

Ferreting around in her pocket, she found her mobile and called Ben. The phone clicked straight to voicemail.

'Ben? It's me. I'm in Long Field and I've found something. Ring me as soon as you get this message, will you? It's urgent!'

Returning the phone to her pocket, a movement in the field caught her eye. A figure dressed in dark clothing was close to the entrance gate at the village end of the path, a brown dot ran around the figure's ankles. Jumping down from the tree, she quickly made her way back to the main path and recognised Reverend Johnson, out for a walk with his spaniel.

She waved. 'Andrew! Hi!'

He looked up, raised a hand in greeting and walked towards her.

'Stacey. How lovely to see you. What a beautiful day it is.'

'Yes, isn't it. A good-to-be-alive day.' She felt her cheeks burn as she realised what an inappropriate remark that was, given the circumstances and the location, but Andrew seemed to ignore it, sparing her embarrassment maybe. The dog galloped over the grass and flung himself at Stacey's legs, bouncing up and down excitedly.

'Sami! Cut that out! I'm so sorry, my dear, he's pretty highly strung, but spaniels tend to be like that. Sami!'

'It's OK, Andrew. I'm used to dogs and it's not as though I'm dressed in my best, more mud won't hurt.' Stacey crouched to stroke Sami's long, silky ears. 'He's like a rag-dog, isn't he? All floppy, like the rag-doll I owned as a kid.'

'I see we've got our field back,' Andrew said. 'Don't know about you, but I felt *invaded* by all those policemen. I'm surprised they cleared out so fast really.'

'Yeah, me too, but I don't think they found much and as soon as Danny had been moved, I guess there wasn't any reason not to reopen the path.'

'I saw the paper this morning, read your article about poor Mrs Read. Whatever is going on?'

'Wish I knew, I'm as shocked as you. Nothing happens here year after year and now this – two deaths in a week.'

The vicar nodded. 'Dreadful business. The police have certainly been busy. Your article said Mrs Read was found somewhere off the Llandovery Road.'

'That's right, the large picnic area on the left, last one before the hill down to the main road. I don't know too much and obviously can't ask Ben, it'd make things difficult for him. I'm not sure his boss approves of his choice of girlfriend, the press is always viewed as the enemy. Do you walk this way often?' Stacey asked.

'Every now and again. Emily is busy with final preparations for the fair this afternoon, so I took this little monster for a walk to keep him out of the way and try to wear his legs off. Wish I had half his energy. How about you, pleasure or business?'

'Bit of both really, that and my insatiable curiosity.'

'Find anything?' he asked.

'No,' she lied, 'but the local boys in blue have been over the area and if they couldn't find it, it isn't there to find. I thought I might go over and see if the Reads fancy talking to me.'

'I was there this morning, they don't know what's hit them. Poor Bob, losing your wife must be dreadful, but to lose her under these circumstances is unimaginable. They are like lost souls. The police offered them a visit from Victim Support, but they refused. They've always kept themselves to themselves.'

Stacey nodded. 'I've lived here eight years now and I know them, obviously, but they don't socialise much. Can't say I blame them. Some of the villagers don't like the way they live and aren't afraid to make their feelings known. God, it must be awful for them!'

Andrew whistled for his dog.

'Well, my dear, good to have seen you, but I must be getting along. The fair opens in a few hours and I can't leave all the work to Emily. Are you and Ben planning to attend?'

'I was, but there's a press conference arranged for one o'clock this afternoon in Victoria Hall, so I'm not sure I'll be able to get to you if it runs on and it'll be the same for Ben, but I promise I'll do my best. My editor wants a follow-up article on the flower festival, so I'll try hard to get there.'

He patted her arm.

'I know you will. The piece earlier in the week was excellent, the pictures of the church were quite beautiful. Come on, Sami, you reprobate, let's get home.' He strode away, busy dog scampering at his feet, barking excitedly.

Stacey returned to the car and leant on the bonnet while she took a long drink from her water bottle. The sun had burnt away the last early morning mist and the day warmed up. She shrugged off her sweatshirt as her mobile buzzed.

'Ben.'

'Hi, Pumpkin. Make it quick, will you? Things are mad here, we're setting up the press conference and it's all go.'

'I'm in Long Field and think I found something. There's a bloody great oak tree not far from the path, and it looks as though it's been climbed recently. Maybe the sniper used the spot to shoot Danny. I've taken pictures, but reckon someone should come and look.'

'Right little Dr. Watson, aren't you? Sure it's not just kids who've been up there?'

'I don't think so and the marks look fresh. We haven't had any rain since last weekend and there are patches of mud fairly high up. I climbed up and found I had a clear view of the kill site.'

'OK. I can't come myself, but I'll get hold of Mark and send him. Can you wait? Where exactly are you?'

'In the lane at the bottom of the field, Llanagethin end, and yes, I'll wait. Tell him to be quick though as I want to go to the conference.' She peered at her watch. 'It's nearly noon now. I can be here until twelve forty-five at the latest.'

'I'll do my best and let you know.'

'You around tonight?' Stacey asked.

'If I am, we need to have a chat about you crashing my scene. Can't get into it now, as I said. I'm busy. I'll text. Gotta go now, sit tight.'

* * *

Ten minutes later, Stacey heard the sound of an engine and Mark pulled up by the entrance gate.

'Hi, Stace,' he called. 'Ben says you've been sleuthing. What have you got to show me?'

They walked along the edge of the field and Stacey pointed out the narrow track leading to the base of the ancient oak. Mark peered into the branches, searching for the mud and bark damage before hauling himself up to the lowest branch and peering some more.

'Hang on, what's this?' he mumbled.

'What'd you find? Come on, tell me!'

'Looks as though someone has used a knife on the bark, there's a small engraving above my head. I can just about see it. Hang on, I'll see if I can get higher.' He puffed and panted and wriggled his way further up the thick trunk. His shirt caught on a sharp twig and there was a quiet tearing sound.

'Bugger! That's a new shirt,' he grumbled.

'Never mind your bloody shirt. What have you found?'

'Well, it *is* a carving, recently done too, the wood is still damp and very white. It's small though, can't make it out. Not initials or anything, more like a rune.'

'I'm coming up.' Stacey swung herself up to stand on the lowest branch and peered over Mark's shoulder. 'I see it. What *is* that?' She pointed her camera at the spot then studied the resultant picture on the small screen. 'Looks a bit like a fish, especially if you turn it sideways, something a kid might draw – basic shape, tail, no fins… Here, take a look.' She passed the camera over.

'I think you're right, very odd. I'd better get on the blower and update Ben. He'll be tied up with the conference until later, but I'm sure he'll want to see this. Well done, Stace.'

'I bet it'll turn out to be nothing, but you never know.' She fiddled with the memory card, finally popping it out of the slot. 'Take this to Ben and tell him *not* to lose it or I'll flay him alive, I've got other stuff on there. Anyway, matey, must dash, need to get cleaned up for this afternoon. Like you, I have to be in two places at once today. Sam still wants me to do a piece on the flower festival, although with all this excitement around I don't know who's going to read it. You coming back too?'

'No. I'll wait here until SOCO takes a look. How about that meal you promised me?'

'I'd forgotten with everything else. Fancy a late Sunday lunch? I think Ben has the afternoon off, so maybe you can skive too. Check with him and if one of you lets me know, I'll cook a roast – let's say three thirty, four o'clockish.'

'OK, will do.'

'If you don't, you'll go hungry or end up with beans on toast. Gotta run, Mark, press conference to attend, see you later.'

## Chapter five

Stacey arrived at the Victoria Hall in Llanwrtyd Wells with time to spare. Even so it was difficult to find anywhere to park. Vehicles of all shapes and sizes nearly blocked the narrow road completely. Reporters milled around chatting and smoking, while locals leaned on their garden gates and kept an eye on them. She counted two radio cars and recognised representatives from nearly all the national dailies. A couple of police cars were parked in the small car park, both empty. Shouldering her bag, she pushed through the crowd and managed to find a seat halfway back. She checked her watch; nearly one, kick-off due anytime.

'Stacey!'

Scanning the room she spotted Sam Jenkins waving at her from the front.

'I saved you a seat,' he called.

Stacey wiggled out from her row and joined him.

'Wow! Front row seats, you must have been here for hours, either that or paid some hefty baksheesh.'

'Used my local press status.'

'And your funny handshake.' Stacey chuckled. 'Is that the chief constable?'

'Yep. They're pulling out all the stops on this one. I was amazed how many hacks had turned out until I worked out the royal connection.'

'Royal connection? What the hell are you talking about?'

'Think about it. Charlie Boy has just moved in, got that place outside Llandovery, so I guess the authorities can't *really* entertain a nutter rambling around randomly shooting dog walkers.'

'Honestly, Sam, this would be big news even if Prince Charles *didn't* live down the road. Two people shot dead and no clues?'

'Do you think we'll learn anything today?'

'Don't know, maybe…' Her mobile buzzed in her pocket. Digging it out, she checked the screen and saw a text from Ben. 'DON'T mention the carving to ANYONE.' That couldn't be clearer.

'What?' Sam asked.

'Nothing, only Ben telling me he loves me.'

'Ah, how sweet. You wanna watch it, you'll ruin that roughy-toughy-independent-woman image. So tell me, what have you accomplished today to earn your vastly inflated wages?'

'This and that – hunting for an angle. Anyway, I work damn hard for you. After this little bun-fight is over, I've got the flower festival to cover. I don't think you pay me enough.'

'No chance, you're not pulling that one. We're a *local* paper not a national. You want more money? Defect!'

'God, Sam, you really are all heart. If I don't feel appreciated, I might just do that. Hang on, here we go.'

The chief constable emerged from the wings together with the assistant chief, Ben and two others. Stacey recognised Bob Read but didn't know his companion. She nudged Sam. 'Who's the woman?'

He shrugged his shoulders. The buzz in the room rose at their entrance before becoming so quiet Stacey could hear Sam breathing. The chief constable ushered his team to their seats, then stood near the front of the raised platform and cleared his throat.

'Ladies and gentlemen, I ask you listen to what is said without interrupting. There will be a short opportunity for questions at the end. I'm pleased to introduce DS Ben James who is heading the enquiry under my direct supervision.' He sat and Ben took his place.

'Good afternoon,' Ben said. 'As I am sure you are aware, we have called this press conference to provide you with details we can release regarding the ongoing murder investigations. On Monday morning the body of Daniel Evans, together with that of his dog, were found on the edge of Long Field, close to the village of Llanagethin, and two days ago another body was discovered on forestry land off the Llandovery road – that of Mrs Kathy Read. Her dog was found at the scene – also shot. After considerable work behind the scenes, it is likely they were both killed with the same gun, a high-powered rifle. We are unable to release any further information at this time, but I would like to introduce you to Mr Bob Read, Kathy's husband, and Mrs Joanne Evans, Daniel's wife. They wish to make short statements.'

A reporter at the back of the hall raised his hand.

'No questions until the end please.'

Ben sat and Bob Read glanced at the assembled press. He looked dreadful, tired and drawn with darkly shadowed eyes. Clearing his throat, he began to speak, sandpaper dry voice cracking.

'I want to appeal to anyone who has any information regarding the death of my wife, to come forward and speak to the police. They have assured me any information provided will be treated in strict confidence. Please, if *anyone* knows *anything*, get in touch.' He looked around, bewildered, and ran out of steam.

Ben leant towards Joanne Evans and put his hand on her arm.

'It's OK,' he whispered. 'You don't have to say anything if you can't manage it.'

She shook her head and spoke in a tiny voice.

'I'm OK.' She wiped her eyes, sniffed, then said, 'Please, please help us.'

Reporters leant forward, trying to ensure they didn't miss a word as digital shutters clattered loudly.

'I have lost the most wonderful man in the world. We were childhood sweethearts, met at school and were married for nearly ten years. He was my life and my soulmate and I don't know how I am going to cope. The children miss their daddy so much and all we do is cry. Please,' she implored again, 'someone must know something. Has a member of your family been acting strangely, or been away from home, or…'

She couldn't continue and wilted in the chair, hiding her face behind a tissue. Bob Read patted her shoulder as she sobbed loudly.

Ben got to his feet and cameras whirred. A forest of arms waved in the audience and reporters yelled questions from the back.

Ben held up his hand to calm the pack. 'One at a time, please. You, there.'

'Peter Stamford, *Daily Herald*. Can you tell us if the police are looking for one suspect? Have the killings been linked?'

'At this point in time we have no reason to think these crimes have been committed by different individuals or are unconnected. The circumstances of each are certainly very similar, but we're keeping an open mind. Yes?' Ben pointed to a small woman at the back of the hall.

'Annie Noonan, *The Mail*. Have police any idea as to the motive behind these killings?'

'Not at present, no. Yes – you, there.'

'Dan Starkey, freelance. Do you think these crimes have been committed by a local person or by someone from outside the area?'

'We aren't ruling out anything. Well, ladies and gentlemen, I'm afraid that's it for now…'

The room erupted as questions were flung into the air from all directions. Joanne looked like a wild animal caught out in the open and Bob's head slumped into his hands.

Ben raised his voice. 'I'm sorry, but that's it for now. As soon as we have something to tell you, we will arrange another conference. Thank you all for coming.' He led the way off the stage, followed by the top brass, Bob and Joanne. It was over.

'That wasn't up to much,' Sam grumbled. 'I came all the way from Brecon for that and don't know any more now than I did before. And what was wrong with you? Couldn't think of anything to ask? I wonder what I pay you for sometimes.'

'Don't be a grouch, Sam. Let's be honest, if the police haven't got any clues, how can they tell us anything? It's early days yet. Let them do their jobs.'

'You know what this spectacle was all about, don't you?' Sam said. 'Put the victims' relatives in front of the press to see if they have anything to hide. There's an army of bobbies in a back room somewhere studying every blink and twitch those two made, trying to see if they've got guilty body language. After all, your nearest and dearest are the folk most likely to kill you.'

'Now there's a pleasant thought – but yes – I agree. It all looked pretty genuine to me, although I'm not an expert.'

'Anywhere round here we can get a drink?' Sam asked.

'Pub at the end of the road, but you'll have to go on your own. I've got a flower festival to cover, remember? Come with me, it'll be fun.'

'Not my idea of fun, lots of old ladies oohing and aahing over bunches of daffodils – no chance! Better things to do, like get a drink.'

'They'll have a beer tent I'm sure.'

'Beer? No, I'm after a Scotch to fortify me for the drive across the ranges back to Brecon.' He leaned in and planted a dry kiss on her cheek. 'Go get 'em, kid.' He swept out of the hall, using his bulk to clear a path through the noisy crowd.

Stacey glanced round and saw the room was emptying quickly. Ben was nowhere in sight, Bob and Joanne spirited away. Seeing no reason to stay, she went out to her car and drove slowly to St David's church in Llanagethin.

* * *

The event was in full swing when Stacey arrived. A local band was performing at the far end of the village hall field and visitors wandered around the stalls and in and out of canvas marquees housing the floral displays. She was surprised to see how many people had turned out – given the general mood in the area – but guessed the glorious spring weather probably had something to do with it.

Hanging the Nikon from her neck, she ambled slowly round the field, pausing every now and again to take photos and examine the wares for sale on the stalls. Following her nose to the tea tent, craving a caffeine kick, she bought a strong coffee. The sunshine and the early morning start were beginning to have an effect. Snagging a folding chair, she plonked herself down to take the weight off. Sipping slowly, she watched the fair-goers, waving and nodding at those she knew.

Not far away, she spotted a young woman sitting under a tree fiddling with her mobile. She looked familiar and Stacey tried to remember where she had seen her. Of course, Samantha Phillips, the head girl who'd been Danny's muse. Stacey watched for a while, then tossed her paper cup in a nearby bin and wandered over, taking a couple of candid shots as she got closer. Samantha didn't look up and when Stacey said hello, she jumped.

'God. You gave me a fright!' the girl snapped. 'You shouldn't sneak up on people.'

'Sorry, didn't mean to startle you.'

'Who are you anyway? I don't know you, do I?'

'Don't think so. I'm Stacey Logan. I live on the mountain in Llanagethin and work for *The Times* – the Mid Wales one, not the national.'

'You're a reporter then?'

'Yeah, that's right. Mind if I sit down?'

'Please yourself.'

Stacey dropped to the ground and leant against the tree. 'Beautiful day,' she said.

'I suppose,' Samantha mumbled.

Stacey studied the girl from under her fringe of curly hair. 'You OK?'

'What's it to do with you?'

'Nothing, just didn't think you seemed very happy. Not like your portrait in the school. You have a lovely smile.'

'Oh. You've seen it then?'

Stacey nodded. 'When I went to see the head the other day. It's very good, makes you look like the Mona Lisa. Daniel was a great painter, wasn't he?'

Samantha didn't answer and seemed to shrink into herself while staring out across the field. Stacey saw the sparkle of tears in her already swollen eyes.

'Are you sure you're OK?'

'You've asked that already, and yes – I'm as OK as I can be.'

'What's upsetting you so much, Samantha? Is it Danny?'

The girl hunched over, hugged her knees and sobbed. Once she got going it didn't look as though she'd ever stop. Stacey put an arm across her shoulders, but Samantha didn't notice.

'I miss him,' she wailed. 'I miss him *so* much. He was a wonderful, wonderful man and I *miss* him. It's breaking my heart. I can't believe he's not here anymore. Why on earth would someone kill my Danny?'

'*Your* Danny? How d'you mean "your Danny"?'

'I loved him with all my heart and now he's gone and there's this huge hole in the middle of my chest. I feel as though I can't breathe. What am I going to do without him?'

'Were you having an affair?' Stacey asked gently, worried she might be pushing her luck.

Samantha hiccupped. 'Why the *hell* am I talking to you? You just told me you're a bloody reporter. It'll be all over the papers tomorrow. God, I'm a total prat!' She struggled to her feet and Stacey stood with her, took hold of her arm before she could dash off.

'Wait, love, please wait. Don't go off like this. You're upset, stay a while and calm down. I promise you I won't put this in the paper. Honest injun.'

'Yeah, like I believe you! *Everyone* knows you can't trust the press. If you care that much, just pretend you never saw me. If Danny's wife finds out about this, she'll come after me… bound to.'

Samantha shot off across the field and disappeared behind the hall, leaving Stacey standing on her own, mind racing. Danny may have been loved by all, but he wasn't an angel. It looked as though there was a side to him his wife didn't know about.

## Chapter six

Stacey glanced up from the range as Ben and Mark sauntered in through the open back door.

'Hi, guys. How's it going?' she asked.

Ben pecked her on the cheek. 'Not bad. Busy – obviously.'

'I guessed as much – you haven't darkened my door for a while and I suspect you're only here now for the food.' She leaned closer. 'I was worried I'd overstepped the mark the other day.'

Ben gave her a squeeze. 'No, it's OK. You're only doing your job. I was just surprised to see you there when I'd left you cuddled up in bed.'

'Hi, Stace.' Mark added another kiss to her cheek and waved a bottle of red wine at her. 'Where are the corkscrew and glasses?'

'All on the table, go and make yourselves comfortable. Dinner's nearly ready and I'm best left alone in the kitchen.'

'She's right, Mark, you'll get your ears chewed off if you get in the way. She watches too many TV chefs, picked up all of their bad habits and not many of the good ones. You should hear her curse.' Ben laughed, hopping out of the way as Stacey flapped a tea towel at him.

'Cut that out, Sherlock, or you'll get bread and water. Go on, shoo!'

Ten minutes later she followed them into the dining room carrying a large plate with an equally large chunk of beef sitting on it, surrounded by roast vegetables.

'Ben, can you fetch the gravy and the other veg?' she asked.

'Blimey, mate.' Mark chuckled. 'You've got your feet well under the table here. Wanna swap for my lonely bachelor pad? I'm sure Stacey could put up with me far better than she can you.'

'No chance. Anyway, she knows what a pain you really are. I've told her you only behave properly in company, and all about the nasty personal habits you have.'

'Like what?' Mark was indignant.

'Let's not go there, after all, I haven't eaten yet.' Ben headed for the kitchen, returning with a large china dish and a gravy boat.

'You've outdone yourself, Pumpkin, smells wonderful and I'm starving.'

'Bet you haven't been eating properly with all this excitement and you can't run an engine without putting any fuel in the tank. Mark, don't be shy, dig in.'

No one said anything for a few minutes as they piled their plates high and took large mouthfuls of food.

Mark raised his glass. 'A toast! To Stacey, best cook in Wales.'

Stacey grinned.

'Creep, but thanks, won't get you out of the washing-up though.' She looked at them. 'Well?'

'Well what, Pumpkin?' Ben mumbled, round a mouthful of beef.

'How are you getting on, and why have I been sworn to secrecy over the fish thing on the tree?'

'We've decided not to make that public yet,' Ben answered. 'It may be nothing, but if it *was* done by the killer, only him and us know about it and we want to keep it that way. Bloody well done though. Perhaps you should leave the paper and become a copper, we could do with some good ones.' He fixed his gaze on Mark who blushed.

'What do you think the carving is?' she persisted.

'Still working on it. God, Stace, this is *good!*'

'We aim to please. What about the gun, any further forward?'

'Can't tell you,' Ben said. 'Your little tricks won't work on me, I'm immune to them all.'

'OK, how about this then? A trade.'

Ben put his fork down and chewed, studying her. 'What do you mean "trade"?'

'I know something that you don't know,' she trilled, fluttering her eyelashes.

'Give it up. You can't withhold information from the police, that's an offence and I may just have to…'

'Yeah, I know, arrest me. We've been here before. In all seriousness though, I *do* have something to tell you. Remember I told you about Danny's paintings hanging in the school corridors? I showed you a couple on the camera. Well, I bumped into Samantha Phillips at the flower festival yesterday afternoon, recognised her from the portrait. She was there alone and looked pretty unhappy so I made it my business to try to cheer her up.'

'And your point is?'

'Give her a chance, Ben, don't get on at the girl,' Mark grumbled.

'Thank you, Mark. Anyway, as I was saying, she was sitting alone and I wandered over and she broke down, sobbing hysterically and then let it slip.'

'Let *what* slip? Don't drag it out,' Ben huffed.

'That she was heartbroken over the loss of "her Danny".'

'*Her* Danny?' Ben spluttered.

'Yep. She more or less admitted they were lovers and now he's gone, she doesn't know if she'll ever be happy again. Real heart-rending stuff. I guess Mrs Evans doesn't know anything about it, or maybe – just maybe – she does and bingo! You have a motive. Maybe, your killer, this *him* you're talking about, is a *her*. What d'you reckon?'

'That's a bit of a leap – even for you!' Ben said.

'What do you think, Mark?' Stacey asked. 'It's got to be worth checking out, hasn't it?'

'It ought to be looked into, but how did you get her to tell you and, more to the point, how did they *ever* manage to keep their affair quiet? I only have to fart in Builth and someone in Llandovery knows about it.'

Stacey laughed. 'She was crying, distressed, instantly regretted opening her mouth and ran off. As to how they kept it a secret, I haven't a clue; must have been careful, I guess. More meat, anyone?'

Ben helped himself to another plateful, adding more vegetables and Mark followed his example.

'Seems like you two haven't eaten in a month. Good job I know coppers have hollow legs and cooked extra. Leave room for apple crumble, won't you?'

Ben groaned. 'Wish I'd known there was crumble before I started.'

'I'm sure you'll squash it in. So, where do we go from here?' Stacey asked.

'*You* don't go anywhere with it,' Ben muttered. 'You're a reporter not a copper. That's our job and again, you can't print anything about this.'

'Don't worry, I already promised Samantha I wouldn't. If you speak to her she'll know I grassed her up.'

'Not necessarily,' Mark said. 'We can easily concoct a story about phone records or something, but we'll have to talk to her – Joanne Evans as well. Bloody hell, this is going to get sticky. I can't imagine Joanne climbing a tree and blasting her husband and the family pet to death with a high-powered rifle cos he was cheating on her. Even if she did – and it's a huge *if* – that doesn't explain the shooting of Kathy Read, not unless she thought that's who Danny's lover was and I *really* can't see that. I mean,

Danny Evans and Kathy Read? Do me a favour.' Mark shovelled in another mouthful. 'Pass the gravy, Sarge.'

Ben pushed the jug in his colleague's direction.

The meal finished, they retreated to the back garden, sprawled on garden benches and listened to a robin singing from the depths of a nearby bush, as the light softened towards evening and the mountain air cooled rapidly.

* * *

Both officers left well before six the next morning. Stacey showered and took her coffee out to the garden to enjoy the coolness of early morning on her face while she planned her day. She wondered if she could get into the picnic area now for a sniff around, just in case the police had missed anything. She couldn't be that lucky twice, but you never knew.

Half an hour later, driving out of Llanagethin she passed the Reads' place and spotted Stevie, at nineteen the youngest of the three boys, sitting on the fence bordering the lane, and pulled over.

'Hey, Stevie, how you doing?'

He looked up, a blank expression on his face.

'It's Stacey. I live on the other side of the village in the white cottage.'

He nodded, jumped off the wall and wandered over to the car, leaning in at the window.

'Sorry, miles away, didn't recognise you.'

'How you doing, matey?' Stacey asked. 'I'm *so* sorry about your mum. Are you and the others OK? Can I do anything to help?'

'Nah, it's OK, ta. Pa's not here, gone to Birmingham to see Ma's sister and the others haven't got up yet.'

'How are things?'

'Pretty grim. No one knows what to do. Ma did everything, running the house, cooking and stuff and now she's not here, well, nothing's getting done.'

'What have the police said?'

'Not much. Useless bastards if you ask me. They look at Pa as though he did it and won't tell us anything. I know her and Pa weren't getting on, but he'd never kill her. The worst thing is, this time next week she wouldn't have been here anyway.'

'Was she going somewhere?'

'Yeah, back to Birmingham. She'd had enough of the village, us as well I expect, and definitely enough of Pa. She was going to stay with family.'

'What, for a holiday?'

'No, for good. Like I said, she'd had enough, couldn't put up with the way things were anymore.'

'I didn't know your mum and dad weren't getting on.'

Stevie shrugged. 'Hadn't for a while. She was worn out, I guess. They'd worked it out between them and were still friends – but she didn't want to live here any longer, said it was too remote.'

'Did you tell the police?'

'Yeah, they grilled all of us. I guess that's why they're coming down so hard on Pa. Don't blame him for buggering off, I'd do the same. It's crazy though, they might not have been getting on, but Pa would never kill her or Sabre. That's mental. It's not even as though he's got a gun, never mind knowing what to do with one.'

'Did Kathy walk near the picnic area often?'

'Yeah, nearly every day. Usually in the evening for an hour or so, there are forestry footpaths that lead from there to the village, she walked those. When she didn't come back, Pa and David went to find her and…' He paused. 'They rang here in a state then called Old Bill.'

'Must have been awful for them.'

'Yeah, right cut up they were.' He fell silent.

Stacey put her hand on his arm. 'Look, Stevie, if there's anything I can do, give me a shout. If I'm not in, put a note through the door and I'll come down. I mean it.'

'Ta, Stacey, we will.' He stepped away from the car. 'Where are you going now?'

'Only town,' she lied. 'Can I bring anything back for you?'

'No, ta, we've got what we need, but thanks for stopping. Nice to know someone in the village has a heart.'

'See you later then.'

'Laters.' He returned to his perch on the wall.

Stacey drove away watching him in her mirror, staring into space and swinging his legs. She didn't realise things had got so bad that Kathy was planning to leave home and wondered briefly whether Bob *did* have something to do with her death, but dismissed the idea. That was bonkers. Bob might have an alternative lifestyle, but Stacey couldn't see him as a killer.

She left the village behind and headed along the Llandovery Road. The lanes were full of hedgerow birds fluttering in and out of tall undergrowth on the verges and, passing open grassland, she spotted a hare lolloping slowly up the side of a hill. She pulled over to watch until it vanished over the ridge. It was another glorious day, the kind of day that banished memories of the cold, frost and snow of winter and the long, dark nights, reminding her why she loved living here. Mid Wales in good spring weather was hard to beat.

A few stray lambs shot out from a gateway and galloped along in front of her car, bleating for their mothers. Stacey drove slowly behind the tiny flock until they sprang to the top of a high verge allowing her to pass. It didn't take long to arrive at the picnic area, but she was disappointed to see the tape was still in place and a couple of coppers stood guard at the entrance. No getting in there then, she thought and drove on past towards the main road. While she was this far along the lane she may as well nip into town and pick up some groceries. Yesterday's lunch had cleaned her out of fruit and fresh vegetables and an extra bottle of wine for the larder was always a good idea.

The supermarket car park was nearly full and it took Stacey a while to park. Grabbing a trolley, she wandered between the aisles absent-mindedly picking things from the shelves. Rounding a corner, she bumped head-on into another trolley with a loud crash.

'Oh, God. I'm so sorry!' she said and looked up to see Emily Johnson smiling at her.

'Hello, Stacey. That's OK, no damage done. How are you? I loved the piece in the paper, the photos were very pretty. Any chance of some copies of the ones you took inside the church? Andrew was very impressed.'

'I'm glad you approved, thank you, and yes, I'll print some off and drop them in at the vicarage next time I'm passing. It's nice to be able to write good stuff with all this nastiness about.'

'I know what you mean,' Emily said. 'This is not what you expect in a rural community, one of the reasons we took this parish when it was offered – a bit different from Hackney.'

'I didn't realise you came from the city. How long have you been here now?' Stacey asked.

'We arrived just before you did and don't miss London at all. Hackney was a stopgap when Andrew came home with the troops. He was a chaplain, not a soldier.'

'He was an army chaplain? I didn't know that.'

Emily nodded. 'He spent a lot of time away when he was younger, but I'm glad we settled in Wales. I love the freshness of the air here and of course the glorious mountains. "God's Own Country" is about right, couldn't go back to a city now. Andrew loves it too, although these murders have affected him badly. He's not sleeping well and seems to have lost his appetite. Caring for the bereaved can be very wearing day after day; it was bad enough after Danny was shot, but now poor Mrs Read.'

'It must be hard for him. I saw Stevie this morning as I was driving through the village. He looked so lost and sad. His dad's gone to Birmingham to see Kathy's sister and the lads have been left to their own devices. I don't think they know what to do with themselves. How did we manage to attract a nutter out here?'

'You think it's someone from outside then, do you, not a local?'

'Emily, do you honestly think that someone living here would do such awful things?'

'I'd like to think not and why shoot the dogs? It's not like they could be witnesses or anything.'

'No, that's got everyone puzzled. Ben – like Andrew – has been working flat out all week.'

'I'm not surprised. How is he? I haven't seen him for a while now. You two still getting along?'

'Yes, very well, thank you. I've got used to having him around, although I'd like him to be able to slow down, go back to nicking the local bad boys in Llandrindod for weed. He's never handled a case like this before, a touch above his pay grade, but all the local stations are short of staff.'

'His boss must think he's up to it.'

'Yes, I guess. Anyway, I must get on. Good to see you, Emily, please give Andrew my best. I hope he feels better soon.'

'I will, take care.'

## Chapter seven

Stacey was working in the back garden when she heard a car pull up outside in the lane. Struggling to her feet, she brushed off her hands, walked round the side of the building and saw Ben making his way towards her.

'Hi, how's it going? Skiving again I see,' he said.

'Not at all.' She leaned into his kiss. 'Umm. Missed you too, Sherlock. What are you doing here, accusing me of skiving? How about you?'

'Technically, I'm on duty.'

'Guess my number came out of the hat today then and you're here to run me in. I *knew* my past would catch up with me eventually.'

'Not today, it hasn't.' He brushed a lock of hair away from her face, tucking the long strand behind her ear. 'I'm returning your memory card and thought I'd beg a coffee while I'm here.'

'I'm overdue for one myself, thirsty work gardening. Come in and I'll get the kettle on. Hungry? I missed lunch and was going to make a sarnie. Want one?'

'When did I ever refuse anything you offered me?' He chuckled and led the way to the kitchen. He sat at the table and watched Stacey dig around in the fridge.

'Ham and cheese OK?' She waved a wrinkled-looking tomato in his direction. 'Want to risk some of this as well?'

Stacey began buttering bread and slicing cheese. 'How's the case? Any news on the gun yet and was anything found at the picnic area? I went there yesterday, couldn't get in, still cordoned off.'

'One question at a time, OK? The answers, in no particular order are: no, yes and sort of.'

'Put them in the right order, will you, it's too late in the day for your cryptic ways.'

'Look, Stace, this is between us, OK? You *cannot* mention this to anyone or send anything to that editor of yours. I'd be skewered if my boss knew I was telling you this, but so far you've discovered more than the boys in blue have, so I owe you.'

'You know I'll keep quiet, just remember to let me know when I *can* go public. Sam loves a scoop and it can't do my career any harm. So go on – give.'

'OK, here goes. The same gun *was* used for both shootings. It's a military weapon, issued to the army and

Royal Marines, been in service for a while and is still used as a sniper weapon – long distance stuff.'

'An *army* gun? Are you saying a soldier shot these people?'

'No, that's not what I'm saying. I'm saying it was an army issue rifle, but that doesn't mean a soldier used it, if you think about it.'

Stacey nodded.

'These guns are available without having to join up to get one, but the army does use them. I don't know if you remember a few years ago, Dai's son – Nicholas – found an assault rifle left on the ranges at the back of the village and brought it home with him?'

'Yes, I do remember that, his mum had a fit when he walked in the back door with it.'

'So that proves you don't have to be a soldier. They've tightened things up considerably since then and don't tend to leave weapons lying about, but it's not impossible. Until we actually get our hands on the rifle we won't know, but at least we know what we're looking for. Nothing was found at the Llandovery Road picnic area, other than the bodies of Kathy and Sabre. No funny carvings, no footprints, no tyre tracks, nothing, but – because of your discovery at Long Field – they tried harder, hence the site was shut for longer. We're working on the theory these crimes *are* linked and we're looking for one individual, rather than treating them as two separate incidents.'

'Let's be honest, Ben, you don't have to be Einstein to come up with that. Two people and their dogs shot by the same rifle in the same week? It would be bloody odd if it *was* two separate killers.'

'I agree, but until the back room boys had officially confirmed the evidence, it could have been two separate, unconnected killings. But yes, very unlikely.'

'Do you think whoever did this came from outside the area? Have the police checked with locals to see if there were any unusual vehicles about on those days? If an unknown *anything* pulls into Llanagethin, at least three sets of curtains are twitching, so an out-of-town vehicle would have been noticed, surely?'

'We've checked, and nothing was out of the ordinary. No cars, vans, bikes, nothing that doesn't belong here was spotted either before, or after the killings and no witnesses – to *anything*.' Ben sighed and rubbed his eyes.

'What about checking people who hold gun licences?'

'That's happening as we speak, but most of the issued licences relate to shotguns owned by farmers, a rifle like this is a different thing altogether. Seeing as this would appear to be a military-type gun not a sporting weapon, it will probably be unlicensed. However – according to the experts – it was fired by someone who *really* knew what they were doing. If our killer *did* make his shot from the oak tree – a distance of about 200 yards – he's good, better than good. We found no extra bullets, so it would appear that only two shots were fired and both bang on target.'

'Then you're hunting for someone who knows how to shoot, owns a high-powered, military rifle and doesn't stand out. Maybe it *is* a rogue soldier from the barracks? Came down off the ranges and fancied trying his hand at killing real things, fed up with cardboard targets. That's a bit scary, don't you think?'

'Yes, very, but I'm not sure that's the answer. We're liaising with the military police at Sennybridge Barracks and they're checking records to ascertain if any rifle, or ammunition, has gone missing or been reported lost. As I said, they've tightened things up since Nicholas frightened his mother half to death, so I don't hold out much hope. At the moment, we're floundering. There's going to be another press conference in a couple of days, keep the press-pack happy, but other than informing them the same gun was used and that we're officially linking the crimes, nothing else will be released.' He rubbed his eyes again.

Stacey was concerned. 'You look tired, love, are you OK?'

'Yeah, I'm all right – just bloody frustrated. We know a little, but what we do know only throws up more questions and without evidence we're going round and round in circles.'

'What about the scratching on the tree? What did your experts say about that?'

'Not much. They agree it was fresh, probably done on the day of the shooting, they can tell apparently by looking at the newly exposed wood and how much oxidation has taken place. There's no guarantee the killer did it, but also no evidence anyone else did. It isn't a symbol they recognise either. Like you, they describe it as a fish shape.'

Stacey refilled the coffee cups and stood at the sink staring out of the window.

'It's not much is it?' she said.

'No, it isn't, but it's all we've got. The house-to-house is still ongoing and we're checking again with local farmers in case they spotted anything in the lanes, any strange vehicles driving about or parked in odd places, so we might turn up something. To be honest, Stace, I don't hold out much hope. It's over a week now since Danny was shot and we're no further forward at all.' He rubbed his eyes. 'I shouldn't really be leading this investigation, but the station is an inspector down and DCI Ambrose says he has faith in me, whatever that means.'

'Have you spoken to Samantha yet?'

'That's where I'm going when I leave here, followed by – I'm sure – a very difficult interview with Joanne. I'm meeting Mark in town in half an hour, so better get going. Thanks for the hospitality, I needed that.' He walked over and wrapped his arms around her.

'Any chance of seeing you later?' she asked.

'Don't know yet, I'll keep you informed. If I can, I will. You know I'd rather be here than anywhere else. Besides, I need to protect my assets. I don't want to find Mark sneaking in here while my back's turned.'

'You've got no worries there, love. I'm a one-man woman.'

* * *

After Ben left, Stacey went to the cramped office and phoned her editor.

'Hi, Sam, it's me.'

'Hi, Stace. How you doing, any scoops for me? Any more murders?'

'No, thank goodness. Just checking you received the updates I sent.'

'Yeah, got 'em all. Not very exciting though. Appeals to save local churches, Easter events, and Sheep Week in Llandovery – hardly in the same category, are they?'

'Ben's been here and says there will be another press conference in the next few days so obviously I'll go to that, but I don't think they've got much to report. Maybe we *have* got a mad stranger running around the Powys countryside picking off residents and their dogs, but that doesn't feel right to me. Psychopaths are rare – regardless of the impression the media likes to give – and to have one turn up here doesn't make any sort of sense. There *has* to be more to this story than any of us know. It's a matter of getting a handle on it, some clue to give the police a starting point. Anything in the in-box for me?'

'Nothing new. You'll have to find something to occupy yourself. Have a root around over there, collect some local vox pops, you never know, you may turn something up.'

'I'll do my best, Sam, but don't hold your breath. I think this has reached stalemate for the moment.'

She said her goodbyes and returned to the garden to finish tidying the vegetable patches in fading sunshine.

* * *

Ben knocked on the door of the Phillips' household, Mark standing by his side, warrant card in his hand. The door was opened by a tall and willowy, dark-haired girl in her mid-teens.

'Hello.'

'Samantha Phillips?' Ben asked.

'No, I'm her sister, she's up in her room. Who wants her?'

'Police.' They held out their identification.

'What do you want?' she asked, scrutinising their open wallets.

'To speak to Samantha, please,' Ben said.

'What's she done?'

'Nothing, as far as we know, just need a chat.'

'Come in and I'll fetch her.' She showed them into a small living room, went to the bottom of the stairs and hollered, 'Sam! Sam! Two hunky coppers here to talk to you. *Sam!*'

She walked into the living room. 'Fancy a cuppa?'

'No thanks, we're on a tight schedule,' Ben answered.

There was an uncomfortable silence for a few minutes before the door opened and Samantha came in looking wary. Her sister escaped into the hall and disappeared.

Ben stood and extended his hand. 'Hello, Samantha. I'm DS Ben James and this is DC Mark Jefferies. We'd like a few words with you. Please sit down.'

She shook his hand reluctantly and perched on the edge of the sofa.

'What's all this about then?' she asked.

'We'd like to talk to you about Daniel Evans.'

'What about him?'

'We understand you were good friends.'

'That poxy reporter, she's been on to you, hasn't she? Bitch! Told me she'd keep it to herself.'

'I'm not sure what you're talking about,' Ben said. 'We've been checking Danny's mobile phone records and your number appears often. In a murder case we check everything. Can you tell me what your relationship with him was?'

Samantha looked distressed and twirled a strand of her dark hair around her fingers. 'He was my teacher at school. That's all.'

'We think there might be more to it than that. For a start, he painted a portrait of you. It's hanging in the school, near the main entrance.'

'So? I was head girl. Danny painted all the head girls. No crime in that, is there?'

'No, not at all, but we've reason to believe your relationship was of a more *personal* kind.'

Samantha didn't answer and the silence stretched awkwardly.

Mark joined in the conversation. 'Samantha, we have to ask, it's difficult, I know, but if we are to stand any chance of catching the person who killed Danny, you must co-operate with us. *Were* you lovers?' he asked gently.

Samantha gave a slight nod of her head and tears began to leak from the corners of her eyes.

'How long were you with him? Was it a recent affair or had it been going on for a while?'

She mumbled something.

'Please speak up,' Ben implored. 'We'll try to make this as easy as possible for you. You're not under arrest, but it would be helpful if you would answer us.'

Samantha sniffed, pulled a crumpled tissue from her pocket and blew her nose. 'We were lovers, had been for a while.'

'How long? Did it start when you were at school or after you had left?'

'I was in the last year of sixth form. I wasn't underage or anything, if that's what you're getting at. Danny wasn't a paedo! I was eighteen, so he hadn't committed any crime.'

'How did the affair start?' Mark asked.

'When he painted my picture. He'd nearly finished it, asked me out for a drink and I went.'

'You knew he was married?'

'Of course I did. Oh no! You're going to tell Joanne, aren't you? Oh God.' Once again, tears began to leak from her eyes.

Mark pulled out a clean handkerchief and handed it to her. She took it and blew her nose loudly.

'Are you OK to go on?' he asked kindly.

'Yeah. Let's get it over with and then you can bugger off before Dad gets home. He'll be mad at me.'

'OK. So you started seeing Danny, what, nearly two years ago?'

She nodded. Mark scribbled in his notebook.

'How often did you see each other?'

'As often as we could. It was difficult – round here everyone knows your business before you know yourself – we were careful.'

'Did Joanne know?'

'Don't be stupid! Danny made it plain at the start that she must *never* find out and if she did, it would be over. We used to meet in out of the way places. Trecastle tea rooms sometimes, Brecon every now and again and there was a little pub in Sennybridge we liked.'

'And no one ever saw you?'

'Once. We bumped into Mr Jones – the headmaster from school – but Danny was brilliant. He made up a story on the spot and nothing ever came of it.'

'So you're *sure* his wife never found out? She didn't have a clue what was going on?'

'No, I'm sure. If she had, she'd have given Danny such grief over it. We were very discreet.' She paused. 'She'll know now though, won't she? She'll go crazy.'

'I'm sorry, but yes,' Ben answered. 'If there was a way we could avoid telling her, we would, but as I said, this is a murder enquiry.'

'Will it get in the papers? If it does, I'm going to be painted as a right slag, a home wrecker, but it wasn't anything like that. We loved each other, really loved each other. What we had was special and now it's going to look like a scuzzy affair. Dad's going to kill me when he finds out. And what about everyone else? You know how people are.'

Ben nodded sympathetically. 'Yes, I do, people can be very unkind. Did Danny ever say he was going to leave Joanne to be with you, or was he happy to keep the affair going?'

'We talked about it, but it was difficult for him because of the kids. He wanted to wait until they'd grown up a bit before he did anything like leave home – but yes – we'd planned for the future. He was so unhappy at home.'

'Did he say why?'

'Everything he said, told me Joanne didn't understand she was making him miserable.'

Ben got to his feet. 'Thanks, Sam, I know this can't have been easy.' He handed her a card. 'My number's on there, so if you want to talk, or think of anything that might help the investigation, give me a call.'

Sam took the card and showed the officers out.

Back on the street, the policemen got in the car and Mark drove towards the Evans' household.

'His wife didn't understand him,' Ben growled. 'Honestly, Mark, what is it with women? That's such an old line, yet men use it time and time again, always seem to get away with it and look at the misery it causes. I'm *not* looking forward to this.'

Mark pulled up outside a modest house and killed the engine.

'Let's get it over with, Sarge.'

## Chapter eight

'Hi, Pumpkin, it's me!' Ben called, stepping inside the low-ceilinged kitchen.

Stacey emerged from her office and smiled. 'You're a sight for sore eyes. Didn't think I'd be seeing you again today, did I miss your call?'

'No, didn't make one, sorry, had a real bummer of a day.'

She wrapped her arms round his middle and squeezed.

'You poor thing. Come for a bit of TLC, have you?'

'Hiding more like, I shall be glad to keep away from the world for a while. I've been flat out today with difficult interviews. Samantha Phillips followed by Joanne Evans and neither of them at all pleased to see me. Honestly, Stace, days like this make me wonder why I ever joined the force.

'Samantha's dreadfully upset, believed Danny was going to leave the wife, who "didn't understand" him, and set up home with her. Not yet though, when the kids were older. Same old, same old.' He rattled the ice cubes in his glass. 'It was an awful interview, but worse followed. Mark and I went from there to Joanne Evans' house. That was *terrible*! We had the whole gamut, tears, shouting, ranting and raving, the works. She plainly had no idea about the affair. At one point I thought she was going to punch Mark, he thought so too, never seen him so pale. Luckily the kids were away.'

'Where are they?'

'With their grandparents in Bristol, so we didn't have them to cope with as well. First of all she accused us of making it up, refused to believe anything we said, and then

– when she finally accepted the truth – dissolved into hysterical sobbing that effectively ended the interview.'

'How awful,' Stacey said.

'There's no way she had anything to do with Danny's death; I don't think you can fake that sort of despair. Mind you, at one point it did cross my mind Danny was actually lucky to be already dead – I'm convinced she'd have done him in otherwise. I'd forgotten how frightening some women can be.'

'Where do you go from here? If Joanne didn't kill him, who did?'

'Wish I knew. The brass are in a right state. Royal protection officers have been on to them now. Seems as though Charlie Boy and Camilla were planning a visit during the next few weeks, but there's no way that's going to happen while we have a crazed gunman running round the mountains.'

'You're back to the psychopath theory then?'

'Can't think what else it could be.'

'How about Kathy Read, any further forward with that?'

'Not an inch. We had a good look at Bob after we learned she was planning to leave him and leaned pretty hard; got nowhere. Yes, she was going, and yes, he was upset about it, but it seemed as though they'd come to an amicable split. He hoped after she'd been away a while, she'd want to come home and everything could get back to normal. We've accepted the killings are connected, same gun, same MO and dogs shot in both cases. What is that all about, why shoot the dogs? None of this makes any sense.'

* * *

Once Ben had left for work, Stacey made up her mind she'd go for a snoop around at the Llandovery Road site. She was pleased to see the police had deserted the picnic area and pulled up overlooking the open fields at the back of the site. Perching on the bonnet, she breathed in fresh mountain air and watched a group of four red kites swirling high above her, wheeling and dipping, chasing each other across the sky. They were such beautiful birds, resembling enormous swallows with deeply forked, red tails. As they turned and tumbled, sunlight flashed across their rust-coloured plumage making it glow like burnished copper. They called to each other and she closed her eyes to listen, wild sounds of the mountain filling her senses.

Flocks of sheep sang in the distance, the high-pitched bleating of spring lambs answered by the deep throaty grumble of their mothers, and skylarks twittered nonstop. Behind her in the forest, chaffinches peeped at each other and chiffchaffs repeated their fluting notes over and over again. Stacey felt herself relax, taking deep, steady lungfuls of crystal clean air.

Opening her eyes, she ambled around the large clearing, searching for anything out of place. The ground beneath the trees was brown, covered by a deep mat of fallen needles, free of undergrowth. Ducking her head she entered the twilight, eyes taking a while to adjust to the gloom. It was quieter under the trees, bird noise muted by the thick canopy. A movement close by at the base of a huge larch caught her eye. A small, dark brown face, with cream-coloured cheeks peeped out from behind the trunk and she recognised a polecat rummaging around in the layers of leaf litter. Smiling, she held her breath. Last year she'd had one living under her garden shed and had been delighted to see three tiny kittens running along beneath her kitchen window, holding on to each other's tail with their teeth, looking like a string of fluffy, brown sausages. After a few minutes the little animals looked up, spotted her and melted away.

Stacey heard a car on the lane, the rumbling engine noise loud and alien, but it passed on by and peace settled again. Returning to the open space of the isolated picnic area, she scanned the rough ground, before making her way to the spot where Kathy's body had been found, but apart from trampled earth there was nothing to see. Walking back to the car, she dug out a flask of coffee and carried it to one of the many picnic benches built by the Forestry Commission. The opposite hillside rose up in front of her, fresh new grass, bright amongst the brown of last year's bracken and small patches of purple ling glowed against the vivid green of spring. She became aware of movement and spotted a distant figure walking along the valley bottom. From this distance she couldn't see who it was, but assumed one of the local farmers was out checking stock.

A sharp crack from somewhere behind made her jump and look round. She saw nothing, but when she looked back in the direction of the walking figure she couldn't see it and wondered where the individual had gone. There was certainly no cover in the valley and even Usain Bolt couldn't have made it to the edge of the forest in the seconds she'd looked away.

Grabbing binoculars from the car she searched the area and was shocked to see the figure lying prone on the grass. A movement close by caught her attention and she refocused. A brown animal was running about. What the hell? Feeling uneasy, Stacey crossed over the cattle grid at the edge of the field and jogged down to the valley bottom. The closer she got to the fallen person, the more dread settled in her heart. One part of her brain – the optimistic part – tried to tell her that maybe whoever it was had tripped, or was lying on the grass to watch skylarks, but the other part – the darker part – whispered to her. She shuddered as her grey matter invented horror stories she couldn't push out of her head.

Within minutes, she was close enough to see the brown animal was a dog and the figure on the grass was Emily Johnson. Stacey broke into a run. She saw a dark stain on the front of Emily's light coloured jumper and her legs threatened to stop working. No-no-no! *This couldn't be.*

Stacey shouted as she ran. 'Emily! Emily! Are you OK?' No reply, but on hearing her voice the spaniel ran to her, trying to jump up and as Stacey reached Emily's side, the dog got under her feet and she tumbled to the wet grass, face level with Emily's.

'Oh, God. Emily!' She gently shook her friend, but there was no response. There was blood everywhere. Fresh blood, a dark stain grew rapidly on Emily's chest. The dog tried to get on Stacey's lap and she pushed him away roughly. Removing her jacket, she folded it, placed it under Emily's head and checked her mobile. No bloody signal. Standing, she frantically waved the device above her head and eventually the screen flashed, 'Emergency calls only'. She dialled 999.

'Emergency. Which service do you require?'

Her voice shook uncontrollably as she answered, 'Police and ambulance.'

The operator worked her way through the set script as Stacey jiggled with impatience, worried the signal would drop out. Why was this taking so long? Finally, the operator finished her spiel, informed Stacey the police were on their way and to stay where she was. In the distance, across rolling mountains, she heard the howl of sirens as police cars left the station in Llandovery, eight road-miles away, and hurtled along the winding main road. Within ten minutes they were pulling into the clearing, kicking up thick clouds of dust, followed by an ambulance that skidded to a halt behind Stacey's car. Uniformed officers leapt out of the vehicles and galloped down the grassy slope towards her.

She waved frantically. 'Here! Over here. Come quickly,' she yelled.

Paramedics, loaded down with equipment in large cases, followed the police and moments later were on their knees in the wet grass by Emily's side.

Stacey felt herself being lifted, her legs numb, unable to support her weight, a hot, nauseous feeling spreading in her chest. She heard herself moaning as a policeman tugged at her arm.

'Come on, miss, come away. Julie!' he called. 'Give me a hand, will you?'

A female officer ran over, positioned herself on Stacey's other side, helped to gently pull her to her feet and move her away before lowering her on the grass.

'Stacey! Oh my God,' Julie said. 'Come on, love, look at me.'

Stacey nodded and raised her eyes.

'You'll be fine,' Julie said. 'Deep breaths now, it's OK, I've got you.'

'Emily?' Stacey stammered.

'The paramedics are with her. You don't need to worry, they're looking after her and I need to look after you. You've had a hell of a shock. Sit here with me a minute and take deep breaths, you're shaking like a leaf.'

'Is she… is she dead?' Stacey asked, voice quavering.

'Don't worry about Emily, let the guys do their job. Do you think you can walk a little way? Be good to get you up to your car. Take my hand.'

Stacey struggled upright, wobbled alarmingly before regaining her balance, then slowly started up the long haul to the picnic area. Julie sat her in the passenger seat of the car, feet outside on the ground. Stacey was still shaking – teeth actually chattering.

'Have you got anything to drink?' Julie asked, rummaging about in the glovebox.

'There's a flask in the door pocket,' Stacey mumbled.

Julie found the flask, poured a cup and held it out. When Stacey didn't reach for it, Julie took her hand and wrapped the fingers around the sides of the plastic mug.

'Take a sip, slowly – it's hot. It'll help calm you down. You're in shock. Come on, another one please.'

More vehicles pulled into the picnic area. Car doors slammed and many boots pounded the ground. Stacey stared at the cup in front of her feeling numbed, completely unaware of her surroundings.

'Oh, my God. Stacey!'

She raised her head slightly and saw Ben running towards her. He dropped to his knees on the dusty ground and took her face in his hands, gazing intently into her eyes.

'For heaven's sake,' he said. 'Come on, Pumpkin, breathe, you're as white as a sheet. You're safe, it's OK.' He looked at Julie. 'What's going on?'

'Looks like there's been another shooting, Sarge, on the far side of the valley. Stacey called it in, I guess she found her.'

'Have the paramedics checked Stacey out?'

'Well, they have sort of got their hands full.'

'Who is it over there, do we know?'

'Emily Johnson – the vicar's wife,' Julie said.

'Bloody hell. Is she dead?'

'Don't know, didn't look good, but I needed to get Stacey away. You can see what a state she's in.'

'Do me a favour, go and get an update. I don't want to leave Stacey while she's like this.'

'No probs. On my way.' Julie negotiated the cattle grid and quickly crossed the open grassland towards the huddle of officials. Ben gently took the cup from Stacey's hands, placed it on the dashboard and hugged her, rocking slowly, stroking her hair. Gradually the quivering lessened. He held on. Then, with a great shuddering breath, Stacey started to sob. He held her tighter, continued rocking and let her cry.

Julie returned in a few minutes and shook her head. 'I've had a word with the medics, one of them will be over soon. There's not much they can do down there.'

'Thanks, Julie. As soon he gets here, I'll go over. Can you stay with Stacey?'

'Of course.'

Suddenly, a spaniel appeared from underneath the car and launched himself at Stacey.

Ben put out his hand to fend him off. 'Whoa, you. This is Emily's dog, isn't it? Here fella, here boy.'

The excited animal ran up to Ben who caught hold of its collar.

'Julie, put this chap in the car with Stacey, can you? We don't want him running off. Tell you what, though, he's a lucky dog if our shooter *has* been at it again.'

'Sarge!' shouted one of the uniformed officers. 'We need you down here!'

Ben glanced at Julie. 'Jules, can you take Stacey home once she's been checked and stay with her? I'll be there as soon as I can get away.'

'No problem. What about the dog?'

'Better take him as well. Keep an eye on both for me. I've no idea how long I'll be, but guess I'll be a while and Stacey shouldn't be on her own.'

One of the paramedics appeared by the car.

'Take a look at Stacey, will you, mate?' Ben asked. 'Make sure she's OK, then Constable Smith will take her home. If we need to, we can get the local doctor out. Bloody hell, this gets worse and worse.' He turned away and hurried down the steep slope to the valley bottom.

## Chapter nine

An hour later, Stacey was huddled up on the sofa in her living room, a blanket round her shoulders and a cup of hot tea on the table by her side. Sami was curled up next to her and she absent-mindedly fondled his ears.

'You'd be better off in bed,' Julie said. 'Let me help you upstairs, Sami can keep you company.'

Julie helped Stacey up to her bedroom under the eaves and settled her down. Sami ran up the stairs and jumped on the bed, lying closely against Stacey's side, burrowing his nose under her arm.

Julie stroked him. 'You'll have to go home eventually, little fella, don't get too comfy.' She straightened the duvet. 'I'm going downstairs now to give you some peace. You may sleep and that would be good, but I'll still be here. I'm not going anywhere. If you need me – bang on the floor.'

'Tell me when Ben arrives, will you?'

'Of course, but he may be a while yet. Is there anyone else I can call for you?'

'Maybe Ali, Alison Williams, my friend who works in Hawthorne House, the vet's in Llandovery. Her number's in the red address book by the phone.'

'I'll call her now. Anything else you need? Warm enough? I can refill your bottle for you if you like.'

'No, I'm fine, thanks, just horribly achy and tired. I wish this headache would let up, can't think straight with it.'

'That's probably not a bad thing to be honest, *cariad*. Try to rest and I'll check on you in a little while.'

Julie left the room, quietly pulling the door shut behind her and went down to ring the vet's surgery. Ali was horrified when she heard what had happened and promised to be there within the hour. Julie made another pot of tea for herself and waited, listening to the quiet tick of the kitchen clock.

Ali arrived a little while later and walked in through the open back door, frowning.

'Hello, I'm Alison Williams, you called me. How's Stacey doing?'

'I think she's sleeping,' Julie said. 'I haven't heard anything from upstairs. Emily's dog is up there too, curled on the bed like he owns the place. I think he's good for her.'

'Dogs can be remarkably sensitive. They pick up on emotions with an amazing empathy. He's probably wondering what's going on himself. Do you think I should go up?'

'Have a cuppa first. I told Stacey to bang on the floor if she needs me and we'll hear her if she moves about so I'm sure she's sleeping. I'd leave her be, while she's quiet.'

Ali sat at the table and gratefully accepted a mug of tea.

'What happened?' she asked.

'I'm not entirely sure, to be honest. Stacey found Emily Johnson in the valley beneath the large picnic area off the Llandovery road. Looks as though she'd been shot just before Stacey found her.'

'God, how bloody awful!' Ali was horrified.

'I brought her home. Ben told me to wait until he arrived, but I haven't heard from him yet. There's no point in ringing as the mobile signal is so crap, but he could be a while. I asked Stacey if there was anyone she wanted me to call and she said you, so…'

'You called and here I am.' Ali paused. 'Was Emily shot like the others, is it another murder?'

Julie was non-committal. 'Bit too soon to say, we'll know more when the boss gets here. How long can you stay?'

'As long as I'm needed, told *my* boss there was an emergency. He's good about things like that, I can make up the time later.'

* * *

Ben climbed the stairs quietly, pushed open the bedroom door and peered in. Sami looked up and growled softly.

Stacey stirred and opened her eyes. 'Ben?'

'Yes, sweetheart, it's me. I'm so sorry, I didn't mean to wake you.'

'You didn't, I was awake, sort of dozing.'

He moved to the bed and perched on the edge, taking one of her hands in both of his.

'How are you, Pumpkin? Are you OK? I've been *so* worried, but couldn't get away until now.'

'Better. Tired mainly with a bloody awful headache that won't give up.' She stroked Sami's soft fur and he settled down again, snuggling against her body.

'He looks at home here with you,' Ben said.

'Poor little thing. He was as shaky as I was when we came to bed, but seems calmer now.' She struggled to sit up, holding her arms out towards Ben, who moved closer and hugged her tenderly.

'You're a poor little thing as well.'

'Oh, I'm tougher than I look,' she said. 'What about Emily?'

Ben took a deep breath and shook his head. 'I'm so sorry, she didn't make it I'm afraid. The paramedic said she died almost instantly, wouldn't have known anything about it. Mark has gone over to the vicarage to tell Andrew what's happened and I need to meet him there in an hour or so. I'm here with you, not only because I love you, but to find out what you saw. Are you up to answering a few questions?'

'I think so.'

'Can I get you anything?'

'A cuppa would be nice. I'm so thirsty.'

'Hang on, I'll go and fetch you a drink.'

'No, I'll come down. Help me up, would you? I don't want to lie around like some bloody invalid. Is Ali here?'

'Yes, in the kitchen.'

'Well then, the sooner I get downstairs with you guys, the sooner I'll feel better. Up here, with only Sami for company, I keep going over and over it in my mind and that can't be healthy.'

'You sure?'

'I'm hardly gonna run a marathon… I really do feel better, not as achy – apart from my head – and the shakes have gone. I don't want to stay up here. Come on, Ben, give me a hand, will you? Sami, get down, there's a good boy.'

The spaniel obediently jumped off the bed, following them down the stairs and into the kitchen, claws clicking on bare wooden boards.

Ali looked up from the table. 'Stacey! What are you doing out of bed? Ben, I *told* you not to wake her.'

'I have rested and I'm not made of glass, just didn't expect to see what I saw today and it caught me out. As I told my man here, I'm tired, have a horrid, banging head, but I'll live and want some company.'

Ali got up and hugged her friend gently.

'Someone get the kettle on. I'm parched.' Stacey sat and rested her elbows on the scrubbed wood of the table.

Ben sat opposite, gazing at her with concern. He covered one of her hands with his own. 'You're cold. Can I get you another jumper or something?'

'I don't feel cold. I feel a wuss to be honest. I mean, poor Emily's dead. Andrew's going to be devastated, he's lost his wife, and poor little Sami is going to miss her, they were such good friends. I think what *really* shook me was that one moment she was alive and walking along the valley bottom and the next… I only looked away for a second and when I turned back she was lying on the ground.'

Ben stared at her. '*What?*'

'I said, one minute she was walking her dog, and the next…'

Ben interrupted, 'I heard what you said. Do you mean you were actually *watching* when she was shot?'

'No, I looked away. I saw her walking the lower path on the other side of the picnic area. There's a small stream that runs along the valley bottom.'

Ben nodded. 'I know it. Carry on.'

'At first I thought I was watching a farmer, out checking on sheep or something, then I heard a sharp crack noise. I looked behind me, it seemed to come from the forest further up the mountain, and when I looked back, I couldn't see the walker anywhere, so got the binoculars out. I spotted whoever it was, lying on the grass and thought maybe they'd fallen or something, so ran down to see if they were OK. Bloody hell, Ben, when I saw her… realised it was Emily… all that blood soaking her jumper.' She shuddered.

'You were there when she was killed?'

'Yes, I suppose I was. The sound I heard must have been the shot.' She shivered, eyes filled with tears. Ali put a steaming mug of tea in front of her and bent to give her friend another hug.

'You poor thing, that makes it even worse,' Ali said. 'No wonder you were so freaked. Bad enough to find her, never mind be there when she was killed.'

'Stacey, you must concentrate, love,' Ben said. 'Tell me *exactly* what you saw and heard. You're the closest thing we have to a witness and I need to know every tiny detail. Run through it slowly in your own time and I'll take notes. Don't leave anything out, however insignificant you think it is, it could be very important.'

Stacey took a deep breath and Ben removed his notebook from his top pocket. 'Ready?' he asked.

'As I'll ever be.' She swallowed a gulp of tea, wiped her face and began to speak. 'I'd gone out to the picnic area to see if I could find any clues to do with Kathy's death. It was a beautiful morning. The sun was warm and I spent a while staring at the view over the open fields from the back of the car park by the cattle grid. I was watching kites, listening to skylarks, you know how I love them.'

Ben nodded, scribbling hard in his notebook.

'I went for a wander around under the trees, saw a polecat.' A brief smile crossed her face at the memory. 'Didn't find anything, walked back to the clearing and a car went past on the lane, I remember that. I was annoyed because the noise spoiled the peace and I could tell by the sound it was travelling too fast.'

'Did you see the car?' Ben asked.

'No. It was up on the lane, drove by and didn't stop. I went back to my car, poured a cup of coffee from the flask and sat on the bonnet to drink it. That's when I saw Emily. Well, I didn't know it was her until later.' She paused and sighed deeply. 'As I said, I thought it was a farmer. I spotted her walking close to the edge of the stream in the base of the valley, saw Sami too, running around. I watched for a few minutes, then heard a noise. A sharp crack sound. I never dreamed it was a gun, sounded like the snap of a Christmas cracker, but louder – obviously.'

'Where do you think the sound came from?' Ben asked.

'Forestry land, behind me somewhere, maybe in the direction of the Roman road. You know, the steep rocky track that leads up from the sharp corner on the lane, just before the long straight?'

Ben nodded.

'I can't really be sure, but it seemed to come from that direction. Anyway, I looked back at the valley and couldn't see her. It was like she'd vanished into a hole in the ground. That's when I got the binoculars out and spotted her lying on the grass. I ran down the hill thinking she'd fallen. It was only a couple of minutes until I reached her… Well, you know the rest.'

'No I don't. Come on, Stace, you're doing great, just a little more. What did you do when you found her?'

'Knelt by her side, saw the blood, pushed Sami away, folded my jacket into a pillow, put it under her head and rang 999. I had to wave the phone about to get a signal, you know how bad it is there. I waited until the police and ambulance arrived and well… that's it.' Exhausted, she dropped her head on her arms.

Ben stared at her, his face full of concern, then moved his chair to her side and draped an arm across her shoulders.

'That was brilliant, Pumpkin, well done. Do you need a rest?'

'No, I'm OK, anything else?'

'The car you heard, you didn't see it?'

She shook her head.

'Are you sure it didn't stop?'

'I wasn't really paying attention. I was cross because it had disturbed me, but I think it drove on. To be honest though, I'm not really sure.'

'OK. The "crack", like a Christmas cracker you said?'

She nodded.

'Was there more than one crack or a single sound?'

'I'm sure of that – only one.'

'Was it close by, or a long way away? Did it sound like the army when they're firing up on the ranges behind the village, or nearer than that?'

'Definitely nearer. As I said, it seemed to come from behind me, but not that close. A little way away I guess, and I am guessing. I've no idea how to judge distance from a gunshot sound.'

'When you drove *to* the picnic area, did you pass any other vehicles? See anyone else at all, maybe someone walking along the lane?'

'No one, a few lambs bouncing about, but no people and there can't have been anyone else in the picnic area, I saw that polecat, remember, and they're really shy, so it must have been quiet for a while. Emily was a long way away, I couldn't see who she was until I ran closer.'

'Did you hear anything else? How about after you found her? Hear anything then?'

'No, nothing, but when I was with her, everything else was blotted out. All I could see was the blood. Sami tried to get on my lap and I pushed him away, but that's all. I can't remember anything after that.'

Ben kissed Stacey's cheek and gave her a quick hug.

He glanced up. 'Ali, do you mind staying overnight, keep an eye on this one?' He nodded at Stacey.

'Not a problem. You don't need to worry, I'll take good care of her.'

'Thanks.' He got to his feet. 'Right. Better take Sami back to his owner and relieve Mark. Julie, you can get off now.'

'I'm happy to stay,' Julie said.

'No need. I'll send Mark to run you back to town. Here, Sami, let's take you back home.'

## Chapter ten

After Ben left, Ali tucked Stacey up in bed.

'Thank you for being such a wonderful friend,' Stacey said.

'Steady on, you'll make my head swell and you'll be stuck with me forever cos I'll be too big to get out of the door. Now, listen, if you wake in the night, are worried about anything or need a chat – call me. I'll leave both bedroom doors open and I'm a light sleeper, so I'll hear you. I don't have to go into the surgery tomorrow, gave my boss a ring and told him I'm needed here and he's fine with that. So, any problems at all, holler – I mean it!'

'I will, you've been very kind.'

'What are friends for?' she said, kissing the top of Stacey's head. 'Now, settle down. Are you warm enough? Need another hot water bottle? More pillows, less pillows? Anything?'

'No, I'm fine. Go and get your head down, you look tired too. If you get cold in the night, there are extra blankets in the airing cupboard on the landing. Help yourself.' Stacey yawned.

'Thanks. Night night. See you in the morning.' Ali pulled the door half closed and Stacey heard her moving about in the spare room, before she drifted off.

* * *

Not far away in the vicarage, Ben sat opposite Andrew Johnson. The man looked awful, pale, drawn and older than his sixty years. Sami had been delighted to be reunited with his master and snored next to his slippered feet.

'Is there anyone who can sit with you, Andrew?' Ben asked. 'There are people we can call on. I'm not sure you should spend this evening on your own.'

'Thank you, but I'll be fine,' Andrew mumbled, 'and I am not alone, God is with me.'

'What about family?'

'Emily and I had no children and I come from a very small family, no brothers or sisters… oh.'

'What?'

'Emily has a sister, in Newtown and she should be told, but I'm not sure I want her to come down here. I'm better off alone and I have Sami.' He sighed. 'Can I see my wife? Where is she now?'

'We've taken her to Brecon, and yes, you can certainly see her, but not today. I'll arrange for one of my officers to drive you over tomorrow, but it's too late now and they'll need to examine her.'

'Yes, of course, you have your procedures. She'd been shot you say, like the others?'

'It's a bit early to say for sure, but we think so. Looks like she was killed with a rifle, same as the other victims, but we won't know for sure until we recover the bullet and have forensics look at it. Obviously, we will let you know as soon as we can.'

The vicar hauled himself upright, walked to the large picture window at the back of the room and gazed out at the little church, nestling in a small hollow by the river.

'My beautiful Emily,' he murmured. 'Such a good woman, stood by me all my life, was my rock and now she's gone. I know everyone has to die eventually, there's nothing surer in this life than our death and I *know* she's in a better place, but I feel so empty.'

Ben placed a hand on the vicar's arm, but Andrew didn't seem to notice.

'The word *why* twists in my head and heart and I have no answer.' He paused, deep in thought, fingering the cross that hung from his neck. 'No, Ben. I don't need company. I shall spend the evening in prayer and maybe He will provide some answers. I've been a believer all my life and He has never let me down, has always walked by my side and will not desert me at this time of tragedy.' The spaniel pawed at his master and Andrew bent to pick him up. 'Yes, Sami, I have you too, we have each other. Really, Ben, you don't need to be concerned. I've coped with disasters before, mine and others, so I'm well trained in the art of self-reliance, although I would be grateful if you could contact Emily's sister, spare me that burden. They were very close.'

'Of course, I'll help however I can.'

'Let me find you her phone number. Please – when you speak to her – tell her that I'm OK and don't need her to come rushing down. I'll call her tomorrow, I really need an evening of peace and prayer. Oh!' He stopped talking abruptly.

'What?' Ben asked.

'I have Daniel Evans' funeral tomorrow. It's being held in the green cemetery off the A40, close to Abergavenny. I'm not sure I can manage that. I'm only human and his family won't want a grief-stricken minister. I'll have to contact the bishop to ask if he can provide another officiate.'

'Can I do that for you, vicar? If you give me his number too, I'd be happy to call him for you.'

'My dear man, I feel pathetic, but that would be kind of you. As I said, I'd like to be alone with my thoughts and although the bishop is an incredibly compassionate person, I don't think I could bear his sorrow.'

Andrew moved back to the sofa and sat down heavily. Sami immediately jumped up by his master's side and whined, sensing his distress. The vicar covered his face with his hands and Ben was sure he was crying, but when the man looked up again, his eyes were dry and stared ahead.

'Are you sure you're OK?' Ben asked. 'I'm worried about you, Andrew. Shall I call the doctor? Maybe he should check you over or – as I said – I can arrange for someone to come and spend the night at the vicarage?'

'No, I'm OK, really I am, you don't have to worry. Emily and I would have been married for forty years in August – a lifetime – and now she's gone. It'll take a while to get used to, but I'll be fine, I'm a strong person, been in some terrible situations before. Really, Ben, I'd like it if you'd leave now, give me time to adjust. I'll get you those numbers before you go and please let me know when I can visit Emily. Will you be back tomorrow?'

'If it isn't me, it'll be DC Jefferies. I'm planning on attending the funeral tomorrow, but may well look in after – if you don't mind – see how you're doing. Of course, we will need to ask you some questions, but all that can wait until then.'

Andrew went to the desk, flipped through a tatty address book and scribbled on a piece of paper. 'Here are the numbers. Do you mind seeing yourself out?'

'No, not at all.' Ben passed the vicar a business card. 'My home number is on there as well as my direct line at the station. If you need me, or anything at all, don't hesitate to call. If I'm not there, they'll find me.' He stood, held out his hand and the vicar took it weakly.

'Thank you, Ben, you haven't got an easy job, delivering such dreadful news to the bereaved. I know, I have to do it myself sometimes, but not usually in the same sort of circumstances.'

Closing the door behind him, Ben walked to the car and checked his watch. It was late, Stacey would surely be in bed. He didn't want to disturb her and knowing Ali was there, decided to head home.

* * *

After the sergeant had left, Andrew poured himself a large whisky and took it into the conservatory to drink. The glass was black with night, the church not visible. He sat in his favourite chair and Sami leapt up, snuggled close to his master's thigh and Andrew absent-mindedly ruffled the soft golden fur. He wasn't the only one who would miss Emily, wasn't the only one whose life had been so dramatically changed; Sami's life would be different too. Andrew thought they were very lucky to have each other.

He sipped his drink and his mind rolled back a decade to his time in Iraq, working as chaplain for the army. He'd seen many lives changed beyond recognition by events they couldn't control. He'd counselled and prayed with recruits distressed because their buddies had encountered roadside bombs; because they had killed for the first time; because of trouble back home.

Corporal Mason's face appeared behind Andrew's closed eyelids, a young man who should have never signed up but only realised he was unsuited to army life eighteen months in. He had a pretty wife and wanted to spend time with her, so he was preparing to buy himself out when he was sent to Basra, where Andrew met him. Halfway through the tour, Mason visited his padre and showed him a letter. 'She's leaving me,' Mason had mumbled. 'Gone off with my best mate. I can't stand knowing she couldn't wait for me, didn't actually love me enough.'

Andrew shuddered, poured more whisky and groaned, disturbing Sami who stretched, yawned and settled down again. The remaining section of the memory played out in the vicar's brain, how he had talked to Mason, tried to comfort him and what a waste of effort it had been, how he'd watched Mason stride out into the compound, march towards the main gate and out into No Man's Land, where he stood on a landmine and was killed instantly.

Andrew rubbed his eyes, gulped the whisky, clicked his fingers at Sami and went to bed.

* * *

Early next morning, a police conference was held at Brecon Headquarters. The room was full, buzzing with conversation that ceased as soon as Ben and DCI Charlie Ambrose entered the room.

Ambrose addressed the assembled group. 'Good morning, everyone. I don't have to tell you the rest of the UK is watching us at the moment. We have now had three killings, the brass are demanding a head and it's your job to provide them with one. The national press is having a field day because we don't have anything to tell them. In a moment or two, I'll hand you over to DS James who is heading this inquiry under my supervision, but before I do, I need to inform you all that when I talk about "brass", I mean *high-up* brass. As you are aware, HRH the Prince of Wales and the Duchess of Cornwall were due to visit the area in the next couple of weeks. That visit has been cancelled due to security concerns. The Royal protection officers are in close contact with the Chief Super and it has been *suggested*, due to our woeful staffing situation, that officers from Scotland Yard should take over this inquiry.'

A murmur of dissent rippled around the room. DCI Ambrose held up his hands for quiet.

'I don't like it any more than you, but if we can't show some results quickly, it *will* happen. However, I have every confidence in DS James and all my officers. Leave is cancelled forthwith and I want you to pitch everything you've got into this investigation. There's a cliché about leaving no stone unturned, well I want you to go further, I want you to leave no pine needle unturned. We have *got* to get a handle on this, and soon. I am available to any officer at any time and anything you uncover, however insignificant you may think it is, I want to know about it. DS James…'

Ben stood. 'Morning, all of you. I want to provide an overview of these murders so we all know what's been happening and make it clear where we are with the investigation.

'We have three killings and forensics have confirmed that all three victims were killed with the same gun. The gun has been identified as an RPA Rangemaster.' Ben held up an A3-sized colour photograph. 'This is a 50-calibre sniper rifle, used by the British Army after it entered the tactical market in 2001 and according to the manufacturer, these rifles are in active use by a significant number of police and security organisations across the world. The barrels are threaded to accept a muzzle brake or silencer and can be fitted with a variety of day or night sighting equipment. This is a big, heavy gun. Not something you would want to carry any distance. It is also incredibly accurate over long range. The use of this weapon links all three murders beyond any doubt, even though the victims appear completely unconnected.'

He pinned the poster on the noticeboard and sipped from a glass of water. 'One male and two females have been shot. In two cases, their accompanying dogs were also killed. All were shot in isolated spots on or around the Epynt Mountain. There is no obvious motive behind these murders, although we have discovered that the first victim – Daniel Evans – was having an affair with an ex-pupil of his, Samantha Phillips. We have interviewed Mrs Evans and Mr Read and are satisfied they did not have anything to do with their partners' deaths. Mrs Evans was genuinely shocked when she found out about her husband's adultery and we leaned heavily on Bob Read without turning up anything. Yesterday Emily Johnson was shot while out walking her dog. The dog survived, maybe our shooter was disturbed before he could fire a second shot. We have a witness who saw Emily alive just moments before she was killed.'

A quiet murmur rumbled round the room.

'Stacey Logan – who some of you may know – the local *Mid Wales Times* reporter, was close by and heard what we believe was the shot that did the damage. She didn't see anyone, but maybe the shooter saw her and legged it. Ms Logan only heard a single shot and that means we are searching for someone who not only has access to this type of weapon, but knows how to use it effectively. Ms Logan also heard a car on the lane. She said it sounded as though it was travelling fast. No description, but if we could track down the driver, they might have seen something.'

A hand rose at the back of the room.

'Sir? Is it possible a squaddie has gone rogue? I mean, army gun, up there, so close to the Epynt Ranges. Maybe he fancied having a go for real?'

'That's a possibility we're considering and we're liaising with the Commanding Officer at Sennybridge Barracks. They are conducting their own investigation, checking all weapons, ammunition and whether any of their personnel have taken any unexplained absences. So far they've drawn a blank. This could be a stranger killing, although I find it difficult to imagine why a serial killer would pick this area to ply his trade and I'm sure some planning must have gone into these crimes. At the site of the first, we believe we've discovered where the sniper hid to make the shot.' Ben pointed to a photograph tacked to the wall behind him. 'We found this symbol scratched into the bark of a large oak tree overlooking the field where Daniel Evans and his dog Mollie were found on the morning of the 16th of April. It was carved about twelve feet off the ground and SOCO have confirmed it is fresh. We also found a track leading to the tree and fresh mud on the branches.

We believe this mark may have been carved by the killer while he waited. What we don't know is whether this was an opportunistic killing, or if Danny was the intended target. Nothing similar has been found at the second site. We're still combing the fields surrounding the Llandovery picnic area, but as yet have been unable to discover where either shot was fired from.'

Ben drank more water and frowned at his audience. 'Please, take a good look at these photos before you leave today and keep your eyes and ears open. DC Jefferies and Constable Smith, call on Reverend Johnson and take a statement, he may want a lift to the morgue in Brecon. I'm planning to attend Danny's funeral at the green burial site – I'll take Constable Bradshaw with me – you never know, maybe the killer will turn up to gloat.'

Another quiet, hopeful murmur rolled around the room.

'The rest of you, divide into three groups. Group one: hit the phones. Ring anyone connected to the victims, talk to them, no matter where they live, see if you can uncover anything interesting. The second group are on house-to-house. I want you to knock on the door of every house in the area and I mean *every* house. Group three: you're stuck with the paperwork. Read every report, study every photograph, find that link between the killings. If the same person was responsible, there *will* be one.'

The meeting broke up noisily and Ben called Constable Bradshaw over. 'Ian?'

'Yes, Sarge.'

'Got a dark suit with you?'

The constable nodded.

'Good. Get it on, will you? I want you in civvies today, don't want to frighten anyone off. Go and change and be quick – I'll be out front in ten minutes.'

## Chapter eleven

The sunny weather of the last few weeks finally gave way to more typical Welsh dampness. Thick drizzle blew across the open fields and mountains making the morning dark and dreary. Constable Bradshaw drove and the officers travelled in silence, lost in their own thoughts. Traffic was light so they made good time and arrived at the cemetery nearly an hour before the service was due to start. Mourners from the previous funeral hung around in sad, damp groups, but many had already left and there were plenty of spaces in the car park.

'Pull over to the side, Ian,' Ben said. 'Tuck us behind the chapel a bit. We don't want to be the first thing grieving relatives see when they arrive for Danny's service.'

Ian did as he was instructed and turned off the engine.

'What now, boss?'

'I can't see much point in wandering around in the rain, may as well sit in the dry until kick-off. We've a good view of the entrance, so we'll keep an eye on it and see if anyone stands out. Since we know who the main attendees will be, we're looking for anything or anyone who seems out of place.'

'Bit of an abstract science, isn't it?'

'Yeah, but you never know. The force ought to be represented anyway, so two birds with one stone and all that.'

'Mind if I smoke, boss?'

'I'd rather you didn't and you can't *really* stand by the entrance of the chapel for a fag, can you?'

Ian looked crestfallen.

'Oh, go on then, but open the window. Poison yourself by all means, but leave me out of it.'

Ian lit a cigarette and took a deep drag, before blowing smoke out of the car window.

'Junkie,' Ben muttered.

Twenty minutes passed and the car park gradually emptied. After a little while, a compact 4x4 pulled in and parked near the entrance of the chapel. A woman dressed in a black cassock stepped out and Ben recognised Marion Pike – local lay-reader – Andrew Johnson's replacement. She hurried inside out of the wet weather. The car park slowly began to fill again and mourners made their way into the chapel. Five minutes before the allotted time the hearse arrived, followed by a dark limousine containing the family of Daniel Evans.

His widow, Joanne, sat with her arms around each of her children and an older couple travelled with her. Ben recognised them as Danny's parents, faces set hard as they worked to control their emotions. The children looked scared and Ben wondered why they had been allowed to attend, surely they were too young for this? The glossy black cars pulled up at the door of the squat building. Funeral directors climbed out first, put on their black top hats and gently slid the coffin out of the hearse. Four younger men from the main body of mourners moved closer to assist. Lifting the coffin high on their shoulders they carried it slowly inside, Joanne and the children followed.

Ian nudged Ben in the ribs as a rusty, green Fiat pulled into the car park.

'Look, boss, that's Samantha's car, isn't it? Not sure that's a good idea.'

'Watching brief, that's what we're here for. Best not get involved. I'm not surprised she came though. Stacey said she was in bits when she met her at the flower festival. I *am* surprised she's come alone, you'd think she'd have brought someone with her for moral support. Got to admire her balls; Joanne's not going to be pleased to see her.'

Samantha parked close to the entrance and slipped in through the door.

'Right then, Ian, better get in. Looks like that's all there is. Let's try to do this without being noticed, sit at the back.'

They left the car and hurried out of the drizzle.

The interior of the chapel was a pretty space. Spring flowers filled the alcoves and an organist played sombre music quietly in the background. A large, plate glass window looked out towards the Brecon Beacons, a peaceful scene, but dull and misty due to the bad weather.

There was a good turnout and Ben recognised several staff from the school, including the headmaster and his receptionist. A group of seven teenage girls sat in the middle of the congregation – most probably students – pictures of abject misery as they snuffled into their hankies. The family were seated at the front, Joanne holding tight to her children's hands, more for her own comfort than theirs, Ben guessed. They looked so lost and bewildered and his heart went out to them. Samantha sat in a row on her own near the back, looking dreadful, face red and swollen; black eye make-up smudged both cheeks. She dabbed repeatedly at her nose with a tissue.

Marion Pike stood at the front of the congregation, the organist stopped playing and the service began.

Shortly before the end of the ceremony, Ben and Ian left the chapel and found a vantage point a short distance from the open grave, watching as pallbearers carried the coffin into dreary dampness. The drizzle had finally given up and through a chink in the clouds a narrow shaft of sunlight played on the green grass. The brightness struggled, but failed to lighten the mood of a deep, respectful sadness. Sorrow hung in the air, an invisible mist swirling gently between the mourners. Even the birds were silent.

The slow procession wound along narrow paths to the chosen spot and reassembled on the edges of a deep grave. Marion Pike opened her prayer book and read from the committal. As soon as she began to recite the final prayer, the undertakers took hold of the webbed strapping and gently lowered the coffin into the ground. As the lid disappeared from sight, Joanne began to weep openly. Danny's father stood by his daughter-in-law's side and draped an arm across her shoulders as the children clung to their mother's legs, sobbing.

There was a sudden movement from the rear of the group and a wailing sound sliced through the damp atmosphere. Samantha pushed through the mourners and for a moment it appeared she was going to fling herself into the grave. One of Joanne's hands shot out, snagged the younger girl's wrist and swung her round.

'You little bitch!' she screamed. 'How dare you. How bloody *dare* you come here?'

Samantha tried to pull away, but the angry woman's grip was too strong and she couldn't free herself.

'Why are you here?' Joanne demanded. 'Don't you think you've done enough damage? I can't believe you've got the nerve to come today.'

Samantha yelled back. 'I loved him and he loved me. You certainly didn't! If you'd made him happy, he wouldn't have needed me.'

'Shut your dirty mouth, you tart. Don't you *dare* criticise me. He was my *husband*, for crying out loud.'

Other mourners were shocked at the outburst, frozen to the spot, no one quite knowing what to do. The lay-preacher looked horrified and Danny's father tried to pull Joanne away while his wife gathered the children in her arms and steered them back towards the car park. A couple of bright flashes lit up pale, shocked faces and when Ben looked round, he spotted a couple of photographers and sent Ian to deal with them. Joanne managed to break free and lunged at Samantha, fists flying.

A lucky punch caught the younger girl on the nose and blood splattered across her face. Ben pushed past the mourners and wrapped his arms round Joanne's upper body, while a pallbearer grabbed hold of Samantha to stop her fighting back.

'Joanne, stop it!' Ben implored. 'This isn't the time or the place.'

Joanne was having none of it. 'Don't tell me what I can or can't do. What the *hell* has it got to do with you? Get off me!' she bellowed.

'I'm not going to let go until you calm down.' Ben glanced over at the young man holding Samantha. 'Can you take her back to her car, get her in it and make sure she leaves?'

He nodded, tugging at the younger woman's arm. Eventually she went with him, sobbing loudly.

'Joanne, look, she's going. Come on, stop it. Danny wouldn't have wanted this.' Ben shook her gently, forcing her to look at him. Then, as quickly as her outburst began, she wilted in his arms and he held on as her legs collapsed. The anger left and was replaced by a mournful sobbing that wracked her entire body. Ben led her gently towards a nearby bench and helped her to sit.

'Mr Evans,' he called. 'Sir, please, can you sit with her?'

'Who are you?' asked the distressed man.

'DS Ben James, Llandovery CID. Please, help me out here, will you?'

Mr Evans hurried over and sat next to his daughter-in-law. He wrapped his arms round her body and she collapsed onto him, still sobbing, but calmer. He mumbled soothing words and her body relaxed.

Ian returned, puffing slightly. 'The paparazzi won't be back.' He waved a couple of stamp-sized squares of plastic. 'I confiscated their memory cards.'

* * *

Ben and Ian travelled back to Llandovery, both rattled by the scene at the burial ground.

'Bloody hell, boss.' Ian chuckled. 'That was worth the trip.'

'Show some respect, Constable. Not only has that poor woman lost her husband under dreadful circumstances, she didn't have any idea about his affair. I tend to agree with her, Samantha should not have come. Stupid girl, but then, wisdom comes with age I suppose. It's those poor little kids I feel sorry for, at least Mrs Evans had the sense to get them away.'

The silence lengthened.

'Sorry, boss.'

'I should bloody well think so.'

They travelled a few more miles in silence, Ian's face pink with shame, before Ben asked, 'Well? Did you see any unexpected attendees?'

'Can't say I did, to be honest. Once it kicked off, we sort of had our hands full. There were a few I didn't recognise, but no one who looked like a psychopath.'

Ben smiled, no longer angry. 'And what, may I ask, does a psychopath look like?'

Ian had no answer and they drove the rest of the way to town immersed in their own thoughts. As they passed Llanagethin village, Ben asked Ian to drop him off at Noddfa. He desperately wanted to check on Stacey and there was little more he could achieve today. Ian pulled up in the narrow lane outside the cottage, Ben climbed out then leant back in through the open door.

'I'll see you early in the morning at the station. Take the car back, write up your report and then you can clock off. And, Ian?'

'Yes, boss?'

'Emphasis on the *early*. I'll be in around 7am. We've a lot to do and I want an update on what the others have accomplished.' He slammed the door and watched as the car disappeared round the bend at the end of the road.

Ben strolled up the front path, followed it round the side of the house and tapped on the stable door. He found it unlocked and walked into the kitchen.

'Hey, Pumpkin, it's me, where are you?'

'In the office.'

He walked through the house and discovered Stacey working at her computer, fingers flying over the keys.

He kissed the top of her head. 'Hi there, you. How you doing?'

'Good thanks. Back at work as you can see.'

He peered over her shoulder at the screen. 'Working on what?'

'This and that. Follow-up pieces. How did the funeral go?'

'Oh God, Stace, it was pretty horrendous to be honest.'

'Funerals aren't usually much fun.'

'No, not many laughs to be had at this one.' He sighed. 'Samantha turned up and caused a dreadful scene.'

Stacey shut the computer down and swivelled in her chair.

'Let me get you a drink. Coffee or whisky? The sun *is* over the yardarm after all.'

'Whisky'd be great.'

'Let's go through to the living room, you'll be comfier there. There's some chilli in the freezer, I'll heat it up and boil some rice, that way you won't have to worry about cooking when you get home.'

'I'm going home, am I?' he asked, eyes twinkling.

'Well, not if you don't want to. I've changed the sheets on the spare bed.' She laughed, heading for the kitchen.

Later, after they'd eaten and the washing up was out of the way, they lounged on the sofa. Stacey cuddled in the crook of his arm and he stroked her hair.

'So, any out of place mourners at the funeral?' she asked. 'Did our murderer turn up?'

'Oh, I don't know,' he groaned. 'There didn't seem to be anyone odd. A few from the school, the headmaster, you know, Anthony Jones?'

Stacey nodded.

'Danny's parents, although I didn't see Joanne's, and a few pupils, a group of about seven, all girls and all sobbing, looked like sixth formers. There were some I didn't recognise though, and of course – the lovely Samantha. God, she was in a dreadful state. As soon as Joanne saw her, she lost it completely. It started with shouting, Joanne calling her a tart and Samantha screaming back, telling her how much Danny loved her, before Joanne went loopy, snatched hold of Samantha and started swinging her fists about. Thank God for pallbearers! Joanne caught Samantha a good one on the nose, blood everywhere. You know, Pumpkin, I *really* think I'm getting too old for this.'

'You poor, old man. At thirty-six? I don't think so, you're just not used to murder and mayhem. You've been a rural copper for too long.'

He humphed. 'Enough about me and my day. How about you? You seem a lot better.'

'I'm fine, Ben, you worry too much. It was a shock, that's all, but I'm fine now, back in harness. Sam's been pressurising me to write front page articles full of gore, but I'm resisting. Rang the station earlier, but they said there's nothing new to report, no second press conference in the foreseeable. Have you heard anything?'

'No, nothing. Early start in the morning though, I'll catch up then and hope the others have made some progress.'

'Sam can't quite get his head round it. A huge story on his doorstep and nothing to say about it.'

'That's the thing, it's an apparently motiveless crime. Until we discover the *why*, or uncover some hard evidence, crimes like these are very difficult to solve. You know the royal visit has been cancelled, don't you?'

'No, I didn't. Can I write about that? It'll shut Sam up.'

'Yeah, that's common knowledge so go ahead, hack, scribble away.' He yawned. 'It's no good, I'm whacked. Am I really in the spare room?'

'What do you think?' Stacey kissed him soundly and they made their way upstairs together.

## Chapter twelve

Ben was long gone when Stacey made up her mind to visit *The Mid Wales Times* offices in Brecon and catch up with her boss. They'd spoken the evening before and he'd promised her lunch if she made it into town.

The weather was still gloomy, but mild. She dressed for comfort and by ten thirty was driving across the military ranges towards the main A40. She loved the narrow, mountain road. Satnavs didn't recognise the route, as it crossed MoD land, so the few vehicles she did meet tended to be driven by other locals, or convoys of military trucks. On a clear day the views were incredible, stretching across the wildness towards the edge of the Brecon Beacons and the peak of Pen-y-fan, the highest point.

The MoD had appropriated this huge patch – tens of thousands of acres – in the 1940s and cleared the land of people. Small villages sat within the newly acquired land and their residents were moved to towns and villages outside the new range's boundary, an action reminiscent of the Highland Clearances in Scotland. Several churches still remained and twice a year – when the firing ranges were closed – folk who had relatives buried in the churchyards were able to visit the graves. One of the old cemeteries had been completely overtaken by daffodils that spread out to cover almost two acres of land in a bright splash, as though a gigantic pot of yellow paint had been emptied over the green and brown of the mountainside. A wild, lonely place, with a severe kind of beauty, Stacey thought.

On warm summer days heat hazes shimmered over the tarmac, but during the winter snows the road was pretty much impassable. Several times, visitors making their way to see Stacey had been caught out. One or two even having to spend the night in their cars and wait to be discovered by squaddies the next day, who invariably had to tow them out. Today though, it was dull and the visibility bad. She drove slowly with headlights on, keeping her eyes open for the sheep and lambs that wandered all over the winding road. She carefully negotiated the steep, downhill section at the end to join the main road and made it to Brecon in good time.

Parking at the back of the old building housing the paper's headquarters, she pushed through the large glass doors and climbed the stairs to Sam's office. He was on the phone when she arrived and waved her to a seat. Plonking herself on a chair, she waited until he'd finished talking.

Slamming the phone down, he glared at her. 'What do you want?'

'Charming, I'm sure. Thought you were going to take me out to lunch today, being that I'm your favourite reporter an' all that.'

'I don't have any favourite reporters. Tell you the truth, I can't stand any of you.'

'Bloody hell, Sam, you're in a good mood today. Where would you be without us? You wouldn't have anyone to bitch about, no one to shout at and certainly no paper. Did you get out of bed the wrong side today, or is Mrs Jenkins giving you shit about your smelly feet again?'

He sighed. 'Sorry, Stace, not having a good day.'

'Why, what's up?'

'All I've had this morning is the great unwashed phoning up to moan at me. "You didn't spell my name right; I'm not forty-four, I'm thirty-four; you promised it'd go in yesterday". Same old, same old. I think it's time to retire.'

'Don't talk daft, you'll die with your boots on. Give up being editor? No way. You'd last a week at the most. I can't even remember when you weren't here.'

'That's what I mean. Too long, Stace, I've been here too, too long.'

'I'll get my violin out in a minute. How ever does your wife stand you? Come on, you grumpy old bugger, shift your arse and take me to lunch.'

They left the office together and found the weather had cheered up a little, at least the drizzle had stopped. They walked to The Wellington, a short distance from the offices, and took a table at the back. Sam was a regular and always ordered steak if the paper was paying and expected his guests to eat the same, so menus were unnecessary. A bottle of his favourite wine appeared in front of his nose, Stacey was served a long fruit juice with ice. She drank deeply before reaching in her bag to pull out a cardboard folder and dropped it in front of Sam, next to the wine bottle.

'What's that?' he asked, round a mouthful.

'A very padded out piece for you. The royal visit's been cancelled, protection officers aren't prepared to take the risk. There are a few local vox pops about how much the residents and neighbours were looking forward to the occasion, a quote from the Mayoress, the usual stuff. I fleshed it out with a nice photo we used when Charles and Camilla toured the villages a few months ago and added an update on the investigation, but there's really not much to say about that.'

'You know more than you're saying. How could you not, with that great, hunky copper of yours snuggling up to you most nights? *Everyone* pillow talks.' He sipped his wine. 'So, what is it you're not telling me?'

'Really, Sam, the police haven't got any clues.' She gestured at the folder. 'It's all in there.'

'Indulge me – talk. Saves me using my eyes and wearing them out.' He peered at her over the rim of his glass.

'I give in. Motiveless crimes, two female victims, one male and two dogs, all shot with the same rifle, possibly an army or ex-army weapon. Remember, Sam, I was a short distance away from Emily when she was shot, more or less in front of my eyes, and I didn't see anything.'

'Maybe we *have* got an outsider picking off the locals. Not hunting season for them, is it? No, you're right,' he said, noticing the look on Stacey's face. 'Tasteless.'

'As I said, Sam, that's why they're struggling. I don't know any more than you, if I did – and it came from pillow talk – I wouldn't tell you *or* use it in the paper. I don't want to lose that hunky copper of mine, thank you very much.'

Food arrived and they tucked in, too busy chewing to speak. Moments passed and Stacey sipped her drink.

'Got anything for me then?' she asked. 'I'm anxious to get back in the groove.'

'There was something.' Sam looked puzzled. 'Uh… not anything very exciting. Uh… something to do with… got it! St David's church, where the flower festival was? They're having a push to renovate the churchyard. I think they're mapping it, graves and stuff, then contacting the living relatives and begging for money. Something like that anyway.' He stuffed a huge piece of meat into his mouth and chewed vigorously.

'Yeah, I'd be up for that. That's Andrew Johnson's church, Emily was his wife. I'd like to see how he's getting on and haven't spoken to him since she was killed; been wondering how he's coping. Good timing, Sam.'

Sam took a slurp of red.

'I'll take that, and send the piece over the wires when it's done. Any deadline?' Stacey asked.

Sam shook his head.

'I'll see if I can take some good pictures, it's such a pretty church, tucked on the banks of the river. Maybe a mini feature, with colour, give their appeal a boost,' she said.

She heard him grumble under his breath, something about being the only editor in history that no one listened to, but pretended she hadn't noticed and concentrated on her food.

* * *

After lunch, Stacey drove back towards the ranges. Pulling up in a lay-by, she tapped the number of the vicarage into her mobile phone.

A woman answered, 'Hello. St David's Vicarage.'

'Hello. Is Andrew Johnson there, please?'

'Who's calling?'

'My name is Stacey Logan. I live in the village, not far from the church. I, uh, I found Emily.'

She heard the woman catch her breath.

'Is he there or is it inconvenient? I'd like to call in to see him in about an hour. I understand he wanted help publicising a fundraising drive for St David's. I'm a journalist for *The Mid Wales Times.*' She paused. 'I'd also really like to see how he's doing, whether there's something I could do for him.'

'I'm Sarah Gilbert,' the woman said. 'Emily's sister. I arrived yesterday to look after him. He's OK, still in shock I think, not a wreck but not really *present* most of the time. His faith keeps him going, but it's been so long since he had to look after himself. I'm sure he'd love to see you and he is at home. I'll take your number and if he says he's not up to it, I'll call you. Otherwise, please visit. It will be good to meet you.'

* * *

An hour later, Stacey parked tight to the verge in the centre of Llanagethin, walked to the vicarage and tapped on the polished brass knocker. A few moments passed before the door was opened by a woman in her late fifties, short and slightly rotund, with grey crinkling hair. She wore a pretty floral apron and was wiping her hands on a tea towel.

'You must be Stacey!'

She held out her hand and Stacey took it in greeting, surprised by the strength of the grip.

'I'm Sarah. Sarah Gilbert. Do come in.'

'Good to meet you. I am very sorry it's under these awful circumstances. How are you?'

Sarah sniffed. 'Struggling if I'm honest, such a dreadful shock, difficult to believe I've lost my sister.' She closed the door behind her guest. 'Andrew's in the conservatory at the back of the house. You go through and I'll bring some drinks. Tea? Coffee?'

'Coffee please, if it's no trouble.'

'None at all. Go on now, I won't be a minute. Andrew knows you're coming so won't be surprised when you walk in on him.'

The dumpy woman turned away, heading for the kitchen and Stacey walked along the narrow hall towards the rear of the house. A small living room filled with floral-covered chairs opened out into a spacious conservatory. The clergyman sat in a wicker chair overlooking the lawn that swooped gently downhill towards St David's church and the winding river beyond.

'Hello, Andrew,' Stacey said.

He didn't move, didn't make any sign he'd heard her, eyes fixed on the church.

'Andrew?'

Eventually, he turned to face her and a brief smile flittered across his face.

'Stacey, sorry, miles away, how nice to see you. Do come in and sit down, won't you? Now the sun has finally broken through, it's quite beautiful out here. Amazing how a little sunshine can make everything seem better.'

Stacey nodded and sat in a matching chair to his right.

'How are you, Andrew? I've been meaning to visit before now, but wasn't sure you'd want company.'

'You're not alone, my dear. It seems these days no one knows how to treat the bereaved, what to say, how to behave, so they stay away and that's probably the worst thing they could do.' He spotted her slight frown. 'Oh, my dear, I don't mean you. Please don't think that. I should have been in touch with you – to thank you.' He smiled again.

'Thank me?' Stacey was puzzled.

'Yes, for being with my Emily, you know when… The police told me you were there when she was killed, that you tried to help her. For that, I thank you. It must have been very hard.'

The man had such sadness about him, such loss, yet he was able to thank her for the little she'd done. She didn't know what to say, so reached out and took his hand in hers as he smiled at her.

Sarah bustled in carrying a large tray laden with a coffee pot, mugs, milk and cream and a plate of homemade scones.

'Here we are then. Stacey, could you move that small table over from the window for me? I can put the tray on that and we can all help ourselves.'

Stacey dragged over the table and Sarah put her burden down, puffing slightly with the effort.

'Please, tuck in, don't wait to be asked. We don't stand on ceremony here – well, only on Sundays.' Her face wrinkled with amusement as she turned to her brother-in-law. 'Andrew, shake a leg or the scones will be gone. I made them for you this morning and they're always better fresh.'

The older man shuffled forwards in his seat and poured three mugs of coffee while Sarah buttered scones.

Stacey had just filled her mouth with a huge bite when Andrew asked her. 'You're here to help with our fundraising I understand?'

She struggled to clear her mouth and took a sip of coffee, which promptly went down the wrong way and sent her into spasm of coughing. Sarah leapt to her feet and pounded her enthusiastically on the back.

Stacey nodded at Andrew, eyes streaming. 'Sorry. Yes, that's right. I met Sam – my editor – this morning. He told me you're raising money for renovation work, said you were mapping the churchyard or something?'

'Yes, that's right. It was Emily's idea, you know. She thought if we were able to trace living relatives of the souls buried in the churchyard, we could contact them and appeal for donations. They may be more inclined to help since we are custodians of their ancestors.'

'Make it difficult for them to say no, you mean?' Sarah said with a chuckle. 'Emily was good at dreaming up all kinds of ideas to raise money, a very creative person. I miss her so much.' She hesitated. 'Stacey, can I ask you something?'

The reporter nodded.

'When you were up there, when you found Emily, was she… was she dead when you reached her? What I mean is, did she say anything to you?'

'No, she didn't. I'm sorry, I think she was already dead. It didn't take me long to run down the hill and the police say they think she died instantly. She wouldn't have known much about it.'

'Strange the things we are sometimes grateful for, don't you think?' Sarah paused again before asking, 'Did you see anything? When you were up there I mean, before. Before she was shot.'

'No, I didn't. I told the police I heard a car pass on the lane and heard the shot, but didn't see anyone at all. I'm so sorry for you both, it must be incredibly hard. Can I do anything to help?'

Andrew shook his head. 'No, my dear, we're fine, we'll manage. Time is a great healer, as is thinking about other things. Get out that notebook of yours and see if we can't write a piece between us that Emily would approve of.'

When the interview was over, Sarah walked Stacey to her car.

'Thank you so much for coming. I know Andrew was pleased to see you and I've enjoyed meeting you, hearing you talk about Emily. She was my little sister, I've always felt protective and her passing has left such a hole.' Sarah's eyes reddened and a couple of tears slipped out. 'Who'd have thought things would end like this? We had a holiday booked – just the two of us – a bit of sisterly bonding. We'd been saving for years and booked a three-month cruise round the coast of South America. She was so excited about it. Emily worked incredibly hard all her life, it's not an easy job being the wife of a vicar and Andrew can be very set in his ways. She needed a proper rest, that's why we dreamed up the idea. Andrew wasn't very pleased about it to be honest, but men can be grumpy, can't they? Soon as they think they have to cook their own tea and wash their own socks – even the best of them.'

'When were you going?' Stacey asked.

'End of the summer – August – we'd have been back in time for Christmas. Emily wouldn't desert Andrew at one of his busiest times of the year.' She sighed. 'I could understand him being a bit put out if she'd planned to be away during the festivities, but she was clear she wanted to be back, so we booked a trip that would fit in.'

'That's such a shame when you'd saved for so long.'

'Yes and I don't know what to do now. I was looking forward to it too, but I'm not sure if I want to go alone and can't make up my mind who to take if I did decide to go. I mentioned it to Andrew but he wasn't interested. Maybe it is too soon.' She wiped her eyes with the back of her hand. '*Listen* to me, rambling on. I'm so sorry, you have more important things to do than listen to my problems. Go on, off with you and write that article, the better you write it the more donations we'll encourage and it might help Andrew deal with this awful tragedy.'

## Chapter thirteen

Ben stood at the end of the long incident room gazing up at a large corkboard covering the wall. The entire investigation was on this wall. Photographs of people, places and evidence, maps, pages of names and addresses, lists of witness statements – it was all here. Pinned to the buff-coloured surface with multicoloured map pins.

The board was divided into three. At the top of each section was an enlarged photograph of each victim, Danny Evans, Kathy Read and Emily Johnson. Immediately beneath the large pictures, were smaller photos of significant people in their lives, husbands, wife, children, and in all three cases, photos of their dogs. At the bottom of each section were landscape shots of the areas where they were found and close-ups of the ground where they fell, complete with dark splashes of dried blood. Lots of it. Human blood and in two cases, smaller patches of animal blood.

In the first section, under Danny's name was another photo of the scratching Mark had found on the tree overlooking the murder site. Ben frowned. It didn't make any sense to him and still looked like a fish, if you turned it sideways, but he wasn't convinced this was the work of the killer. The field was popular in good weather and used by gangs of children from the surrounding area. It could have been carved by anyone and nothing similar had been found at either of the other sites.

The door at the far end of the room suddenly banged open, ricocheting off the wall. Ben whirled round angrily and saw Mark Jefferies storming into the room.

'Hell's teeth, Constable! You nearly gave me a heart attack. What on earth's wrong with you, crashing about like that? Consider yourself reprimanded.'

'Sorry, boss, you gotta come. Brass want you.' Mark shot back out the door and Ben struggled to catch him up on the stairs.

'Hold on, Mark. What's going on? Why all the urgency?'

'There's another body. Found first thing this morning. They're going ballistic upstairs.'

They ran up the stairs to the top floor and as soon as their faces appeared in reception, were ushered into the inner sanctum. There were already three men in the office. DCI Charlie Ambrose sat in front of the wide wooden desk, the Chief Super – Dennis Oliver – sat behind and off to the right was a man Ben didn't recognise.

Dennis Oliver cleared his throat. 'Thank you for being so prompt, DS James. I'm sure DC Jefferies has filled you in. Another body was found in the early hours of this morning, believed to be Mrs Amber Atkins from Llandovery. She was discovered on the banks of the Tywi River by a David Little, not far from town. The call came in an hour ago and uniforms are securing the area. We took a call yesterday from her husband – Jimmy – around midnight, saying she hadn't returned home and he was worried about her. I suggest you make a quick visit to the site, then get over to see him as soon as you can. I'd prefer the news coming from you rather than some rookie, so that's a priority.

'Before you go, I'd like to introduce DS Jack Trent, from Scotland Yard. As you know, there's great concern over these killings due to the royal residence on the outskirts of Llandovery.'

Ben frowned. 'So Scotland Yard doesn't think we're capable of handling this or what?'

'Dyfed Powys is seriously understaffed, you know that, so I'm happy to accept DS Trent on secondment.'

'But–'

Oliver held up his hand. 'You can't blame London for being twitchy when the heir to the throne has a property within five miles of these killings, especially as we don't seem to be making much progress with the investigation. I've been informed DS Trent is on a watching brief, but will of course help you all he can. He's an experienced officer, so use him. Don't waste his talents because you feel your noses have been put out of joint. This is *not* because we don't have confidence in you, this has been dictated from on high and is not open for discussion.' He glared at everyone in the room, reinforcing his words.

'Good! On with it then and as soon as you've got something to tell me, I expect to hear it.' He began to shuffle papers on his desk and the uncomfortable interview was over. All four men struggled to their feet and didn't speak until they were on the stairs.

Charlie Ambrose broke the silence. 'What can I do to help, Ben? Could you use any more manpower? I've been granted unlimited overtime on this, so anything you need, just ask.'

'Thanks, boss. Until I visit the crime scene, I don't know what'll be useful. As the guv said, I have to call on Jimmy Atkins, so we'll talk as soon as I'm back in the station. No idea when that will be. I'll take Mark with me and we'll keep you posted.'

'Don't forget DS Trent, Sergeant.'

Ben and Mark glanced at the newcomer who smiled broadly.

'I won't get in the way – promise.' DS Trent held up one hand, three fingers together forming a scouting salute.

'Make sure you don't,' Ben growled, pushing past him making for the car. Mark sat in the driver's seat and DS Trent ducked in the back.

They headed towards the river and the Londoner tried again.

'Look, I don't like this gig much either, get dead nervous in the country – all this wide open space stuff, wild animals like cows and sheep, mud and foul smells everywhere. I'm a city boy through and through, perfectly comfortable with thousands of strangers round me, grey concrete and buildings, but not at all happy with this agoraphobia inducing, outdoor space. Right culture-shock. I'm so rattled I probably won't speak again, unless one of you buggers says something to me. I need the energy to hang on to my paranoia.'

Ben chuckled, reached over the back seat and awkwardly the men shook hands.

'Call me Jack, will you?' the seconded officer said. 'I don't do rank and stuff.'

'I'm Ben and this is Mark. Welcome to our world.' Ben looked back at the road. 'Here we are then. Are you intending to leave the car, Jack, or will the fields freak you out too much?'

Mark pulled into a large lay-by behind a transit van and several patrol cars. An ambulance waited at the far end. The officers ducked under the tape and made their way to the bank of the river where a group of people congregated. As Ben approached the small crowd parted and he spotted a body lying on the ground. There was a splash of red on the grass that glowed in the early morning sunshine. He trotted over to the group and recognised Constable Julie Smith.

'Hey, Julie! Been here long?' he asked.

'In the first car, boss.'

'What have we got?' Ben asked, bending down to examine the dead woman.

'Another shooting. Her name is Amber Atkins, lived just outside town, had a wallet on her.' Julie held up a plastic evidence bag containing a small leather pouch. 'She's been shot with a large calibre rifle – hence all the blood – the bullet leaves a huge hole on the way out. She was walking her dog.' She pointed to the left. 'He's over there, also shot. We're searching, SOCO's here, Doc's been and the body is ready to be moved. We waited so you could see the scene intact.'

'Thanks, good work. Mark, go and check with the guys organising the search, see if they've found anything. Have them check the undergrowth in a radius approximately three hundred yards from this point, *before* they trample any evidence. Tell them to search for tracks or small paths, then for vantage points a sniper could use. Make sure they don't cock it up, I'll be pissed off if they miss anything this time like they did at the Long Field site.'

Mark scurried off and Ben signalled to the waiting paramedics. They moved forward and gently collected the body on a stretcher, carrying it to the ambulance waiting on the road. The ground where Amber had lain was then searched thoroughly – nothing found.

Ben called Jack over. 'Here's an idea. I need someone to keep an eye on this lot. Can you get the agoraphobia in remission long enough to do that for me? I'll leave Mark here and take Julie to talk to Mr Atkins.'

'No worries, happy to be useful.'

Ben leaned into his car, dragged out a cardboard file and threw it towards Jack. 'There's some photos in there of the other kill sites. Take a look and see if you can find anything *here* that matches *anything* in any of those. I'm not afraid to admit it, Jack, I'm getting desperate and if you can help… well, I'd be grateful.'

'That's what I'm here for,' Jack said. 'I'll be fine as long as those sheep keep their distance – they look manic to me, with those intimidating, yellow eyes – not what I'm used to at all.'

* * *

Ben and Julie arrived outside a green door with chipped and peeling paint. A handwritten note pinned to the frame read, 'Please knock' – a piece of electrical tape was stuck over the bell push.

Ben rapped loudly and sounds filtered through the wood, running feet followed by silence. Ben knocked again.

'Who is it?' a young-sounding boy asked.

'I'm a friend of your dad's – Ben's my name. Is he in?'

'Yes, but he's asleep.'

'Can you wake him up, son? It's important.'

A younger girl spoke. 'Is it about Mummy?'

Ben looked troubled. 'Can you go and wake your dad please and ask him to open the door?'

He heard scampering sounds. There was a long wait until a heavier footfall approached and at last the door was opened.

The man standing in the hall was dishevelled, short hair stuck up in all directions and his eyes were bloodshot, the whites tinged yellow. He was unshaven and his once white T-shirt was stained with at least three different substances. A waft of stale alcohol floated out of the house.

He frowned at Julie's uniform. 'You took your time. I rang last night to report Amber missing.'

'Can we come in?' Ben waited and when the opening didn't widen, he added, 'It will be easier to talk than out here on the doorstep.'

'Found her then?'

'If we could come in for a minute?'

The door finally swung open to reveal a scruffy hall, wallpaper peeling in places with large patches of black damp on the plaster. No carpet, but grubby bare boards were littered with toys, newspapers and a large pile of junk mail. Peering round a door halfway along the hall were two small faces, a young boy and girl, quite obviously siblings being dark in colour with identical, rounded faces, like a pair of Welsh pixies.

'Well?' the man prompted.

'Jimmy Atkins?'

'That's me.'

'I'm afraid we have bad news for you. Yes, we have found your wife, but–'

The man drew in a deep breath and rubbed his hand over his unruly hair. 'Where? What happened?'

Julie stepped forward and laid a hand gently on his forearm. 'Maybe we could sit down somewhere. Let's go into the kitchen and I'll make some tea, then you and DS James can talk while I keep the little ones amused in the living room.' She skilfully eased him towards the back of the house, Ben following. Once tea was in the cups, Julie went to find the children while Ben perched on a stool to talk to Jimmy.

'She was found down by the Tywi,' Ben said, 'on the outskirts of Llandovery. There was a dog with her, a large, leggy mongrel.'

'Bramble, bloody thing. Amber was always out with that damn animal. I swear she loved it more than me. You sure it's my wife?' Atkins' voice wavered.

'Yes, sir. I'm very sorry, looks as though she's been shot. I'm afraid Bramble is dead too.'

'Shot like the others?'

Ben nodded.

'Why the *hell* haven't you caught this sick bastard yet? He's been running round for weeks now and you useless buggers haven't nabbed him. He's still out there, free to keep on killing innocent people and you lot aren't doing anything.'

'Is there anyone who held any bad feelings for your wife? Anyone who'd want her dead?' Ben asked.

'Apart from me, that is?' he growled. 'Don't suppose I should have said that… I don't mean it. We didn't see eye to eye a lot of the time, but I wouldn't kill her.'

'When did you see her last?'

'Yesterday evening. She took that animal out for his last walk, I told her she wasn't up to it. She's got MS and isn't very stable on her pins sometimes, but whenever she has a good day she'll be out with the dog. I tell her to take a mobile, but she says the signal is so bad there's not much point. I went out for a quick look about ten thirty but couldn't find her. Didn't have anyone I could leave the kids with, so came back and rang your lot. Now you come here and tell me she's dead. This is all too barmy for me.' He gulped from his mug, then looked at Ben. 'So, what are you going to do about it? Are you going to sit here all bloody morning drinking my tea, or are you going to get out, do your job and catch whoever did this to Amber?'

'Please try to remain calm, sir, we're doing our best and have to start by talking to everyone who knew her – including yourself – to try and piece together her last movements. Did she often walk by the river?'

'I don't know where she went, never told me anything,' Jimmy huffed. 'If she was up to it, she'd go out with the dog as soon as I got home from work. She'd put the meal in front of us and then wander out. Lately it seemed if I was home, she was out.'

'You said you hadn't been getting along recently?'

'That would be easy for you, wouldn't it? Instant suspect. Husband and wife in the middle of a difficult patch so it's bound to be the husband. Well, I've got news for you, copper, I had nothing to do with it. I went out to look for her, couldn't find her, came home to ring you and stayed with the kids. How could I leave them? You're barking up the wrong tree and now I want you to go.'

'There are a few more questions…'

'That's tough, isn't it? Take your questions – and that mate of yours – and get out of my house. I know my rights and I don't have to talk to you. It's bad enough Amber's dead, without having to put up with your suspicious mind trying to make a killer out of me. I'm not having it! Go on, sling your hook and only come back when you've got something to tell me. I've got two little kids who've just lost their mother to look after and don't have time for your crap. Go on – get out!' He slammed his mug on the table and stood, towering over Ben who remained seated.

'Please, sir, calm down. This is a dreadful time for you, I understand that, but we need your help. We must ask questions if we are to stand a chance of catching her killer. We're not accusing you of anything, please…' Ben gestured at the chair, hoping Jimmy Atkins would sit back down, but the irate man was having none of it.

'Let me arrange a family liaison officer,' Ben said, 'someone to help you with the little ones.'

'No, I want you to go.' His voice rose and Julie returned to the kitchen to see what was going on.

'I mean it!' Jimmy shouted. 'Get out and don't come back until you've got something useful to tell me.' He herded them out of the kitchen, down the hall and out of the front door, slamming it violently behind them.

Ben and Julie walked to the car.

'What now, boss?' she asked.

'Get onto Social Services and arrange for a health visitor to call. Atkins has definitely been drinking, whether it was a late-night session or Special Brew on his cornflakes, I don't know, but I'm concerned about the kids. Make sure the station's FLO attends and maybe Jimmy will calm down enough to be interviewed. We can't force him unless we arrest him and we don't have any evidence to allow that. No sense carrying on with this while he's so aggressive. In the meantime, we'll get back to the murder site, find out how the others are getting on.'

## Chapter fourteen

As Ben pulled into the muddy car park close to the river, Mark ran over and yanked open the driver's door, almost before the car had stopped.

'Sarge, we've found something! This way, quickly.'

Ben and Julie struggled out of the low car, followed his scurrying form across the water meadow beside the river and deep into a patch of scrubby deciduous woodland. A group of officers congregated under the trees and Ben spotted Jack Trent in the middle of them.

'Jack!'

The large man looked round.

'What's got Mark so animated?' Ben asked.

Jack grinned and held up two small, plastic evidence bags.

'Not much to get *quite* so excited about, but we have a collection of three cigarette butts and… a shell case, from a 50-calibre rifle no less.' He flourished the bags again, obviously pleased with himself.

'Good on you, Jack. Who recovered them? I want to shake him by the hand.'

'Constable Bradshaw? Over here, boss wants you,' Jack shouted.

The uniformed officer came at a trot and Ben thumped him good-naturedly on the shoulder.

'Well done, Ian, at last we have a couple of clues we can work with. Show me where you found them, will you?'

Ian nodded and led the way along a narrow footpath for a hundred yards or so, then cut off to the right. The covering of bluebells under the trees was crushed and trampled where many feet had pushed through during the search. He pointed to a bright yellow marker, close to a patch of nettles growing along the bottom of a leaning, wooden fence.

'The dog-ends were there, at the base of the old gate, see the marker?'

Ben nodded.

'The shell case was further over, this way.' He led Ben between the trees and a few feet away there was another marker. 'That's where the shell was, in that thick patch of grass.'

Ben stared at the ground hoping for another clue to miraculously appear out of the earth, but there was nothing, no footprints – other than those of the police – no tracks, nothing.

'Ian, have you had anyone up in the trees looking for carvings, any sign that the sniper used one of them as a vantage point?'

'Yeah. DS Trent got us doing that, but so far we've found nothing else.'

'Can't have it all I suppose,' Ben muttered as he made his way over to Jack. 'Get those sent off as soon as you can,' he told him, 'and keep looking. That's the first shell we've found and you're right, it looks big enough to come from a fifty. I guess our man missed it. Heartening to see he *can* make a mistake. I'd better get back to the incident room and–' Ben's mobile rang. 'DS James.'

'Hello, sir. Constable Lowe – Llandovery. We've had a call from Social Services. They've left the Atkins' house now but there's been trouble. Mr Atkins lost it and he's been brought here. Social Services have the kids and are in the process of finding them a place of safety. Atkins was so out of control there was no calming him, so we had no option but to arrest him. Thought you should know, sir.'

'You're right, I'm on my way.'

'Oh and, sir?'

'Yes.'

'We've also brought in David Little, the guy who found Amber this morning? We went to take a statement, but he was way too cagey, to be honest – not at all cooperative, abusive in fact, so he's cooling his heels in the cells as well.'

Ben disconnected the call.

'Atkins got himself nicked. Sounds like he kicked off when the council arrived and a witness is being a pain in the arse. Bloody hell, I've gotta go. Jack?'

'Yes, boss?'

'Can you stay here and finish up? I want to take Mark with me. We've got two bodies in the cells and both need interviewing. I'll leave Constable Smith with you. Julie?'

'Yes, sir?'

'Stay here and give DS Trent a hand to finish the search, we'll catch up later. If I don't get to speak to you again today, we'll have an early morning get together in the incident room. Pass the word, will you? I don't want anyone missing. Mark!' he shouted.

'I'm here.'

'Come on, people in cells are waiting on us.'

* * *

Ben and Mark checked in with the custody sergeant and decided to leave the interview with Jimmy Atkins for later. He was still raving, shouting obscenities and bouncing off the cell door. Leaving him to cool down seemed a sensible option. They went straight to the interview room and, a few moments later, David Little was escorted in. He sat on the plastic chair and stared sullenly across the table at the two officers.

He was exceptionally tall and very thin with sallow skin. His hair was short, almost black and a scruffy beard obscured his chin. He sported a dark blue baseball cap, T-shirt with a checked shirt worn over the top, and camouflage combat trousers.

Ben began the interview, switching on the recording equipment and stating his name and rank, as well as the names of others in the room.

'David, I am DS James, this is DC Jefferies and we are interviewing you under caution. Do you understand?'

'Yeah, I get it.'

'Would you like a solicitor present?'

'No, cos I haven't done anything, so why don't you get on with it?'

'Fair enough, if you change your mind, just let us know. We'd like to ask you about the events of this morning. Can I get you anything, coffee?'

'A fag u'd be good and yeah, coffee'd be nice as well. Ta.'

'We can do coffee, but no smoking in the station I'm afraid.'

'Not surprised.'

Mark stuck his head out of the door and yelled down the corridor for coffee.

'Right then, David,' Ben said. 'Tell me what happened today.'

'Like I said, I was out for a walk – early – and I found her by the river.'

'OK. Let's take things slower. I need to know everything you did this morning from when you got up until you found Mrs Atkins. What time did you leave home this morning?'

Little stared at the table and mumbled something.

'Come on, son, it's not difficult,' Ben prompted. 'What time did you go out this morning?'

'Well, I sort of didn't go home, so I can't tell you what time I left if I was already out, can I?'

'What are you talking about? Make some sense, will you?'

'I'd been out all night. I was coming *home* when I found her. I always come back along the river.'

'Where had you been?'

'Just out.'

'You can do better than that and I'm gonna keep asking until you do. Where had you been?'

'Walking the dogs.'

'What, in the middle of the night? All night?'

'Yeah. That's right.' Little slurped coffee.

'You're telling me you were out walking your dogs since yesterday? All night? Isn't that a bit odd?'

'Not for me it ain't.'

'Where do you walk?'

'Here and there. You know.'

'No. I *don't* know. That's why I'm asking.' Ben sighed heavily. 'I have to say you're not being very helpful, David, quite the opposite in fact and if you don't start talking soon, we'll nick you for obstruction.'

Little said nothing and drank noisily from the polystyrene cup.

Mark said, 'Give it up, Dave. We're not really interested in what you were doing, we want to know if you saw anything or anybody. We're not bothered about a spot of lamping and if you play ball, I can't see us being particularly interested. You were out working your dogs, weren't you?'

'Yeah,' he agreed reluctantly. 'After rabbits – no pheasants or anything – just rabbits.'

'Get any?' Ben asked, anxious to stay in touch with the conversation and try to build bridges.

'Couple. Not many about last night.'

'So, what time did you come back along the river?'

'About seven.' He smiled fleetingly. 'Mum usually cooks me a lush breakfast when I've been on a night out.'

'And what did you see?'

'Like I keep telling you, nothing. I walked along the river with my two girls on the lead. They were tired, I was too. I found the woman just off the path and, not far away, her dog. Blood everywhere. Spooked me I can tell you, not what you expect to find, is it?'

'Did you see anyone else? Someone walking their dog? Hear anything?'

'What, like a shot you mean? No. Why won't you listen to me? I went out, caught some rabbits, came back along the river, found her, rang you. That's all there is to it. Nothing else to tell. Now are you going to keep me here or let me go? You can't charge me with anything, I've done bugger all.'

'Well, nothing apart from poaching a few rabbits and swearing at my officers.' Ben paused. 'Go on then, Mark will show you out. But don't leave the country and next time a policeman asks you a few questions, bloody well answer them, it'll save all this bother.'

David Little was led out and released, on the understanding he could be contacted at any time for further questioning.

* * *

Ben and Mark drank coffee in the staffroom and took a breather before tackling Jimmy Atkins.

'I don't think Dave saw anything, boss,' Mark said. 'I'm sure he was only playing hard to get cos he'd been out poaching, been at it since he was a nipper and not one of our biggest fans. He doesn't take deer or anything, just a few rabbits, brace of trout now and again and unlikely to stop any time soon. Apart from that, he's a good lad. Looks after his mum well, I often see him working in the garden, doing the heavy spade work for her.'

'I tend to agree. I caught him once when he was about sixteen, sharing a spliff with the town's bad boys behind the market, other than that – nothing.' Ben drained his coffee and refilled the mug from the machine in the corner. 'You ready to tackle Mr Angry now?'

'Yeah, guess so.' Mark shrugged. 'Lead on, Macduff.'

* * *

Jimmy Atkins was brought to the interview room in handcuffs by the custody sergeant.

Ben glanced up from his notes. 'Have you calmed down now, Jimmy? Do we need to leave those cuffs on, or shall I ask the sergeant to remove them so you're more comfortable?'

Jimmy's voice cracked. 'He can take 'em off. Ta.'

The cuffs were removed and Jimmy sat on the opposite side of the table. Again, Ben started the tape machine, stated date and time and who was in the room, reminded Atkins he was under caution and began the interview.

'Would you like a solicitor present or are you happy to speak with us without representation?'

'Just get on with it,' the man growled. 'I don't need a solicitor.'

'What on earth are you doing here, Jimmy? You should be at home with your children, yet you lost your temper, got yourself arrested and have spent a few hours in the cells. What went on?'

Jimmy took a deep breath. 'They came to take the kids off me.'

'Who did, the council?'

'Yeah, those bastards! Steamed into the house, picked them up and were halfway out the bloody door before I realised what was going on. What did you say to them? Why did you tell them to take my kids?'

'I didn't tell them to remove your children, Jimmy. I asked them to visit, ask if you needed any help, either with the children or for yourself – on the grounds of your bereavement. I sent a family liaison officer with them to see if we could support you in some way.'

'Well, that's *not* how it went. I opened the door and two of 'em marched in and made for the kids. They were watching a cartoon, I thought it might take their minds off their missing mother. Anyway, I let the buggers in and the next thing I know they're carrying my kids out the door. They were crying and screaming for their mum and I wasn't allowed anywhere near them. They're young, four and seven, and hadn't a clue what was going on. They were frightened and I couldn't do anything to comfort them – wasn't *allowed* to. As if it isn't bad enough losing the missus, now – thanks to you – I've lost my kids as well.' He banged his fists on the table in front of him.

Mark leapt to his feet, but Ben waved him back to his seat.

'Look, Jimmy, I don't know anything about this. I'll have to go and find out. Stay calm and you can wait here with DC Jefferies while I do that, rather than go back to the cells. I'll bring some coffee back with me, OK?'

Jimmy nodded and Ben left the room making for his office on the next floor. He yelled at the desk sergeant, 'Get hold of the FLO who went out to the Atkins' place this morning and send them to my office as soon as. Who was it anyway?'

'Don't know, boss, someone from Brecon. I'll get onto it.'

* * *

Twenty minutes later there was a tap on Ben's door and a small, blonde officer entered.

'Sir? I'm Molly Burton – Family Liaison.'

'Sit down, Molly, and tell me *exactly* what went on this morning. I've got a *very* unhappy Mr Atkins banged up downstairs. He's lost his wife, now his kids have been snatched by Social Services and no one has told me anything.'

'It wasn't like that, sir, we had no choice. We arrived ten minutes or so after you called. The front door was wide open and – although we shouted – there was no sign of Mr Atkins. The children were in the living room watching the telly. The council's care team went inside to speak with the little ones, then – all of a sudden – Mr Atkins came galloping in from the garden, shouting and screaming. He had a nearly empty bottle of vodka in his hand and took a swing at me with it on the way past. Social Services had no option other than to remove the kids and I arrested him – attempted assault of a police officer. The bluster went out of him fairly quickly when reinforcements arrived, by then the alcohol had arrived at his brain and all of a sudden he was too pissed to stand. Oh, sorry, sir.'

Ben waved away her apology. 'You're saying he brought it on himself?'

She nodded. 'He'd drunk an awful lot in a short period of time, sir, a mental case, and the team were concerned about the state of the house, disgusting. They were worried the little ones weren't being cared for properly and I didn't have much of a choice but to arrest him, especially when he started to get physical. The bottle missed my face by an inch.'

'OK, Molly. Get all that down on paper before you leave the nick. Drop it off with the desk sergeant for me. Needless to say, Mr Atkins' version isn't quite the same as yours.' He sighed heavily. 'I'd best get back down there, I've left Mark holding the fort. Thanks for coming by so quickly and don't forget to leave your report at the front desk.'

'No, sir. Thank you, sir.'

Ben hauled himself to his feet, trudged down the stairs to the interview room, took a deep breath and opened the door.

* * *

Nothing seemed to have changed since he'd left, the still air pungent with tobacco smoke and stale alcohol.

Jimmy looked up. 'About bloody time! Where the hell have you been? Don't you think I got better things to do with my time than hang around here? Where are my bloody kids? Get me my kids and we'll all go home, then maybe we can start to deal with the loss of their mother.'

'Mr Atkins,' Ben began, 'I've been talking to Constable Burton, the liaison officer we sent to visit you. Her version of events differs somewhat from your own. She says the door to your house was open when she arrived and that you were nowhere around. The children were found watching telly in the front room on their own. She also told me you came charging in the back door like a bullock, waving a bottle about, pissed as a fart. Says you wouldn't calm down and even took a swing at her, which was why you were arrested.'

Jimmy said nothing and stared at the grubby tabletop.

'Well, is she right? Did you take a swing at her?'

'Might have done.' Jimmy was quieter now. 'But you'd lose it if you thought someone was stealing your kids. Yes, I was in the garden and I'd had a *bit* of a drink, but it was Dutch courage, had no idea what to say to the nippers, didn't know how to *start* to tell them even. They were happy watching cartoons and so, yes, I had a drink or two. There's no crime in that, is there? You buggers don't seem to understand, I've just lost my *wife* for God's sake.'

There was an uncomfortable silence and Ben changed tack. 'What do you do, Jimmy? Where's work?'

'Security guard on the industrial estate, other side of town.'

'Been there long?'

'Just over two years.'

'What about before that?'

'Army. Enlisted as soon as I was old enough, served fourteen years, quit a couple of years ago, not long before Nathan's third birthday.'

'Did you see active service?'

'Yeah, a bit. Afghanistan, Iraq, usual stuff. The army's so undermanned now everyone gets plenty of tours.'

'Why did you leave?' Mark asked.

'Told you, cos of Nathan. I missed his second birthday, spent it in some dust filled hole in a desert full of ungrateful ragheads and thought, no more. Left as soon as I could after that. Might have stayed in if it wasn't for the family – it's a good life – but Amber was happy to have me home.'

'When did you start having problems with your drinking?' Ben asked.

Jimmy glared across the table. 'Who said I had a problem? You? You know nothing about me. The only reason we're having this conversation is because some nutter out there murdered my wife. All you seem to want to do is give me a hard time and make my life even worse than it already is.' He leapt to his feet, eyes full of anger.

'It's OK, calm down, I understand how difficult this is for you, but you *really* must stop shouting at us, and *sit down* or you'll be in handcuffs again.'

The red-faced man sat and stared defiantly across the table.

'Look, Jimmy,' Ben said. 'We're not unfeeling bastards, you've had an awful shock and it's hard on you, but we must be sure your children will be safe. If you've drunk as much as I think you have, not only are you a danger to them, but to yourself as well. You have my word we are working as hard as we can to find out what happened to your wife – and the others who have died. We are asking lots of different people lots of questions and of course we have to ask you questions too. Somewhere, someone has an idea about this. There's a little piece of information out there that could help us and we must find it.'

'I get it,' Jimmy snarled, 'but I'm not that person.'

'I think it'll be best for all concerned if we release you on police bail and take you home. You'll be bailed to your address and will have to come back here in a couple of days so we can have another chat. What do you think?'

'I want my kids,' Jimmy growled.

'Yes, I know you do, but you must understand why that can't happen, at least not today. They'll be well looked after and when you are sober, you can contact the council. In the meantime, I'll speak to them on your behalf, put your side of things, but I strongly advise you *not* to ring them until tomorrow.'

Jimmy's head slumped lower on his shoulders as the sense of what Ben was saying at last sank in. He looked defeated and Ben experienced a twinge of compassion. Jimmy was in a bad space and Ben wasn't sure he could do anything to help the distressed man.

'Right then, DC Jefferies will drive you home, he'll make sure you've got all you need and I'll be in touch soon.'

## Chapter fifteen

Stacey poured two glasses of wine and lit candles. Supper was almost ready and Ben was finishing off in the bathroom, she heard him moving about on the boards above her head. He'd arrived an hour ago looking utterly done in, so she sent him upstairs to wash and change while she rustled up a meal. She was opening the oven door when he walked into the kitchen with a towel wrapped around his waist, hair damp and sticking out at crazy angles.

Stacey stared at him. 'Not dressing for dinner?'

He grinned. 'Do you mind if I don't? I'm so tired I don't think I could summon up enough energy to dress and then a couple of hours later, undress, and the kitchen is warm.'

'Course I don't mind. A bit of eye candy with food is always welcome, helps with the digestion I find.'

He chuckled and kissed the back of her neck before sitting at the table.

'Smells wonderful, thanks for this. Didn't fancy going back to mine and flopping in front of the telly with a ready meal.'

'You know you're always welcome. My work's up to date so Sam's stopped griping at me and *anything* is better than housework.'

'I'm not just eye candy then, but an excuse as well?'

She laughed and carried a steaming lasagne to the table and settled opposite him. He raised his glass in her direction.

'To the best little chef I know.'

Stacey giggled. 'With three caveats: one – you obviously don't get out enough to meet new people, two – flattery will *not* get you out of doing the washing-up, I keep telling you that, and three – I am *not* little.'

He laughed, sliced up the pasta and loaded their plates high, adding a mound of fresh green salad.

'Right then, Sherlock, if you can bear to think about it, unload all that gungy stuff swimming around in your brain. You know by now you can trust me, so unload, you'll feel better for it.'

'Oh God, Stace, I don't know where to start. I can't believe we've got *another* murder. The killings are far from a perfect match, they share the same weapon and all victims were shot while walking dogs, but other than that? The brass have brought in a guy from Scotland Yard – Jack Trent – watching brief, they said.' He paused to fill his mouth.

'That's pretty shit of them. Don't they think you're doing a good enough job or something?'

'Actually, it's OK. I must admit I felt exactly the same when I found out, but – if I'm truthful – I *have* got my hands full and he's not a bad bloke. Has way more experience than I do with this sort of crime and it seems the main reason he's here is because Prince Charles has that new place in Llandovery. I can see the higher-ups would be concerned. Jack doesn't seem to mind at all if I delegate. He just says, "yes, boss" – even though we're the same rank – and gets on with it.'

He recounted the rest of his day while Stacey listened.

'You have had a day of it.'

'I'm only halfway through. You reporters don't know how easy you've got it. Nosey about for a bit, write something salacious and move on. Us coppers? We gotta get right down and dirty.'

'Yeah, yeah, heard it all before. Move on,' she said, flapping a hand at him.

'An afternoon of interviews. Can't help feeling a little sorry for Jimmy. He kicked off and we had to handcuff him. Husbands are always suspects, we don't usually handcuff them until we have firm evidence, but he was pissed and lost it when Social Services removed his kids. Nothing else we could do.' He groaned.

'How awful.' Stacey topped up the glasses. 'Do you think Jimmy is a serious suspect?'

'Don't know, ugly brute, but a killer? Anyway, we found out what had gone on, calmed Jimmy down, explained the situation and took him home. Hopefully, he'll be able to deal with this better after a night's sleep and no alcohol. I finished my day with a couple of hours of paperwork and now I'm here, eating this wonderful food with my own bit of eye candy. Thanks.'

Stacey removed the plates and carried a large glass bowl filled with fruit salad to the table.

'Afters,' she announced. 'Ice cream or cream?'

'You need to ask? Both.'

She spooned out the fruit. 'What's next? Where do you go from here?'

'Waiting on forensics and fingerprints. That stuff should never have been outsourced. When it was all in-house we could keep a better eye, have more control, still at least this time we have some physical evidence. No doubting really that the shell case is linked, but not sure about the dog-ends. They were found close by, so it's possible. Then more interviews. Gotta go and see Jimmy Atkins again, hopefully he'll be in a better frame of mind to answer questions, more house-to-house… And I need to chase the army, they haven't been back to me yet. I *still* don't know whether any of their soldiers had unexplained absences in the last few weeks. It's like trying to get blood out of a stone getting anything out of Sennybridge Barracks. Enough! What have you been up to?' He picked up a spoon and stirred ice cream into the fruit.

'Went to Brecon to meet Sam,' Stacey answered. 'He doesn't improve with age, just gets more grumpy. He took me out to lunch though, so I must be doing something right. I called in to see the vicar on the way home and met his sister-in-law, she seems nice. Andrew thanked me for being with Emily. Imagine being able to think about other people at all when you've been so badly wounded yourself. Maybe there is something to this God lark after all.'

Ben looked up from his food. 'Do you really think that?'

'Probably not, maybe it's just spirituality or empathy, maybe God doesn't have to be involved. Andrew's obviously throwing himself into work, we spent a good hour on the article for his fundraising project. Turns out that was Emily's idea, this business about contacting the living relatives of the occupants of the graveyard to try and raise money to renovate the building. It's a novel idea. Anyway, I've already written the piece and sent it off to Sam, so–'

'You have the rest of the night off,' Ben said.

'Yep. All yours if you want me.'

'How could I say no?'

* * *

Soon after Ben left for the station, Stacey drove into town. She needed to stock up on supplies and thought she'd see what the locals were saying regarding the latest murder.

Parking in the Castle car park, she wandered through the narrow back alley to the main shopping street, calling in at the post office, chemist and charity shops. In every establishment locals were gossiping in hushed tones, the general mood one of horror and amazement that something so terrible could happen in their home town. There had never been anything like it in their lifetimes, and memories needed to reach back a long way into the past to come up with anything remotely similar. The drovers who herded sheep through the town many years ago were known to be hard men. You didn't cross them and disagreements sometimes ended in violence, but nothing in more recent times. Theories ranged from an army recruit going rogue, to a killer from one of the big cities – usually an English one. It appeared the townsfolk were unable to contemplate that these crimes could have been committed by one of their own.

Stacey stepped out of the bank and nearly collided with Suzie Thomas who was out with her dog.

'Hi, Suzie, seems like ages since I've seen you. How are things?' Stacey asked.

'Not bad, thanks. Been away for a while, that's why you haven't seen me.'

'Anywhere nice?'

'Parent visiting, nothing exciting.'

'You look well.' Stacey ruffled Charlie's ears.

'Yes, I'm fine now, thanks. All that nasty business rattled me a bit, but I've bounced back from worse. I don't take Charlie to Long Field anymore, doesn't seem the same, I stay closer to town where there are more people.' She paused. 'Do you know if the police are any nearer catching anyone? I walk around town now looking at people and find myself wondering if they'll be next.'

'Awful, isn't it? I don't think they have any suspects yet.'

'Those poor people and their families.' Suzie sighed. 'I knew Amber Atkins. Lovely woman.' She leaned closer and lowered her voice. 'Had a lot to put up with, though, with that husband of hers.'

'How do you mean?' Stacey asked.

'Well, you must have seen him about. Hulking great brute, tattooed arms and skinhead haircut, works as a guard down on the industrial estate. Drinks a lot, I heard. Amber never said he walloped her, but I don't think they were happy. I used to meet her out with her dog, Bramble. He was lovely. Did you know Amber was ill?'

'No, I didn't, what was wrong?'

'Multiple Sclerosis. I always knew when she was bad cos we didn't see her, but if she was well enough she'd spend as much time as she could out walking. She loved her kids dearly, but Jimmy was a handful.' Suzie leaned even closer and dropped her voice to a whisper. 'He was having an affair, you know?'

'What, Jimmy was?'

'Yeah. Amber reckoned it was someone at work. She wasn't happy about it, but somehow managed to accept the situation. Maybe she was too ill to deal with it and didn't want to upset the *status quo*. With Amber, her kids always came first and a divorce would have been awful for them. Who knows what goes on behind closed doors? I only know what she told me, she wasn't happy though, such a shame, she was a lovely person.'

'Do you think Jimmy knew he'd been caught out playing away?' Stacey asked.

'Haven't a clue. Didn't have much to do with him and never went round the house, only ever met Amber out walking and we'd chat our way along. I shall miss her. Everything seems to be changing.'

'Yes, it does. Andrew seems a little better since Emily's sister came to look after him. Have you met her? She seems a nice person, too.'

'Yes, bumped into her at the weekend when I was sorting out flowers for the service on Sunday. Told me she'll stay as long as he wants her to and I agree, the vicar does seem better, he took the service on Sunday, although Marion Pike was there to support him; good job really.'

'Why do you say that?'

'Well, he drifts off a lot, stares into space, but I guess that's to be expected. Must be awful to lose your partner. Sarah said he's planning to conduct Emily's funeral himself, doesn't want anyone else to do it. I think that's so brave.'

'Yes, isn't it. Anyway, Suzie, good to see you. I'm glad you're feeling better.'

'Me too, but you have to get on with it, don't you?'

They parted company and Stacey called in at the supermarket for much needed supplies. On the way home, she pulled in close to the bridge over the Tywi River and visually scanned the banks, using a small pair of binoculars. The police were still in attendance, a couple of uniforms standing guard at the start of the path. SOCO hadn't left either and were poking about in the undergrowth. Stacey snapped a couple of photos before tucking the camera away and beginning the drive home through the narrow lanes.

Reaching the top of the hill she spotted a figure with a couple of dogs, walking along the lane some distance ahead. She slowed to pass and recognised David Little. Pulling over in a lay-by a little way ahead, she waited for him to catch up.

'Hi, Dave,' she said brightly. 'How you doing? How's your mum?'

He looked up and recognised her.

'Stacey, hi. Mum's not bad, ta, and I'm fine.'

'Where are you going? You're a long way from home – did you walk up here?'

'Yeah, good exercise for the girls and Mum can get on with things better when I'm out, or so she says. I'm on my way to see Stevie Read.'

'Want a lift?'

'No thanks, I'm fine, anyway, the dogs are muddy, they'd make a right mess of your car and it's not far now.'

'You sure? It's still three miles to Llanagethin. I don't mind the dogs. My car's never that clean so more mud won't make any difference.'

He considered for a moment. 'Oh, go on then, that'd be good.' He whistled the two skinny lurchers, opened the back door and they jumped in obediently. Dave folded his long frame in the front seat and Stacey set off.

'You found Amber Atkins, didn't you?' she asked. 'That must have been nasty.'

'Wasn't nice, but – well – it was only a dead body. You won't *believe* the grief I got from Old Bill over it, made me wish I hadn't rung them. All over me like a rash they were, anyone would think I'd done it.'

'I'm sure they didn't think that, but they had to find out if you saw anything.'

'They bloody well *arrested* me, Stacey, took DNA an' all.'

'They have to do that to anyone who's arrested these days.'

'Well, it's not right, is it? All that happened was I was walking back along the river after a night out, found Mrs Atkins and rang them. They got right arsey with me, and I admit I got arsier.' He grinned. 'Next thing I know I'm in a cell. I'll think twice about helping them in the future, I can tell you.'

Stacey decided to change the subject. 'You said you're off to see Stevie, I didn't know you two were friends.'

'Went to the same school – different year – got to know him then. We see each other now and again, sometimes he comes fishing with me. I haven't been up since his mum died and felt bad about it, so I thought I'd walk up today and see how he's doing.'

'I bumped into him a week ago. He was pretty down. I think they're all struggling. Kathy used to do all the house stuff and, now she isn't there, I don't even know if they're cooking or anything. He'll be pleased to see you.' She slowed the car and pulled up outside the Reads' yard.

'Thanks, that saved me some time. One of them might give me a lift back, but if not it doesn't matter, all downhill from here and I like walking.' He stepped out, opened the back door for the dogs and peered in at the back seat.

'It's not too bad, they weren't as dirty as I thought, thanks again.' Slamming the door, he walked in through the wide gate, dogs trotting by his heels and Stacey drove the half mile to Noddfa. She had an afternoon in the office ahead of her, much easier to cope with while the weather was grey and damp.

## Chapter sixteen

Ben and Mark were pouring over results from the labs. Unfortunately, the fingerprint found on the shell was only a partial and not good enough for identification purposes. However, the forensic lab had been able to collect good quality DNA samples from the cigarette ends. The really exciting news was they had a match on the system.

'Now we're getting somewhere, Mark,' Ben said. 'Where's Jack? He in yet?'

'Saw him filling that bucket-sized mug of his in the staffroom, boss. He's a real coffee hound, isn't he? I'm surprised it doesn't make him jumpy.'

'You're having a laugh, any more jumpy and he'd leave his skin behind – you've seen him with sheep.'

'He puts that on surely… doesn't he?'

Ben shrugged as Jack strode into the room.

'Morning, boys. How's it hanging?' He grinned broadly at them.

'The lab results on the fingerprint and DNA sample have come back. Print not a lot of use, only a partial, but there's a positive match on the DNA,' Ben told him.

'A match? Brilliant! So why are we all sitting here? Let's mount up and go and get the bad guy.'

'It's not quite as easy as that,' Ben said, 'we have a bit of a problem.'

'What problem, what are you on about?'

'It's a match to Jimmy Atkins, husband of the last victim.'

Jack opened his mouth to say something and then shut it again.

'Exactly. We've no choice, we'll have to bring him in for questioning and you've seen him angry. Mark and I are going to see him this morning and wondered if you'd come along to make up the numbers, in case he gets stroppy again. He was a right handful last week I can tell you. Spent an hour bouncing off the walls of his cell until his alcohol-soaked brain *finally* worked out it hurt. I'll be honest, I'm not looking forward to this.'

Mark stood. 'Let's get to it, Sarge, get it out of the way. There's probably a logical explanation, Jimmy will tell us all about it in a quiet, reasonable manner and then we can get back here to start shit-shifting again. I thought once computers took hold we weren't gonna have paper any more – look at this lot,' he groaned, running his hands over the piles.

* * *

Twenty minutes later, all three were outside the battered green door of the Atkins' house. Ben banged loudly on the wood and almost immediately it was flung wide open, catching him by surprise. Jimmy Atkins stood in the doorway looking even more dishevelled than the last time they saw him.

'Heard you pull up,' he said. 'You got news then, about my Amber? Or the kids? Bastard council won't tell me anything.'

'Can we come in?' Ben asked. 'We need to talk to you. You know DC Jefferies and this is DS Trent from London, Scotland Yard.'

'Good to see you're taking things seriously at last.'

The officers followed him through the hall to the kitchen, carefully stepping over piles of assorted debris. The kitchen was in a dreadful state, sink piled high with dirty pots and pans and every available work surface was buried under empty ready meal containers, more greasy crockery, old newspapers and dirty laundry. The air smelt musty and the stink emanating from the overflowing pedal bin in the corner made their eyes water.

'Let's have it then,' Jimmy said. 'What's the news? Caught the murderer yet? My kids coming home today?'

Ben cleared his throat. 'No, Mr Atkins, we haven't caught the killer, but we do have more evidence to work with now. Due to the nature of that evidence, we'd like it if you could come to the station with us.'

'Down the nick, why? What evidence are you talking about and why does finding it mean I have to go down there again? Saw enough of that place a week ago. I thought you were here to tell me when my kids were coming home.' Atkins sat down heavily on a high stool and lost his balance, his elbow caught a plate poking out from the unstable pile on the draining board, which started an avalanche that crashed and clattered to the floor.

'It won't take long, Jimmy, but it *is* necessary. You want to help us catch whoever did this, don't you?' Ben didn't wait for an answer. 'The best way you can do that is to come with us. We have a few questions we need answering and it'll be much easier and quicker to do it there, so get your coat.'

The angry man hesitated for a second. Jack stood in front of the doorway, tensing in case there was trouble, but

Jimmy's shoulders relaxed as he realised he couldn't win. Picking up his jacket from the back of a chair, he walked out of the house, ducked into the back of the car and Jack drove to the station.

* * *

The group gathered together in the claustrophobic interview room. Ben started the recording machine, ran through the required script and then addressed Jimmy.

'Now, Jimmy, you haven't been arrested today. You are officially helping the police with their enquiries and that means you are free to leave at any time you like. You are also able to have a solicitor present. If you don't have one, we can arrange one for you. Do you understand?'

'I don't want a solicitor, haven't done anything wrong so don't need one.'

'That's up to you, but if you change your mind, we'll stop and call one in. We need to ask you some personal questions and I'm sorry I have to do this. The purpose behind these questions is to try and piece together the last period of Amber's life, who she was friends with, where she went, stuff like that. I will try to be as uninvasive as possible. OK?'

Jimmy nodded.

'You'll have to speak, Jimmy,' Ben said. 'The machine can't record nods.'

'Yes then, it's OK. Get on with it so I can go home, got things to do.'

'We'll be as quick as we can. You told us you and Amber weren't as happy as you might have been; going through a difficult patch. Is that right?'

'Not that it's any of your business, but we hadn't been very happy lately. What couple doesn't argue now and again? Wouldn't be normal if you didn't.'

'What was the problem?'

'Just stuff. You know, day-to-day stuff, just got on each other's nerves. She couldn't keep the place tidy, managed the kids all right, but was crap at looking after the house. It really wound me up, dirt and muck everywhere.'

'You told us she was ill, MS I believe. Maybe she struggled with the cleaning, can't have been easy, especially with two little ones.'

'She didn't try hard enough! Oh… whatever. We rubbed along. Separate, but together – sort of – mainly cos of the kids.'

Mark chipped in. 'You had a lover, didn't you?'

Jimmy's face darkened. 'Who have you been talking to? Some chopsy local no doubt. That's none of your bloody business!'

'Sorry, mate, but we've got to ask.'

'You are *not* my mate. You said I was free to leave as I was only helping you with your enquiries, so that's what I'm doing – leaving. I've had a gut-full of this rubbish. Now, out of my way and go and catch my wife's killer.'

He made a lunge for the door only to find the solid body of Jack Trent blocking it. Jack smiled at Jimmy and that made him angrier. He grabbed the detective by the arms and tried to pull him out of the way. Ben and Mark joined the fray and Mark caught Jimmy's arms, pinning them to his sides.

Ben put a hand on his shoulder. 'Jimmy Atkins, I am arresting you on suspicion of murder, you do not have to say anything…'

'Let go, you bastards, let go of me! You're mad, all of you.'

Ben finished reading him his rights and Mark spun Jimmy round to face the room, pushing him roughly onto a chair.

'We just wanted a chat,' Ben said, 'but you got angry again. It doesn't help you.'

'I don't understand this at all. What is it, got-it-in-for-Jimmy-week or something? I can't *believe* you're arresting me for killing my wife. Whatever's the matter with you? I tell you we aren't getting along, you find out I've got a bit on the side, then all of a sudden I'm a killer? What about the others who died? Am I supposed to have shot them too? For crying out loud, no wonder the police have lost respect. How on *earth* can you think I had anything to do with this? Amber's the mother of my kids, for Christ's sake.'

He glared across the table at Ben, eyes flashing angrily.

'All you had to do was keep hold of your temper and talk to us,' Ben said. 'Behaving like you did makes us suspicious and we do need you to answer our questions. Give us the right answers and this could all be over.'

Jimmy folded his arms across his chest and glared at the detective, saying nothing.

'Right, Jimmy. Let's have another go. Is it true you've been having an affair?'

He nodded.

'Told you once – nods won't do. Please answer me.'

'Yes!'

'Who with?'

'No one you know… look, she's married all right. I don't want to get her into any bother at home with her old man.'

'Just tell us who she is. We'll be as discreet as we can, but remember, Jimmy, this is a *murder* investigation, we have to do whatever it takes to catch your wife's killer.'

'Mary Saunders – and you better not drop her in it,' Jimmy mumbled. 'Works in the builder's office on the industrial estate.'

'Has it been going on long?'

'About a year, nothing serious, a bit of a fling – with things being bad at home.'

Jack made a quiet sarcastic noise from the back of the room and Ben hoped Jimmy didn't notice. He'd have to speak to Jack later.

'Did Amber know you were having an affair?'

'Don't be daft, of course she didn't. She'd have gone loopy. Me and Mary were very careful, no one knew, not even our mates. We kept it between the two of us.'

'Army trained you in the art of subterfuge, I suppose,' Jack muttered from the back of the room. Ben glared at him and Jack looked away, but now the subject had been broached, Ben took the questioning in that direction.

'What rank were you in the army?'

'Sergeant. Did thirteen years give or take, had Nathan and packed it in just before his third birthday, been home a while now. I've told you all this.'

'I know you have, but I'd like you to tell me again. What did you do in the army?'

Jimmy stared at his hands, picked at hard skin and ignored the question.

'Jimmy, what did you do in the army?' Ben persisted.

'For crying out loud! I was a sniper, all right? That's what you wanted to hear and now you have. I was a sniper and good at my job. I loved the army, certainly better than civvy street. I'm a bloody security guard on a poxy industrial estate in the middle of nowhere, same day in, day out, nothing to get the blood pumping.'

'Is that why you shot those people, to get the blood pumping?' Jack asked sharply.

Ben couldn't believe it, he was so angry, but determined to carry on and couldn't reprimand his colleague in front of Jimmy. Frowning at Jack, he hoped he'd keep quiet, but the situation was already out of control.

Jimmy was on his feet again, waving his arms around. 'Tell that bastard to keep his mouth shut, better still get him out of here. I'm not saying another word until I get a solicitor and he gets gone. Go on. Bang me up in one of your nasty cells and go get me a lawyer. I mean it, that's it. I'm not listening to any more of this shit!' He sat down again with a thump and leaned back, arms crossed over his middle.

'OK, Jimmy, we'll do it your way.' Ben opened the door and shouted into the corridor. 'Sergeant Jones, where are you?'

'On my way, sir.'

'Book Mr Atkins in, will you? Mark will give you the details. We've arrested him on suspicion of murder.' The custody officer raised his eyebrows. 'And can you get Dick Nyle on the phone? Mr Atkins has asked for the duty solicitor.' He turned towards Jimmy. 'I'll see you later when Mr Nyle gets here. Mark, you do the honours. Jack? Come with me.'

They ran up the stairs to the incident room and Ben was pleased to find it was empty, not only because it meant that work was actually happening, but he didn't want anyone to witness his next conversation.

He turned to face Jack. 'Have you lost it? What the *hell* was that all about in there? You're here as an observer and I'm cool with that. I'm even cool when you help, you've proved to be good at that, but your interview technique stinks, absolutely bloody stinks!'

'I don't know what you mean,' Jack said. 'I've never been told that before. Seems to me you're pussyfooting around the issue rather than getting on with it. His DNA is on the dog-ends, he used to be in the army – *a sniper* no less – and doesn't seem overly cut up about his wife's death. Lean on him a bit, crack him open and he'll confess. You get a result and I can go back to London,' he said, a broad smile on his face.

'Jack, this isn't funny. How the hell are you going to be able to continue with your watching brief if the suspect won't let you sit in the interview room with him? I can't have you in there, you see that, don't you? That sort of aggressive formula may work wonders in Brixton, but it's different out here. The people are different and you need to know how to handle them.' Ben took a breath and asked, 'Do you really think he's our man?'

Jack shrugged. 'Oh, who knows, but you could find out quicker, that's all I thought.'

'Well, now it's slowed things up considerably. We have to wait for Nyle to get here and who knows how long he'll be. We haven't even got to the issue of the DNA and now I've a hostile prisoner to deal with.'

'OK, boss, I get it. I'm sorry, didn't mean to cock things up, only speed them up a little for your sake and mine. Sooner this is wrapped up, the sooner I can get back to the concrete. What can I do to help while you finish up with Atkins? That is if you want me to help anymore.'

'I'd send you home if I could, but I can't, so while you're here go through the statements, those from folk close to the victims and the ones collected door-to-door. See if you can find anything to link the victims, maybe the same friend, a shared interest, anything. I want you to re-read every word and then do it again, to make sure. Oh, and, Jack?'

'Yes.'

'We won't speak about this again. I've vented my spleen, you've listened and – I hope – learned. Now, we'll move on. OK?'

Jack half smiled and sat at the large table running along the side of the incident room and began shuffling paper into piles. Ben left the room, found a coffee and took a few moments respite before returning to the cells.

Sitting in the waiting area he found a small man, wiry like a whippet, with wild fluffed-up, greying hair and a battered briefcase that matched his battered shoes. He wore a scruffy dark suit, the hem of the jacket hung down a little at the back and a pair of tortoiseshell rimmed glasses dangled from a chain round his neck. Dick Nyle, from the local solicitor's offices.

'Dick. Hi. Good to see you. You ready for your client?'

'Yep. Let's get on with it. If I decide we need time to confer, I'll let you know.'

Ben led the way to the interview room and called for Jimmy to be brought up from the cells.

## Chapter seventeen

Ben and Mark sat on one side of the table, Jimmy Atkins and Dick Nyle faced them. The room appeared even smaller and being windowless, was hot and stuffy. The recording machine whirred quietly in the corner and Ben was about to begin the interview, but before he could say anything, Jimmy spoke up.

'About last time, I'm sorry, all right? That big copper wound me up. I want to say that I *really* haven't killed Amber. Why would I? And I've certainly not shot anyone else, crazy to suggest I have. I'm under a lot of stress at the moment – you must see that – wife dead, kids taken off me to God knows where? The council will never let me have them back after all this, will they? How can you possibly arrest me for murder? I don't understand it.'

Dick Nyle placed a hand on his client's arm to stop him speaking. 'Mr Atkins, let the officers ask their questions and then we'll be closer to getting this matter cleared up.' The solicitor glanced at Ben. 'DS James?'

'Thank you, Mr Nyle. Right then, Jimmy, let me recap what you've already told us, OK?'

'Get on with it,' Jimmy growled.

'You've been having an affair with Mary Saunders, from the industrial estate and have been doing so for some time. You told us you don't believe Amber knew about it. That's right, isn't it?'

'Yes, I'm sure she didn't know.'

'Do you ever walk by the river where Amber was shot?'

'Hardly ever, once or twice maybe.'

'When did you last go there, can you remember?'

'No idea. Not for a while.'

'Where were you on the evening your wife went missing?'

'At home with the kids, you know I was. I rang from there to say she hadn't come home.'

'You didn't call us until getting on for midnight. What were you doing before then?'

'Told you, looking after the kids. Where else would I be? I couldn't leave them on their own.'

'Did anyone visit, someone who could confirm you were there? Anyone phone you?'

'I didn't go anywhere, no one came to see me and who remembers phone calls?'

'OK, fair enough, we'll check the phone records. We do have a problem though.' Ben opened the folder in front of him and took out a sealed plastic bag. He held it high so Jimmy could see it. Three cigarette ends languished at the bottom.

'What's that?' Atkins asked.

'Dog-ends. We picked them up in the wood, overlooking the path where Amber was killed.'

'Your point is?'

'We found your DNA on them, Jimmy, proves you were up there and not that long ago either.'

'They can't have! How would you know anyway? You haven't got my DNA.'

'Yes, we have. Don't you remember or were you too drunk? We took a swab when you were arrested the other week, just like we do to everyone who has been arrested. Your DNA is a perfect match to the samples we've taken from these.'

Ben waved the bag again. Jimmy said nothing.

'We *know* you were there. You need to tell us when and what you were doing.'

'I took Mary up there, all right?' Jimmy grumbled. 'Happy now? We went there a couple of weeks ago, something like that – when the weather was nice. It was our place, nothing special, but quiet. Not many people walk in the wood – they all stay down by the river – so we were never disturbed. It was difficult, with both of us being married.'

'Why didn't you tell us you'd been there before?' Ben asked.

'Didn't think you'd believe me and it was at least a week before Amber was shot. Can I go now? I've answered your questions and I want to get back home.'

'Sorry, Jimmy, this isn't over by a long shot, but we've made a good start. The next move is to check out what you've told us. We *will* have to go and talk to Mary but we'll be gentle, I promise. We'll also need to search your house.'

'What?' Jimmy growled. 'Why do you have to do that? There's nothing there.'

'We have to look. We won't conduct the search in your absence and we'll arrange it as soon as we can. I'll get a squad together and then you can come with us. You'll have to stay here in the meantime, but we'll be back to you as soon as possible.'

The custody sergeant returned Jimmy to the cells. Mr Nyle filled in the required forms for his attendance, shook hands with Mark and Ben and returned to his office in town. Ben went to the incident room, to see how Jack was getting on and begin the process of putting a search team together. As soon as he sat down, his mobile rang.

'Hi, Pumpkin, how's it going?'

'Yeah, good thanks – same, same. Wondered if you and Mark wanted to come over for food tonight. I've been using up last year's veg from the freezer and seem to have ended up with too much stew.'

'I'm definitely up for it and I'm sure Mark will be too. What time?'

'Any time. I'll stick the pot on top of the wood burner and it'll be ready whenever you arrive.'

'Great, I'll let you know when we're on our way. Gotta go, still mad here.'

'I can imagine. See you later. Bye.'

A couple of uniformed officers stood by the coffee machine and another sat at one of the desks, sorting through photographs.

'Ah good,' Ben said. 'Just what I'm looking for, a couple of bodies. You two,' he called to the coffee drinkers, 'we've got a search to conduct and need to take Atkins with us. Go down to the cells and get him booked out. If he's in a reasonable state of mind, you can leave the handcuffs off. But any sign of trouble, cuff him. Mark? Bring the car to the back door, we'll take him out that way. I'm not expecting any trouble, but you never know and news tends to travel fast round here. Meet you out back.'

* * *

An hour later, the small group entered the house on the edge of town. The uniformed officers were unable to hide their disgust at the state of the place and Ben issued protective gloves from a box in the boot of his car. The team began their work upstairs, taking Jimmy with them so he could watch proceedings. They worked one room at a time and searched through everything, even lifting edges of the carpet, running hands along the seams of curtains and pulling out the contents of every drawer and cupboard. Jimmy protested a few times, but was mostly ignored. Moving into the bathroom, they bagged all the dirty laundry. Next they searched the children's room and lastly the little box room, which looked as though it had once been used as an office.

Mark was pulling drawers out of a cheap desk when he heard something drop down with a heavy clunk. Removing the drawers completely, he pushed a hand into the space beneath and felt around. His fingers brushed a coarse, hessian-like bundle and with a bit of stretching, he managed to snag it with two fingers and pull it towards him. Grabbing it properly, he dragged it into the light.

The bundle was about eight inches long and looked like a tool roll, dark green and stained in places with spots of oil, tied in the middle with a length of twine.

'What's this, Jimmy?' Mark asked.

Jimmy said nothing, staring at the parcel.

Mark untied the string and slowly unrolled the package, hearing a few soft clinks from inside, metal on metal. As it was opened completely, several shiny objects rolled out from the folds of canvas and tinkled to the floor.

Mark picked one up and held it high so the others could see.

'Jimmy, why have you got bullets in your house?' he asked.

The silence lengthened, all eyes on the contents of the material roll. Mark flattened it on the carpet and laid out round after round of ammunition, all different shapes and sizes, and all live.

'Jimmy, do you want to tell us what this is all about?' Ben asked.

'Souvenirs,' Jimmy mumbled.

'What?'

'Souvenirs, one from every gun I've ever shot, began collecting them as soon as I started training and never got out of the habit.'

'Well hidden, weren't they?'

'Wouldn't you hide them properly if you had kids in the house?'

Mark held up a 50-calibre shell. 'Got the gun for this as well, have you?'

'No. I haven't got any guns, only ammo.'

'We'll see.' Mark looked up at Ben. 'We're about done up here, Sarge. Let's move downstairs.'

One of the uniformed officers took the bundle from Mark and placed it in a large evidence bag, scribbling on the label. The rest of the house was searched, but nothing else was discovered, the garden shed was ransacked, followed by the coal bunker – nothing. Jimmy was taken back to the station and once again locked up. The ammunition was despatched to the labs to see if the 50 calibre matched the shell case found at the scene and the daily reports were compiled. By eight o'clock they were done for the day and Ben and Mark made their way to Noddfa and the supper waiting for them.

* * *

The aroma hit them the moment they entered the kitchen. A rich, beef stew simmered gently on the wood-burning stove, filling the air with the most amazing, mouth-watering steam. Ben called for Stacey who appeared from the direction of her office.

'Hey, you two… Thought you might be later than this.' She planted a kiss on Ben's rough cheek. 'Hi, Mark, how you doing?'

'OK, ta, Stace, a bit tired. Thanks for the invite.'

'You're always welcome. Take your coats off and sit down, there's wine on the table so get it opened and I'll dish out.'

Ben busied himself with the corkscrew and poured three large glasses of a deep red wine. A fruity smell hung over the table, mingling pleasantly with the meaty richness of stew. Stacey placed a good-sized bowl in front of each of them and carried over a basket filled with freshly baked rolls.

'Homemade bread as well,' Ben exclaimed. 'You spoil us.'

'I know, but I think you're worth it. Tuck in, boys.'

After supper they made themselves comfortable in the living room, lounging on overstuffed chairs. Stacey had lit a fire in the small grate and golden light flickered across walls and ceiling.

'That was exactly what I needed, Pumpkin, thanks. We've been full at it again today,' Ben said.

'With what?' she asked.

'Interviewing Jimmy mainly. We've got a bit of a natural lull now while the guys in the labs do their thing. How about you? What's the number one lady reporter of Powys been up to?'

'Funny you should ask that, bit of sleuthing actually.'

'God, I don't like the sound of that. What have you been up to this time? No good, I'll be bound.'

'I don't know why you'd say such a thing. Anyway… do you remember the photographers at Danny's funeral?'

'Yeah, we confiscated their memory sticks and sent them on their way.'

'Well, I know them – one of them actually – Sid Barker, bumped into him this morning, both covering the building of a new scout hut. He wasn't best pleased with you for nicking his pictures, moaned on a bit and then said you hadn't been that clever. He had a small point and shoot camera in his pocket and had snapped off a couple of shots before and after you spotted him.'

'The cheeky bugger,' Ben said. 'We asked him if he had any other pictures and he said he hadn't.'

'You don't expect the truth from journos, do you? Not even the photo variety? The point is we went back to his house and he gave me a couple of copies. He'd only kept them because they were good pictures, knew he couldn't use them. They're in the office.'

She uncurled from her chair and padded out of the room, returning a minute or two later with a brown envelope. She removed the photos and passed them to Ben who switched on a nearby reading lamp.

He peered at the images. 'They are good, aren't they? Look at that one, he managed to take it just as Joanne's fist landed on Samantha's nose. What an action shot.'

'Never mind that,' Stacey said. 'Look at the rear of the picture where the chapel is. See the corner of the building? Now, look to the left towards that little bush. Is that someone standing there, do you think?'

Ben concentrated, screwing up his eyes. 'I can't see anything… oh, hang on a mo… yes, I see what you mean, it *does* look like a person. Here, Mark, what do you think?' He passed the photo over and began to examine the second one.

'You know, Sarge, I think she's right. That could be an arm, leaning on the corner of the chapel and further down, maybe a bit of a leg and a shoe. I can't see a face, only the arm. Dressed in dark clothes yes, I'm sure that's a person. Who was that then?'

'I don't know,' Ben said. 'Don't remember seeing anyone back there and everyone dresses in black at a funeral. Mind you, this picture was taken when the girls were starting their boxing match and we only had eyes for them – as it were. I'll check with Ian tomorrow, ask if he noticed anyone.' He took the print back from Mark and again held it in the pool of light under the lamp. 'The more I look at it, the more I'm convinced. I wonder why someone would hang about so far away from the proceedings. If they'd come to pay their respects, you'd think they'd want to see the interment.'

'Maybe that's our man, Sarge.'

'An outside chance, I guess, could have been a groundsman or gravedigger watching the graveside scrap and checking on progress before getting ready with the shovels, but worth checking out. I'll send these over to the boffins for enhancement and find out what happened to the confiscated memory cards, bet no one's even bothered to take a look. I hope Constable Bradshaw put them somewhere safe. Well done, you.' He pecked Stacey on the cheek. 'Now, who's for coffee and maybe a brandy nightcap? All right if we stay over? Another early shift tomorrow.'

'No problem. I'm on a day off tomorrow, so as long as you leave quietly and let me sleep, I don't care. The spare room is always ready for unexpected guests, so help yourself, Mark. I'm going to leave you guys to it, been busy today and it's caught up with me so I'm off to my bed. Sleep tight both of you. Nice to see you, Mark.' She gave Ben a quick hug and made her way upstairs.

## Chapter eighteen

Stacey surfaced late next morning and wandered downstairs in pyjamas searching for coffee. Ben and Mark were long gone, two dirty mugs on the drainer the only sign they'd been there. The weather had cleared and sun shone brightly through the back windows. Putting the kettle on the Aga to boil, she ambled to the front door to collect the post and morning newspapers. The first she unfolded was one of the red tops and she gasped at the headline: ARREST MADE IN MID WALES MURDERS.

Hurrying back to the kitchen, she made coffee and plonked herself at the table to drink while she read the main story.

> A man from Llandovery was arrested yesterday on suspicion of murder. Mr Jimmy Atkins, 36, has been held overnight at a local police station. His wife, Amber, 31, was found dead earlier in the week and it has been confirmed she was shot, together with the family dog. Amber is thought to be the most recent victim of the killer known to locals as, "The Stalker". The killer is believed to have been responsible for four murders during the last month in the area surrounding the sleepy market town. Llandovery is situated on the edge of the Brecon Beacons National Park and within a few miles of a

> country residence owned by HRH The Prince of Wales and the Duchess of Cornwall.
>
> Mr Atkins is a well-known local figure who works as a security guard on the nearby industrial estate, a position he has held since leaving the army several years ago. He was arrested yesterday morning and his house searched. He has two small children who have been taken into care by the local authority. No one was made available for comment at the council offices in Brecon or at the local police station.
>
> Residents are concerned tourism to the area will be affected and recent events could attract the "wrong" type of visitor. The Lady Mayoress, Mrs Elsie Thomas, expressed her sorrow to the relatives of all victims and added that prayers would be said at the main church in town next Sunday.
>
> According to our information, Mr Atkins has yet to be charged and if police wish to hold him for a further period of time, they will need to apply for an extension from local magistrates.

Stacey put down the paper and poured more coffee, wondering if Ben knew about this. Collecting her mobile from the office, she composed a short text, 'Have you seen the papers today? Check out the Red Tops. S x' and pressed send. As she did so, the house phone rang making her jump.

'Hello. Stacey Logan.'

'Hi, Stacey, it's Sam. What on earth's going on? Have you seen *The National*? They've got a headline inches high – big exclusive article. They've got names, details, the lot, and what has *The Mid Wales Times* got on its front page? Bugger all, that's what!'

'I know and understand why you're angry, but this has to have been a leak. None of this is public knowledge and if I wasn't sleeping with a copper, *I* wouldn't know any of it. You know I keep my ears to the ground so don't ring up and yell at me when I haven't spoken to anyone else yet – it's too early and it's not polite.'

'I don't give a stuff about *polite*. Why haven't we got this on our front page? Why have I got to read it somewhere else? I don't get it, Stacey. All I've received from you is an update on the last shooting and the fact the police haven't made much headway, yet our competitors know the name of the suspect and even where he damn well works.'

'OK, OK, calm down for God's sake. If it's any consolation, I don't think the police know about this and I've only just seen it. It *is* my day off, remember? Look, I'll take a wander around town and see if I can find out where this has come from and I'll check with Ben and ask what I can safely write, now the story's out there. We've gotta be careful with all these new rules and regs, following the Leveson Inquiry you don't want to find yourself in the dock, do you? Or worse, being chased around a ten-by-eight by a hairy inmate who wants to show you how much he cares.'

'Of course I don't – bloody awful idea – but give me *something*, Stacey. This is all happening on our doorstep and we're trailing behind abysmally,' Sam grumbled.

'I'll get back to you as soon as I can and – don't forget – this is my day off and now you owe me.'

* * *

Later she was sitting at a table outside her favourite café, watching the foot traffic on Stone Street. The sun brought out more folk and they wandered back and forth, stopping to chat to friends and neighbours or stare in the windows of the charity shops. She recognised nearly every face. Even if she didn't know their names, she'd seen them all in and around town during the years she'd lived here. A few tourists were about too and they were easy to spot as they were dressed up, locals – in the main – didn't bother. From her vantage point, she looked across the road towards the Craft Centre and watched as a young couple studied the display of Welsh gold jewellery.

She was startled when someone sat at her table and was even more surprised to see it was Ben.

'Hello, you,' he said.

'I wasn't expecting to see you today. Have you seen the papers?'

He glowered. 'Yes. Charlie Ambrose is going ballistic and the Chief Super is on his way over. How did *The National* get all that stuff?'

'You must have a leak somewhere, that's all I can think of. Sam's pissed off at me cos we didn't have it on *our* front page and I must admit, I'm less than pleased someone got the jump on me. Any ideas who it might be?'

'Not a clue, but I agree, it must have come from inside the nick. Jimmy's still cooling his heels in the cells, so it can't have been him and there's no way his solicitor would have pulled a stunt like this. As if I haven't got enough on my plate.'

'What you up to now, got time for a coffee?' Stacey asked.

'Not a chance. I'm meeting Jack to drive through to Sennybridge Barracks and finally pick up the army's records. We've also asked for a copy of Jimmy's service record, so I hope we're going to get hold of that at the same time. I'll be glad to be out of the way while CS Oliver is stomping about the station, he's like a bear with a sore head because of this.'

'Will I see you tonight?'

'Not sure, but probably not. The paperwork is really mounting up and we'll come back from the barracks with another pile – I hope – so I'll pull a late one then crawl home in the wee small hours.'

'There's always the key under the pot, in case you get lonely.'

She leaned into his kiss and watched as he walked quickly towards the police station.

Finishing her drink, she paid the bill and set off towards the car park. As she rounded a corner, a large man barged into her.

'Hey!' she protested.

'Oh, sorry, in a hurry.' He kept walking without looking back, striding purposefully up the road in the direction of the vets.

Stacey didn't recognise him and he didn't have the aimless air of a tourist, so – curiosity aroused – she changed direction and followed him. He was a portly man, dressed in a scruffy suit and puffed slightly as he hurried along. Reaching the end of the street, he vanished into the front door of the posh Boutique Hotel. By the time Stacey arrived outside the door, it was shut and having no good reason to go barging in, she thought she'd call on her friend, Ali. Maybe she could be persuaded to come out for a late lunch. She was disappointed. Ali had taken leave and gone away for a couple of weeks. Her colleague thought she'd gone back home for a visit, but wasn't sure. Stacey felt a little put out, Ali hadn't said a word to her the last time they spoke. She wondered why her friend hadn't mentioned her time off and hoped nothing was wrong.

Leaving the surgery, she caught a glimpse of the stranger emerging from the back door of the hotel with a small suitcase in his hand. On a sudden impulse she walked over.

'Hi there!' she called.

He studied her. 'Hello again.'

'Don't I know you?' she asked. 'I'm sure I know your face, but can't remember your name. I'm very sorry, good with faces, crap at names. Are you from the college? Maybe I've seen you there?'

'No, I'm not local.' He held out his hand, smirking, giving her the eye. 'Fred Murray – *The National*.'

Stacey took his hand and shook it. 'There's a coincidence, Stacey Logan, *Mid Wales Times*.'

'We're both in the business then. Perhaps we covered the same story somewhere along the line?'

'I know,' she said. 'Weren't you at the press conference a few weeks ago, when all these murders started?'

'Yeah, I covered that,' he said.

'Good story this morning. Where'd you get your info?'

'Must protect my source at all costs.' His lips twisted in what Stacey assumed passed for a smile. 'I'm surprised you're even asking, do I detect sour grapes? I found the story and you didn't, is that it?'

'Hardly, you painted Jimmy pretty black. Aren't you worried about prejudicing any trial?'

'Oh, I know where the line is, don't ever cross it,' he answered cockily, sure of himself.

'No, but you seem to be jumping up and down on it at the moment. Have you got a police source? You know they'll find out who it is, don't you? When they do, his career will be ruined. It's not like the cities out here, nothing ever stays a secret for long.'

'What *is* your problem?' he asked. 'You know how it works, how we get our stories. It'll be forgotten tomorrow and we'll all move on to something else.'

'I don't think your story will be, "forgotten tomorrow", not here. You don't have a clue do you, or any idea of the damage you might cause? I'm glad I work where I do and not somewhere that encourages such a lack of morals, or even any feelings for the lives of the people you destroy – whether or not they're guilty.'

'Don't be so naïve,' he snapped. 'You haven't been in the game as long as I have. You'll learn.' He opened the boot of the car, dumped his case and laptop bag inside, slammed the lid and without another look at Stacey, walked round to the driver's side and squeezed behind the wheel. Starting the car, he began to reverse out of the narrow space and while his attention was elsewhere, Stacey snatched a candid photo of him, hiding the camera behind her back when he looked in her direction. Raising a hand in a sarcastic wave, he drove away.

Stacey made her way back to the main car park and drove towards home. On impulse she stopped at the picnic area. It was the first time she'd been there since finding Emily. She parked overlooking the open hillside, needing space and fresh air to calm down. A couple of buzzards circled lazily on the rising thermals and the ever-present skylarks twittered away overhead. It wasn't the same, though, something had changed this spot and it didn't take a genius to work out why it felt so different.

She had only been sitting there for a few minutes when she thought she heard something – a noise from the edge of the forest plantation. Turning to stare at the wall of trees, she listened carefully. There was a faint scratching sound, a sort of wispy, crackly noise, slightly to the left of the trees. Listening intently, she wandered slowly towards the start of the plantation and heard it again. She couldn't think what it was – didn't sound like an animal. A cold shiver washed over her skin and she wondered what on earth she was doing. She was in the middle of nowhere, in an area where people were dying, trying to track down a mystery noise. Shoving her hand in her pocket, she discovered her mobile was missing, lying on the passenger seat in the car, and quickly decided it was a bad idea all round and walked back to her car as fast as she could.

Once she gained the safety of the driver's seat, she fired up the engine and drove slowly past the spot, eyes scanning dark shadowy patches under dense branches. She thought she caught a movement out of the corner of her eye and pulled to a stop, but peering intently into the darkness couldn't see anything, the gloomy twilight under the trees stealing colour from the day, turning everything into a dull monochrome. The window was open, but she couldn't hear anything over the rumble of the engine and didn't feel brave enough to switch it off. In the end, she gave up and drove back to her cottage.

Pulling into the drive she spotted Bob Read by her front door and tooted the horn. He looked up and raised a hand in greeting.

'Hi, Bob,' she called, opening the car door. 'How are you? I haven't seen you for a while. Are you doing OK?'

'Yeah, guess so, just come home from Kathy's funeral up in Birmingham – where her family are. We ended up spending a week there, you know, doing the rounds, staying here and there, putting off coming back really. Strange without her here.'

'Must be difficult. How are the boys doing?'

'What they always do – getting on my nerves and winding up the neighbours. They haven't talked about it much, seems as though they miss her most at mealtimes – I'm not much of a cook and daren't let any of them near the kitchen. Goodness knows what we'd end up with.'

'Fancy a cuppa? I'm just going in to put the kettle on.'

'Yeah, go on, if you can spare the time.'

Stacey led the way round the back of her cottage and unlocked the stable door.

'Take a seat, builder's tea for you, isn't it, milk, two sugars?'

'Yeah, thanks.'

'What can I do for you?'

'Nothing really, I wanted to thank you for sending those flowers, the ones for Kathy's funeral. It was a smashing arrangement, she'd have been pleased and I was touched. Didn't think anyone from the village would bother.'

'I'm glad they arrived, wasn't sure I had the details right. Your Stevie gave them to me and he didn't seem too sure.'

'Miracle they got there at all then.' A faint smile played across his face, but didn't reach anywhere near his eyes. 'Out of all of us, I reckon it's hit him the hardest, spends most of his days sitting on the wall outside the house gazing into space. His mate Dave's been up a couple of times, but even he's finding it difficult to get him out. He never did say much before all this, but we hardly get a word out of him now, "Silent Steve" we've started calling him, even then he ignores us.'

'Maybe you should get Dr Chalmers to take a look at him.'

'No, he'll be all right, too sensitive, that's all. Oh, thanks.' He took a mug from Stacey and drank, wiping his mouth with the back of his hand. 'Nothing beats a good cup of tea. Can I ask you something, Stacey?'

'Yes, of course, ask away.'

'Well, you're friends with Ben James down at the nick and I wondered if they think they've caught the guy, this Jimmy Atkins bloke? Don't know who he is, never met him and I'm sure Kathy didn't know him either so why would he kill her? Doesn't make any sense to me.'

'I don't know any more than you do, Bob. Ben can't talk to me about his work and if you want my opinion *The National* has jumped the gun. I bumped into the scumbag reporter who wrote the article in town today, not a very nice character. I can't get my head round the fact that people will believe anything – "if it's in the paper it must be true" – that's daft.'

'So you don't think there's much in it or what?' Bob persisted.

'I really can't say because I really don't know. The police have a few more leads now, so who knows? Maybe they're on the right track after all.'

Bob finished his tea and put the empty mug on the table.

'Thanks, Stacey, and for the tea. If you do hear anything will you let me know? I got such a hard time at the nick after she died – and when I should have been grieving too. Life's hard,' he muttered philosophically.

He left the kitchen and Stacey heard his boots clumping away along the lane.

## Chapter nineteen

The investigation team crammed into the incident room above Llandovery Police Station. Tasks were quickly assigned and most of the uniformed officers were once again sent out to knock on doors or patrol the lanes around Llandovery, in the vain hope of stumbling across the killer. At least seeing patrol cars reassured the natives.

Stacey had written a more reserved article on the Atkins' arrest for *The Mid Wales Times* containing a warning for people to think before they walked alone in particularly rural areas, especially dog walkers. The article was pinned up on the long noticeboard together with the one from *The National* the day before. Ben stood at the board contemplating the mass of information collected over the past weeks and still couldn't see anything that helped move the investigation forward. He turned to face his remaining colleagues.

'Jack, I want you to go over to Sennybridge Barracks with Mark and meet the officer in charge. I was due there yesterday, but they cancelled at the last minute. In good army fashion, the officer's name seems to be on a need-to-know-basis, but they *are* expecting you and have agreed to the meeting. Check their personnel registers for any absences among the squaddies – or officers if it comes to that – on the dates the murders were committed, and pick up a copy of Atkins' service record. Make sure you don't leave without it. We've managed to get an extension to hold him on the strength of the ammo we found, but can't hang on to him forever and what evidence we have got is circumstantial. Also check whether any guns or ammunition have gone missing from the ranges. I guess the army probably won't admit it if they *have* lost anything, but at least we'll be seen to have asked the question. Any problems, call me. If all goes according to plan, we'll meet back here around three. OK with you?'

Jack nodded and left the room, Mark in his wake.

'Julie, you come with me. We need a chat with Mary Saunders, Jimmy's girlfriend. I've promised him we'll be discreet, but after the headlines yesterday, I can't see it'll make much difference. Still… go and get your civvies on so it's not obvious who we are, and I'll meet you in the car park in ten.'

'OK, boss.'

Ben gazed up at the board again, sweeping his eyes over the many photos, maps, notes and lists of names, people who had been interviewed on their doorsteps, other dog walkers and friends of those who had died, their relatives and partners. It appeared nearly half the town had some mention on the board.

A new photograph had been tacked up in the centre. It depicted the corner of the funeral chapel at the green burial ground, had been enlarged from the original and didn't include the brawling women. There was most definitely a person standing there. With the enhancement the labs had managed, it was easy to recognise a hand and arm and even a shoe, poking out from behind the grey stone. Ben had hunted for the memory card Ian confiscated from Sid Barker and – once found – it had been handed over to the geeks in the back office who printed off the photographs. The shots taken at the funeral had been deleted and the rest returned intact to the journalist with a compliment slip.

In this new photo, the figure was slightly more visible. Ben thought he could make out the side of a head, but nothing more. It was infuriating. It could be one of the groundsmen, but Ben would like to know, to be sure. Shaking his head to clear his thoughts, he took his jacket from the back of a chair and went out to the car park. Julie was already waiting in the car, suitably dressed.

'You OK with me driving, boss?'

'Yeah fine. Do you know Mary Saunders, ever met her?'

Julie started the engine. 'Once I think, in passing. Her kids go to the same school as my sister's boys, I was introduced to her at the Christmas show, but wouldn't say I knew her.'

'Any impressions?'

'What, from that one meeting?'

'You *are* a copper, you're supposed to be more observant than the rest of Joe Public.' He chuckled.

'Yeah, right, but no, nothing really. Ordinary mum, not outstanding to look at, quite pretty, but nothing exceptional, bit shy maybe. I only chatted with her for a few minutes, can't remember what about – kids probably, or the show.'

Within a few minutes they arrived outside the small industrial park at the bottom of town and parked the car by the administration block. A noticeboard hung on the wall listing businesses renting units, together with a map showing where on the estate they were based. Ben ran his finger down the names and stopped at one that read, "D. A. Jones and Sons, General Builders".

'This is what we're looking for,' he said. 'Mary works in the office and all things being equal, we can get in and out without anyone else noticing we've been here. We've got enough trouble without setting husbands and wives against each other if we can avoid it. Come on, Jules, let's walk.'

They wandered along the narrow road passing by units of various sizes from tiny lock-ups to bigger, almost warehouse-sized buildings. Inside one of the smaller buildings, a blacksmith worked at his forge, large doors wide open, a ringing sound echoing around the estate as he hammered and shaped a bar of red-hot metal. Some units looked empty, but most had a few cars parked outside and people coming and going.

'How's Stacey doing, Sarge? I've been meaning to pop in, but with everything going on I haven't managed to squeeze in a visit. We're busy on the farm too.'

'She's doing well, thanks, back at work with no lasting effects. I'll pass on your good wishes.'

They arrived at the builder's unit and studied it from the pavement. The place didn't look very open and the car park was empty, but there was a light on inside so they pushed open the door. The small room was bisected by a long, chest-high counter. On the far side were a couple of desks, some filing cabinets and an odd selection of office machines. Piles of paper were tidily arranged on a wide windowsill and at one of the desks sat a small woman with straight brown hair, typing intently in front of a computer screen. She didn't appear to have noticed them, so Ben cleared his throat a couple of times, eventually managing to gain her attention.

'Sorry, didn't see you there, can I help?' she asked and walked over to the counter.

'I hope so. Are you Mary Saunders?'

Her face quickly lost its smile and she nodded warily.

'Yes I am. Who are you?'

Both officers held out their warrant cards.

Mary studied them. 'You want to know about me and Jimmy, don't you?'

'That's a good guess,' Ben said.

'Obvious, isn't it? Jimmy's been arrested for killing his wife and I'm his bit of stuff, so it stands to reason at some point you'd find your way here.'

'Are you OK to talk? Thought it'd be better to come here rather than your house – we haven't got much to ask you, ten minutes at the most, is that OK?'

'I guess it has to be, doesn't it?' She sighed. 'Go on, ask your questions and I'll do what I can to help.'

'Here, or is there somewhere else?'

'No, this is it, but stop if anyone comes in.'

'No problem. You've already told us you were having an affair with Jimmy Atkins.'

Mary nodded.

'How long has it been going on?'

'A year, thereabouts. Didn't take much notice, to be honest. It wasn't – *isn't* – a serious thing. Neither of us had any illusions about setting up home together, I've got my two boys and he's got his kids. It was a bit of fun, a diversion.'

'Did Mr Saunders know, or Amber? Did she find out?'

'Neither of them knew. If either had cottoned on we'd have known about it. Amber would have gone ballistic and I can't think my old man would have been pleased.' She pulled a face.

'So, you'd been seeing each other for about a year, were you together the day Amber was killed?'

'No, he couldn't get away. We *were* going to meet, but around teatime he sent a text to say Amber had decided to go out walking with the dog. She was having a good day with her MS and once she'd made up her mind to go out there was no deflecting her. Poor Jimmy just had to let her go and stay to look after the kids. I think that was part of the problem.'

'What was?' Ben asked.

'Her selfishness. Jimmy says since she got ill, she put herself first. Not before the kids – her little angels – but before Jimmy, definitely. If she wanted to go out, she was going and he had to lump it. He often had to cancel a date.'

'Where did you go when you were together?' Julie asked.

'Nowhere special. Sometimes we'd go over to Llandeilo for a meal. There's a quiet place behind the main street that does nice food, far enough away to be safe. Twice we went to Aberglasney – you know, the gardens and house? Places like that mainly cater for tourists and it's rare for a local to pop in. They do really good food, grow a lot of it in the kitchen garden and the grounds are beautiful, more my thing than Jimmy's.'

'Anywhere else? What about round here, did you ever meet locally?'

She blushed and spoke quieter. 'We'd meet about once a week by the river on the edge of town.'

'Where exactly, Mary? Was there one place or several?' Ben asked.

'Only one really. There's a wood above the water meadows on the far side of the Tywi. No one goes there. Anyone who walks that way tends to stick to the bank to watch the water. We used to sit in the wood looking down on them, giggling when we recognised someone from town cos they couldn't see us. It was like being a couple of teenagers again.' She smiled at the memory.

'What did you do there, or is the answer obvious?' Julie asked gently, trying to sugar-coat what she was suggesting. 'How long did you spend there with Jimmy?'

'Depended on how much time was available and what the weather was like. If it was wet we'd go for a walk hidden behind the trees, for a chat and company.'

'Does Jimmy have any guns, Mary?' Ben asked.

She looked horrified. 'You don't think he killed her, do you? I know you've got him in the cells, but you can't *really* think he shot Amber? That's crazy, Jimmy's not a killer for heaven's sake.'

'That's not quite true is it?' Ben asked. 'He'd been in the army – you knew that?'

'Yes I knew, he was a *cook*. He didn't kill people. He worked in the mess.'

'Is that what he told you?'

'Yes. We didn't talk much about our pasts, but I knew he'd been in the army, he told me that much. He knew a bit about me, where I grew up, stuff like that, but we didn't delve deep, why would we? We were having a bit of fun, no strings attached. I liked him – of course I did – but wasn't planning on running away with him. There wasn't going to be a happy-ever-after for us, so why would I pry? He told me what he wanted me to know and I did the same. Anyway, what about the other victims? Are you trying to say he killed them too? Why would he do that?'

Neither officer answered, busying themselves with their notebooks.

Finally, Ben spoke. 'I think that's it for now, Mary. Thank you for talking to us.'

'When are you going to let him out then? He's all right, is he?' she asked.

'He's fine. Fed up at being in the cells, but we're working as fast as we can. Can you write your name and address down for me? I assume the phone number here is the best one to reach you.'

'Obviously only during working hours, but yes, it'll be better if you don't ring the house.'

'Can you write that number too, in case we need to get in touch quickly? We'll be discreet and only use it if we have to.'

Reluctantly, she scribbled on a piece of photocopier paper before handing it over. Ben glanced at it and tucked it in his inside pocket.

'Well, thanks again,' he said. 'We'll ring if we need to ask you anything else.'

The officers stepped out of the dingy office and sauntered back along the sunny street to the car park at the entrance of the estate.

'She thinks he was a cook?' Julie said. 'What's that all about, Sarge? Most of these ex-army types – and some that aren't, to be honest – say they were in *The Regiment*, ex-SAS, trained to kill, yet here's a guy who was a sniper and *was* trained to kill, telling his bit of stuff he was a *cook*.'

'It's odd, I admit. I wonder why he told her that? Maybe he *was* a cook and he's lying to *us*?'

'That can't possibly be it,' Julie huffed. 'You said he didn't like admitting what he did in the army, hated having to tell you guys he was a sniper. If he was a cook that's what he'd have told you, makes him look less guilty, don't you think? He'd be *pleased* to tell us he was only a cook, just as an accused forger would be delighted to be able to tell you he was colour-blind.'

'What do you feel about this, Julie, do *you* think he's the killer?'

'Don't ask me. I'm only a lowly copper, you're the detective, you're the one who should be coming up with answers. I do plod work, you lot do clever stuff.'

'Go on, I want to know what you think,' Ben prompted.

'Well then, no, actually I don't. I don't know why I think that as we have evidence pointing neatly his way, the collection of bullets and – in his opinion – a selfish wife. He's a drunkard, ex-army sniper and his DNA was found close to the scene. I can probably see him doing Amber in – aggrieved husbands sometimes do strange things – but I can't understand why he'd kill the others. Have we established whether he knew any of them?'

'He admitted to knowing Danny, they'd gone to school together. He also knew Danny was seeing Samantha, but wasn't a church-goer so only knew Emily by sight and says he's never met Kathy Read or any of the family. He knew *of* them, but most people round here have heard of them for one reason or another, or at least read about their exploits in the local rag, but he hadn't met any of them – so he says.'

'We aren't getting very far, are we?'

'No and it's beginning to do my head in. I'm not sure what more we can do. We've spoken to nearly every single resident in town, visited local hill farmers to ask if they've seen anything in recent weeks, questioned families and partners and the best we can do is Jimmy. Like you – I'm not convinced.'

'What does DS Trent think?' Julie asked. 'He's probably handled more of this sort of crime than we have, coming from the city. Does he think Jimmy's guilty?'

'I don't know what he thinks. He helps when I ask him to and stays out of the way when I want him to do that. You can tell he's a city boy, has his own ways of doing things, but hasn't come to me with any revelations. If Scotland Yard thought their wonder boy would solve this, they were wrong.'

They arrived at the car and Julie sat in the driver's seat.

'Who do you think leaked that stuff to the press – was it one of ours?' she asked.

'I can't see how it could have been anyone else. Dick Nyle – the duty solicitor – isn't going to queer his pitch and we've used him for years without any problems. We kept the arrest quiet so it was only us who knew what was going on.'

'What about the council, would they know? I mean, they're still looking after the kids, aren't they? Someone there must know Jimmy's whereabouts, the circumstances of the case. Would they have said something?'

'I'd like to think they wouldn't, but it's a point. I'll give them a ring this afternoon and see if I can find anything out. Better idea, *you* give them a ring, you might get more out of them. My rank sometimes puts people off, especially the ones who've done something they shouldn't have done.'

'Yes, and I'm a girl – people talk to women more than they do men.'

'No, *women* talk to other *women* more, but I'll concede it's a point in your favour.' He laughed.

'I wonder how Jack and Mark are getting on with the army?'

'No idea, but nothing is ever easy when the army is involved. Thought Jack's manner was more suited to

Sennybridge Barracks than coming to see Mary. He's on the brash side, an archetypal bad cop – hulking great lump.'

'He's a townie, boss, and they're all like that in England – not just the coppers.'

## Chapter twenty

A young soldier stuck her head round the waiting room door.

'DS Trent and DC Jefferies? The captain is ready for you now, this way please.' Without waiting to see whether they followed her instructions, she vanished from the room. The officers struggled to their feet and hurried to catch up with her retreating back. Arriving outside a door at the end of a long corridor, she knocked smartly then held the door open for the two men.

'DS Trent and DC Jefferies, sir,' she barked.

The military man behind the desk stood to greet them, shaking their hands as he introduced himself.

'Captain Harford-Brown, Military Police. Pleased to meet you, officers. Can I get you some coffee?'

'Pleased to meet you too, sir,' Jack said. 'Thank you for agreeing to see us and yes, coffee would be good.' Jack unbuttoned his jacket and sat.

The captain picked up a phone and ordered refreshments. He was a small, busy man, slightly overweight, officious in his manner and a touch effeminate. His uniform was immaculate, buttons shone, the gleam on his boots almost blinding under harsh, fluorescent lighting.

'Now then, gentlemen, what can I do for you? I'm sorry I had to cancel yesterday, but something came up, I'm sure you know how that feels.'

'Only too well at the moment,' Jack agreed. 'We're very busy in Llandovery.'

'Yes, you must be. The Colonel sends his apologies, but he's tied up today so I've volunteered to assist you. I understand you want to know if any of our boys or girls have been nipping out AWOL. DS James sent me a list of dates and times and I've had one of my staff work through it. I'm pleased to inform you we haven't discovered any unauthorised absences that match.'

There was a tap on the door and the female soldier returned, carrying a tray laden with coffee cups, which she placed on the large desk.

'Thank you, Annie,' said the captain. 'Shall I be mother?'

The policemen gave each other a sideways glance and Jack raised his eyebrows a fraction.

'How do you like it?' Harford-Brown asked.

'Black, two sugars in both, thank you,' Mark said.

The captain poured mugs of coffee then settled back in his leather chair.

'No unexplained absences at all, or only those dates and times?' Jack asked.

'Not at those times. Of course we *do* have the odd incident, youngsters in training sometimes stay out longer than they should, but not often. My MPs are an effective bunch, quick to round them up. It's rare though, we have a pretty good group in at the moment.'

'What about any missing weapons or ammunition?' Mark asked.

'Nothing at all unaccounted for,' Harford-Brown said confidently, displaying a broad grin that stopped at his nose. 'We run a tight ship here and these days the lads are required to bring back empty shells after target practice.

Count 'em all out and count 'em all back in again, that's the drill. Nothing goes missing – ever.'

'You seem very sure of that, sir,' Jack said.

'That's because I *am* sure, DS Trent. You don't think the army is lax in any way, do you? You're not trying to suggest we don't know what we're doing? The kit we use is not only deadly, but expensive. Everything, and I do mean *everything*, is accounted for.' He buried his face in his coffee cup.

Jack caught Mark's eye and shrugged. 'Well then, sir, I guess that's it. Oh, one more thing, DS James said we were to pick up Jimmy Atkins' service record.'

'Yes, that's right, I have it here… somewhere.' He rifled through folders on his desk and made a triumphant sound as he discovered the file at the bottom of a large pile. 'Here we are. This is a copy, you understand – can't let you have the original – but it's all there, all the sordid little details. I hope you enjoy it.'

'In what way *sordid*, sir?' Mark asked.

'You'll understand when you read it.' The captain got to his feet. 'That's us done then, thank you for coming over, gentlemen, and I wish you luck with your case.' He held out his right hand while opening the office door with his left. The policemen had little choice but to walk through it and make their way back to the car. The meeting was over in under twenty-five minutes.

'Blimey, Jack, he didn't want us there, did he?'

'No, not the most welcome I've felt since I came to Wales.'

'Do you think he was being difficult, or is that just the way the army is?'

'Bit of both I reckon. The army doesn't enjoy talking to the likes of us, never been great fans of civilian coppers. I think he'd been told to be nice, tell us what he thinks we wanted to know, then get rid asap.'

Mark folded himself behind the steering wheel and started the engine as Jack opened the thick cardboard folder.

'Drive smoothly, can you, Constable? I get carsick if I have to read on the move, but I'm not patient enough to wait until we're back at the station.'

'I'll do my best,' Mark said and pulled away. He drove through the compound past rows of barrack buildings, under the red and white pole at the main gate, and out onto the main road. They hadn't travelled many miles when Mark heard Jack whistle.

'What have you found?' he asked.

'That Jimmy Atkins is a liar, that's what I've found.'

'Don't keep me in suspense.' Mark peered over at the file.

'Keep your eyes on the road. Give me a minute, will you?'

They drove a few more miles before Jack started to speak. 'According to this, Jimmy was a sniper – a bloody good one – won lots of tournaments for his regiment, quite a star. Went out to Iraq and conducted himself honourably – so it says – showed courage in the field, but not enough for a medal, other than a campaign one. You know, an I've-been-to-Iraq-and-came-back-alive badge. Didn't have long in Blighty before they sent him out again, this time to Afghanistan for another six-month tour.' Jack was silent as he read. 'Four months in and everything goes pear-shaped for Jimmy. Out on patrol one evening, he shot an Afghani woman and her two young children.'

'Nasty. It was a mistake, right?'

'That's just it. The army investigated it from all angles and although Jimmy said it was self-defence – thought the woman was wearing a suicide vest under her clothes – the brass weren't impressed. Shipped him back to England and quietly discharged him, citing PTSD, you know, Post Traumatic Stress Disorder.'

'Yeah, I *do* know, I'm not as thick as I look thank you.' Mark thought for a moment. 'Did he lose it, do you reckon, or did he truly believe they were a threat?'

'Not a clue, mate, and until we go over these records properly, I can't get much of an idea about it, but it doesn't look good. People suffering with this condition can often act without thinking about what they're doing. No wonder Harford-bloody-Brown wanted us out of his office, so we couldn't ask questions. If we went back now he'd be unavailable or in a meeting – something. Put your foot down, Mark, and get us back to the office, let's see what Ben makes of it.'

* * *

Later in the afternoon, the team finally managed to all be in the same place at the same time. Jack handed over Jimmy's service record, then went to fill up on coffee. Ben speed-read the important parts of the file, then called Mark over.

'How did it go? Jack behave himself?'

'Yeah, all fine, boss. He's a good bloke, Jack, but that funny little captain had him beat. Dished out what he wanted us to know, nearly *threw* the file at us and we were out the door before we had time to finish our coffee. How did he do that without seeming rude? Wish I knew, I could try it with Mam next time she drops in unannounced.'

The door swung open and Jack entered carrying a tray of coffee. 'Have you had a look at the file, boss? What d'you reckon, think he's our man now?' He waved an envelope in the air. 'If not, perhaps this will convince you. I've just been handed the lab results from Jimmy's clothing – the stuff we took when we searched his place. Gunshot residue on a leather jacket and shirt. Does that do it for you now?'

Ben gazed at him, open mouthed.

'Yeah, I knew you'd be surprised. Guess we gotta chat to Jimmy again. I know he doesn't want to see me, but he shouldn't get to choose who interrogates him. Go on, boss, let me show you how it's done in the city. Let me push a little, I'll be so gentle he won't even know he's being leaned on and I bet we'll get some answers. What d'you think?'

Ben took the results from Jack and placed them in front of him on the desk, next to the service record, and stared at them.

'OK, I guess we'll give it a go – give *you* a go,' he said. 'Jimmy's got some explaining to do and maybe this time we'll get the truth, but remember, Jack, just because we've got this evidence it does *not* mean he's guilty. People make mistakes and if he was suffering from PTSD when he shot those civilians in Afghanistan, then he wasn't entirely liable. That matter has been dealt with by the army and we cannot let that affect our judgment here. There may be an explanation why GSR is on his clothes, so don't get carried away and I'll be there to make sure you don't.' Ben drained his mug. 'Right then, someone get Dick Nyle on the blower and call him down here. Mark, get Jimmy into the interview room, I'd like the three of us in there. The rest of you – clean this place up. The paper mountain is overtaking us and we'll miss something if it's not in order. Julie, can you make a quick copy of this file and the lab results and run them up to DCI Ambrose? Let him know we're going to interview Jimmy again, he may want to sit in the observation room. Let's get cracking.'

* * *

They met Jimmy in the interview room with Dick Nyle at his side. Ben and Jack sat at the table facing them, while Mark switched on the recording machine before leaning on the tiled wall near the door. Jimmy was not at all pleased to see Jack.

'What's that ugly bastard doing in here? I told you, I'm not talking when he's here, so get rid of him.'

'Sorry, Jimmy,' Ben said. 'That's not an option and there's no need to get personal. You can't choose who interviews you, that's not how we do things.'

'Fine, I won't speak then. He'll be wasting everybody's time.'

Dick Nyle leaned in towards his client. 'Jimmy – as your solicitor – I advise you to listen to the officers' questions and be as cooperative as you can. This attitude won't help your case at all and will only make things difficult for me – *for us* – later on. Listen to what they have to say at least.'

Jimmy glowered, folded his arms across his chest, leaned back in his chair and grinned cockily at Jack.

'Go on then, copper, talk. My brief says I have to listen, so I'll listen, but no guarantees I'm gonna answer any questions.'

Jack nodded. 'We've been to see Mary at the industrial estate. She confirmed that you have been with her in the wood above the river on several occasions.'

'Told you I was telling the truth.'

'Thing is, she also told us she thought you were a cook in the army, said that's what you told her. A cook – not a sniper. Did you tell her that?'

'Yeah, I said I was a cook.' Jimmy sounded bored.

'Why did you do that?' Jack asked.

'Didn't think she'd like it if she knew I'd shot people for a living and it sounded better.'

'Did you shoot people, Jimmy?'

'Yeah, sometimes. What else would a sniper do?'

'I guess that is pretty much what they do,' Jack agreed. 'Who did you shoot? What sort of targets? Is that what you call them in the army, "targets", or is it "marks" these days?'

'Bad rag-heads, that's who I shot. Taliban in Afghanistan, groups of leftover Republican Guards from Saddam's time in Iraq, other snipers waiting to ambush my guys.'

'You were good too, weren't you?'

'Not bad.'

'Won trophies for your regiment, quite the star… in the early days anyway.'

Jimmy peered at Jack through half-closed, suspicious eyes. 'What do you mean, "in the early days"?'

'Went a bit tits-up after you'd been in Afghanistan for a few months, didn't it?'

'Don't know what you mean.'

'I think you do, Jimmy, in fact I *know* you do. We've obtained a copy of your service record, so we know you were sent home early. What was that all about? Women and children?'

Jimmy didn't speak and glowered at Jack who held his gaze. Minutes passed, before Jimmy lowered his eyes and studied the backs of his hands.

'Well, Jimmy? Tell us what happened.'

'Nothing to do with any of you bastards, that's for sure. Served Queen and country to the best of my abilities. Yes, I was discharged, but not *dishonourably*. You read that, copper? I wasn't discharged dishonourably, but on health grounds.'

'Yes, it does say that,' Jack said. 'You were suffering from PTSD. Not quite the tough guy you thought you were and it's not what you told us before. You said you left to be with your wife and kids. You lied to us, Jimmy. I said you were a liar.'

'Bollocks! I'm not listening to this. You – DS James – tell him to shut up, will you? It's all in the file. You've read about it and if I don't want to discuss it, I don't see why I should. The army dealt with it, case closed. This has *nothing* to do with my wife, nothing to do with Amber at all.'

'No, you're right. It doesn't have anything to do with Amber, interesting though, don't you think?' Jack flashed him a smile.

'Tell him to shut up, he's doing my head in,' Jimmy muttered.

'Would you like a break, Mr Atkins?' Dick Nyle asked. 'I'm sure we could stop for a while.'

'No, let's get it done, but I don't want to talk about the army. That's in the past and I've moved on, so tell that *thug* to stop going on about it.'

'DS Trent, I think my client has made his feelings clear and he does have a point – this matter was dealt with. Is there something else we can move on to?'

Jack nodded, still smiling, and slowly opened the folder in front of him, took out a piece of paper and held it in front of his eyes as though reading it for the first time. He made a few grunting noises, rubbed his chin, put the paper on the table in front of him and looked Jimmy in the eye. The prisoner shifted uneasily in his seat, wary. Ben had to admit Jack was good at this and enjoyed watching him work. He wondered what DCI Ambrose was making of it on the other side of the false mirror.

'OK then, no more army stuff – well, for now anyway. When did you last shoot a gun, Jimmy?' Jack asked.

The question caught the prisoner off guard. 'When I was in the army, that's when I last shot a gun. I can't give you the exact date, but I'll bet someone can. It's probably in that precious file.'

'Are you *sure* about that? You've never shot a gun since you left? No shooting clubs, rabbits, targets, nothing?'

'Yes, I'm sure, I'd know, wouldn't I?'

'Why did you stop? Shooting was such a large part of your life for so long, how could you give it up like that? Must have been hard.'

'No, it was easy. I haven't got a gun, or a licence. I don't want a gun in the house with the kids and Amber would never have allowed it. That's what I did for a job, I don't do that job anymore, end of.'

'But you were so good at it, all those trophies. Why not join a club here? There are plenty around and they'd be pleased to have someone as good as you.'

'Never bothered. Came home and gave it up.'

Jack cleared his throat, picked up the piece of paper again and studied it, saying nothing.

Jimmy couldn't stand it. 'What's that?'

'Lab results,' Jack muttered.

'Of what?'

'Well – as you're interested – it says here that GSR, or gunshot residue, has been found on the sleeve of your jacket and also on one of your shirts. How do you reckon that got there if you haven't shot a gun for years?'

Jimmy looked horrified, all colour seeped from his face. He started to sweat and wiped his face with his hand.

'It can't say that, how can it?' he asked. 'I haven't shot a gun in years. I'm being set up here. Wake up, Dick, you're my solicitor, can't you do something? Are you going to let them get away with this? They're framing me!' He surged to his feet and shouted, 'I didn't shoot my wife, do you hear me? I didn't shoot her!'

Jack calmly slipped the paper back into the folder, not reacting to the angry man's outburst.

'That's all for now, Jimmy, we could all do with a break. You should talk to your solicitor, see what he advises and later – when you've calmed down – we'll do this all over again until you tell us the truth.' Jack stood and swept out of the room, Ben and Mark following on behind.

'Let's get another extension from the magistrates,' Jack said. 'Leave him to cool off overnight. We'll do this again first thing tomorrow – give him some time to think about it.' Jack chuckled, satisfied with his performance.

'OK,' Ben said. 'Shouldn't be a problem with the new evidence and we're nearly at the point where – if an extension was going to be difficult – we could charge him. It's all still a touch circumstantial, but it would take the heat off and I reckon we can get another forty-eight hours without too much trouble. You were good in there, Jack.'

'Thanks, boss. We'll play things differently tomorrow. We'll chat beforehand. Right, I'm off. Big day tomorrow and I want to get my head down. The King's Head isn't always the quietest place in the evening and – as you've doubtless already noticed – I need my beauty sleep. See you in the morning, boys and girls.'

They listened to him skip his way down the stairs, and a jaunty whistle as he hit the street.

## Chapter twenty-one

Stacey was at her desk trawling the internet, searching for similar shootings in the rest of the UK. She still thought it was unlikely Jimmy Atkins had shot four people and if he hadn't – who had?

Her main research area was the digital libraries that nearly all newspapers maintained. Crimes of this magnitude were always well covered, but so far she'd been unlucky. The phone on her desk rang and she jumped, dropping her pencil into half a mug of cold coffee.

'Oh, bugger,' she said and picked up the receiver. 'Hello, Stacey Logan.'

'Hi, Stacey, how are you doing?'

'Julie. Good to hear from you. I'm OK thanks, you?' Stacey tucked the handset under her chin, pulled a tissue from a box balanced on top of her screen and mopped up.

'Busy, obviously. Sorry not to have rung before. Have you got time to chat?'

'Yeah, no worries. All I'm doing is surfing the net.'

Julie sniggered. 'I hope you're not distracting yourself with unsuitable stuff.'

'No, gave up porn for lent. What I'm actually doing is searching for crimes in the rest of Britain which might match what's going on here.'

'That's a good idea. Don't think we're doing that. Any luck?'

'Nope. As you'll know, serial killers are rare and always generate more column inches than a royal baby, so I'm trawling newspaper archives.'

'Another bloody good idea.'

'Would be if I'd come across a series of unsolved, multiple murders, but I haven't. Anyway, why did you call?'

'Only to see how you're doing. Da was asking after you and Mam says it's too long since she's seen you.'

'Tell them not to worry, I'm fine, really I am. No nightmares or flashbacks. That's down to you, I'm sure. I was so glad when I saw it was you looking after me the other day, rather than someone I didn't know.'

'No problem, it is my job after all. When there's time, we should go for a drink, maybe supper at the farm.'

'Yeah, that would be nice.'

Julie hesitated. 'Have you met the English copper? DS Jack Trent?'

'No, not yet. Ben talks about him though and seems to think he's OK – for an English townie. Why?'

'No reason really.'

Stacey giggled. 'You fancy him, I can tell by your voice. Does he know?'

'Not entirely sure I do yet, he's growing on me and must admit I'm drawn, but can't work out why. Don't say anything to anyone, will you?'

'Course not, our secret, but you should go for it. Time you got yourself settled down.'

'You sound just like Mam.'

'We can't both be wrong.' Stacey changed the subject. 'On a work issue, I was wondering why The Stalker shot the dogs and their owners.'

'And? Any ideas?'

'Only one really and no doubt impossible to prove, but what if he shot the dogs first? The owners would be bound to stop, kneel by their pets. The killer would know he was on target so the second shot would be easy.'

'God, that's calculated, makes perfect sense, although that didn't happen when Emily was shot.'

'Maybe he missed the dog, hit Emily instead, then spotted me and didn't shoot again.'

'Yeah, possible I suppose. Have you told Ben?'

'No, haven't seen him, he's busy, and it's such a vague idea and as I said, could never be proved, but it might help identify the individual responsible, someone cold, as you said, calculating.'

'I agree and yes, I'll tell him. We're all in early these days so I'll let him know first thing.'

'Thanks. So, you gonna ask Juicy Jack Trent on a date?'

Julie laughed. 'Bit soon for that, I'm still in thinking mode.'

'Make sure you keep me up to date.'

'I might. Sorry but I gotta go, Mam's just put supper on the table. Take care.'

'You too.'

Stacey finished mopping her workspace, made a fresh coffee and returned to cyberspace, unwilling to give up her search.

* * *

The next morning, Ben and Mark were studying the noticeboard when Ian Bradshaw called from his desk.

'Hey, Sarge, come and have a look at this, will you?'

Ben moved to Ian's side and bent over his shoulder.

'What you got?'

'I know the print on the shell case we found at the scene wasn't good – only a partial – but I've been playing around with it, pulled up a copy of Atkins' prints and been trying to line them up. Look, if I turn his thumbprint this way, then lay a copy of the partial over the top, it sort of fits.' He twisted the papers slowly. 'See? That matches, doesn't it?'

Ben peered at it then carried the documents over to the window. He studied them in the daylight.

'God, I hate these fluorescents, crap light to see anything properly… you know, I think you have a point, Ian, it does look like there's a match.' Ben moved the prints around again in bright sunshine. 'The little we *have* got on the shell does seem to line up with the middle section of Jimmy's thumbprint. I wonder if it's good enough to hold up in court. If you add it to everything else we've got, you'd think so.'

The door at the far end of the room banged open and Jack stomped in with a tray of coffee, a carrier bag dangling from one of his wrists.

'Morning, campers, breakfast,' he announced. 'I called in at the baker's on the way, managed to convince the young girl there to let me sneak in before they opened and make off with a bag of freshly baked Danish pastries. Help yourselves, I have a feeling this is going to be a long day.'

Everyone instantly downed tools and were soon munching, mumbling their thanks through crummy mouths.

'Morning, Sergeant. What's this in aid of?' Ben asked.

'Got a good feeling about the next part. I tell you now, I think Jimmy did it. There's too much circumstantial stuff to be explained away.'

'We've possibly found some more,' Ben told him. 'Ian's been playing around with the fingerprint evidence and reckons we can match the partial on the shell casing to Jimmy's thumb.'

'*Really?* Now that *is* good news. Think I'll have another bun to celebrate. You told the brass yet?'

'No, not yet, only just heard. I'll get Julie on it, she is liaising with DCI Ambrose for us, has the sort of mind that doesn't forget anything and keeps it all nicely ordered. Anyway, I'm sure he'd much rather spend an hour in the office with her than any of us buggers.' Ben chuckled.

'Do you think it's good enough if we go to court? Will it be admissible?' Jack asked.

'Not sure, but we'll certainly give it a go. Maybe we can use it in this morning's session with Atkins, see if we get any response? How do you intend to tackle him today?'

'You play the good guy to my bad. Start the interview and take him over the same ground to check we're still getting the same answers. Don't mention the fingerprint, we'll leave that until further in, nice little surprise for our boy. I'll probably chip in now and again, wind him up a bit. Don't forget – even with his problems – we have a hard man here, ex-army with training in interrogation techniques, makes him more difficult to question. I've had experience with squaddies before.'

'What was that then?' Mark asked.

'We had a case in Battersea a few years ago – a couple of brothers. They were both in the same regiment and one of them was busy breaking into little old ladies' houses and making off with their cash and jewels. They could have been twins, less than a year between them and they played us one against the other for days after we'd nicked them, each blaming the other for their misdeeds. We had a witness, but he couldn't tell them apart.'

'How did you sort it out?'

'Pushed and pushed until we finally got a confession, turned the tables and played *them* against each other. I'm sure we can get a result here. Jimmy will confess.'

'Say you *do* get a confession,' Mark said, 'how are we going to link him to the other killings? Even if he confesses, we'll need to prove he shot those people. We need more than bullets to connect him to the other murders.'

'I can't see him killing one and not the others,' Jack muttered. 'He's our man, take my word for it. PTSD got out of control again, a nagging wife, disappointing life, depressed – maybe he was practising with the first three before the main event, as in getting rid of Amber.' Jack shoved the last mouthful of pastry between his lips and followed it with a swig of coffee that emptied his mug.

'Right then, lads, let's have at him. I'll grab some more coffee first – anyone else?' Ben and Mark shook their heads. 'OK, see you down there. Good work with the fingerprint, Constable Bradshaw. Make me a quick copy, will you? I've discovered Jimmy doesn't like it when I wave pieces of paper in his face.'

* * *

Jimmy was escorted to the interview room accompanied by his solicitor. Dick nodded at the officers then sat by his client's side. Ben started the recorder, went through the usual preamble and the interview began.

'Morning, Jimmy,' Ben said. 'Slept well I hope? Have we given you any breakfast?'

'Yeah, I've been fed.'

'Good. I've heard our custody sergeant rustles up a mean bacon and eggs.'

Jimmy didn't respond and stared sullenly straight ahead.

'Have you had a chance to talk with Mr Nyle?' Ben asked.

'Yeah, done that too. Look, when is all this going to be over? I'm going to lose my job if you hold me here much longer. The bosses aren't keen to keep me on as it is with all the publicity, but you knew that when you told the press you'd nicked me. Dick showed me a copy of the paper, paints me as a right nasty piece of work. When all this is over, I'll sue you for telling them all that. And what about my kids? I still don't even know where they are, haven't seen them for over a week.'

Ben cleared his throat. 'The press shouldn't have got hold of this. It wasn't an official release and we are investigating the leaking of your personal information. I can only offer my apologies and assure you that your children are being well looked after by Social Services, you don't need to worry about them.'

'Like I'm supposed to believe that! Everyone knows what coppers are like, a reporter waves a few quid under their noses and they can't keep their mouths shut.'

Before Ben could reply, Jack interrupted, 'You want me to feel sorry for you? Poor, hard-done-by Jimmy Atkins. Killed his wife and couldn't face the consequences?'

'Shut up,' Jimmy snapped. 'I'm not talking to you.'

Jack leaned back in his chair and folded his arms.

Ben took a deep breath. 'I am sorry the information was printed. All I can do is try to assure you I will find out what happened and I'll make sure there isn't a repeat.' Ben paused. 'Now let's move on. Have you thought over what we talked about yesterday?'

'Bugger all else to do in your smelly cells, yeah, I thought about it.'

'And?' Ben prompted.

'And what?'

'For a start, have you remembered how you got gunshot residue on your clothes?'

'I told you yesterday, I haven't fired a gun since I left the military and I stand by that. Maybe my clothes were cross-contaminated. Doesn't that happen all the time? I hear about it a lot on telly, or perhaps you just planted it on there to frame me, help your clear-up rate. I tell you over and over again I didn't shoot my wife, yet you are still bothering me with these stupid questions. Why are you doing this?'

'Because we don't believe you. Because you're a liar,' Jack muttered.

Jimmy turned to his solicitor. 'What *is* it with him? Why is he even here? He's not a local cop, he shouldn't be allowed to be in here.'

'He's a representative from Scotland Yard and has every right to be here,' Dick told him.

'Well, I don't like him.'

'Tough,' Jack muttered again. 'You know something, Jimmy, I don't like you much either. Nasty drunken slob who – I'm sure – bullied, then killed his sick wife. Shagged around, spinning lies to your bit on the side – comes easy to you doesn't it, lying?'

'You don't know anything about me, copper. You know nothing about my life, what I've done, where I've been. You'd *never* be able to deal with the stuff I've had to, fighting abroad, crap conditions and natives who'd shoot you as soon as look at you or worse, pretend they're your friend, get close, then blow themselves – and you – to kingdom come. You've no bloody idea! Got a cosy life up in London I'll bet, nice place to live, good job, plenty of money. I was out in the dust and shit of the Afghan desert, fighting to keep the likes of you safe. Look at the thanks I'm getting.'

'I'm sorry, Jimmy, I didn't know you wanted me to *thank* you for that. Well then – thanks.'

'You sarcastic bastard! Did you miss charm-school day when you were – *trained*?'

Ben butted in. 'Is it possible you've forgotten about going shooting? Maybe went with a mate, shot some clays, that sort of thing. It says in your record you were discharged due to ill health, suffering from PTSD. That sometimes causes memory problems, doesn't it?'

'Sometimes it does, but not this time. You'll be saying I'm mad next and ship me off to Rampton or somewhere equally disgusting. Listen to me. I did *not* shoot my wife, I did *not* shoot those other people and I have *not* shot a gun since I left the forces. Happy now?'

'Not by a long way, sunshine,' Jack growled. He leant forward, opened the cardboard folder and took out two sheets of paper he studied for a minute or two.

'What's that?' Jimmy asked.

'More evidence. More evidence to prove you shot your wife.'

'Not possible, I didn't do it. You can't have anything.'

'We've got part of your thumbprint on a shell case. A shell case that was discovered near the cigarette ends with your DNA on, remember them? Missed this, didn't you, Jimmy? Picked up all the others, but forgot this one. You're slipping, losing it.' Jack leaned menacingly over the table until his face was only a few inches from Jimmy's sweating skin. 'You lost it a while ago, didn't you? Lost it in Afghanistan when you shot those kids and their mother and you've lost it again now – haven't you?' Jack roared.

Jimmy pulled away from the table, looking shocked.

'That's it,' he said. 'I've had enough. Do what you like, you will anyway, so get on with it. If I have to go to court to prove I'm innocent, then so be it. You bastards'll end up with egg on your face, you'll be a laughing stock, maybe they'll even sack you. I'll have the last laugh here I can tell you. Come on, Dick, get me out of here. Make them put up or shut up, I know my rights!'

Dick nodded. 'You heard him, gentlemen, and I tend to agree. Charge or release. He's been here as long as you can hold him.'

Ben and Jack conferred quietly.

'OK.' Ben nodded at Mark who was leaning on the wall by the door. 'Jefferies?'

'Yes, Sarge.'

'Take him away. Charge him with the murder of Amber Atkins, then bang him up. Court in the morning. Jack and I have other things to do.' The sergeants left the room together, listening to Jimmy loudly protesting his innocence.

* * *

Stacey wondered if Ali was back home so she gave her a call from the office, pleased when she answered. 'Hi, you, good break?' she asked.

'Yes thanks, Stace, pretty good.'

'Didn't know you were going anywhere, you didn't say.'

'No, sorry, short notice. Dad's not been too well and Mum wanted a hand, so I went to stay for a week or so.'

'Nothing serious I hope?' Stacey asked.

'No, a bad cold and a bit of a chest infection, but he's much better now and back to firing on all cylinders. What's been going on since I've been away?'

'That's why I'm ringing. It's such a lovely day I thought you might like a picnic and a catch-up. I could collect you at lunchtime, drive out somewhere with a view, feed you homemade sandwiches, cake and other goodies, then drop you back at the surgery. You up for it? I can fill you in with all the gossip then.'

'What a lovely idea, I'm definitely up for that. How about twelve thirty? Will that do? I can probably swing an extra half hour.'

'That'll be perfect. See you soon.'

* * *

Two hours later, with Ali sitting in the passenger seat, Stacey turned off the main drag and up the Llandovery road towards the picnic area on the edge of the forest. The weather was perfect. The lanes were filled with birds swooping over hot tarmac to catch insects that congregated there. Swallows were particularly adept, speeding along a few inches from the ground then zooming up to swish over the tops of thick hedges. Vegetation on each verge was dense and lush. Cow parsley and new foxgloves almost crowded out the grass and every few yards Stacey saw the flash of a common spotted orchid, sheltering between thicker stems, pale pink in contrast to the fresh green. The friends chatted amiably on the way up the hill, but Ali was surprised when Stacey pulled into the picnic area.

'What are we doing here?' she asked. 'Isn't this where you were when Emily was shot?'

'Yes, it is, but it's also one of my favourite places, you have to admit there's a great view. Look at it, Ali.' Stacey stopped the car close to the cattle grid so they could gaze across the valley to the open mountains.

She climbed out of the car and dragged a couple of folding chairs from the back seat together with a wicker picnic basket and small folding table.

'Give me a hand will you, Ali?'

Ali joined her reluctantly, took the table and opened it out. Stacey put the basket on the bonnet, opened the lid with a creak and removed a white tablecloth covered with red spots.

'Blimey, you *are* doing it properly,' Ali said. 'I thought we'd end up with a plastic bread bag and a few curly sandwiches in the bottom. What's all this in aid of?'

'Thought it would be nice, that's all. Juice or coffee?'

'Juice first, coffee later.' Ali smiled and filled her lungs with the clean mountain air. 'I have to admit it, this is lovely, proper stunning. We are lucky living in such a fabulous place with so few people. Tend to take it for granted when you live here.'

'I hear you. I used to visit in school holidays to stay with Auntie Alice – who left me the cottage…'

Ali nodded.

'I loved it,' Stacey continued. 'The train journey up from Swansea in that funny little carriage, like a bus on rails, the twisty line and all the viaducts. The one closest to Cynghordy is the best, out of the tunnel and instantly hundreds of feet up. Amazing how they built stuff like that all those years ago.' Stacey passed her friend a glass filled with apple and elderflower juice and she drank deeply.

'This is gorgeous, did you make it?'

'Yeah, easy when you know how. Auntie didn't only leave me the cottage, but all her cookery books and recipes too. Most of the things I make come from those. Nigella Lawson, with all her cream and sugar, leaves me cold.'

They took large bites of overstuffed sandwiches and gazed at the scrubby mountain land. Ali pointed out a large hare lolloping over the grass a few yards away, oblivious to the fact it was being watched. Stacey passed over the binoculars so her friend could take a better look and was delighted when Ali's face split into a wide grin.

'Magic, isn't it?'

'Just amazing,' Ali sighed. 'Yes, we live in the right place. This is *nice*, Stace, thanks. I'm worn out having had to look after my folks, came back to work for a rest. Sorry again for not letting you know I was going, it slipped my mind completely. You know how Mum can be – bit of a drama queen – she made it sound as though Dad was on his last legs, so I dropped everything and went. He wasn't, of course.' She took another bite of her sandwich. 'Bit of a chest infection that vanished within two days of antibiotics and a sniffly cold. Mind you, it was a *man-cold*, so pretty serious.'

They laughed.

'What's been going on here?' she asked. 'I read about Jimmy Atkins in the paper. Did he really kill Amber and the others?'

'I don't know, Ali. Ben's been working more or less round the clock, haven't seen him for a while now, but he may come over this evening. They've got a copper from Scotland Yard helping them – keeping a watching brief, something like that. The authorities are pretty spooked cos of Prince Charles' country residence being just down the road.'

'I can see how that would worry them, but surely they wouldn't arrest Jimmy unless they were convinced he was guilty. It said in the paper his kids were with Social Services. Poor little tykes when they've lost their mum too; must be dreadful for them.'

'Let's have a wander round,' Stacey said, 'shake lunch down and then I'll take you back to work. I need to do some shopping – especially if my man's coming later.'

They packed away the chairs and put everything back in the basket before loading it in the car, then strolled slowly round the open space, breathing in the fresh air. They were nearly back at the car when they passed a picnic table and bench set provided by the Forestry Commission; a big heavy lump of furniture, made with thick wood and coach bolts, legs sunk into the ground and anchored with concrete so no one could pinch it. Ali sat down and fiddled with her shoelaces, then glanced over. 'Here, Stacey, come and see.'

'What? You found something?'

'Yeah. Look at this.'

Stacey bent and stared at the wooden tabletop. Gouged deeply in the weathered surface was a carving, a strange, flowery symbol that resembled calligraphy, carefully executed with great skill.

'It's pretty,' Ali said. 'What is it?'

'I don't know, it's not initials or anything, not quite Chinese, but that sort of thing.' Stacey traced the mark with her finger. 'This must have taken some time and I'm sure it wasn't here last time I came, at least I didn't notice it, looks sort of Celtic to me – how odd.'

She shivered, not sure why, but maybe this had something to do with the murders of Kathy and Emily. Was this another potential clue? Returning to the car for her camera, she took some photos of the mark, then drove down the hill to drop Ali back at work.

## Chapter twenty-two

Leaving the vet's after dropping Ali off, Stacey drove to the police station on the edge of town. Walking into the lobby she met Mark on his way out.

'Hi, Mark, how's things?'

'Fine thanks, busy. I'm on my way for lunch supplies, we've been working with Jimmy Atkins most of the morning.'

'Is Ben in?' she asked.

'Yeah, up in the incident room. Shall I give him a shout before I go for food?'

'Yes please, matey. It is work – not pleasure.'

'Makes no odds to me. Hang on, won't be a tick.' He dashed up the stairs. A few minutes later he returned with Ben who was jacketless, sleeves rolled to the elbows, tie missing completely.

'Hi, love, you OK?' he asked.

'Fine thanks, but you look tired. Are you coming round tonight?'

'Is that all you've got me down here for?' he grumbled. 'You have no idea how busy we are.'

'No, grumpy ass, I have something to show you.' Removing her camera from its pouch she switched it on and scrolled down until she found what she was searching for. 'Here, have a look at this.' She passed over the camera and Ben angled the screen so he could see better and peered at the small picture.

'What am I looking at, Stacey?'

'An interesting bit of graffiti carved on a table at the picnic area on the Llandovery road.'

'What?'

'I said, an interesting…'

'Yeah, I heard you. Have you just found this?'

'Ali did. We went there for lunch and after we'd eaten, wandered around and Ali spotted it carved right in the middle of one of the tables. It's not small – bugger – I should have put something in the picture for size comparison, but it's possibly four inches in diameter and looks new. The wood is freshly cut and I'm sure it wasn't there last time I went.'

'When was that?'

'Little over a week ago. I didn't stay long, a bit freaked out to be honest, the last time I'd been there was when Emily was killed. I had a bimble around then spooked myself cos I thought I heard noises in the wood, so I left.

I'm sure I'd have spotted this before if it had been there. What do you reckon it is, Sherlock? Anything to do with the case?'

'No idea at all. We've been working on the principle that the killer *might* have carved that little fish-shaped thing you found at Long Field – well – had it in the back of our minds and now you find this.'

'Ali found it, not me,' Stacey said.

'Can I borrow your memory card and print a few of these pictures off?'

'No problem. You on for tonight then?'

'Yeah, think so. I'll bring a takeaway. Not sure what time I'll arrive, but it'll save you cooking – Indian again?'

'That'd be lovely. Sorry to drag you downstairs.'

'No, it's OK, sorry I was short. The case is stressing me out, making me snappish.'

'I can tell.' She smiled. 'I'll see you later – try not to overdo it.' She walked out of the front entrance as Mark rushed back in, his arms full of paper bags containing food.

'Stacey, are you off?'

'Yep, getting out the way of all these working men. See you later, Ben,' she called over her shoulder.

* * *

Ben followed Mark into the incident room and dropped Stacey's memory card on the desk in front of Ian Bradshaw.

'Work your magic on this, will you?' he asked. 'Don't wipe anything though, it's Stacey's and she'll have my hide if we lose any of her precious pictures. There's a wood engraving on it somewhere, an odd sort of swirly shape, that's what I'm after. Print off a couple, quick as you can.' Ian leapt up to carry out Ben's orders and nearly knocked Julie off her feet.

'Hey! Careful, you big oaf, look where you're going, can't you,' she grumbled.

'Sorry, Jules, in a hurry.'

'Yeah, aren't we all. Sarge? I've been onto the council and spoke to a nice woman called Mrs Brown in Social Services – twin set and pearls type. You asked me to see if I could find out anything about the leak to *The National*?'

Ben nodded. 'I remember. Any luck?'

'She was horrified at the mere suggestion it might have been one of them. Spouted all the rules about confidentiality, but by the end of the conversation agreed it was a possibility, someone in her department could have spilled the beans. She says she'll make discreet enquiries, see what she can uncover and let me know later in the week. I think she was quite thrilled at the prospect of being a spy for the police.'

'Funny what turns some people on,' Jack said, getting up from his desk.

'Yeah innit?' Julie smiled at him and he winked.

'Right then, Ben, that's all the Jimmy paperwork done,' Jack announced. 'He's in front of the beak tomorrow – morning session – ten thirty in Llandrindod. I've had a word with the prosecution solicitor and informed him we obviously want Jimmy remanded. I also called a mate of mine in London who works for the CPS in my neck of the woods. We had an informal chat about the fingerprint and I asked whether he thought we'd be able to use it. He reckoned if we get as far as Crown we could enter it into evidence, but thought a good defence barrister should be able knock it into touch. Said not to give up on it though. Will you need me at court tomorrow?'

'I don't think so, Jack. Mark and I are probably enough. Isn't it about time you had a day off?'

'I did wonder when you'd remember I'm human.' He grinned. 'Yeah, a day off would be good. It's been a bit full on and we won't be talking to Jimmy again tomorrow. He'll be getting himself settled into Cardiff nick with a bit of luck. Hey, Julie?'

She glanced up from the back of the room.

'You've got a day off tomorrow too, haven't you? Fancy showing me some of the local sights while keeping me away from the wildlife?' Jack looked pleadingly at her, a smile dancing across his lips.

'I *was* thinking of spring cleaning tomorrow.'

'Really? Even taking me out should be better than that. I'll buy you lunch if you prove to be a good tour guide.'

'Go on then, you've convinced me. I'll meet you in the market square about ten, that OK?'

'Great, I'll look forward to it. How about I knock off early, boss? I've done about all I can do here and promise to be back in on Saturday morning, bright-eyed and bushy-tailed.'

Ben chuckled. 'That's what you think. You don't know our Jules very well, do you? Yeah, clock off, I'll be out of here before too long myself, rest up before the rigours of court in the morning. Enjoy your day off.'

'Thanks, see you later, campers.'

Ian returned with some printed photographs from Stacey's memory card and Ben took one to pin on the investigation board. He positioned it next to the other engraving they had found, fixing it with a bright red map-pin. There was nothing similar about the marks. The first was a thin carving – more of a scratching really – this second one looked as though it had been crafted with a narrow chisel, cut deeply into the dark wood and much larger.

Ian looked over his boss's shoulder. 'What do you think it is? Is it connected?' he asked.

'Bloody hell, Ian, I don't know.' Ben ran his hands through his hair, exasperated. 'It's on one of the picnic tables at the Llandovery Road site, close to where we found Kathy and where Stacey saw Emily die. I've sent a couple of lads over to take a look. Stacey says she was there a week or so ago and didn't see it then; she can't be *sure* it wasn't, but it must have been carved since the search teams finished. Maybe it is only graffiti and has nothing to do with the case. Have a look on the net before you pack it in today, see if you can turn up anything like it. Find out if it actually means anything, or as is more likely, an idle act of vandalism by a townie on his holidays.'

'Will do, boss. You coming in after court?'

'Yeah, as soon as I'm done there I'll be in.' He raised his voice to address the room. 'Right then, you horrible lot, keep your noses to the grindstone. Mark's in charge and he'll know where to find me. Mark?'

'Yes, boss.'

'Meet you here at nine tomorrow to take Jimmy to see the judge.'

'Will do. Have a good night.'

Ben ran down the stairs to the car park, drove to the small Indian takeaway and bought far too much food. Stopping at the convenience store on the edge of town, he picked up a bottle of suitable wine, before heading out to Llanagethin. On the way up the hill he pulled into the picnic area to look at the carving for himself, but even seeing it first-hand provided no further clue. Ten minutes later he walked through Noddfa's back door.

'Hey, Pumpkin!' he shouted. 'Where are you? Food!'

'Office,' she yelled back. 'I'll be there now in a minute.'

'You've been in Wales too long, talking like that. Come on, it'll get cold.'

Stacey padded into the kitchen wearing woolly socks on her feet and pecked him on the cheek.

'That smells good, what is it?' she asked.

'Bit of everything, I've probably overdone it. There's some wine in the carrier bag.'

Stacey rummaged about and pulled out a dark green bottle in one hand, a small bunch of flowers in the other.

'Flowers?'

'For being a pig earlier. Sorry, I didn't mean to bite your head off.'

'You're forgiven – you always are. These are lovely, thanks.' She collected a vase from the windowsill and while

Ben spooned out curry and rice she arranged the small bouquet and placed it in the centre of the table.

'Thanks, Sherlock, the food looks amazing. How many did you buy for?'

'Told you, I got carried away. I'm finding it difficult to keep my mind on mundane stuff these days.'

'How did it go with Jimmy this morning?'

'I hate to admit it, but Jack was good. He has a different interview technique to us and I think he's beginning to wear Atkins down, he's definitely looking unhappy, but still not telling us anything, just keeps on and on denying everything.'

'Well, maybe that's cos he didn't do it? Have you thought about that?'

'I think about it all the time, but we have all those pieces of evidence against him. They add up to give him suspect status and he's the only one we've got. He's refusing to talk to us now, said he wants to go to court to prove he's innocent and as we'd run out of time to hold him without a charge, we charged him. Court in the morning.'

'You charged him?' Stacey was shocked. 'Really?'

'Yes, really, we've few other leads to go on. One of the lads is researching that engraving thing and another couple are getting statements in order, sorting out those we can use and those we can't.' He took the empty cartons to the bin. 'Jack's on a day off tomorrow, first he's had since he arrived. He's conned Julie into taking him to see the sights – can you believe that?'

'Is there an office romance in the air?' Stacey asked innocently.

'Maybe. I think he's keener than she is, but she agreed to the outing pretty quickly for Jules.'

After supper, Ben and Stacey sat outside in the back garden watching the lengthening shadows and the colours of the flowers gradually changing as the sun sank over the ranges in a magnificent display of magentas, deep oranges and violets, reflected on evening clouds like left over fireworks. Bats crawled out of their daytime hiding places and flittered around the bushes hunting, and somewhere they could hear a tawny owl hooting to his mate.

'It's very peaceful out here, isn't it?' Ben said. 'I can see why you love your cottage so much.'

'It is pretty quiet, the only traffic you really hear is a local coming home. I'm glad I'm just outside the village, the residents might be noisy during the day sometimes, but they're usually quiet at night. Couldn't live in a town again – even Builth after this. In the morning, I can hear the seven o'clock train on the Heart of Wales Line – all this way away, and sometimes, in the spring and early summer, curlews sing on the ranges and their calls waft down here. I'm very lucky. I have a job I love, live in a house I adore and which actually belongs to me and not the bank, and I'm seeing a pretty special fella too. What more could a girl ask for?'

## Chapter twenty-three

'Mark, would you bloody credit it!' Ben snapped, as he stormed into the incident room and slapped a folded newspaper under his colleague's nose. 'Our damn mole's been at it again, this is *not* going to make things easy today. How I *wish* I could get my hands on them, I'd throttle 'em – I swear I would.'

Mark unfolded the paper, spread it flat on the desk and read the front-page article.

> The National – 11th May
> ATKINS IN COURT TODAY ON MURDER CHARGE

Jimmy Atkins has been formally charged with the murder of his wife on the 28th of April this year and will appear at Llandrindod Wells Magistrates Court this morning. The body of Amber Atkins was discovered in water meadows on the banks of the Tywi River in Llandovery. She had been shot and lying close by was the body of her pet dog, Bramble. The shooting of Amber Atkins is the fourth local killing in recent weeks. Other victims were Mrs Kathy Read of Llanagethin, Mrs Emily Johnson, the wife of the vicar of St David's church in the same village, and Mr Danny Evans of Llandovery.

An unnamed source confirmed Mr Atkins is the only suspect in the case and significant evidence was recovered at the home he shared with his wife and two small children. Mr Atkins is a veteran army sniper and completed tours in Iraq and Afghanistan before settling in the town, where he works as a security guard at the local industrial estate.

Mark skimmed the rest of the article then glanced at Ben. 'Bloody hell, Sarge, Jimmy's not going to be happy about this.'

'That's the least of our problems, the entire press pack is going to be waiting for us outside court. Wish I hadn't given Jack the day off, we could have done with his muscle. I *was* hoping you and I could drive Jimmy over with the minimum of fuss and leave him in the capable hands of the screws from Cardiff nick, but now…'

'We could drum up reinforcements though, couldn't we?' Mark said. 'I can give Builth a ring. In the absence of a van, I could round up a couple of extra cars, one in front, one behind and I'll contact the station in Llandrindod, get them to turn out too.'

'Good idea, get onto it will you? I'll speak with Dick Nyle, be best if he talks to Jimmy about this. We'll have to warn him and get him inside court quickly, we don't want photos to go with this as well. Honestly, I'll swing for that damn mole!'

* * *

Stacey was on her way to Llandrindod Wells when her mobile rang and she pulled into a lay-by before answering.

'Stacey Logan.'

'It's Sam. They've done it again, haven't they? You've seen the paper I take it?'

'Yes, Sam, I'm ahead of you. I'm on my way to court now.'

'Who are they getting this stuff from and how come we haven't got it? This is ridiculous, a case like this, so close to home and they keep stealing our thunder.'

'Look, Sam, it's no good getting wound up about it. I told you – I'm on my way. I'll ring you as soon as it's over and send an article via cyberspace for tomorrow's edition.'

'Tomorrow's edition! That's the problem, tomorrow's no bloody good!'

'Well, it's the best I can do, keep your hair on. I'll write you a good piece and if I get there early enough, try to get a photo to go with it. After all, I know who I'm looking for, everyone else will be guessing. Don't worry, it'll be fine. Gotta go or I'll miss the perp-walk and then you *won't* get a picture.'

* * *

On the pavement outside the court a crowd had gathered – much larger than Ben had anticipated. It seemed as though half the town had turned out and the press pack was well staffed. Radio cars lined the street and the car park by the railway station was crammed with 4x4s and large saloons, vehicles of choice for your average roving reporter. Ben took small satisfaction that the weather was truly awful. The best rain Wales had to offer fell in torrents, drowning everyone waiting outside the old Victorian building. A forest of umbrellas sprouted from the concrete, joining together to create a fabric lobby in front of the doors.

Jimmy had been warned what to expect by Dick Nyle at the station, then he'd been handcuffed, helped into the back of an unmarked car and driven towards the pretty town of Llandrindod Wells, thirty-two miles away. He sat in the back seat glowering, refusing point-blank to speak. As the car passed through Builth Wells, they picked up a couple of squad cars as an escort and a short while later pulled up outside the court building.

'Bloody hell, there's hundreds of them!' Jimmy was horrified. 'I can't walk through that lot! For God's sake, take me round the back.'

'You've got no choice I'm afraid,' Ben said. 'This is the only entrance. Let's do it fast before they realise what's going on. Mark, move yourself. Throw this jacket over his head, try to minimise the damage.'

Mark leapt out of the car, opened the back door and was just about to cover Jimmy's head when a flashgun went off. He whirled round quickly, but couldn't see where the flash had come from. Indeed, most of the reporters gathered on the steps hadn't even spotted the car yet. Covering Jimmy's head and shoulders, he took hold of the prisoner's arm and helped him out of the back seat. Ben joined them on the steps and local uniforms closed around them to form a human box, accused in the middle.

As soon as they began to move, the pack spotted them and all hell broke loose. Screamed questions filled the air and cameras clicked and whined. A large fluffy microphone was thrust under Ben's nose and he angrily knocked it away, glaring at its handler. Jimmy stumbled, unable to see where he was going and Mark held him up while he regained his footing. The pack pushed and shoved like stormy waves on a beach and the noise generated was shocking. Within seconds they entered the relative safety of the lobby, local coppers stood against the main door like a blue wall so Ben and Mark could relax a little as they walked Jimmy down to the cells and booked him in.

'Blimey, Sarge, that was mental,' Mark said. 'Glad it wasn't me they were after. Reckon they'd have ripped Jimmy apart if we'd let them.'

'That damn *National* reporter is to blame for this – him and his mole, we've *got* to get a lead on that,' Ben grumbled. 'I'll carpet whoever it is when I catch them. Julie's been onto the council again and doesn't think the leak came from there, so it *has* to be one of ours. Just what we need. Oh, God, let's get a cuppa before kick-off, we've done our bit.'

The men strode down the corridor in search of a coffee machine.

* * *

Outside court things had quietened down quickly and reporters were gradually being allowed in to fill the public gallery. Stacey was right at the front of the pack and more or less first in, so had her pick of the seats and positioned herself in the front row where she had a good view of the dock. Seats behind her filled up quickly, the room hissing with whispered anticipation. She recognised Fred Murray from *The National* and tried to catch his eye, but he didn't – or wouldn't – look in her direction.

At exactly half past ten, the magistrate took the bench and proceedings began. The room fell silent as Jimmy Atkins was brought in and led to the dock. He was asked to confirm his name and address and sat while two sets of solicitors argued the case for bail. Stacey had to admire Dick Nyle, he gave it a go and for a minute or two she thought bail might be granted, but the prosecution eventually won the day and Jimmy was taken away, to appear again in seven days.

The court emptied quickly, but Stacey remained seated having no wish to get involved with the crush. A young lad was brought in, accused of cultivating cannabis plants in his dad's greenhouse and she scribbled notes about the case for a *News in Brief* article, before following the rest of the journalists out.

The heavens were still chucking it down, so she dashed through the torrent to the nearest café for a spot of breakfast. The eatery possessed one of the rare wi-fi connections in the town, so she fired up her laptop and while she waited for her food, composed a quick draft article for Sam to shut him up. He'd tweak it and send it back, by which time she'd be in a better position to craft a decent piece.

The coffee arrived first and while she drank she uploaded shots from her camera, face splitting into a wide grin as a photo appeared on the screen. It was brilliant and showed Jimmy sitting hunched on the back seat of the car, handcuffed wrists plainly visible, Mark helpfully standing to one side, about to cover his prisoner's head. Jimmy looked pale and frightened, a sweaty film made his skin shine, hair unruly, eyes wild. Stacey had to admit that – in this picture at least – he *did* look like everyone's idea of a murderer.

She knew she was the only one who had this photo, knew she'd got the jump on the rest of them and smiled as she wondered how Fred Murray would react when he saw *her* front page in the morning. She didn't need leaks, she had her skill – and her local knowledge. The waitress delivered a large plate of food to the table and Stacey shut the laptop to concentrate on it, enjoying the feeling of a job well done.

* * *

Jack waited in the shadow of the town clock on the edge of market square, sheltering from gallons of water gushing out of a grey sky, rendering the town's fountain redundant. Tiny rivers ran between grey cobblestones and there wasn't a single person on the street. Turning up the collar of his coat, he shivered. What a dreadful day he'd picked for sightseeing.

He thought about his date while he waited. Julie seemed very committed to the job, but up for a laugh; quite good looking too, with a strong face and dark, serious eyes, framed by short, almost-black, curly hair. He liked her mouth best – there was nearly always the suggestion of a smile playing across her lips. She was tall and slim and that was good too. He'd had such hopes for today, but as he watched rain tumble from heavy clouds, he wondered what on earth they could do in such awful weather. He could hardly take her back to his room at the King's Head, they didn't know each other well enough.

He caught sight of a farmer in a flat cap, scurrying between the buildings towards him, dressed in blue overalls and wellies, a tatty, waxed-cotton jacket over the top. He was shocked when the farmer spoke to him.

'Hi, Jack! Ready?'

'Julie?' he asked incredulously, trying to peer under the cap.

'Yep, it's me. Got a Land Rover in the car park so it's run or get drowned.' She shot off the way she'd come and Jack had no choice but to follow. He caught up as she pulled open the passenger door of a battered blue Land Rover.

'Get in quick,' she said.

He wedged himself on the narrow front seat, Julie slammed the door behind him, climbed in the other side and looked him up and down.

'Not exactly dressed for it, are you?' she asked.

'Dressed for what?' Jack asked. 'I thought you were going to show me the sights. This is the best suit I've got with me, I *am* living out of a suitcase.'

'Oh no, you look great.' She smiled again. 'You always do, but it's not the garb for today.'

'Why, what are we doing?'

'Going to cure your fear of sheep.'

'How's that then?'

'My da has a flock on the Epynt Ranges. We bring them down off the mountain at this time of year to shear them, check them over and sort out the lambs, and today's the day.'

'We're going sheep herding? You've gotta be kidding, right? What's the matter – your pa not got a dog? Don't *dogs* do sheep herding?'

'Course they do and yes he has – three actually – but we have to get them up to the sheep and it's big up there, difficult for dogs without *some* human assistance. Don't look like that, it'll be fun.'

'You *said* you were going to show me the sights,' Jack grumbled.

'And I'm going to! Wait till you see the mountain… If only the rain would ease.'

Julie turned the key and the old vehicle coughed and wheezed into life. She drove out of the car park and along the main road towards Trecastle, turning off eight miles further on at Llywel and pulling into a large yard in front of a slate roofed farmhouse, dodging soggy-looking chickens.

'Come on, boy,' Julie said. 'Let's get you dressed properly, then we'll get the quads out.'

'Quads?' There was a twinkle of interest in his eyes.

'You didn't think we'd do it on foot did you? Come into the house, I think we've got a pair of overalls that'll fit, but you'll have to lose the suit. Da might have some old stuff you can borrow – be way too short though.'

'No one will see if I'm wearing overalls, will they?'

Ten minutes later, they splashed through the yard to one of the barns and Julie showed him the quad bikes.

'You ever done this before?' she asked.

'No, but I've got a motorbike back in The Smoke, I guess it's not that different.'

'Not much, but the handling will take some getting used to with four wheels instead of two, so take it steady until you get the feel of it. Da's already up there, so follow me. Hey look!' She pointed at the sky. 'A tiny patch of blue, maybe the weather'll improve. Ready then, cowboy?'

'Sheepboy, surely. Here, Julie, how close are they gonna get?' Jack asked nervously.

'What, the sheep?'

'Yes, of course the bloody sheep!'

'You'll be fine, the dogs'll keep them moving. We're only there to reinforce their efforts.' She started the engine and set off up the hill towards the mountains.

It was a steep pull up from the farmyard, but by the time Jack reached the top, he felt confident with the machine and could relax a little. As soon as they gained the edge of the range, Julie headed off the tarmac and out across the rough ground, Jack on her tail. The quad bike ironed out the bumps a little, but he soon discovered standing up – rather than sitting down – was more comfortable, using his knees as extra shock absorbers. He soon managed to catch up with his date as she hurtled over the scrubby grassland.

They travelled a few miles before Julie stopped at the top of a steep ravine divided by a gushing stream full of waterfalls. Jack manoeuvred his bike close to hers and gazed out at the breathtaking mountain scenery. The sky had cleared and large blue patches jostled with clouds. Bright splashes of sunshine lit up the earth and rushed across the forests as though an enormous torch was being shone from on high, while a stiff wind blew the clouds around.

'Wow, Jules, this is incredible!' Jack stared at the wildness. 'What's that?' He pointed at some buildings on his right.

'A fake village built by the army to teach recruits how to shoot round corners. See how there are no doors or windows and how it looks vaguely Germanic?'

'Even I can see it's not Welsh.'

'The sheep will come over this way,' Julie said. 'The flock tends to stay in roughly the same place, so we usually know where to find them. We'll wait here to stop them getting down by the water, it's a struggle to get them back up again.'

Jack looked around. 'How many are we waiting for?'

'About two hundred, with their lambs.'

'*Two hundred!* Christ, that's a lot of sheep. You sure they'll be OK?'

'Fine, unless of course any have picked up a cloudberry worm.'

'What's that?' he asked.

'Sheep disease – not catching – but tends to send them a bit mad. Only sheep with cloudberry worms will bite, but when they do…'

Jack looked at her horrified, then spotted the smile hiding behind her lovely eyes.

'You cow! I fell for that,' he grumbled.

They stared over the borderless land. A pair of ravens appeared from behind a stand of conifers and floated across the sky croaking at each other. The sun was out now, most of the storm clouds had blown away and the temperature had risen. Julie took off her jacket and peered into the distance.

'Here they come,' she said. 'See? Over there?'

Jack screwed up his eyes and on the far hill spotted a white patch creeping slowly towards them, growing larger as more and more animals crested the rise.

'Bloody hell, Julie, that *is* a lot of sheep. I'm not sure this is fun anymore.'

'You'll be fine, chill out. Let's move up to be ready for them.'

They bounced across more wiry grass and were suddenly surrounded by animals surging round the quads like a flood of water. Jack was aware of them bumping his machine and felt a flutter of panic, but the flock passed by and before he could worry about it, Julie was off after them, beckoning him to follow her.

After three hours of hard riding the sheep were safely off the hill, quads back in the barn and Jack was sitting next to Julie at the kitchen table in the farmhouse. Her mother was busy at the stove, while her father sat by the fire at the other end of the room warming his feet.

'That was great, Julie,' Jack said. 'I can't remember having so much fun in a long time, just what I needed.'

'You're a proper country boy now. Wait till the others hear you've been rounding up sheep, they won't believe it.'

'I'm not sure I am. Great day, though, you certainly showed me the sights.'

'It was a good opportunity. All that land is closed off most of the year, but we obviously have to get the sheep down and the army leave off firing for a week so we can. It's so beautiful up there and great to have an excuse to bomb about on the quads. I'm glad you enjoyed it.'

Mrs Smith turned from the Aga and started to load the table with plates and dishes piled high with vegetables. She placed a large platter in the centre, a steaming leg of lamb resting on the china surrounded by roast potatoes and golden shallots, the aroma thick in the warm air.

'Come on, *bach*, tuck in now,' Mrs Smith said. 'Da, come and eat.'

Mr Smith joined them at the table and they fell on the food as though they hadn't been fed for a week.

In the evening, Julie drove Jack back to town.

'I don't suppose you fancy a nightcap, do you?' he asked. 'In the hotel bar I mean.'

'I was hoping you'd invite me in. Are they OK about guests?'

'Yes, there's a public bar, no problems.'

'I meant *overnight* guests…'

## Chapter twenty-four

Ben was surprised to see how many of his officers were already in the incident room. Ian Bradshaw worked at a computer while a couple of uniformed officers read through statements, sifting out those that weren't useful. Mark was on the phone and Jack and Julie were standing together at the noticeboard.

'Morning, people,' Ben said.

He received various grunts and nods in response.

'Jack, Julie, good day off?'

Jack's face split into a wide smile. 'The best, boss, thanks, played at being a cowboy all day.'

'You did what?'

'He means a drover, boss,' Julie said. 'I took him up to the ranges to get the sheep in.'

'I thought you were scared of sheep?'

'Not anymore,' Jack said. 'Julie's aversion therapy cured me completely, I had a blast racing over mountains on a quad bike. Didn't know you could have so much fun in the middle of nowhere, maybe I should have been a farmer and not a copper.'

'I think that's a bit of a stretch.' Ben laughed. 'But I'm glad you had a good day. You'll be more use to me if you're rested.'

'Rested?' Jack spluttered. 'Every bloody muscle I've got aches and I didn't sleep too well last night.'

Ben thought he saw a look pass between the officers, but chose to ignore it. As long as nothing interfered with the job, it was their business, after all.

'Right then, to work.' Ben removed his jacket and sat at his desk. 'Ian, any news on that graffiti yet?'

Ian moved over to Ben's desk. 'Yes and no. I've been at it for a while, you have no idea how many odd signs and symbols civilisation has collected during its history and that's without all the different scripts like Chinese, Japanese, Thai, Nepalese – you get the picture. I've narrowed it down though, it's Islamic, Arabic to be precise and although it isn't identical I *think* it's the symbol for Allah. Take a look.' He passed over some papers, together with the photograph Stacey had taken and Ben studied them for a minute or two.

'I think you're right,' Ben said. 'It's almost the same, isn't it? But what's this doing out in the middle of nowhere? I can't see how it can have any bearing on the case, can you?'

'Not really, boss. It's nothing like the fish thing we found at Long Field – the closest I can get to identifying it is as a Christian symbol but it wasn't carved in the same manner. This looks *professional* somehow, artistic, possibly done with a chisel rather than a penknife. Maybe a sleeper unit of Muslim fundamentalists has moved into Powys.'

'Oh God, Ian, don't even joke about it,' Ben groaned. 'We've enough on our plates at the moment without anything else and let's be honest, even if a group *has* moved in, they wouldn't stay hidden for very long, would they? Mid Wales isn't known for its ethnic diversity; they'd stand out like a sore thumb.' Ben studied the diagrams again. 'Stick it on one side, I'm not sure this has anything to do with the matter in hand. Anyone else?'

Julie moved to stand by Ben's side and placed a photograph in front of him.

'Who's this, boss?' she asked.

'Fred Murray, reporter with *The National*.'

'Is he the one we've been having trouble with? I saw the article yesterday, must have given you a few problems.'

'Didn't it ever, I'm never going to give Jack another day off again, we could have used his muscle to get through the press pack, a real feeding frenzy. Once we were inside it all went much as expected and luckily by the time Mark and I came out, they'd gone off to bother someone else. Some of them are such bottom feeders, swimming around in muck all day, I don't know how they stand it.'

'Get paid more than you, I guess, boss.' Julie giggled. 'Anyway… this guy, Fred Murray, I saw him in town this morning, about seven thirty.'

'How come you were in town so early, Julie, don't you live out Llwyel way?'

Again, Ben caught a quick glance pass between Julie and Jack.

'OK, none of my business. So you saw him in town, Stacey said he stays at the Boutique Hotel in Stone Street.'

'Well, that wasn't where I saw him. He was coming out of one of the terraced houses round the back of the High Street, looked as though he'd stayed the night there, you can usually tell when someone has been out all night.' She blushed.

'And your point is?' Ben enquired.

'I'm fairly certain it was Molly Burton's house, you know the FLO, works over at Brecon. She lives in Llandovery and it looks like she knows this Murray bloke.'

Ben stared at her, his mind racing. 'That can't be right, Murray's an out-of-towner so how would he know Molly Burton? Oh no… Do you think she's our mole?'

'What else?' Julie asked. 'I mean it is *possible* they knew each other before all this, but I think it's more likely they met here. It may be innocent, a fling, but I'm not happy knowing a serving police officer is entertaining a hack who just happens to have used leaked stories in the press. Leaks give us all a bad name and with that fuss at the *News of the World*, we can't ignore it. You'll have to go and see her.'

'Yes, I will, won't I?' Ben said. 'One step forward and another back. Seems as though that's all I've been doing for weeks.'

'Want me to go, Sarge?' Mark asked from the other side of the room.

'No thanks, better be me and I'll go on my own, keep it unofficial at this point. Can you find out if she's on shift? I'd rather go to her house than Brecon station.'

'I'll do it now.'

'Well spotted, Julie, I knew you were more observant than you let on. As a reward you can team up with DS Trent today and go through the paperwork, begin building the case. If this does go to Crown we'll have to be ready, nothing winds up judges like coppers not getting their act together.'

Mark returned to Ben's desk. 'Molly's on a day off today, should be at home. Sure you don't want company?'

'No thanks, Mark, help the others and I'll be back as soon as I can. I need this like I need a hole in the head.'

* * *

Ben ran down the stairs and out into the early summer sunshine. He left the car at the station, hoping the walk would help focus his thoughts. Warm weather had brought people out of their houses and the streets became busier the closer he got to town. Strolling past the exclusive private college, a gaggle of pupils in burgundy and gold hooped rugby gear streamed out of the gates, making their way to the playing fields. They passed by, chattering loudly, studded boots rattling on the pavement. Turning past the post office, Ben nodded to a farmer he knew, before ducking up an alley behind the main street towards Molly Burton's house.

It was a narrow two-up, two-down, with a red front door opening onto the street. Taking a deep breath, he rang the bell and heard the loud yapping of a small dog from inside and a few moments later Molly opened the door.

She was surprised to see him. 'Oh… hello, DS James.'

'Can I come in, Molly?'

'Yes, of course. Tigger, get down!' She pushed a small terrier-type away with her slippered foot and opened the door wider. 'What can I do for you, sir?'

Ben walked into the living room, sat without being asked and waved Molly to the seat opposite.

'I'm not sure how to start this conversation,' he admitted. 'Have you seen the paper today?'

She gave an involuntary gasp and a hand flew to her mouth.

'I guess I don't need to say anything else, do I? How much did he pay you?'

'He didn't pay me,' she whispered.

'Of course he did. Why else would you risk your career – cos that's what you've done – you've put your whole career in jeopardy. Why did you do it?'

'I didn't mean to, not at all, it just sort of slipped out. Fred took me for a meal and I guess I had one glass of wine too many, he asked about the case and I told him.'

'But *twice*, you did it *twice*! Honestly, you can't be that naïve, you're a copper, for heaven's sake. You of all people should know what the press is like. So, tell me, what happened? Came along and chatted you up, did he? Wined and dined you with dessert to follow at your house and you blabbed confidential information – to a reporter. Where's your brain, Molly? You have no *idea* how difficult you've made things, never mind prejudicing a future trial. If this reporter friend of yours has overstepped the mark, we'll be ruled against as we can't guarantee Jimmy Atkins a fair trial. All that work will go up in smoke and Murray may face criminal charges – so might you, come to that. Is that what you wanted?'

'No, sir.' Her voice was quiet and shaky.

'The *only* thing you've got going for you at the moment is you didn't take any cash for passing this stuff on.' Ben paused. 'I'll have to report this, you know?'

'Yes, sir, I realise that.'

'I'm sure your commanding officer will agree with me that you should be suspended until he's made a decision about your future.'

Molly started to cry quietly and Ben felt himself soften.

'You realise you've been very foolish, don't you? I always thought you made a good copper and would go places. Maybe you still will, but it'll be up to the brass, not me. Personally, I hope you get a second chance, Molly, I really do. I don't think you'd make the same mistake again.'

'No, sir, I wouldn't.'

'We'll leave it at that for now then. I expect Brecon'll be in touch fairly quickly and it'll be better for you if you're here when they call, they won't like wasting their time on this. I'll see myself out, Molly, look after yourself.'

Ben left her sitting on the sofa looking small and miserable and let himself out into the street. The beginnings of a headache tapped against his skull and he suddenly felt old and tired. It was a good job he had a day off tomorrow, he needed to recharge his batteries.

## Chapter twenty-five

Stacey leant on the kitchen sink gazing at the early morning while she waited for the kettle to boil. Ben was still in bed and she'd decided to let him sleep, a lie-in would do him good.

She could see it was going to be another hot day, as soon as the sun got to work and burned away the mist and thin cloud. Night-time temperatures had been low and in the shaded spots of the garden, a glisten of late frost caught her eye. A lone blackbird pecked around at the base of the hedge hunting through the fallen leaves, flicking them in the air with his bright yellow beak, searching for bugs and beetles. She heard a faraway sound and opened the back door to listen. Standing on cold concrete in bare feet she held her breath, then heard the sound again – the wild, wispy call of a curlew somewhere on the ranges. This was her favourite time of the day, while it was still peaceful, before the rest of the villagers were up and about. Even though Noddfa was half a mile from the rest of the houses, the residents could be very noisy. Behind her she heard the click of the kettle as it turned itself off and went back inside to make tea, surprised to see Ben already pouring water into the pot, dressed in only his boxer shorts.

'Sorry, Sherlock, did I wake you?' she asked. 'I tried not to, thought you could do with a lie-in and it is Sunday.'

'No, you didn't disturb me, I'm programmed for early morning starts. Here, have some tea.' He placed a large mug in front of her. 'It's going to be a beautiful day. What do you fancy doing, anything special in mind?'

'No, not really, it'll be great to spend some time hanging around with you. You've been so busy lately, I haven't seen as much of you as I'd like.'

'You mean you'd like to see more of me than this?' He stood and began to remove his underwear.

'No, you idiot, sit down! You'll frighten the horses with that sort of behaviour *quite* so early in the day and on a Sunday too. Auntie Alice would be turning in her grave if she knew you were dancing about in her kitchen – naked.'

'And you're properly dressed, are you? That's my shirt you're screwing up and bare feet – very bohemian.'

'I'm not taking your shirt off, I'll be cold. Fancy breakfast?'

'That'll be good, something light maybe and I'll take you out to lunch later. I've booked a table at the Caer Beris Manor in Builth. You up for that or shall I cancel?'

'Don't you dare, that will be fabulous. Tell you what – as the weather's so good – how about a coffee, a couple of croissants, then we'll go for a walk to build up a proper appetite. Does that sound good?'

'Perfect. I'll get the oven on while you go and get dressed, it'll be ready when you come down. Go on, scoot.' Ben nudged her out of the kitchen.

Stacey ran upstairs, washed, dressed in baggy trousers – comfortable for walking – and a T-shirt, hooded fleece over the top. By the time she was back at the table, Ben was removing croissants from the oven and a pot of coffee stood beside two mugs.

'Good timing, Pumpkin, dig in. Now I know we're going walking, I want to be off. I've spent too many hours indoors lately.'

After they'd eaten, Stacey piled plates in the sink and hauled out a small backpack from the cupboard under the stairs. She packed it with a couple of bottles of elderflower and apple juice, a handful of nutty energy bars, her small camera and a pair of binoculars. Ben was dressed quickly and by half past nine they were out the door and walking through the village, heading towards the river.

They strolled past the Reads' place. Bob and Stevie were outside moving scrap metal about. When Bob saw them he raised his hand in Stacey's direction before scurrying inside, followed by his son. An angry-looking Rottweiler and two white Alsatians stood their ground, barking incessantly.

'They won't talk while I'm with you,' Ben said. 'I don't think they've forgiven me for the grilling I gave Bob after Kathy was killed, but how could I not? You know them, into just about everything and nearly all of it illegal.'

'They are scallies,' agreed Stacey, 'but I really like them. They don't go into the village much, tend to hang around their compound chopping wood and cutting up old cars mainly. They've been a lot quieter since Kathy died, I wonder if they'll stay on or move away?'

'They'll stay,' Ben said. 'Can't think of anywhere else that would have them.' He chuckled, took her hand and they continued on towards the bottom of the village. As they passed St David's church they saw Andrew Johnson walking up the path, surplice folded over one arm, a bible in his hand. Spotting the couple, he called out and hurried to the gate.

'Hello, you two, what a beautiful morning.'

'Hi, Andrew,' Stacey said. 'Yes, it is gorgeous, isn't it? Have you been working already?'

'Just finished the early service, I have to take another in Llangammarch this evening. We're so short of clergy these days we all have four or five churches to look after. Still, it's good to keep busy.'

'Glad you're OK. I saw Sarah a few days ago. She dropped in to give me some scones she'd made, delicious. Could you thank her again for me?'

'Yes, I'll tell her, be warned though, you'll get more. I went back to work as quickly as I could and it's getting easier. Evenings are the worst.' His eyes unfocused. 'I am struggling with my faith, husbands killing wives is abhorrent. Why *does* He allow it?'

'I'm not sure,' Stacey said hesitantly, 'isn't it something to do with free will?'

'What?' Andrew said. 'Oh, my dear. I'm sorry, ignore me, still not quite back to normal I'm afraid. I don't know what's going to happen when Sarah goes home, she can't stay for ever. She's been so supportive, not sure what would have become of me without her, developed scurvy I should think. Cooking is not one of my strengths.'

'She did say.' Stacey giggled. 'Told me she's been trying to give you cookery lessons.'

Andrew smiled. 'She has, yes, but I'm not a very good student. It's all too much like chemistry to me and I hated that at school. Had a very severe teacher who used to throw blackboard rubbers at you if you misbehaved, damn good shot too. Ben, good to see you too. Day off?'

'Yes, vicar, we've been hard at it for weeks now, so today I'm out for some fresh air to work up an appetite before I take Stacey to lunch.'

'I've been following the story in the papers,' Andrew said. 'What a dreadful business this has turned out to be; and Jimmy Atkins charged with killing his wife. I was shocked when I heard, and now he's locked up in prison, is that right?'

'Yes, he couldn't seriously have thought he'd make bail on a murder charge, but his solicitor did try to get him out. Magistrates weren't having any of it though, so he languishes in Cardiff Jail.'

'I may ask if he'd like a visit. Cardiff, you say?'

Ben nodded.

'Can I ask – I know it's difficult for you – but do you intend charging him with the murders of the others? Do you think he killed Emily?'

'I honestly don't know. We haven't got much out of him since he was charged and haven't found evidence to link him with the other killings. We'll be meeting with him again next week, see if he can – or will – tell us anything more, but I'm not holding my breath. The investigation is still very much ongoing and if we learn anything we will tell you, of course, but you're right, it is difficult for me to say too much. I know you'll understand.'

'Yes, dear boy, don't worry about it, I wouldn't be human though if I didn't want to know who changed my life so dramatically, who took Emily from me. I haven't received any answers in my prayers but, like you, I hope for a future revelation. Enjoy your walk, it was good to see you both.' Andrew smiled and carried on up the slight hill towards the vicarage.

'He looks pretty good, Stace, I haven't seen him in a while – you can tell he's still disturbed – but looks better than I thought he would. Like you said, maybe there is something to this God stuff, I don't think I'd be as strong if I lost you.'

'You are a big softie, DS James. I'd hate to lose you too.' She squeezed his hand. 'Let's cut through the forest, there's a stony beach on the river and it's a great place to hang out. A pair of dippers are nesting nearby and the beach is a good spot to watch for them.'

* * *

Ben was just about to put the first forkful of lunch into his mouth, when he spotted a movement across the conservatory dining room of the Caer Beris.

'Oh no, look out, Stacey, Samantha Phillips, one o'clock,' he warned.

'Hey, you!' Samantha shouted, striding across the room, glaring at Stacey. 'You, reporter person! Glad I've seen you. That was a shitty thing you did grassing me up to Old Bill, you promised you wouldn't and I almost believed you.'

Stacey didn't answer, so Samantha had another go. 'Don't try to deny it, you're sitting here eating lunch with a copper, so don't expect me to believe you never said anything. And you!' She rounded on Ben. 'What's all this with locking Jimmy up? He was one of Danny's best mates, you can't think Jimmy shot him. I tell you now, he didn't!'

'How do you know he didn't, Samantha?' Ben asked.

'I just do, that's all. I've known him years and Danny grew up with him. You lot have only nicked him to take the heat off yourselves, haven't got a bloody clue, have you?'

One the waiters hovered uncertainly behind the angry young woman.

'Samantha, I'm off duty. If you've got anything to tell the police that you think might be useful, call into the station tomorrow and I'll meet with you. This isn't the time or the place and I'd hate to see you get walloped again.'

'Are you *threatening* me?'

'No, of course not, but the waiter behind you doesn't look very happy and I know for a fact the chef won't stand to have his lunch ruined, so sit down and finish your meal. If you want to, we'll talk tomorrow.'

There was a second when Ben thought Samantha wasn't going to comply, but in the end she turned, spotted the waiter behind her and flounced off.

'Sorry, Pumpkin, that's destroyed the mood, hasn't it?'

'No, not at all. I'm a hack and you're a copper, we've both seen worse. I can remember being young and in love. Makes you do silly things – being in love.' Stacey reached out and covered his large hand with her smaller one.

'Don't I know it.' He smiled as he spoke, reached into his inside pocket and brought out a small, plush covered box. He placed it on the table between them, the opening facing Stacey who stared at it.

'What's this?' she asked.

'In the words of every film I've ever watched, "why don't you open it and find out?"'

Gingerly, as though the box might bite her, Stacey picked it up and pried open the lid. A glint of gold caught her eye and nestled on a bed of black velvet was a ring, beautifully carved with what appeared to be runes and tiny diamonds, winked at her, skilfully set between the magical markings.

It took her breath away and all she could say was, 'Wow!'

'Is that a good "wow" or a bad "wow"? Don't keep me in suspense,' Ben begged.

'It depends what this is for. It's a beautiful piece of work, I've never seen anything quite like it.'

'You won't. I designed it myself and had it made at Nirjana's – the bespoke jeweller in Llandeilo – she spent ages getting it just right. It's Welsh gold, well a portion of it, not an engagement ring as such – I know you aren't into getting married – more a "be mine" ring. Do you like it?' he gabbled nervously.

'Like it? I love it! It's amazing and yes, I'd love to be yours.' She frowned suddenly. 'Does that mean I have to come to live with you or are you going to come and live with me?'

'Would it matter?'

'Well… I do love my cottage… and my independence.'

'I know you do, so why bother changing anything? At least not yet anyway. I'd be up for living together, but you're happy with things as they are, aren't you?'

'Yes, more than happy, and this? Well, this is the icing on the cake.' Slipping the ring out of the box she handed it to him. 'Perhaps you'd like to put it on for me?'

'I'd be honoured.' He took the ring and gently slid it over the knuckle of her ring finger.

'It even fits! You *are* a clever old Sherlock. How did you manage that?'

'Pinched one I found on the bedside cabinet, luckily not one of your thumb rings.' He chuckled, leant over the table to kiss her soundly on the lips and her cheeks glowed with embarrassment.

'Wait till we get home for that sort of thing, people are looking.'

'Don't care,' he said and did it again.

## Chapter twenty-six

The couple managed a hurried breakfast together. Stacey left early heading for the Royal Welsh Showground at Builth Wells to cover the Smallholding and Countryside festival, one of her favourite annual assignments, while

Ben drove slowly through the lanes to Llandovery station, enjoying the last of his time off.

* * *

The incident room was buzzing and a swarm of pink sticky notes covered the surface of his desk. Other officers nodded at him as he sat and rifled through the messages. Dennis Oliver, Chief Super at Brecon, had rung and asked Ben to call him as soon as possible; taking a sip of coffee, he made the call.

'Oliver,' a gruff voice answered.

'Morning, sir. DS James, Llandovery.'

'Ben, good of you to get back so quickly, I know you're busy over there. Seems as though you're making progress at last with a suspect on remand. Is he responsible for all four killings?'

'With respect, sir, I think that's probably jumping the gun. It's true we have *some* evidence, ammunition rounds at his house, DNA traces on cigarette ends found near an empty shell case we are sure was fired to kill his wife, Amber. We have a partial print on the shell that seems to match with Atkins' thumb and we found GSR on items of clothing removed during the house search a week or so ago, but he still denies killing her. During interview he suggested his clothes must have been cross-contaminated or even that we'd planted evidence.'

'I won't bother to comment on that,' Oliver huffed. 'Honestly, television should be banned, gives our suspects too many ideas, although, on the flip-side, the streets are quiet when the soaps are on. Maybe we should have round the clock *Coronation Street* and *Eastenders,* keep them all in. Now there's an idea.'

Ben chuckled. 'What can I do for you, sir, or did you just want an update?'

'No, I'm getting daily updates from Julie Smith. Pass on my thanks, will you?'

'Certainly.'

'I need to talk to you regarding this business with Molly Burton. We've put her on gardening leave for the time being. You said in your note she insists she didn't take money for passing this information on. Do you think she's being honest?'

'I'd like to believe so,' Ben said, 'and I don't have any reason to suspect she's being untruthful. She was very upset when I visited on Saturday. My partner, Stacey Logan, bumped into the journalist from *The National* earlier in the week, Fred Murray; she said he was a slimeball. Molly is fairly young; this guy must be fifteen years her senior at least and I think it was more his fault than hers. I can easily imagine him working on her to get what he wanted.'

'I agree, that was my feeling when she talked to us. I'd like to give her a second chance if I can, with time she should make a good copper. In order to make this possible, the fewer people know about it the better. This Murray character has been skating on thin ice and I'm not best pleased he involved one of my junior officers. If you can keep a lid on it your end, I'll see that Molly receives extra training after her period of leave, then slowly integrate her back in. I know the leak caused you a lot of trouble, especially at court, and that's why we're having this conversation before I decide exactly what to do.'

'I admit I was steaming mad on Friday morning,' Ben said. 'But when I went to see her, I calmed down. Like I said, I'm pretty sure Murray was more to blame than Molly. I appreciate the call, but really, sir, it is your decision. I'm happy, whichever way you play it.'

'Might be an idea for a couple of your lads to pay Murray a visit if he's still in the area – warn him off. I'm sure you can think of a reason to make Llandovery uncomfortable for him. Thanks, Ben, this has been useful. What's on your agenda for the rest of the day?'

'DS Trent and I are off to Cardiff nick for another chat with Atkins. Maybe a few days banged up in a proper prison has made him more helpful, although somehow I doubt it. His arrest has calmed the locals down – so that's a good thing – but I'd like some more hard evidence. We have nothing at all linking him to the other murders, but found very little in the way of evidence at those sites. Trouble is, with our man using a rifle capable of such long-distance work, he could have hidden himself anywhere up to four or five hundred metres away and the huge forestry plantations provide excellent cover.'

'Well, I wish you luck with your session at Cardiff. You're obviously finding DS Trent useful.'

'He's a good bloke, sir; took a while to iron out the wrinkles, but he's been a help without a doubt. Good interviewer and can always be persuaded to wade through paperwork.'

'Good. All's well then. I'll speak with you later in the week, Ben, let you know what we decide to do about Molly. If I can save her, I will. Just keep it quiet at your end.' He disconnected the line.

'Jack,' Ben called. 'What time are we booked in at Cardiff this morning?'

'Eleven thirty, boss. What is it, about an hour's drive?'

'More like hour and a half, you keep forgetting there aren't really any motorways in Wales. Right, the rest of you – carry on preparing the case papers. I can't think this is going to end up in court any time soon, but we have to be ready when it does. Mark and Ian, here a mo. I'd like you to go to the Boutique Hotel in Stone Street and see if that oily journalist from *The National* is still there. If he is, present yourselves at his door – preferably unannounced – and gently, but firmly, read the riot act to him regarding the corruption of police officers.' Ben lowered his voice. 'I've been talking to the Chief Super who is anxious to give Molly a second chance and I know she wants that too, so we must do what we can to help. When you see Julie, tell her this has got to be kept hush-hush. It's unlikely Murray will say anything about it once you've pointed out the error of his ways. This is unofficial and off the record, so not too much fuss, boys, OK?'

'Yeah, Sarge, no worries,' Mark said. 'I'm looking forward to making Murray's life difficult for *him* after that fiasco at court on Friday. Come on, Ian, this should be fun.'

'Are you ready, boss?' Jack asked. 'We ought to be going, I've rounded up the relevant paperwork together with photos of that carved graffiti, thought we'd wave them under Jimmy's nose, see if we get a response.'

'Good idea. Get the car started and I'll meet you out front in five minutes.'

* * *

Jack drove towards Cardiff looking as though he was enjoying himself.

'You like it here, don't you?' Ben asked. 'Now you've got over your sheep phobia?'

'Funnily enough, I have to admit I do. I didn't to start with, but it's getting better all the time.' He grinned. 'I love the roads, quiet and twisty with great views and friendly drivers. It's not like this in London.'

'No, I wouldn't have thought so. I went there once when I was younger, but wouldn't want to now. I like it here, too.' He smiled. 'Do you know where we're going once you get into Cardiff?'

'Satnav's been programmed, I'll follow that.' He negotiated a particularly sharp bend before asking. 'How are we going to play this today, more of the same?'

'Pretty much, but won't be so easy in the jail. As you know, screws don't like us coppers very much and even though they aren't keen on the inmates either, they protect them to wind us up. I think it's cos they wanted to be coppers, failed the entrance exam and some bright spark suggested they become prison officers. After all, using keys occasionally and wandering about landings isn't too taxing.'

'Ooo, you don't like them, do you? I'm not keen either, to be frank, but they'll often turn a blind eye in the Scrubs and if you can get one on your side…'

'Not here. You can still play bad cop, but you'll have to be subtle, no shouting or Jimmy'll complain and they'll chuck us out.'

Half an hour later they pulled up in the prison car park and submitted to the rigmarole of signing in, before being shown to an area segregated from the main visiting hall. They didn't have to wait long before Jimmy was led in by a prison officer. He looked tired and twitchy and sat reluctantly on the orange chair facing the officers.

'Hello, Jimmy, how's it going?' Ben asked.

'How do you think it's bloody going? I can't believe you've got me banged up in here. This is an effing nightmare.'

Jack leaned over the table and smirked at the nervous man. 'It'll be so much easier if you tell us the truth. To be honest with you, I don't like having to travel all this way to talk to you – very time consuming – and although *you* may have a problem filling the days, mine are very full, so how about it?'

'You really don't give up, do you? I got nothing to say and my solicitor says it's better if I don't.'

Jack removed the photos he'd brought with him from the folder and placed them in front of Jimmy.

'Have a look at these.'

'What are they?' Jimmy asked, reluctantly.

'Photos, they don't bite.' Jack raised his voice slightly and managed to turn a request into an order. 'Look at them!' he hissed.

Jimmy leaned forward and peered at the pictures gingerly. A look of relief flickered across his face and he quickly relaxed.

'What are they then?' he asked.

'You don't recognise this carving?'

'No, looks like initials or something, cut into a tree.'

Ben and Jack exchanged a glance, mentally agreeing the man was telling the truth.

Jack tried a different tack. 'Jimmy, we know you did it, OK? We know you killed Amber. We've got the shell case with your thumbprint on it, your DNA at the scene and gunshot residue on your clothes. It all points very neatly to you. The only thing we don't have is the gun. Why not do us all a favour, including yourself, and tell us what happened. You'll feel better for it, I promise you.'

Jimmy shook his head and his shoulders slumped lower.

'Come on, Jimmy, get it over with. What did you do with the gun?'

Jimmy said nothing, staring into the middle distance.

Jack persisted, asking the same questions over and over again, receiving shorter and shorter answers from Jimmy. After twenty minutes or so, Ben noticed the prisoner was trembling and peering into his face, realised the man was crying.

'Hang on a minute, Jack, will you?' Ben said.

'Borrowed.' The word slipped from Jimmy's lips, his eyes screwed shut, face pale, skin damp with sweat. He moaned softly, then repeated the single word, 'Borrowed.' He enunciated each syllable carefully and deliberately.

Jack leaned closer. 'What are you saying? What are you talking about?'

Again the single word followed by a moan that increased in volume until it was almost a howl. The door of the room flung open and two large prison officers rushed in with four smaller specimens bringing up the rear.

'Oy! What's going on in here?' one of them demanded.

'Not sure, lads, he just started making that noise,' Ben answered.

The officers pulled Jimmy back in his seat. He looked dreadful, face dripping wet, almost purple in colour. He panted in shallow gasps and desperate moans crawled from his mouth.

'God, I don't like the look of him,' the warder said. 'Someone go get the doc. You two, interview over, go on, get out. We've enough on our plates with him, you know the way. Show your visitor's badges and warrant cards to get you through security.'

Neither Ben nor Jack moved.

'You can't possibly think I can allow this to continue, do you?' the man said. 'He's had some sort of a breakdown, so get moving.' He shouted over his shoulder. 'Where's that bloody doctor?'

The detectives had no option but to leave. Jack couldn't take his eyes off the distressed prisoner and nearly walked into the door frame until Ben nudged his shoulder to correct his direction. They passed through numerous metal security doors. All were locked, all needed unlocking and it took an age before they eventually found themselves standing outside the prison in the car park.

Jack leaned on the bonnet of the car and soaked up the warm sunshine.

'What the hell was that all about, boss?' he asked.

'How am I supposed to know? This is a bloody disaster!'

'I didn't push him that hard. You were there,' Jack muttered. 'He must have been close to a breakdown and if it hadn't been us, someone else would have helped him drop off the edge.'

'It's OK, I'm not blaming you. I thought you were quite gentle – for you. Persistent, but not bullying. What was it that he said, "borrowed"? What did he mean, any thoughts?'

'I don't know, can't even remember what I asked him. I detest these interviews, at least if we'd been at the station we could listen to the recording. What on earth did I ask him?' Jack rubbed his face.

'Maybe he meant he borrowed the gun?' Ben said.

'How on earth could you *borrow* a 50-calibre Rangemaster, for heaven's sake? It's not like you can get one at Tool Hire or Exchange and Mart and you're not likely to have a friend or neighbour with one tucked in the umbrella stand. Jimmy can't have meant the gun.'

'What else could he have been talking about?'

'No idea, boss. Jimmy's mental, could have meant anything at all in his addled brain. Let's get back to Llandovery and do a bit of brainstorming with the rest of the team.'

'It must be the gun,' Ben mumbled. 'I'm sure you asked him what he'd done with it right before he broke down, maybe he borrowed it from the army. Does he know anyone serving on the ranges? That's one thing we haven't checked out.'

'Captain Harford-Brown would have a hissy fit if he heard you talking like this, he's convinced nothing's missing in the way of arms and ammo.' Jack paused. 'Mind you, we asked if they'd lost anything, we didn't ask about anything being borrowed, but how the hell would that work? Even if it *had* happened, how could we *prove* it had? Unless a squaddie admitted lending someone their rifle, and I can't see too many soldiers queuing up to tell us they've broken the rules. Mind you,' Jack laughed saucily, 'depends on what punishment our good captain dishes out and whether or not they like it.'

Jack took the wheel and they travelled in silence, both replaying the disastrous interview and both asking themselves the same question, was it *really* possible Jimmy had borrowed a gun? And was that one word *any* sort of a confession?

## Chapter twenty-seven

Ben was working at his desk when the phone rang.

'DS James.'

'Ah, just the man, Governor Hughes here from HMP Cardiff.'

'Morning, sir, what can I do for you?'

'Just to keep you informed, Jimmy Atkins has been transferred. We moved him onto the hospital wing here for observation after your visit, but his condition has remained pretty much the same – deteriorated if anything. At times he's almost catatonic and doesn't speak. The psychiatrist has insisted he be transferred to somewhere he can be observed and treated as necessary. He will not, therefore, be attending court on Friday as he has been assessed as too ill to be aware of what's going on around him.'

'That's all I need! He's really ill is he, not putting it on?' Ben asked.

'The doctor here doesn't seem to think so, given Atkins has previously been diagnosed with PTSD, but I guess I'm an old cynic, I don't trust any prisoner. I've seen some strange things take place so individuals can avoid the consequences of their actions. We had a chap once who nearly disembowelled himself with a sharpened toothbrush in order to be taken to an outside hospital where he launched an escape attempt. You wouldn't believe it.'

'I can imagine. Presumably the court authorities have been informed?'

'Yes, we've taken care of all that and copies of the documents are being couriered over to you as we speak.'

'When will he be going?' Ben asked.

'He's already gone, first thing this morning. Should be arriving at Broadmoor in the next couple of hours or so.'

'Broadmoor? Isn't that a bit heavy?'

'No places at Ashworth or Rampton. Not like we had much choice with only three high security mental hospitals in Britain. No, he's in the best place. They'll assess him properly and if he's putting it on, he'll be back here sooner than he thought. Don't worry, I wouldn't be at all surprised to see him returned in a week or so. If cons *are* trying to pull a fast one, as soon as they see the inside of a place like Broadmoor, they often make remarkable recoveries and can't wait to return to jail.'

'Well, thank you for letting me know, sir.'

'No problem, I'll keep you in the loop.'

Ben called Jack over.

'Sit down, Sergeant, got some bad news. Jimmy's pulling the mental health card, with some help from the shrink at Cardiff and has, as of this morning, been sent to Broadmoor for assessment.'

'So, what do we do now?'

'I guess we walk upstairs and let DCI Ambrose know. I'm not looking forward to telling him, he won't be very happy.'

Jack looked concerned.

'Don't worry,' Ben said. 'We've been over this, it wasn't down to you and I'll make sure Charlie knows that. Come on, let's get it over with.'

* * *

Half an hour later they were still in DCI Ambrose's office. The inspector had been less than pleased and accepted the news badly. He asked his sergeants to repeat everything they could remember about the meeting at the prison on Monday and eventually seemed satisfied with their accounts.

'You know, I'm beginning to think Jimmy is our man after all,' Ambrose said. 'I've looked over his service file in detail and it's obvious he had a serious problem out there in Afghanistan. From what I've read the army did well to keep things under wraps and quietly discharge him on health grounds. It worries me, it really does.' He sighed heavily. 'How many more Jimmy Atkinses are wandering around with mental health problems like this? It amazes me we don't have more trouble than we do. Teach a man to kill another man and obey orders without question, let him do that for a while and then – when it suits the authorities – chuck him out on his ear. They don't seem to leave with useful skills that adapt to civvy street either, these days. It was all a bit different in my time, the army would teach you a trade. Still, we haven't had any more shootings, so maybe that's the biggest clue of all?'

Ben nodded. 'I wish I felt more certain though, sir. It bothers me we have plenty of evidence against him in relation to Amber, but nothing for the others. The only tentative link is Samantha Phillips. She admitted knowing Jimmy, said he and Danny were best mates at school, but says Jimmy would never shoot him.'

'Did Atkins even know the vicar's wife or Mrs Read?'

'He says not and of course we can't ask the victims. The team are trawling through the statements, so maybe they'll uncover something; same with the house-to-house, but we're not hearing anything new.'

'Not easy without a witness or two,' Ambrose said.

'I also wish I could understand that "borrowed" business. We've looked at it from all angles, been back onto the army – nothing forthcoming there, but I didn't really expect them to admit to lending out their kit. With so many guns to choose from we'd never find the right one and even if we did, we'd never discover who lent it out.'

'Yes,' Ambrose said. 'I can see that would be problematic.'

'Perhaps it's a completely random word that only makes sense inside Jimmy's disturbed mind. According to

Governor Hughes, on the rare occasion Jimmy does speak, he just repeats that word over and over. Maybe he was slowly falling to bits, perhaps he held things together during the earlier killings, hence no physical evidence. It's possible when he shot Amber he was closer to his breakdown, so he became sloppy. I wonder if we'll ever know for sure what happened?'

'It depends on whether Jimmy is actually ill or putting it on,' Jack said. Governor Hughes at Cardiff said a lot of these cases soon wind up back inside his walls. Once they see the inside of an institution like Broadmoor, they decide they're not mad after all and beg on bended knees to be allowed back into the main prison population.'

'I guess we have to hope for that then, but it's not very satisfying, particularly for the families of the other victims,' Ambrose muttered. 'How's the paperwork coming, in case we *do* get our day in court?'

'Pretty much up together,' Ben told him. 'In a few days we'll be in a position to hand the lot over to the CPS, see what they make of it.'

'Soon be time to close down the incident room then?'

Ben nodded. 'Certainly downsize it. I'm not sure we can close it completely yet. We need at least a week to try and tie up loose ends. I keep hunting for something that will strengthen the case against Atkins, but until we can prove he knew the other victims, we won't be able to prove he was responsible for their deaths.'

'OK, I'll go along with that. We'll reassess the situation next week and pray for more evidence in the meantime.' DCI Ambrose glared at his officers. 'Right then, gents, on with it.'

The two men walked back downstairs together. Jack stopped halfway down and leant on the banister.

'Can I have a word, boss?' he asked.

'Of course, what's on your mind?'

'Well, it's a bit… delicate.'

Ben raised his eyebrows. 'What is?'

'Constable Julie Smith and I are – how shall I put it – good friends.' He smiled. 'Getting better all the time actually. I just wanted to make sure you were OK with it, with us working on the same team.'

'I'm happy as long as you don't let the relationship affect your work, or Julie's.'

'Great, thanks. We'll keep it quiet in the office.'

Ben grinned. 'Too late, mate. We all know about you and Julie, landlady at the King's Head gave us full details.'

Jack's face lost its smile; it was replaced with a look of astonishment.

'Get used to it, Sergeant, there are people in this town who will *always* know something about you before you know it yourself.'

* * *

The rest of the day was spent reorganising and reducing the team, eventually retaining Jack and three other officers: Julie, Mark and Ian. The paperwork was in good order and in a last-ditch attempt to uncover some useful evidence at the earlier murder sites, Ben sent the team out in cars to patrol the lanes on the Epynt. They were instructed to drive slowly, looking for any tracks in the undergrowth on each side of the road and check out the murder sites themselves, as well as surrounding areas – just in case. He was fairly sure he knew where the shots which killed Danny and Amber were taken, but search teams found no similar foxholes at either of the other murder sites. It was unlikely his colleagues would turn up anything this late in the day, but Ben was unwilling to give up.

He took a large sheet of paper and attacked it with a sharpie, re-writing the main elements of each case, and he gradually created a smaller version of the board hanging on the wall behind him. He headed each section with the victim's name and again noted down the names of family members and friends, circumstances of each crime, adding additional information about their nearest and dearest, hunting for the one thing that linked them all. It *had* to be there.

If Jimmy *was* Amber's killer, it would be wrong not to consider him for the other three, but what was the motive? Was a coincidence of this magnitude possible in such a small community? Or was it as simple as Mark thought: target practice before the main event – Amber's death? What had gone on inside the damaged mind of Jimmy Atkins? Had he picked people at random, found a hiding place, sat there with the gun loaded and waited for someone – anyone – to walk into his line of fire and then shoot them? What was *that* all about? Or, had he targeted particular people? During the extensive investigation, it hadn't been proved Jimmy even knew all the victims, or anyone connected to them. Would you shoot someone you didn't know? Maybe a psychopath would. And where was the gun? Ben realised his knowledge of mental illness was woefully lacking.

He went in search of coffee and when he returned, stood over the desk to study what he'd written. The familiar facts floated on the paper. There really didn't seem to be a single common denominator.

Four people killed: three women, one man, three dogs. One man having an affair, one woman leaving her husband and moving away, Jimmy Atkins had also played away from home. Two lived in or close to Llanagethin, two lived in Llandovery. All four killed while out walking their dogs. Ben read it again. *All* four killed while walking their dogs. That was a link, a small one, but that *did* link the crimes, albeit in a very tenuous way. Dogs – what was it about dogs? Was there a mad farmer out there who'd suffered one too many dog attacks on his sheep and was wreaking vengeance? Ben wasn't sure. Why did the killer shoot the dogs and why not Emily's dog? Did he fire and miss? Stacey said she'd only heard one shot. Was she right? Did the killer target the dogs first to make his second shot easier? If so, why not do the same with Emily? If only he knew where the shots had been fired from maybe there would be more evidence to find. Ben glanced at the clock and hoped the rest of the team was being more productive.

* * *

Jack navigated slowly through the lanes on the Llandovery side of the Sugar Loaf, while the others worked their way into the system from the far side. The damp, dreary weather had finally driven away the sunshine and midges were out in force, dancing in the air forming large, misty-looking patches. Julie peered out of the side window, scanning the verges for any sign of recent foot traffic.

'Had a word with Ben earlier,' Jack said. 'He's fine about us dating as long as it doesn't interfere with work.'

'Good. I thought he'd be OK; after all, he is going out with a journalist and Charlie Ambrose approved that.'

'Not gonna be as easy when I'm back in London, we–'

'Hang on a minute, Jack, there's something, just off that large pull-in. Park up as soon as you can and we'll go take a look.'

He stopped thirty yards or so further down the road in a gateway and they ambled back, hand in hand.

Julie leaned in and kissed him on the cheek. 'London isn't far away, *cariad*, not if this turns into something serious.'

He squeezed her hand. 'Well, while I'm living in the country, I shall certainly be making hay.'

Julie chuckled and pointed out the muddy track on the high grass verge. They peered at the narrow path, studying the wet ground hoping for footprints, and spotted half a boot print further in.

'Nothing for it, Jules. Do you want to stay here while I go and look?'

'No, I'm fine, I'll come too.'

They scrambled over the verge and ducked their heads under the low branches of the thick conifer plantation. It was dark, they waited for their eyes to adjust to the gloom then Jack took her hand and slowly walked deeper in towards the centre of the wood, following the track. They didn't get far before Julie made a noise of disgust.

'What?' Jack asked.

'Dirty bastards! This is a *toilet path*,' she grumbled. 'Some bloody tourist probably. Look at all that paper. I wonder why I do this job sometimes. Come on, boy, let's get back to the road, we're not going to find anything here.'

They returned to the car and continued their slow drive.

'I don't think there's anything *anywhere* to find,' Jack muttered. 'We'd have found it before so I don't know why we're bothering. We've got our man banged up and the fact there's been no more killings sort of confirms his guilt, don't you think?'

'Yeah, I reckon you're right, but Ben likes to be sure and you can't blame him. It's his neck on the line if we get it wrong.'

Jack slowed and pulled into a passing place as a car drove around the bend. It stopped by the side of the unmarked car, Andrew Johnson smiled at them from behind the wheel of his elderly Morris and wound the window down.

'Hello, Julie, haven't seen you for months, how are your folks?'

'Fine thanks, vicar, how are you?'

'Not too bad, thanks. I still have Sarah with me and she's a big help. I'm glad I bumped into you. I've been thinking about going to visit Jimmy Atkins, in a professional capacity. He's in Cardiff Prison, isn't he?'

'Not anymore, no,' Julie told him. 'He's been moved to Broadmoor for assessment.'

'Broadmoor?' Andrew blinked. 'Gosh, that's further away than Cardiff. Maybe I'll write to him first, see if he'd actually like a visit. Why has he been sent there?'

'Breakdown I believe,' Jack said. 'He'll have to be assessed to discover if he's fit to stand trial.'

'Probably due to having to carry his guilt around with him,' Andrew muttered darkly. 'Sin is a destroyer of souls. Is he really ill?'

'Not good apparently.'

'Has he been charged with all the murders?' Andrew asked.

'No, only that of his wife so far, but with his mental health problems, who knows what will happen now.'

'It all looks so easy on the crime shows I watch in the evenings. Psychopaths are always depicted as charismatic, highly intelligent individuals.' He chuckled. 'That doesn't really describe Jimmy, does it?'

'No it doesn't,' Jack agreed, 'but don't worry, vicar, we will keep you informed of any developments, we haven't forgotten about you.'

'My dear man, I didn't think you had. I don't mean to pressure you.'

'You're fine. Anyway, we must get off, DS James will think I've kidnapped his constable if I don't get her back to the station soon. Good to have seen you, take care.'

'I will, you too.'

Andrew drove away round the bend, vanishing in a cloud of meadowsweet and exhaust fumes.

Jack shifted gear. 'What is it with vicars? They come out with some strange stuff and your vicar isn't any different. Has he always been odd?'

Julie giggled. 'A bit, but he's been worse since this awful business began. Hardly surprising, he *has* lost his wife. Let's get back to town, find out if the others had more luck than we have.'

## Chapter twenty-eight

The Reverend Johnson parked his Morris Minor outside Broadmoor Hospital. The gloomy Welsh weather had lifted as he'd left Llanagethin and he'd enjoyed the drive to Berkshire in bright sunshine. He'd written to Jimmy last week and had been surprised to receive a visiting order by return of post. Now he was here, he was afraid his resolve would desert him. He occasionally visited parishioners in prison, but hadn't been to Broadmoor before and didn't know what to expect. Like most people he knew of the secure hospital – mainly because of the notorious killers it housed – but had never given a thought to what the place actually looked like.

He was confronted by a large, red-brick gatehouse, obviously Victorian architecture with a white-faced clock set in the imposing tower. It didn't look very prison-like, or hospital-like come to that, more like a grand country residence. He pulled up outside, climbed out and walked to the gatehouse. A member of staff caught his eye and smiled.

'Good morning, sir, can I help you?' the man asked.

'Yes please. I have a visiting order to see one of your…' Andrew hesitated over the word, what was right? Inmates? Prisoners? Patients? He settled on the latter. 'Patients.'

'Can I see the order, sir?'

Andrew handed the paper over and waited while it was inspected.

'Yes, I see, "A" Wing. You can park inside the grounds if you'd like to, it'll be quite safe. You're visiting someone who is here for assessment in the main building, rather than a sentenced individual.'

'Does that make a difference?'

The warder nodded. 'We have two main buildings here and you'll be visiting in the closest one. You may see patients walking in the grounds, but don't concern yourself, they have been rigorously risk assessed to determine whether they are a danger to themselves or others. You don't need to worry. People arrive here with such heavy hearts expecting something dreadful, but you'll see, it's not that bad.'

Andrew got back in his car, the warder dragged open the tall, wooden barrier and Andrew drove through slowly, watching in his mirror as the gates swung shut behind him.

He was confronted by another red-brick building, windows glinting in the sunshine. It sat in what could only be described as a mini park. The grounds were pleasant, with many mature trees dotting the grassy patches. Off to the left, he spotted a lake surrounded by reeds and yellow flag iris in full flower. Waterfowl glided across the still surface, their calls slipping in through the open car window. He saw a couple of women walking along the path on the bank and wondered if they were inmates or staff.

After parking in the designated area, he made his way to a small extension resembling a single-storey office block. The sign above the entrance read 'Reception'. Pushing open the door, he went inside. There was a counter at one end with two men standing behind it sorting paperwork. The strong scent of antiseptic prickled his nostrils.

'Good morning, sir, how can we help?' one asked.

'Good morning. I'm here to visit one of your charges, Mr Jimmy Atkins. He sent me a visiting order.' Andrew held out the document.

'Ah yes, you're Mr Johnson, the Reverend Johnson?'

'That's right.'

'OK. Let's get you booked in. Our security arrangements are strict, but you'd expect that. We'll need to give you a quick rub down search, take your photograph and full details, then we'll issue you a visitor's badge. The badge will have a unique barcode, don't lose it – you won't get out without it.'

Half an hour later Andrew was waiting in a large hall at a table which looked as though it should have been on the pavement outside a French café, rather than inside a place like this. At the far end of the room was a stage with rich velvet curtains; at the other a small counter where tea and biscuits were being served by the local WRVS. After a short wait, Jimmy was led to the table and helped to sit opposite his visitor.

The vicar was shocked. Atkins looked truly dreadful, skin bone-white and sickly with deeply sunken cheeks coated in an oily sheen; his hair greasy, uncombed and dirty. In fact, nothing about Jimmy looked clean. His fingernails were black, clothes rumpled and eyes crusty with dried tears. He slumped in the chair as though all his muscles had given up at once. Andrew held his hand out to the distressed man, but it was ignored.

'Hello, Jimmy. You asked me to come and see you?' he said.

There was no response.

'Would you like a cup of tea, or coffee?' Andrew thought he saw the man shrug, so left the table, went to the hatch and returned with two mugs of tea and a plate of biscuits on a tray. He placed one mug in front of Jimmy who blinked once or twice, picked it up and began to drink noisily, tea escaping his mouth and running down his chin to splash on the blue and white checked tablecloth.

Andrew tried again. 'Are you being treated well here? Do you need anything?'

Still no response and Andrew fidgeted, feeling awkward and inadequate. Reaching out he placed his hand on one of Jimmy's arms and was heartened when the man glanced up at him. Jimmy blinked again, slowly and deliberately, then with his free hand scrubbed at his eyes. He stared at the vicar's face and his eyes widened – a little. If Andrew hadn't been paying attention, he'd have missed the only recognition he'd received so far.

'You sent me a VO, requested a pastoral visit. Well, here I am. What can I do to help you?' He tried to sound upbeat and cheerful, hoping it would rub off on the disturbed man.

'Borrowed,' Jimmy whispered. 'Borrowed.'

'Do you have something to tell me? Is that why you wanted me to visit, because you want to tell me something?'

Almost imperceptibly the man nodded.

'What do you want to say? Is it about Amber, something about Amber?'

Again Jimmy gave a slight nod.

Andrew took a deep breath. 'What about her, Jimmy? Tell me.'

Nothing. No nod or any acknowledgement.

The older man gazed deeply into Jimmy's watery, blue eyes and watched as a single tear escaped from beneath a sore-looking lid and rolled slowly down his pale cheek. Andrew glanced around the room and spotted a member of staff leaning against the far wall, so raised his hand and waved him over.

'Yes, sir. Can I help?'

'Is Jimmy always like this?' Andrew asked. 'This *disconnected*?'

'Yes he is, doesn't wash, doesn't speak. He'll eat and drink if you put something in front of him, but doesn't interact with anyone else. You're his vicar, are you?' The man asked, spotting the dog collar.

'Yes, he's in my parish, but not a regular churchgoer by any means. He sent me a VO, but doesn't seem to know I'm here.'

'Oh, he knows. He's well aware of what's going on around him, just chooses not to play any part in it. Would you like to leave, sir?'

'I'll stay a while longer. How long have I got?'

'Another hour, but if you want to leave early let me know.' The man retreated to lean on the wall once again and Andrew focused his attention back on Jimmy.

'Let's try it this way. If you don't want to talk to me – or find it too difficult – I'll ask yes or no questions, then you only need to nod or shake your head, how's that? Will that work?' He watched and received a slight nod. Andrew felt he was getting somewhere.

'OK. Do you need me to get you anything, send something in for you?'

A head shake – *No.*

'Do you need money?'

*No.*

'Are you worried about your children?'

*Yes.*

'I can tell you they are quite well and being cared for locally. I've spoken to Social Services and they told me they are being fostered at the moment, but it may be possible for them to go and live with your mother in Llandeilo. She has offered to look after them and as soon as Social Services are happy, they will go there. Does that help?'

*Yes.*

'Good, I'm pleased. You said you wanted to talk about Amber. Is that right?'

*Yes.*

Andrew thought for a moment. What on earth did Jimmy want to say about his wife? It could be anything. He felt he was in the middle of a particularly frustrating parlour game and minutes ticked by as Andrew wondered what to ask next.

Jimmy mumbled something, but it was impossible to understand him.

Andrew took a deep breath. 'Jimmy, you know Amber's dead, don't you?'

*Yes.*

'Is it her death you want to talk about?'

*Yes.*

'Are you sad she's dead?'

*Yes and no.*

Andrew wished he could ask 'why', it would have been the natural next question, but couldn't be answered with a yes or a no.

'Do you know something about how she died?'

*Yes.*

Andrew took a deep breath and asked the only question left to ask, 'Did you kill Amber, Jimmy? Did you kill your wife?'

There was a long pause then a nod – a very definite nod.

'Borrowed,' the prisoner mumbled again.

'Why do you keep saying that, what do you mean? If you don't talk to me how can I help you? I'll ask again, to be sure, did you *really* shoot your wife?'

*Yes.*

The vicar suddenly found it difficult to breathe. The room temperature seemed to have risen. He lifted his mug and drank down the remains of cold tea but it didn't help. He stared at Jimmy who had closed his eyes and was breathing deeply, almost as if in deep meditation.

Andrew gently shook his arm, but received no response at all. It seemed as though the younger man had switched off and – try as he might – the vicar couldn't get any reaction to anything else he said. He didn't give up, but continued talking quietly and intensely to the man until the end of visiting hours, leaning over the table so their faces were close. When the visit had ended and feeling defeated, he raised his hand to summon a staff member who radioed one of his colleagues to collect Jimmy, while he walked the shaken vicar back to reception.

* * *

Stacey was dishing out supper when the phone in the office rang.

'Oh bugger, that's crap timing,' she grumbled. 'Help yourself, love, I'll be right back.' She went through to the office and Ben heard her pick up the receiver.

'Hello. Stacey Logan.' She paused, listening. 'Yes, he is here, I'll get him for you, hang on.' She returned to the kitchen. 'The vicar, for you.'

'Me?' Ben asked, surprised.

'See anyone else here?' She smiled as he got up from the table and padded to the phone.

'Hello, Andrew. What can I do for you?'

Stacey half-listened to the one-sided conversation as she tucked into a plateful of shepherd's pie. She was about to put Ben's meal in the oven to keep warm, when he returned and sat down looking thoughtful.

'What did he want?' she asked through a mouthful of carrots.

'He went to see Jimmy Atkins today.'

'What, in Broadmoor? That's brave, don't think I'd be keen to visit there.'

'Yes, Broadmoor. He told me Jimmy sent a VO asking him to visit.'

'So, is Jimmy talking again now?'

'It would seem not. Andrew said he spent over two hours there and they communicated with nods and shakes of the head. He worked out questions that could be answered with a yes or a no answer and Jimmy would nod – or not. He asked Jimmy if he'd killed his wife.' Ben put a large chuck of pie in his mouth and chewed thoughtfully.

'What did he say? Come on, don't keep it to yourself.'

'According to the vicar, he said yes.'

'Yes to killing Amber?' Stacey was surprised. 'Is that a confession?'

'That's what Andrew wanted to talk to me about. He wasn't happy mentioning it at all. Being a vicar, they have rules about what they do with stuff they've heard in confidence, but he felt it was his duty to inform me.'

'What about the others, did he confess to those as well?'

'No. Andrew said once Jimmy confirmed he'd shot Amber, he sort of switched off, closed his eyes, didn't move or look up again and was eventually taken back to his cell, or room or whatever.'

'Where does this leave you and the investigation then? Is it solved? Jimmy did it?'

'I don't know, I *really* don't know, sounds like Jimmy has completely lost it. I don't know whether anything he says or indicates would be admissible evidence. Anyway, if he's deemed unfit, then he'll never even make court and, in a few weeks, we'll issue one of those completely unsatisfactory statements along the lines of, "Police are not looking for anyone else in connection with this crime", that sort of thing.' He attacked his food again. 'This is – as always – lovely, thank you.'

'No problem, glad you like it.' They ate in silence before Stacey asked, 'What are you going to do, Sherlock?'

'Have a chat with DCI Ambrose in the morning, I guess. That's why he gets paid more than I do, to make the "what now" decisions. The weeks since all this started have been so exasperating. The team who worked on it with me have given their all. You should see the mountain of paperwork the investigation has generated and, even with all that, we didn't solve all four killings. We followed every lead, every tiny scrap of evidence and ended up with nothing. The closest we got to a witness was you and no matter what we did, it wasn't enough, not even close. I keep thinking I did something wrong, it *was* my first major case, so maybe I missed something.'

'You didn't, you know you didn't and if you had, Jack would have picked you up on it. He went through everything with you, same as Charlie Ambrose. Charlie oversaw the investigation and he'd have soon shouted if he thought you weren't up to the job. You know that's true.'

'Yeah, you're right – as always,' he mumbled, 'but it's left such a nasty taste in my mouth, like having an itch I can't reach to scratch. Pretty soul destroying, all that work to end up with a man who's lost his brain, can't be tried and can't – or won't – come clean with us.'

'Maybe that will change,' Stacey said. 'Like the governor at Cardiff said, Jimmy might be putting it on – or might recover. Don't give up, Sherlock.'

## Chapter twenty-nine

Stacey knocked on the old wooden door of the vicarage and admired a large clump of granny's bonnets in full flower, almost glowing in the sunshine while solitary bees buzzed in and out of the blooms. The door opened and a smiling Sarah looked out.

'Stacey! Lovely to see you, how are you?'

'Hi, Sarah, not bad thanks. I hope I'm not disturbing you, but was passing and thought I'd pop in and see how you're both doing.'

'Come in and I'll get the kettle on. I've just finished a batch of Welsh cakes, you arrived at the right time.'

Sarah opened the door wider and Stacey followed her into the kitchen at the back of the house.

'Is Andrew in?' Stacey asked.

'He's down at the church, spends a lot of his time there lately, but he'll be back soon; he couldn't do without his elevenses – hence the Welsh cakes. Do sit down.'

Sarah filled the kettle, put it on the Aga to boil and placed a laden plate on the table together with a block of golden local butter.

'Don't be shy,' she said. 'Help yourself.'

'Thanks.' Stacey spread butter on one of the griddle cakes and bit into it, sugar sticking to her lips. 'Hmm – just how I like them.'

'Where are you going?' Sarah asked. 'You said you were passing.'

'Only down to the river. Can't keep away from mountain streams when the sun is shining.' She sipped her tea. 'How are you and Andrew?'

'Recovering slowly, I guess. It's always shocking when someone close to you dies suddenly – more so when they have been murdered.'

'It must be utterly ghastly. I've thought of you often.'

'That's kind, thank you. I do feel better, time is a healer, but Andrew's struggling. He doesn't say much, but I know he isn't sleeping well, I hear him wandering around in the middle of the night and he's nearly always in the church, praying.' Sarah topped up the mugs from a large teapot. 'Did you know Andrew and Emily were childhood sweethearts?'

'No, I didn't. No wonder he's finding this so difficult.'

'They met at primary school, knew each other nearly all their lives. I always knew they'd marry, Emily was so supportive, a perfect vicar's wife. Found it difficult though when he went overseas with the troops; Andrew completed two tours, Iraq and Afghanistan. The experience changed him, everyone said so, but war does that to a person.'

'So how did they end up in Mid Wales?'

'He came here originally to cover for the incumbent who was off sick. She eventually had to retire on health grounds and Andrew and Emily stayed on, fell in love with the place, who wouldn't?'

The kitchen swung open and Andrew walked in. He seemed surprised to see Stacey.

'Hello, my dear,' he said. 'I wasn't expecting you, was I?'

'No, I was on my way for a paddling session in the river and popped in on the off chance. How are you?'

'Bearing up, thank you, keeping busy – I find that helps.' He sat at the table and helped himself to tea and Welsh cakes.

'Ben told me you visited Jimmy in Broadmoor,' Stacey said. 'How was that? I thought you were very brave going there. Not sure I'd be keen.'

'I must admit, I wondered what I'd find, but you'd hardly know it is effectively a prison. The security arrangements are strict, but once you're inside, it's not bad at all – just like a modern hospital. Long drive over though.'

'Good you had nice weather. How was Jimmy?'

Andrew sighed heavily. 'Not well I'm afraid, looked dreadful, tired and sad, broken.'

Stacey feigned ignorance and asked. 'Did he tell you anything about what happened to Amber and the others?'

'No, he didn't speak and I spent the whole two hours talking to myself. Such a tragic situation, I don't even think he recognised me.'

'Did he know you then?'

'We'd met briefly, in Iraq of all places, a few years ago. I spoke to him after his spotting partner was killed by a landmine. Such a coincidence we both ended up in Wales.'

'Amazing,' Stacey said. 'So were you in touch with each other?'

'No. Until this awful business began, I didn't know he lived here.'

Stacey dug in her backpack and pulled out two photographs. 'I wonder if you'd have a look at these,' she said and held them out to Andrew. 'I'm planning an article on street art and have been taking pictures of any I find. I think the first one might be a fish, similar to the symbols used by early Christians, but haven't a clue what the other one is. It looks like a Celtic knot or something.'

Andrew took the snaps and studied them. 'I agree with you regarding the fish. The other one is Arabic for Allah, see it everywhere in the Middle East. Where did you find these carvings?'

'Sorry, took them ages ago,' Stacey lied, 'and can't remember.'

'Have you discovered any Banksies?' Sarah asked.

'Sadly not, mostly teenagers' tags, but some are very colourful.' She tucked the photos back inside her bag and changed the subject. 'How has your fundraising been going?'

'Very well, my dear,' Andrew said. 'I wouldn't say we're swamped with donations, but there is certainly a healthy trickle – thanks to your article no doubt.'

'More tea, Stacey?' Sarah asked.

'No thanks, my stream-side hideaway is waiting. Your Welsh cakes were wonderful, just what I needed.'

'You're welcome anytime, always good to see you.'

Stacey left the vicarage, took the forestry track at the bottom of the village, then turned off and threaded her way through the dense patch of conifers to the stream. The stony beach was in full sun and she shed her jumper, boots and socks, sat on the bank and dangled her toes in clear icy water. A loud peeping announced the presence of a dipper that zipped past her feet, swooped around a bend and out of sight.

She thought about what Andrew had told her. She wasn't aware that Jimmy and the vicar knew each other and made a mental note to tell Ben, not that she could see the information would make much difference to the investigation. It wasn't as though the pair were friends or had even been in touch since their days in the army. What Andrew had said about the carvings was interesting, but again, she didn't think the graffiti had any link with the case. Maybe she would take a hike in the forest above the picnic area on the Llandovery road. There had to be a foxhole there somewhere and if she managed to find it, there might be more evidence for Ben and the team to work with.

* * *

Stacey was draining a saucepan of new potatoes when Ben appeared at the back door.

'Hey, Pumpkin,' he said, moving closer and kissing the back of her neck.

'Hey, you,' she said, put the saucepan on the drainer and hugged him. 'How's your day been?'

'Not wonderful. Mind if I help myself to a whisky?'

'Of course not. Has it been that bad?'

'Worse.' He poured a stiff measure and gulped a mouthful.

'So, tell me what's up?' she said.

'Jimmy Atkins is dead,' he muttered.

'Dead?' Stacey sat at the table. 'How did that happen?'

'Staff at Broadmoor found him in his room this morning with a noose around his neck. He'd hung himself.'

'That's awful. His poor children, they're orphans now.'

'Yeah. I'm so glad the council got them settled with their granny in Llandeilo, at least she can look after them, rather than them being stuck in the care system.'

Stacey returned to the Aga, removed a steak and ale pie and cut two large slices to go with the potatoes and string beans.

'Do you know what happened – apart from the obvious?' she asked.

'The authorities at Broadmoor rang DCI Ambrose first thing and informed him. It seems as though Jimmy never improved, if anything became more withdrawn and only left his room if one of the staff made him.'

'If he was so ill, how on earth did he manage to hang himself?'

'Made a noose from a pair of jeans which he looped over a ceiling light. Looks like he stood on a chair and kicked it away. There was one on its side in the middle of the room.'

'Bloody hell,' Stacey said, putting a plate of food in front of her partner and helping herself to a finger of whisky. 'Wasn't anyone watching him?'

'He was checked throughout the night as all the patients are, but hadn't been placed on suicide watch. There will be an investigation of course.' Ben loaded his fork with meat and pastry, transferred the food to his mouth and chewed. 'Hmm, that's good, didn't get to eat anything today.'

'Well don't give yourself stomach ulcers, buckets of coffee on an empty stomach isn't good for you.' She sipped her drink. 'I'm surprised Jimmy could do that to himself. I visited Andrew earlier in the week and he told me Jimmy wouldn't even speak.'

'You be surprised what desperate people can do. Charlie Ambrose wasn't best pleased and Jack was furious. He was always convinced Jimmy was faking it and that we'd eventually get him into court.' Ben put down his cutlery and scrubbed his face. 'Christ, what a bloody awful mess. Four dead people, only one suspect and now he's dead as well. For all we know, there might still be a killer wandering around the hills. Doesn't bear thinking about.'

'Did Jack have anything constructive to say?'

'Not really, but probably won't until he's calmed down. Charlie did say that Jack hasn't been recalled to Scotland Yard, so I'm pretty certain his bosses aren't convinced the investigation is over either.'

'Don't beat yourself up, *cariad.* What else could you have done? Not like you found much in the way of evidence – nor me. I've been trekking about in the forest above the picnic area and haven't found a thing. Without any clues, how *could* you have solved the case?'

'You really shouldn't be doing that. I have warned you,' Ben said.

'I know, but I'm careful and if Jimmy *was* the killer, I'm safe.'

Ben sighed and pushed his plate away. 'I'd always thought I'd make inspector,' he said. 'This was my first big chance, wouldn't have had it without the backing of Charlie, and of course the shortage of staff, and it's destined to be labelled as a cold case.'

'Not necessarily surely? If new evidence comes to light–'

'But it won't, will it, with Jimmy dead?' Ben snapped. 'Oh, God, I'm sorry. I don't mean to take it out on you.'

Stacey squeezed his hand. 'It's OK, I know you don't. Jam roly-poly for afters, that'll cheer you up, then after supper you can soak in a hot bath until bedtime. It'll do you good.'

'Only if you keep me company.'

Stacey smiled. 'Can I ask something?'

Ben nodded.

'Can I write about Jimmy's suicide?'

'Yeah, the news is already out in England.' Ben hauled himself upright. 'I'm off to the bath, early shift tomorrow.'

'What about afters?'

'Sorry, maybe later, ate too much pie.'

* * *

Ben was staring at a mound of paperwork when the incident room door banged open and Jack Trent stomped in, two mugs of coffee in one hand. He plonked one in front of Ben and flopped on a nearby chair.

'Still pissed off then?' Ben asked.

'Yeah, pretty much.' Jack gulped coffee. 'Bloody scumbag coward,' he muttered. 'Brave enough to pull triggers but not brave enough to face the music. I really don't like it when bad guys get away with it.'

'Still think he was guilty?'

'Of course he was. He killed Amber, we know that even if we didn't get to prove it in court, so it stands to reason he killed the others. No more shootings, so in my book that confirms it.'

'When do you think you'll go back to London?'

Jack hesitated. 'Ah, that's the thing.'

'What's the thing?'

'I've put in for a transfer. Reckon I've outgrown the city.'

'Oh? Where are you thinking of going?'

'Well… here actually.'

'You want to move to Mid Wales? I thought you hated it here?'

'I did, but it's grown on me.' Jack grinned like a mischievous teenager.

Ben chuckled. 'You mean Julie's grown on you.'

'Yeah, that too. Her da has offered me a cottage to rent on the Epynt – knocks spots off my place in Brixton.'

'How do you rate your chances?'

'Fair to middling. Be bloody marvellous though. I like it here and I'm really not keen on heading back to The Smoke. Breathing is easier in the mountains.'

'I know what you mean and hope it works out for you. I'd be pleased to have you around.' Ben drained his mug. 'I was chatting to Stacey last night. Seems she's been hiking through the plantations off the Llandovery road looking for clues. I've warned her not to, that if the killer is still around she could be in danger, but she hasn't taken any notice.'

'Chill out, boss, like I said, it had to be Jimmy. Stacey won't come to any harm, I'm sure of it.'

'She called in to see Andrew and his sister-in-law a few days ago, told me Andrew and Jimmy knew each other.'

Jack humphed. 'Vicars probably know everyone, isn't that their job? Were they mates? Cos if they were, that didn't come out in the investigation.'

'No, nothing like that. Andrew told her he'd met Jimmy briefly in Iraq, counselled him after one of his comrades was killed. Don't you find it odd they ended up living so close to each other after they left the army? Andrew said he'd only found out Jimmy was living so close when the murders began.'

'Not really, six degrees of separation and all that. Coincidences do happen, boss. Any evidence Jimmy knew Emily? That would be more interesting.'

'No, none at all.'

'There you are then.'

'What does that mean?

'That we are where we are. Without a confession from Jimmy, or some concrete evidence, you can't change the outcome. I know how frustrating this is for you, but you have to let it go and move on. If you don't, this case will haunt you for years. My advice would be not to let it.'

> The Mid Wales Times – 1st June
> ATKINS FOUND DEAD IN CELL by Stacey Logan
>
> Jimmy Atkins, charged last month with the murder of his wife, Amber, was found hanging in his cell at Broadmoor Hospital. He was transferred to the facility for assessment on the 16th of May this year after suffering a suspected breakdown while on remand in Cardiff Prison.
> Atkins was found to be incapable of understanding the charge put to him and was therefore deemed unfit to be tried. He was discharged from the army on health grounds, following extensive active tours in both Iraq and Afghanistan. His condition deteriorated rapidly in the weeks since he was transferred to Broadmoor but he had not been placed on suicide watch and was able to fashion a noose that he tied to a light fitting in his cell. The staff member who discovered Atkins tried for

several minutes to revive him, but he was declared dead at the scene.
He leaves behind two small children who are being cared for by relatives. Police have released a statement, confirming they are not looking for anyone else in connection with the April killings in and around the small market town of Llandovery.

## Chapter thirty

Stacey dashed to open the door and smiled warmly at the group waiting outside. Julie gave her a hug, Jack held out a bottle of wine and Mark brought up the rear.

'Come in! Come in!' she said. 'Great to see you. Ben's in the kitchen, thought we'd eat outside this evening – as long as the midges don't get too bad, it's still lovely and warm.'

'Nice to be asked,' Jack said. 'I've been looking forward to this evening, I'm told you're an excellent cook.'

'Not bad, not sure about excellent. Go on through, all of you, take the wine with you, glasses already out there. Julie, could you give me a hand?'

'No problem, what can I do?'

'Help me carry this lot through to the garden.' She caught hold of Julie's arm and whispered. 'How's it going with Juicy Jack?'

Julie turned a pale pink and smiled. 'Beautifully well. He makes me laugh, if you can believe that, has such a dry sense of humour most people don't even realise he's being funny, but he cracks me up.'

'You certainly look happy.'

'I am, very. Wouldn't change a thing.'

They joined the men on the small patio in the back garden. A slight breeze made candle flames on the table bounce, chasing shadows around and repelling the worst of the midges. It was a soft, warm evening and honeysuckle climbing over the back fence filled the air with spicy sweetness. Shadows lengthened as the sun set over the ranges and although the meal had finished long ago, no one seemed eager to go indoors.

'Jack, I've heard you've transferred from London,' Stacey said. 'How are you settling in?'

'Loving it, absolutely bloody loving it! Best thing I've done in years, moving out here. Found myself an amazing woman, got a great job working with good people and a fabulous little cottage tucked under the edge of the mountain where I can watch sunsets, can't believe how much my life has changed. I was well pissed off when my boss sent me out here, middle-of-bloody-Welsh-nowhere to keep an eye on you lot, but look how it's turned out. You never know what's round the corner.'

'Probably best not to sometimes,' Mark mumbled from the far side of the table.

Stacey giggled. 'Oh, don't be so grumpy, Mark. Mrs Right is out there somewhere, you just haven't met her yet. Maybe she'll be at the Royal Welsh Show tomorrow.'

'I doubt it, Stace, anyway, she's hardly going to be walking around with a sign on her head saying "Mark Jefferies' Soulmate", is she?'

'If it wasn't hard work it wouldn't be worth having,' Stacey said.

They drank in silence for a while before Julie spoke. 'Awful about Jimmy Atkins killing himself, his children are orphans now, having lost their mam and da.' She sighed. 'All that work for nothing. What a waste of time. What a terrible waste… of everything.'

'Not really, Jules,' Ben said. 'After all, if we take it he *did* in fact confess to the vicar, then we locked up the right man. We can take solace in that as well as the fact no one else died after we arrested him, so… that's it.' Ben sipped from his glass.

'Not very satisfactory though, is it?' Jack said. 'Like Jules, I think of all the work we put in and didn't really solve anything. We carried the investigation along for a while, like a huge cardboard box, until we couldn't hold it up any longer, then put it down and walked away. Not good for the relatives either without a court case.'

Ben agreed and there were other nods round the table before they lapsed into a thoughtful silence. The breeze strengthened and stirred the leaves.

Stacey shivered. 'Brr, mountain air, healthy and chilly even in summer, let's go in for a brandy nightcap. Mark, can you give me a hand clearing the table? If everyone else brings something and dumps it in the kitchen on the way through, we'll only have to make one trip. I've lit the fire in the living room, more for show than anything else, but we'll be toasty to go to bed.'

They gathered in the cosy, low-ceilinged room. Jack sat on the floor leaning against Julie's legs, Stacey and Ben lounged on the sofa while Mark collapsed in the leather armchair closest to the fire, kicked off his boots and wriggled his toes.

'It'll be a good day tomorrow,' Mark murmured. 'I love the Royal Welsh, never mind pulling the duty. I can be there all day *and* get paid as well. Good job things have settled down or I guess Her Majesty would have missed it this year. That would have upset a lot of little old ladies.'

'What sort of stuff goes on there?' Jack asked. 'I know it's an agricultural show, so will it all be tractors, sheep and cows?'

'Of course, you haven't been before,' Mark said. 'You'll love it and yes, lots of tractors and big fancy farming machines, livestock of all kinds – not just sheep. There's an antique fair and heaps of stalls selling outdoor wear, guns, dog leads, shooting sticks, Land Rovers, new 4x4s… everything you can think of, and more.'

'Lots of potential trouble spots too,' Ben said, 'but we're mainly there to keep an eye on the local bad boys. There's a fair amount of shoplifting from the stalls and the odd handbag nicking. Occasionally things get a bit lively at one of the bars, but nothing too serious. Not like the Bike Show in May, that's been known to get tricky, but I've never found a hill farmer with his pockets stuffed full of drugs.' He laughed.

Stacey hauled herself to her feet. 'Right then, you lot, that's enough for me. I'm going to get my head down. I want to arrive at the show before it's open and take some shots for the paper without the crowds, so I'll be leaving early. Sorry, Mark, but tonight you're on the sofa in the office. Jack and Julie wouldn't both fit on it, so I've given them the spare room. How about we all try to meet up for lunch tomorrow?'

'That's a good idea, Pumpkin,' Ben said. 'We'll get a lunch break, even if we are working. How about one o'clock in the main bar or do you fancy somewhere else?'

'No, that'll be fine. Don't worry about the clearing up, leave it all where it is and I'll sort it when I get home tomorrow. Sleep tight everyone and thanks for coming, it's been a delightful evening.'

Jack struggled up from the floor. 'No, thanks to you for inviting us and cooking such a splendid meal. It's been great. We'll have to do this again, maybe at my place next time? It'll encourage me to get on with the decorating if I know someone's coming for dinner.' He gave her a brief hug and not to be outdone, Ben dragged himself out of the sofa and wrapped her in his long arms.

'Sleep well, love,' he whispered into her hair.

Stacey climbed the stairs and went to bed. She drifted off quickly, listening to the gentle rise and fall of the lullaby-like conversation downstairs.

* * *

A fine, early mist hung over the showground. Stacey turned up her collar and shivered. The forecasters had promised a warm day, but the sun was slow in burning away the damp whiteness.

She wandered up and down the lines of animals in their temporary pens and discovered everything from alpacas to ferrets, even some hissing cockroaches on a 'Petting stall' and wondered who would want to. Her favourite were the sheds full of prize-winning bulls, hugely powerful, enormously impressive animals, with heads the size of dustbins and legs as thick as lamp posts. Invariably their handlers were small, wiry types and Stacey wondered what would happen if one of the great creatures decided to explore the showground. Would the men holding their halters be able to stop them? She hoped so.

The mist finally began to clear and the fields filled up with people visiting stalls and watching events in the main arena. Stacey often found so many people a touch claustrophobic, so she hiked above the showground to overlook the area from a hill at the back. It was a fascinating and impressive sight, the marquees and stalls looked like a huge patchwork quilt spread out on the grass.

Digging a water bottle from her kitbag, she took a long drink and peered through her binoculars at the show crowd, the noise of visitors drifting towards her on the gentle breeze. She heard the lowing of cattle and the high, singing voices of hundreds of different breeds of sheep. At the far side of the showground, a clay pigeon shoot was operating and the explosions of the guns cut through other sounds and irritated her. She thought she spotted Mark moving with the crowds, keeping his eye out for shoplifters and pickpockets. The crowd gradually swelled as the time drew near for the royal visit. Her Majesty the Queen, as well as HRH Prince of Wales, were due to attend today and people had turned out in force to welcome them. Stacey was glad things seemed to have returned to normal after the dreadful events in the spring.

Jimmy Atkins' death was still being gossiped about in the county's towns, but angrily. Locals were cross because it appeared the man had escaped justice by taking his own life. Stacey wasn't of the same opinion. The man was dead. He had paid the ultimate price for killing his wife, and by his own hand. Even if he had been tried and convicted in the normal manner, he might have only served ten years or so before his release back into the community.

She checked her watch – quarter to one – time to head for the bar. Hanging her gear on one shoulder, she trotted down the hill to rejoin the hordes. By the time she arrived at the beer tent, Ben and Mark were already there, Jack and Julie still on their way from the far side of the site.

'Stacey, what can I get you?' Mark asked, smiling at her.

'A long fruit juice, any sort with ice please. Thanks.' She pecked Ben on the cheek.

'How's it going, Pumpkin?' he asked.

'Good thanks. Great to have lovely weather this year, so many of these shows have been washouts. I haven't seen anyone getting towed out and that must be a record. Took some fab shots, I've been sitting up on the hill for an hour or so watching it all. How about you?'

'Not bad,' Ben answered. 'Couple of run-ins with local kids trying to help themselves to sunglasses from one of the stalls and a bit of an argument between two shepherds, but nothing serious. Mainly, we've been checking the security arrangements for the royal visit this afternoon. The protection officers are a paranoid bunch though, especially after all that business earlier in the year, and Jack's behaving like he's at a school reunion, knows a couple of them apparently. I wish they'd settle down, it's catching.'

Jack and Julie arrived together and ordered drinks.

'Mark, you were right, this is marvellous,' Jack announced. 'Never been to anything quite like it before. Did you see the tractor pulling, how mad is that? Strap a huge, heavy weight on the back of a tractor and see how far and how fast you can drag it. The Axe-men were fantastic! I watched two lads with a bow-saw cut through a huge tree trunk quicker than a guy with a chainsaw.' Jack grinned broadly. 'This is the best gig I've ever had to work.'

Mark chuckled. 'Told you. There's falconry on this afternoon, you'll like that and sheep dog trials in the other arena. That's my favourite, watching the dogs work.'

They drank up and ordered a repeat round with a large plate of sandwiches to share. Lunch was over too quickly and the group broke up.

'Will you still be over tonight, Ben?' Stacey asked.

'I certainly plan to. No idea what time, it depends on what happens here this afternoon.'

'OK, curry from the freezer it is then. I'll head home as soon as I've got some shots of the HRHs and Sam'll be pleased if I get the piece sent off, he can spend the whole of Sunday picking holes in it. I'm not planning on going out, but I may be in the bath, so help yourself to the key. Actually…' She felt around in her pocket and pulled out a key ring, a miniature pair of silver handcuffs, from which dangled a door key. 'I meant to give you this a while ago, Nirjana in Llandeilo made it. The key's for the back door.'

Ben took the key ring and studied the workmanship. 'It's stunning, it really is. Hey, they even open and close!'

'Of course, no point in having handcuffs if they don't work, is there?' She smiled as he gave her a quick hug and a fierce kiss.

'Thank you, Pumpkin, that's very special. Wish I could come home with you now, but… duty calls. I'll be there as soon as I can. Day off tomorrow so we can have a lie-in.' He left the bar and followed his comrades into the crush of the crowds.

## Chapter thirty-one

Stacey was busy in the kitchen when the phone rang. She'd just sent her piece to Sam and guessed he was ringing up to moan.

She snatched up the receiver. 'Yes, yes, I know. You can change it all you want, but don't grumble on!'

A woman's voice sounded startled. 'Oh, sorry. I was trying to get hold of Stacey. It's Sarah, Sarah Gilbert from the vicarage.'

'Hi, Sarah, I'm sorry.' Stacey laughed. 'I thought you were my editor ringing to bitch about a piece I sent him. That'll teach me to assume I know who's calling. How are you?'

'I'm not feeling very well actually, having a bit of a funny turn, very dizzy and unsteady. Andrew's out, not back from the show yet so I wonder if I could ask you a favour. Would you mind popping down? I know it's a dreadful imposition and you're probably busy, but I really could do with some company.'

'I'm sorry you're not well. Yes of course I'll come, can I bring you anything? Would you like me to ring the doctor?'

'No, I don't need a doctor, just company while I feel so unsteady. I've had these attacks before and they usually pass, but I don't like being alone in case I fall or anything. The back door's open, just come on in, and I'm sorry to drag you away from home.'

'No problem. I'll be there as soon as I can.'

Stacey hung up, grabbed her jacket and keys and left the cottage by the back door, locking it behind her before hurrying along the lane towards the village.

* * *

Stacey slipped through the overcrowded garden and made her way along the path to the back door of the vicarage. It was open and as she pushed it wider, she called out.

'Sarah, it's me, Stacey. Where are you?'

She thought she heard a muffled reply from the front of the house and moved further into the kitchen.

'I'm on my way. Are you in the living room?'

She walked along the hall towards the small front room, stepped inside and stopped abruptly, gasping in surprise. Sarah was nowhere to be seen, but resting on a table in the middle of the room was a large rifle. It looked incongruous, on the delicate lace tablecloth and a small drip of oil had leaked from the mechanism to mar the white material. She put her hand to her mouth and started to back out of the room. Something hard and cold touched the back of her neck and a voice spoke directly in her ear.

'No you don't. Stand still!' the voice hissed.

'Who are you? What's going on?'

A hand grabbed her shoulder and began to pull her out into the hall.

'Come on, this way. You've come to see Sarah, haven't you?'

'Andrew, is that you?' Stacey asked. 'What are you doing?'

'Shut up and come with me.' He pulled at her some more and half dragged her along the passageway stopping in front of a narrow door, before shoving her up against the wall.

'Don't move or I'll shoot you.'

Stacey stared at the flushed face of the vicar and was transfixed by a small pistol he held in his right hand. Fumbling a bunch of keys from his pocket he inserted one into the lock, turned it and swung the door open wide.

'In you go.' He yanked her roughly away from the wall and pushed her towards the darkness behind the wooden door.

'What are you doing, Andrew? Where's Sarah? She rang me, said she was ill. Where *is* she?'

'Down there.' He indicated the dark doorway with a jerk of his head and waved the pistol in her face. 'Move!'

He shoved harder and she had no option other than to duck her head and shuffle into the dark. The door slammed shut. She heard the rattle of keys and click of the lock. Pressing an ear to the door, she listened as Andrew moved away down the hallway.

It was pitch-black, the air tainted with an unpleasant mushroomy scent. Feeling around the walls for a light switch, she touched nothing but damp plaster and spiders' webs. Having the sense to test the ground in front of her with a foot, she discovered she was standing at the top of a flight of steps. This must be the cellar, she thought. Rummaging in the pocket of her jacket she pulled out her keys. She had a miniature torch she used as a key ring and prayed the batteries weren't flat. Holding it in front of her body, she pushed the button and a weak beam of white light illuminated the area close to her. Shining it towards the steps she was able to safely navigate her way to the bottom of the long flight. Playing the narrow beam around the floor, she spotted a crumpled form lying near an old packing case. Sarah!

Stacey ran to her side and checked for a pulse. Sarah was alive and seemed to be breathing normally. Stacey tapped the older woman's cheeks gently and called her name. Sarah's eyes snapped open, full of fear until she realised who was looking down at her.

'Stacey! I'm so pleased to see you, but *wish* you hadn't come. Here, help me sit up, will you?'

'Are you OK? Are you hurt?'

'No, I'm fine, just cold. I've been here most of the day – apart from when I rang you – Andrew took me upstairs for that. He gave me some water, I think it must have had something in it because I was so sleepy, couldn't stay awake. What time is it?'

Stacey checked her watch. 'Seven fifteen, I haven't been here long. What on *earth* is going on, Sarah? What's Andrew playing at? He held a pistol to my head to get me in the cellar and he's got a bloody great rifle in the front room. I don't understand.'

'Nor me. He's been acting strangely all day. He was due to go to the show, but said he didn't feel up to it. I gave him breakfast and he went to the church, spent most of the morning there and when he returned he looked different somehow.'

'Different? In what way?'

'I don't know, odd. Maybe calmer, although that seems a weird thing to say given the current circumstances. Anyway, I offered him lunch. He said he wasn't hungry and asked me to help him bring some things up from the cellar. Of course I agreed, but as soon as I'd gone through the door, he shut it behind me and locked it. I shouted at him to let me out, but heard him walking away, muttering to himself.' She shivered and wrung her hands.

'A couple of hours ago he opened the door and had that small gun. He pointed it at me and said he wanted me to call you, get you to come over. I refused, he swore and locked me in again. The next time he came back, he was more forceful. Dragged me up the stairs, put me in front of the phone and said if I didn't ring you he'd shoot me.' She caught her breath as a sob escaped from her mouth. 'I don't understand, Stacey, what does he want? What's going on?'

Before Stacey could answer, a disembodied voice floated down the stairs.

'I can hear you. I can hear you talking about me.'

Stacey ran up the stairs and perched on the top step.

'Andrew, open the door and let us out. This is daft.'

'No, I'm not going to do that, not now I've got you where I can keep an eye on you.'

'What do you want?' Stacey asked. 'At least open the door so I can talk to you.'

'We can talk well enough through it. As to what I want – I want people to keep their promises and stop lying, sinning in the face of God. That's what I want.'

'I don't know what you're talking about. Which people?'

'*All* people would be nice, but I know that's totally unrealistic, so just the ones close to me to start with. So much sinning, so many broken promises and damaged souls, everywhere I look, everywhere I go, *ingrained*.'

Stacey was at a loss for what to say, but felt she should keep him talking.

'Andrew, unlock the door. Let us out and we can talk about what's bothering you. You can't keep us locked up, people will miss us.'

'Yes, people will miss you, but they won't know where you are, will they? Neither of you will ever be found, I mean, who would ever suspect a vicar of kidnap?'

'Who are the people who have upset you, Andrew, these sinners of yours?' Stacey was anxious to keep him close to the door.

'Kathy, Danny and Emily,' he whispered, making the names sound like a prayer.

'What are you saying? Make me understand.'

'You asked who the sinners were and I told you.'

'Oh, God. Tell me it wasn't you who shot them.'

Andrew chuckled. 'Yes, it was me, but you already knew that.'

'No, I didn't. Why do you say that?'

'I saw you. The morning they found Kathy. You were up on the old Roman road with your camera. You looked straight at me, directly at my hiding place in the forest above the picnic area. I couldn't be sure if you'd taken any photos but you *looked* at me for a long time. I knew you'd seen me. And again when I went to the picnic area to leave the mark of God. What I don't know is why you haven't done anything about it.'

'What the bloody hell are you talking about? I didn't see you. This is nuts. Just open the damn door and let us out – now!'

'You can't talk your way out of this and I *know* you saw me.'

'OK, let's say I did. That was *months* ago, why call me down here now?'

He didn't answer but Stacey heard him muttering on the other side of the door. A sudden thought entered her mind and she banged loudly on the old wood.

'What about Amber, did you shoot her too?'

'No, that *was* down to Jimmy,' Andrew said. 'Cheeky sod broke in, took my rifle, used it, and thought I wouldn't notice. As if! I saw straight away it had been moved. I kept it down there, where you are, tucked into a corner behind some boxes. He'd put it back, but I could see someone had tampered with it. Of course, when I heard the news about Amber I worked out what had happened. I wonder how he knew I had the gun.'

'How did you have it?'

'Easy enough to smuggle home when I left Iraq, not like I had to pass through customs or anything. Didn't realise Jimmy was as devious though, fancy him coming up with an idea like that.'

'Like what?' Stacey asked.

'To get rid of his wife while a serial killer was at work in the area. He obviously hoped his crime would be lumped in with the others, could have got away with it too if he hadn't been sloppy. I went to see him, you know, in Broadmoor.'

'I heard,' Stacey said.

'He was in a bad way, a total wreck.'

'You won't get away with this, you know.'

'Oh, I think I will, a bit of housekeeping and I can carry on being the friendly, recently bereaved vicar of Llanagethin, no one will believe otherwise.'

'You're wrong. Sarah and I will be missed. Ben's coming round tonight and when he arrives and I'm not home, he'll come looking for me.'

'Yes, he will look for you I'm sure, but he won't find you – either of you – and why would he think I had anything to do with your disappearance?'

Stacey thought for a moment. 'That's what Jimmy meant when he said "borrowed". He was talking about *your* gun! If only someone had worked out what he was talking about.'

'Yes,' Andrew mumbled from behind the door, 'if only someone had. I did. I knew what he meant. I was shocked when he said it to me at Broadmoor and worried he'd regain his wits, ruin my life. He won't now, though, will he?'

'You're pleased he's dead, aren't you?' Stacey said. 'So he can't tell us what really happened. It's a good job he was locked up or I might think you had something to do with his death as well.'

'But that's the thing – I did!' He giggled, a creaky, high-pitched sound. 'I was surprised he sent me a visiting order, maybe he was going to confront me or something, who knows, he was in such a bad way. After I'd heard him speak the word, I knew I couldn't risk him waking up one day, so I told him – no, *convinced* him – Jesus was waiting, anxious to see him, to forgive him for killing his wife, all he had to do was go to Him. I was *very* persuasive.'

'You talked Jimmy into killing himself? That's sick!'

'Worked better than I thought it would, and no, it's not sick. Jimmy was an adulterer, another sinner, ruining people's lives.'

'Andrew, why did you kill the others? You said they were sinners. What did they do?'

There was no response.

Stacey raised her voice, almost shouting, 'Andrew! Tell me what they did.' Putting an ear to the door she heard nothing. He had gone.

She turned away and shuffled down the stairs to sit beside Sarah on an old garden bench. She could feel the older woman shivering in her thin dress and Stacey took off her jacket to wrap around her shoulders.

'No, don't, you'll get cold,' Sarah protested.

'It's OK, I'm fine. I'm going to have a scout about to see if there's another way out. Stay where you are and if the torch gives out, I can find my way back to you.'

Stacey walked slowly round the walls of the damp room using the torch as little as possible. She searched a shelving unit at the back and yelped in triumph when she found a bundle of candles together with a box of matches. She lit two candles, carried one over to Sarah and stuck it to the arm of the bench.

'At least we can see a bit better now. You OK?'

'Why is he doing this?' Sarah asked. 'I can't get my head round it, I've known Andrew for as long as Emily did. He's been such a good man, an army chaplain for quite some years, been over to the Middle East several times. He was so committed, so tireless in helping the sad and lonely, the bereaved. Did he really call Emily a sinner? Did he really kill her?'

'He did, yes. Look, Sarah, don't worry, we'll be out of here soon. Ben is due at my place this evening and when he misses me, he'll come looking.'

'Yes, but he won't know *where* to look. Honestly, if I wasn't locked up, I'd shoot Andrew myself. My poor little sister, she didn't deserve this.' She swallowed a sob and then asked, 'What do you think he's going to do with us?'

Stacey had no answer so resumed her search of the cellar for a way out.

* * *

Ben wondered where Stacey was when her phone clicked to the recorded message.

Ben waited for the bleep. 'Hi, you. Guess you're in the garden on such a lovely evening. I'm going to be quite late this evening – sorry – but Jack busted a couple of lads with amphetamine in their pockets and I can't leave the station until we've finished with them. It may be as late as eleven and if you can't wait up for me, don't't. I'll meet you upstairs, now I've got my own key. Love you.'

* * *

There was no way out. Stacey had worked around the walls of the dank space twice and all she'd discovered was what must have been the old coal-hole where sacks used to be emptied straight into the cellar from outside. There was still dust and sacks aplenty, but the opening had been solidly bricked over. Glancing at her watch she saw it was nine o'clock and wondered if Ben had arrived at the cottage yet, wishing she'd left a note and not dashed out of the house so fast.

Her spirits were low and – she didn't mind admitting it to herself – she was frightened. She heard a scraping sound and suddenly the cellar was flooded with yellow light as the door at the top of the stairs was opened. Scrambling to her feet she ran for the steps, but by the time she reached the bottom, the door slammed shut. A bottle of water stood on the tiny landing. Stacey dashed up the staircase and caught hold of the door handle, tugging and rattling.

'Andrew! Andrew! Are you there?' she yelled.

'Yes, I'm here. No need to shout, no point either, there's no one to hear you. Thought you'd like a drink, you must be thirsty.'

'Have you dosed it like the water you gave Sarah earlier?'

He chuckled. 'You'll have to try it to find out.'

'Andrew, why did you do it, kill those people?'

'I told you. They were sinners, they had to pay a price for their sins.'

'What sins?' she asked, forcing herself to sound less angry, more interested, anything to keep him by the door. 'What did they do to you, Andrew?'

'Not to me. They did nothing to me except lie, it was God they wronged.'

'God? How did they do that?'

'Broke their promises. They all promised God, made oaths to Him in His house and broke them. They had to be punished.'

'What did they promise? Tell me, Andrew, help me understand, what promises did they make?'

'To honour each other, to be faithful to each other and to obey each other. I married them, all of them. They made those promises in the presence of God in my church and broke them all.' He lapsed into silence.

At last Stacey thought she understood what he was saying. Danny had been having an affair, he had certainly broken his marriage vow of fidelity, and Kathy was planning to leave Bob, hardly sticking by him, but Emily? What had she done?

'Your wife – Emily – you killed her too, didn't you? What had Emily done to you?'

'She promised to obey me. When we married all those years ago, she vowed to obey me, then after forty years she broke her vow.'

'How did she do that?'

'By agreeing to go on that blasted holiday with her sister. It may seem trivial to a heathen like you, but I *forbade* her to go, told her she couldn't neglect her duties to the church or her duties to me. It made no difference. She defied me. Went ahead and booked the wretched cruise anyway. No, she broke her solemn oath to God, just like all the rest.'

'And because of that you killed her? I don't get it. Sarah said they had booked the holiday months ago, why kill her – or any of them – now?'

'He spoke to me, told me what I needed to do. I didn't have a choice in the matter, I am a servant of God.'

'You're distressed, Andrew, I can hear it in your voice. Open the door and we can talk, I can help you.'

'I don't need your help,' he hissed, 'and I'm not going to let you out. You and Sarah are part of the housekeeping.'

'What do you mean? What are you planning?'

'I'm going to get rid of you both – but not yet. Shots would be suspicious at this time of night when the firing ranges are quiet. I'll wait until they start early morning training on the Epynt, then I'll shoot you. No one will notice a couple of extra bangs. There's a space for you in the crypt of the church – you will *never* be found.'

Stacey heard him move away from the door and sat heavily on the top step hugging her knees. She glanced across the room at Sarah. The older woman seemed even smaller in the pale puddle of light from the candle, frowning as she tried to digest what Andrew had said.

'Stacey, what can we do?' she asked. 'How can we get out?'

Stacey didn't know what to say, so said nothing, hoping that someone would come and find them before the army began target practice in the morning.

* * *

Ben quietly let himself in through the back door of Noddfa. All the lights were out so he switched on the kitchen lamp, guessing Stacey was already in bed. A saffron rich curry was sitting in a saucepan on the drainer waiting to be heated up and on the worktop sat a bag of basmati rice. He had eaten before he left town, so put the curry in the fridge, padded into the living room and poured himself a small tot of brandy as a nightcap, downing the liquid in one. Hoping the bedroom door was shut so he wouldn't wake his partner, he switched on the landing light and crept up the stairs, managing to avoid the creaky step. He used the bathroom, cleaned his teeth, walked quietly along the landing and pushed open the bedroom door. He peered in the direction of the bed and was shocked to discover it was empty.

He flicked on the overhead light and saw the bed was neatly made, Stacey's nightshirt folded tidily on the pillow. He ran downstairs and back to the kitchen, searching the table and worktops, looking for a note and didn't find one. A twinge of panic rose in his chest. He went into the garden and round to the front of the house. Stacey's car was parked in the drive, so wherever she was, she was on foot. Pulling out his mobile he dialled her number. He heard the ringing tone in his left ear at the same time as he heard the ringing of her mobile from the kitchen. He dashed back in and discovered the phone on top of the microwave. Now he *was* worried, she never went anywhere without her phone.

He cut the connection and dialled again, listening to the ring tone, praying his call would be answered quickly.

'Yeah,' growled a sleepy voice.

'Jack, Stacey's missing! I'm at her place now and she's nowhere in sight. Get your ass over here, will you? Something's not right!'

## Chapter thirty-two

Ben heard a car pull up outside the cottage and ran out to the lane in time to see Jack and Julie climbing out of her battered Land Rover.

'Ben, any news?' Jack asked.

'No. I've been all over the garden in case she'd fallen or anything, searched the kitchen for notes and found nothing. I can't understand it – she *always* leaves a note.'

'Maybe she forgot you were coming round, double-booked herself or something?' Julie wondered.

'No chance! This is Stacey we're talking about, not some dizzy airhead. She's got to be the most organised woman I know. She'd never do anything like that, or leave the house without her mobile, so she must have left in a hurry.'

'OK, calm down, Ben,' Jack said. 'Let's go in, we'll have a cuppa and work out a plan of action.' Jack took him by the arm and gently propelled him along the side path and into the kitchen. 'Get the kettle on, Jules, strong and sweet, that's what they say. Ben, sit down. Now tell me, what were the arrangements for this evening?'

'Only that I'd get here when I could and might be late. We were going to have curry, she'd got it out of the freezer, it was sitting on the drainer ready to be heated up.'

'Have you checked *your* phone? Did she leave you a message, send a text or anything?'

Ben pulled his phone out of his pocket and scrolled through messages, checking to see if there were any missed calls.

'Nothing! I don't understand it, she's never done this before. I rang about seven fifteen to say I might be late but only got the answer phone. I thought she was in the garden. God, that's hours ago, it's nearly midnight, she's been gone for hours!'

'Maybe she got wind of a story and dashed off to cover it?' Julie said as she put three mugs of strong tea on the table.

'What, and forget her phone *and* her car? Do me a favour,' Ben snapped. 'You know her – she wouldn't do that.'

'It does happen.' She sounded miffed. 'Why not ring that editor of hers? If a story came in, he'd be the one to send her, wouldn't he?'

Jack pounced on the idea. 'Good thinking, Jules. Where's the landline, Ben? Got any idea of his number?'

'Office is the best place. There's a phone in there with an address book.' He started to get up.

'No, stay with Julie and drink tea. I'll ring him. Try and calm yourself, you're not much use when you're in such a state.'

Ben sat and Jack disappeared into the side office. He quickly found the number and dialled. It seemed an age before the phone at the other end of the line was answered.

'Hello,' a gruff, creaky voice filled his ear. 'Who's this?'

'Am I speaking to Sam Jenkins, editor of *The Mid Wales Times*?'

'Yes, this is he. Who the hell are you and what do you want? It's bloody late, you know!'

'Yes, I know, sir, sorry to bother you. DS Jack Trent here, Dyfed Powys police. Do you have any idea where Stacey Logan is?'

'No, I haven't and why on earth would I? Has she been caught up to no good? I always told her nosiness would get her into trouble eventually.'

'Nothing like that, sir. I'm at her house with Ben, DS James. She's not here and she's supposed to be.'

'I'm not her keeper, man, she's a grown woman. I *really* can't see what this has got to do with me?'

'Listen, you grumpy bugger!' Jack lost his temper. 'I'm ringing to see if you'd sent her on a job. I'm *sorry* if I've woken you, but this is serious. We don't know where she is.'

The bluster suddenly went out of Sam and he spoke in a quieter voice. 'OK, I apologise, not at my best when I've been woken up in the middle of the night. Is there anything I can do?'

'Not unless you know where she might have gone.'

'Sorry, no idea and as far as I know, there isn't any breaking news around that would require her presence. How long has she been gone?'

'We saw her last at the Royal Welsh. She left there about three, said she was going home to write an article for the paper and send it to you.'

'Yes, she did that, I received it this afternoon.'

'What time?'

'Five thirty, or thereabouts. Certainly before dinner, that's for sure.'

'Did you speak to her?'

'No, the stuff she sent was first rate, great pictures and a good write up, didn't have to change anything, so I sent an acknowledgement to say it was OK.'

'Look, Sam, we're going out to search for her, but we'll be leaving Julie – Constable Smith – at the cottage in case Stacey turns up. If you think of anything, or hear from Stacey, give Julie a ring, she'll know how to contact us, OK?'

'Yes, fine. Let me know, will you? When you find her.'

'I will.' Jack hung up and returned to the kitchen. Ben looked hopeful until Jack shook his head. 'No news, sorry. Finished your tea? Good, let's take a drive round the local area, we'll cover more distance than on foot. Jules, you stay here in case Stacey turns up or rings and keep in touch.'

The men went out to the truck, started it up and chugged along the narrow country lanes searching for their missing friend.

* * *

'Stacey, I'm so thirsty, let me try that water,' Sarah begged.

'I don't think it's a good idea. He's drugged you once, he could do it again and might put something else in it, something worse.'

'What do you think he's doing?'

'I don't know, things are very quiet upstairs, I haven't heard him move about for a while, maybe he went to bed?'

'Perhaps we should try to get the door open while he's not around?'

'Yeah… maybe, but he seems so unstable, I wouldn't put it past him to shoot us. Let's be honest, Sarah, he's already shot three people. I wonder where he got the gun?'

'I guess like he said, from when he was an army chaplain in Iraq – obviously learned to shoot there too.'

'He wouldn't be allowed to walk off with a piece of kit like that surely?' Stacey asked.

'I don't expect they knew. My granddad had all sorts of stuff in his shed he'd brought home from France at the end of the Second World War, even some hand grenades, I remember Mum finding them and going loopy. The police sent a bomb disposal squad out to – well – dispose of them, I guess. He had a couple of service revolvers too, Mum didn't know about them, but I did, handed them in after he died.'

'But that was a long time ago, the authorities couldn't be as lax these days.'

'You wouldn't think so would you, but who knows? They were at war after all, busy trying to stay alive and he must have got it from somewhere.'

They lapsed into silence and Stacey felt the older woman trembling on the seat next to her. As the night advanced the temperature in the cellar dropped. The first candles had burnt low, Stacey tipped another couple out of the box and lit them. It was no good, she couldn't just sit here.

'I'm going to have a look at the door, see if I can get it open somehow,' she told Sarah. 'I'll be quiet and keep an ear out for Andrew, so don't worry and stay here.'

Stacey climbed the flight of steps, placed a candle on the small stone landing and shone her torch at the door. She worked her way round the edges and studied the old-fashioned lock, before trying the handle, pulling as she did so, but the door didn't move an inch. She pulled harder, trying to ascertain if there was any give anywhere, but it was solid. A noise on the mountain made her jump. Gunfire! The army was playing war games again. Oh, God, no, gunfire! Maybe Andrew wouldn't wait for the morning training session on the ranges? If he heard the shots, would he take advantage of them? She tugged at the door, not caring how much noise she made now. They must get out of the cellar and quickly.

* * *

At half past two, Ben and Jack returned to the cottage empty-handed. Ben looked awful, tired and stressed and Jack was worried. They drank tea, but it didn't help. The sound of a mini-battle starting on the edge of the ranges and rapid gunfire startled them after the silence. A couple of parachute flares illuminated the countryside as they floated slowly earthwards.

Julie stood and went into the garden for a breath of fresh air.

'What do we do now, Jack?' Ben asked.

'Don't know, mate, I really don't. Sit and wait until morning I guess, then round up the cavalry from Llandovery and organise a proper search.'

'She might be lying injured somewhere. It's cold tonight with clear skies. We can't wait that long, she could die of hypothermia.'

'Only if she's outside and wearing a T-shirt. In case you haven't noticed, it isn't snowing. Let's take a wander around the village and see if…'

Julie dashed in from the garden. 'Come quick, you two, there's someone out there! I saw someone walking down the lane.'

The men shot out the door, ran to the front of the house and stared down the lane towards the village. The army sent up another flare and for a second or two, they saw a hurrying figure on the outskirts of Llanagethin. Ben immediately set off after it with Jack close behind. The figure vanished as it reached the end of the road and turned off the tarmac. Ben ran faster until he found himself standing outside the vicarage. A movement caught his eye close to the front door. He galloped into the garden and reached the door in time to see it close.

He hammered on the wood. 'Andrew, is that you? Open up! Police!'

The door suddenly swung open, but no one stood in the gap. Tentatively, without waiting for Jack to catch up, Ben walked into the hall straining his eyes in the darkness and stood still – listening. He heard the deep throated ticking of a grandfather clock standing to his right, but nothing else. Moving further into the house, he heard a muted rattle somewhere in the hall. He followed the sound until he stood outside the cellar door.

He called out softly, 'Hello, is someone there?'

'Ben! Oh, thank God!'

'Stacey?' he raised his voice. 'What the hell are you doing in there?'

'Shhh! Andrew locked us in. Sarah's with me. Ben, he killed Danny, Kathy and Emily, he murdered all of them.'

'What? Are you saying that Andrew – the vicar – is the killer?'

A voice spoke close behind him, 'Yes, that is *exactly* what she's saying.'

Ben started to turn, but felt something sticking in his ribs.

'Don't move, I've got a gun,' Andrew warned. 'Now, step *slowly* away from the door – and Stacey? Get down the steps. If I open this door and find you behind it, I'll shoot your boyfriend in the head, so *move*!'

Ben heard Stacey scurry down the stairs as Andrew unlocked the door with difficulty, unwilling to take his eyes off his captive. As soon as the door was open, he ordered the policeman into the cellar. Ben hesitated, angry, desperately worried for Stacey and wondered about trying to tackle the man.

'Don't you dare!' Andrew hissed. 'Don't even think about it, you'll be dead before you hit the ground and then I'll finish off the women.'

Reluctantly, Ben stepped over the threshold and Andrew slammed the door, locking it again. Stacey ran up the stairs and hugged Ben fiercely.

'I'm *so* glad to see you,' she said. 'I thought you were never coming.'

'Not doing much good though, am I? Now I'm a prisoner too. How long have you been here?'

'Since about seven this evening. He forced Sarah to ring me, tell me she was ill and to come over. As soon as I got in he locked me down here. He says he's going to kill us.'

Ben wrapped his arms around her, stroked her long hair and tried to work out what to do next.

* * *

Andrew stepped away from the door and made his way towards the kitchen. He fumbled for the light switch and flicked it on, the sudden brightness making him blink after the darkness of the hall.

It was now or never.

Jack's fist suddenly shot out from the space behind the fridge and caught the vicar square on his jaw, knocking him off balance and tumbling him to the floor. The fallen man raised one of his hands and for the first time Jack spotted the gun, just as it was fired. He ducked back into the gap between the fridge and the wall, took a deep breath and sprang out, landing heavily on the gunman's upper body.

Another shot shattered the air and Jack felt a hard thump on his thigh, followed by a burning hot pain. He screamed an angry war cry and lashed out with both fists, forcing Andrew roughly to the floor. The back of the vicar's head hit slate flagstones with a sickening thud. He lay still. Jack reached out, wrenched the gun from Andrew's hand, flicked on the safety catch and tucked it in his waistband.

Pulling himself into a sitting position he felt the pain of the bullet wound slice up his leg. It was so hot. He nudged Andrew's crumpled form with his good foot, but received no response. The older man was out for the count. Jack fumbled for his mobile to call Julie, only to find he had no signal.

'This poxy-bloody-middle-of-nowhere-shit – nothing works,' he growled and tried to heave himself upright, only to fall again – badly. Blood seeped through his trousers and formed a sticky puddle on the floor. His injured leg wouldn't bear any weight at all, so he shuffled along on his bottom and out into the hall.

'Ben! Where are you?' he shouted.

'Jack! In the cellar! Are you OK?'

'Been better.'

'Get this door unlocked, can you? Stacey's with me, Sarah too. Where's Andrew? He's got a gun.'

'Yes, I'd worked that one out. The bastard shot me with it before I took it off him.'

'Shit! I heard something, thought Andrew was just banging about. You sure you're OK?'

'Yeah, of course I'm sure, it's only a flesh wound, but I can't stand.' Jack investigated the door. 'Bugger, no key. Guess he's got it on him, I'll have to go and look.'

'Have you called for reinforcements?' Ben asked.

'Not yet. Let's get you out then you can take over. Hang on, stay where you are?'

'As if I'm going anywhere, you prat! Hurry, will you? And check on Andrew. Stacey says he's got a rifle as well as the pistol. Be careful OK?'

'Yeah, yeah.'

Ben heard Jack drag himself away from the door and back to the kitchen. The vicar hadn't moved and didn't stir as Jack searched his pockets for the key. He made the slow return journey to the cellar door, managed to lever himself high enough to insert the key in the lock and opened the door before collapsing on the carpeted floor, exhausted by his efforts. Ben rushed past him making for the phone while Stacey knelt by his side.

'Bloody hell, Jack, there's a lot of blood,' she said. 'You ever been shot before?'

'Never. All the time I spent in the big bad city I've never really come close. Gotta come to the middle-of-bloody-nowhere-Wales to get shot, didn't you know that? The peaceful Welsh countryside – yeah right. Ow! Steady on, girl!'

'Sorry, only having a look. I've never seen a gunshot wound before.'

Sarah joined them and asked, 'Where's Andrew?'

'In the kitchen, well, kitchen floor to be precise,' Jack told her. 'I knocked him out, Ben's with him. It's OK, I've got his gun.'

Ben returned to the hall. 'The boys are on their way, together with the ambulance – the lengths some people will go to just to get a ride in a helicopter.'

'What do you mean?' Jack asked.

'Gunshot wounds can be nasty, so they've whistled up the air ambulance to whisk you off to hospital. I've also given Julie a ring and she's on her way. You pulled a blinder there, Jack. What would we have done without you?'

Jack almost smiled. 'Nice to be useful.' He groaned. 'That's bloody sore now.'

'Just lie still and take deep breaths.'

The front door banged open, Julie ran into the hall and dropped to her knees by Jack's side. 'Oh, *cariad*, look at you. Are you OK?'

'Yes, I'm fine, bit tired that's all and my leg's bloody killing me,' he said and closed his eyes as the distant sound of sirens filled the cool night air.

# Epilogue

The Mid Wales Times – 16th July
LOCAL VICAR HELD AFTER SHOOTING – Exclusive!! by Sam Jenkins

The Revd. Andrew Johnson, priest-in-charge at St David's church, Llanagethin, was arrested early on Sunday morning at his home and has been charged with the attempted murder of a police officer.
Police arrived at the vicarage after Detective Sergeant James, of Llandovery Police Station, discovered his partner missing and together with two other officers, went in search. At 2.30am, DS James and DS Trent arrived at the vicarage in Llanagethin to discover Johnson had imprisoned Ms Logan, together with his sister-in-law, Sarah Gilbert, in the cellar of his house. DS James was briefly taken prisoner by Johnson who was eventually tackled by DS Trent. During the course of the struggle, a pistol was fired twice and DS Trent was hit in the upper leg. Even though he was injured, he managed to wrestle the gun from Johnson and free his captives.
It is believed Johnson may be responsible for three murders in the area earlier in the year and further charges are expected to be made. Ammunition together with two firearms was removed from the vicarage and is being

examined by forensic officers before any further charges are brought.
Johnson has been remanded in custody and is expected to stand trial in the autumn.
The Chief Superintendent of Dyfed Powys Police – Mr Dennis Oliver – said he was proud of his officers. "They acted with clear heads to free Ms Logan and Mrs Gilbert and showed great bravery. I am pleased to be able to inform you that DS Jack Trent has been nominated to receive the George Medal, awarded to those officers shot in the line of duty. He is making a good recovery and will be back on duty in the next few weeks. I am also pleased to announce that, due to his actions on the night of 15th July, and the tenacity he showed during the murder investigation earlier this year, DS Ben James has been promoted to Detective Inspector and will continue to be based in Llandovery. Constable Julie Smith, who also played a part in the spring investigation and rescue, is promoted to Detective Constable. I wish them well in their new roles, roles they certainly deserve."

Extract from The Mid Wales Times – 18th October
REVEREND JOHNSON: GUILTY! by Stacey Logan

Andrew Johnson – former vicar of St David's in the village of Llanagethin – was found guilty yesterday at Cardiff Crown court on three counts of murder, the attempted murder of a police officer, illegal possession of a firearm and false imprisonment. He was sentenced to four life sentences with an indefinite tariff…

THE END

## List of characters

Stacey Logan – reporter at *The Mid Wales Times*
Sam Jenkins – editor of *The Mid Wales Times*
Daniel Evans – victim
Joanne Evans – victim's wife
Suzie Thomas – villager
Reverend Andrew Johnson – vicar
Emily Johnson – vicar's wife
Sami – Rev Johnson's spaniel
Sarah Gilbert – Emily Johnson's sister
Samantha Phillips – head girl
Mrs Kathy Read – victim
Sabre – Mrs Read's dog
Mr Bob Read – victim's husband
Stevie Read – victim's son
Mrs Amber Atkins – victim
Jimmy Atkins – victim's husband
Mary Saunders – Jimmy Atkins' lover
Dick Nyle – duty solicitor
Sid Barker – photographer
Captain Harford-Brown – military police
Mrs Elsie Thomas – Lady Mayoress
David Little – villager
Marion Pike – local lay-reader
Peter Stamford – reporter at the *Daily Herald*
Annie Noonan – reporter at *The Mail*
Fred Murray – reporter at *The National*
Anthony Jones – headmaster
Alison Williams – Hawthorne House vet
DS Ben James
DC Mark Jefferies
DS Jack Trent

DC Julie Smith
DC Lowe
DC Smith
DC Ian Bradshaw
DCI Charlie Ambrose
Chief Superintendent Dennis Oliver
Molly Burton – family liaison officer
Governor Hughes – HMP Cardiff

**Acknowledgements**

With many thanks to my hard-working reading panel – Bill, Sue L, Helen, Pauline, Sue P, Erica and Kerry. The Writer's Circle at the Cammarch, and of course, The Book Folks.

If you enjoyed this book, please let others know by leaving a quick review on Amazon. Also, if you spot anything untoward in the paperback, get in touch. We strive for the best quality and appreciate reader feedback.

editor@thebookfolks.com

www.thebookfolks.com

## More fiction by Nicola Clifford

### THE CONSORTIUM (book 2)

Whilst reporter Stacey Logan is investigating illegal raves in the Welsh countryside, her boyfriend DI Ben James is dealing with a suspicious death. When drugs enter the picture, their two separate inquiries will collide. Can they find a way to collaborate and catch a dangerous killer?

### NOT FORGOTTEN (book 3)

When journalist Stacey Logan's policeman boyfriend disappears with little more than a note, she suspects he has been abducted. But his colleagues refuse to pursue her leads. She'll have to go it alone, but must brace herself for the worst.

### RIGHT OF SANCTUARY (book 4)

When DC Heidi Holtz's sister Greta joins a cult, she has trouble convincing her superiors of foul play. And there is nothing the detective can do if Greta went by her own free will. Holtz will have to find evidence to discredit the sect, or risk losing her sister for good.

**CODDLING MOLLY (book 5)**

A teenager is found dead after a fall from a bridge on a winter night in Brecon. Identifying her proves a challenge. DI Ben James and DS Erica Bevan discover links to a drugs gang. But when these crooks bother someone dear to ex-detective Heidi Holtz, she too will jump on their trail.

**GONE TO THE DOGS (book 6)**

Reporter Stacey Logan is looking into the case of a missing teenager, but she can't help but put her nose into Detective Ben James' murder investigation. Tensions within the community reach fever pitch as events come to a head.

**MURDER SPIKE (book 7)**

Reporter Stacey Logan lands a scoop when she discovers the body of a man placed on top of a statue in the town square. But that's just the first in a series of bizarre crime cases that hit her small rural town. What is causing the crime spike and will she get to the bottom of the matter before the police do?

**RIVER OF BODIES (book 8)**

When a woman and a man's bodies are found in a flooded car showroom during the night, detectives guess that they are the victims of a cuckolded husband. But once their relationship is explored, strange details begin to emerge. Namely the illicit activities of the woman and her brother, who has mysteriously disappeared. Once again the cops will rely on the increasingly dangerous investigations of reporter Stacey Logan to reach the truth.

## GREEN SHOOTS (book 9)

Police are called out to an commune on a country estate. The owners of the land want the environmentalists off their turf. Someone is going to get killed. Let's hope it isn't journalist Stacey Logan, who is heading there for a scoop.

## **Other titles of interest**

*The nine-book series by Cheryl Rees-Price*

Brought up on a hippy commune, DI Winter Meadows is not your ordinary detective. You could guess from his name, really.
But will a cop with a sensitive side have what it takes to police a remote Welsh community with more than its fair share of crime?
Or will he be seen as a soft touch by locals who have all manner of skeletons in the closet?

*Pippa McCathie's Welsh mystery series*

Having left the police following a corruption investigation, ex-superintendent Fabia Havard is struggling with civilian life. Nonetheless she sets to her new career as an illustrator.

However, when a girl is murdered in her town, old instincts kick in and she is desperate to find the killer. Her former colleague Matt Lambert will have to decide whether to stop her or allow his former boss to assist the floundering inquiry.

So begins a series of cases in which Havard, with her local knowledge and experience, will play a pivotal if unconventional role.

Printed in Great Britain
by Amazon

58557869R00179